PRAISE FOR STEVEN HARPER
AND THE CLOCKWORK EMPIRE SERIES

"If you love your Victorian adventure filled with zombies, amazing automatons, steampunk flare, and an impeccable eye for detail, you'll love the fascinating (and fantastical) *Doomsday Vault*!"   —My Bookish Ways

"Harper creates a fascinating world of devices, conspiracies, and personalities."   —SFRevu

"Inventive and fun . . . a fantastic amount of action. . . . If you are looking to jump into steampunk for the first time, I would recommend these books."   —Paranormal Haven

"The technology is present throughout the story, making it as much a character as any of the people Harper writes about."   —That's What I'm Talking About

"Steven Harper seemed to have this magical way of taking this crazy, awesome, complex idea and describing it in a way that anyone could follow."   —A Book Obsession

"A fun and thrilling, fast-paced adventure full of engaging characters and plenty of surprises."   —SFF Chat

"The Clockwork Empire books are changing what we know as Steampunk! . . . An exuberant novel that takes the reader on an action-packed adventurous thrill ride

IRON AXE

The Books of Blood and Iron

STEVEN HARPER

A ROC BOOK

ROC
Published by the Penguin Group
Penguin Group (USA) LLC, 375 Hudson Street,
New York, New York 10014

USA I Canada I UK I Ireland I Australia I New Zealand I India I South Africa I China
penguin.com
A Penguin Random House Company

First published by Roc, an imprint of New American Library,
a division of Penguin Group (USA) LLC

First Printing, January 2015

Copyright © Steven Piziks, 2015

 REGISTERED TRADEMARK—MARCA REGISTRADA

ISBN 978-0-451-46846-8

Printed in the United States of America
10 9 8 7 6 5 4 3 2 1

To Darwin, forever and always.

AUTHOR'S NOTE

The people of Erda don't much go in for silent letters in their names. Aisa's name is therefore pronounced with three syllables and rhymes with "Lisa." Most vowels have a European flavor, so the A in "Danr" is more like the one in "wander" than in "Daniel."

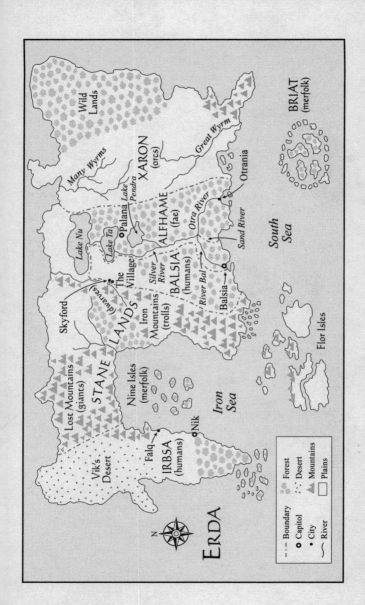

CHAPTER ONE

The stable door creaked open and threw a painful square of sunshine on the dirt floor. Danr automatically flung up his free hand to shield his eyes. His other hand wielded a manure fork. A lone cow, kept in from pasture because of an injured leg, lowed nervously and shifted in her stall.

"Trollboy." Norbert Alfgeirson crossed heavy arms in the doorway. His patchy brown beard stuck out short and prickly, like last year's wheat stubble. "Get out here. Calf fell down the new well."

He left without waiting for a reply, leaving the stable door standing open, showing a large tree inexpertly carved on the outside of it. The square of morning sunlight hung there like a sharp-edged shield. Danr set the manure fork down with a grimace. He was tall enough that his head rapped the ceiling beams if he didn't take care, and his large hands bore the calluses of heavy work. His bare feet shuffled across the dirt floor, avoiding the bright square, though he was only putting off the inevitable. At the door, he lifted a battered straw hat from a peg and clapped it over wiry black hair, then screwed up his face, touched the tree, and stepped outside.

Sunlight slapped him hard. A dull ache settled into the

back of his wide brown eyes despite the shading brim of the straw hat, and he squinted down at the ground, unable to give the clear spring sky even a glance. His wide-set toes clenched at the bare earth of the barnyard. The stories said sunlight turned the Stane to stone. Danr didn't quite believe that, but if the sun caused this much discomfort to someone whose mother was Kin and whose father was Stane, he could understand why the Stane supposedly hid under the mountain during the day.

"Over here, Trollboy!" Norbert called. He was the eldest son of Alfgeir Oxbreeder, the enormously successful herder of cattle and sheep who owned the farm where Danr was currently a thrall. "Move! I don't want this calf to break something because you dawdle."

Danr straightened his back and strode across the barnyard, away from the cool, inviting depths of the stable. Outside, the crisp, fresh air of spring rolled down the western mountains, bringing with it smells of flowers and new leaves and just a hint of snow from the heights. Alfgeir's generous herds lowed in stone-bound pastures in the distance, side by side with recently planted fields. The farm was in the lull of late spring, when calving, plowing, and planting were over and the season's first haying had not yet begun, so there was time for other work, such as repairing thatch, reinforcing fences, and digging a new well for the cattle. Norbert was standing at the latter, hands on hips. So far the well was nothing but a hole in the ground. A formidable pile of earth and rocks stood nearby, and Danr knew it would be his eventual job to move it. From below came a faint bawl.

Danr sidled up to the well, slumping his shoulders and hunching over out of long habit, though it did little to disguise the fact that he had a full head of height on Norbert. His shoulders were broader, his legs sturdier, and his skin swarthier than anyone else's on the farm. Danr's long jaw jutted forward, giving him a pugnacious look, and his lower canines were just a little too long. He had no beard, but wiry hair was making progress over his chest and back. Although he had just turned sixteen, he already had a barrel chest and heavy hands with thick fingernails. He quickly outgrew the castoffs Alfgeir's wife deigned to hand him, and his clothing was always patched and bursting at the seams. Compared to the fine wool tunics and well-cut trousers Norbert and his brothers wore, Danr was a shambling ragbag. His eyes, however, were wide and brown and liquid, and Danr's mother always said they were his best feature, but they were always hidden under his battered hat. In any case, no one seemed to notice his eyes. They only noticed he was that troll boy.

"Well?" Norbert said.

Danr peered down into the well and was just able to make out the form of the calf at the bottom, some fifteen feet down. It was up to its knees in muck. Danr glanced at the calf pen, where the young cattle were kept apart from the rest of the herd during the day so they wouldn't be injured by the larger animals, and knew what had happened. It had come to Norbert that morning to separate the calves from their mothers. He'd been careless and let one run after its mother, whereupon it had fallen into the well.

"It got away from the pen, then?" Danr asked, his voice low and quiet. Mother always said, *"Be gentle, be soft-spoken, and people won't think you a monster."*

"None of your business, Trollboy," Norbert snapped, confirming Danr's suspicions. "I should shove you down that well to join the calf and bury you with the rest of your filthy kind."

The insults stabbed his gut. He'd been hearing them for sixteen years, and it seemed he should be used to them, but like the sunlight that pounded at his eyes, he never adjusted. Each one was a pinprick, or a knife cut, or a spear thrust, and some days it felt as if he were bleeding to death. Other days, the wounds turned his blood to lava, and he felt he might burst out of his clothes from the anger. Anger he could never show, not even once. Thralls didn't get angry, no, they didn't. It wasn't fair or right, but when had the world ever been either, especially to his kind? His clothes felt tight and he worked his jaw.

"I'm sorry, Norbert," Danr said, eyes down.

Norbert punched him in the gut. The air burst from Danr's lungs, and white-hot pain slammed his stomach. He staggered, gasping. Anger flashed.

"I'm sorry, what?" Norbert snapped.

Danr had forgotten—Norbert had recently reached his majority. Danr forced himself to straighten, but not too much. Not so he was taller than Norbert. His gut ached. The monster inside him growled. He would have loved to punch back, but of course he did not. "Yes, *Carl* Alfgeirson."

"What is it? What is happening now?" Alfgeir Oxbreeder hurried over. He was an older version of his son, with thinning brown hair, a bushier beard, and a heavy nose. His fine leather overtunic and thick wool breeches bespoke his success as a farmer, as did the silver buckles on his boots and at his waist.

"This fool let one of the new calves fall down the well," Norbert said.

"What's this, what's this?" Alfgeir peered down the well. "Trollboy, if that calf is injured or killed, I'll add more time to your bonding."

"I—" Danr began, but Norbert made another fist behind Alfgeir's back, and the words died. Norbert smirked. Anger beat a war drum inside Danr, and he ached to smash that smirk. He clutched with shaking hand at the small pouch with two splinters in it that he wore on a thong around his neck. Both pouch and splinters had belonged to Danr's mother, the only legacy she had left him.

"They expect you to be a monster," Mother said. *"Don't give them satisfaction."*

Danr closed his eyes, trying unsuccessfully to make the anger and resentment disappear. His father was a troll, his mother a human, and for that terrible crime, both he and his mother had been banished to the edges of village society. *Carl* Alfgeir Oxbreeder had reluctantly agreed to accept Mother as a servant in his hall, but caring for Danr had brought expenses that had quickly put her in Alfgeir's debt. Before Danr's fifth birthday, he and Mother had both become thralls to the Oxbreeder farm, one step above slaves. No amount of hard work kept them fed and clothed without more debt, thanks to Danr's enormous appetite. Danr continued his grip on pouch and thong. It was unfair, but that was how the Nine ran the world. It didn't matter what a thrall thought. He told himself that over and over, trying to make himself believe it.

"I'm sorry, *Carl* Oxbreeder," he said at last.

"You'll have to pull it out," Alfgeir said. "As the saying goes, 'The price of foolishness is hard work.'"

"I can't do it alone, sir," Danr pointed out. "Norbert will have to help."

Norbert's face grew red and he drew back his fist again, but Alfgeir stepped between them. "Let's just get that calf out." Alfgeir turned to Norbert. "So, how *did* it fall in, then?"

He had already asked that, and it was clear he was giving Norbert another chance to come clean. Danr looked sideways at the young man. At eighteen, Norbert was only two years older than Danr, and when they were kinderlings, Danr had followed Norbert around like an oversize puppy. They had played Troll-in-the-Wood (Danr was always the troll) and fished in the brook and built a castle out of logs and stones. People called Danr Norbert's pet, and they chuckled indulgently. But as they grew, Norbert became less interested in games and more aware of Danr's status as a thrall—and a troll. These days it was as if they had never been friends and were instead a breath away from a blood feud.

Norbert ran his tongue around the inside of his cheek, and Danr held his breath. It would be such a fine thing if Norbert, just this once, would be his friend again, like when they were boys.

"I told you," Norbert growled. "It's Trollboy's fault."

Alfgeir sighed. Danr could see that he knew the truth, but he wasn't going to side with a troll. "All right. On your head be it, Trollboy, if the creature's injured."

The calf bawled again, its voice barely audible above ground. Alfgeir took up a coil of heavy rope. "Climb on down."

"Me, sir?" Danr said in surprise. "I thought you wanted me to pull it up."

"I'm not climbing down there," Norbert scoffed. "It's muck to the knees, and these boots are almost new."

Danr didn't bother to protest. There was no point. Instead he squatted at the edge of the well and lowered himself into darkness, where he hung by one hand for a moment with easy strength before he let go.

The floor of the well and the bawling calf rushed up at him. Danr managed to twist and land beside the calf with a great splat in the mud at the bottom, though his jaw came down across the calf's back. His teeth crashed together and he saw stars.

"You didn't hurt the calf, did you?" Alfgeir demanded from above.

"No, *Carl* Oxbreeder." Danr spat out a mouthful of blood, then pushed himself upright in the cool darkness. The wild-eyed calf bawled, and the sound boomed against the earthen sides of the well. It was actually nicer down here, despite the mud. Danr felt more at ease when he was surrounded by earth or in an enclosed space. He supposed it was his troll half speaking. The pain in his jaw faded somewhat. He scratched the calf's neck and ears.

"You're a pretty one," he murmured. "Everything's fine now. We'll get you out, no need to worry."

The calf calmed. It was covered in mud. Danr sniffed the air. The only way to clear cow manure out of a well was to let the water sit untouched for several months, and that would be disastrous, especially if Alfgeir took it into his head to add the time to dig yet another well to Danr's bonding. But he smelled nothing. That was a small blessing, thanks be to the Nine. He looked up. Even when it was full day above, the sky always looked velvet dark from the bottom of a well. Danr had no idea why. He could even see stars. The fleck of brightness that was one half of Urko shone directly above him. The star that was Urko's other half had moved just into the well's horizon, ready to join with its opposite. Urko, the traitor Stane who joined the Nine Gods in Lumenhame, and had then been sliced in two by his brother Stane for his trouble. Now his right half lived in Lumenhame with the Nine and the left half lived in Gloomenhame with the Stane, and each side thought the other half spied for it. Only once every hundred years did they rejoin, and the two stars showed it in the sky.

"Where does Urko really live?" Danr asked when Mother had first told him that story. "With the Stane or with the Nine?"

"The story doesn't say," she had replied. "I suppose you have to decide for yourself."

The knotted end of a rope hit him in the face. "Let us know when you're ready, Trollboy," Alfgeir called.

With a sigh, Danr set to work tying the rope in a harness

around the calf. It wasn't easy in the narrow, wet space. Mud squished up to Danr's shins, slowing him further. The calf struggled, and more than once Danr had to stop work to calm it.

"What's taking so long?" Norbert shouted down at him. "You're dawdling on purpose to get out of real work."

Danr ground his teeth and kept at it. The knots had to be done just right. If they came undone, the calf might fall on Danr and injure itself. His hands, soaked in muddy water, grew cold, and the rope became stubborn beneath his fingers. The calf continued its restlessness. At last, however, Danr had it in a rough harness.

"Ready!" he called, and tugged on the rope. It tightened, and the calf came free of the mud with a sucking sound. A surprised expression crossed its face as it rose toward the stars like a strange sacrifice. It reached the top, where Alfgeir and Norbert hauled it to safety.

Danr waited a moment, and when nothing was forthcoming, he called up, "Could I have the rope?"

Norbert poked his head over the edge. "We're undoing these stupid knots you tied. Anyway, you're too heavy. Climb up yourself."

The monster snarled inside him again. Danr clutched the pouch at his neck. His mother's soft voice always came back to him better when he did. *"Don't give in. Don't give them an excuse to hurt you. Don't let the monster out."*

"Yes, Mother," he whispered.

He dug hands and feet into the sides of the well, his stony fingers biting into the stiff earth, and climbed toward the upper world. It was hard work. All his strength was in his arms and legs, but this used his wrists, and fiery aches burned in his hands by the time he reached the top. Gasping, he grabbed the rim of the well to haul himself over the top.

"I'll teach the troll some respect, Father." Norbert stamped on Danr's fingers. More pain lanced through Danr's hand. He let go with a yelp and landed heavily in the cold mud.

"Norbert," Alfgeir said mildly at the top, "I don't want you abusing the thralls this way. If you injure him, he won't be able to do his work."

"Sorry, Father." Norbert didn't sound sorry in the least. "I did make him get the calf out."

"Good work, that," Alfgeir said.

Danr levered himself out of the mud, worked his jaw back and forth, and set himself to climb again. There was nothing else to do.

When he finally pulled himself dripping out of darkness, the sunlight slashed his eyes and drilled through his skull. His hat was gone, lost below. He grunted and tried to shield himself with one arm, but the sun's rays thrust sharp pain straight through him.

"Where's your hat?" Alfgeir tutted. "Honestly, Trollboy, you can't keep track of even the smallest thing. Here."

He laid his own broad-brimmed hat on Danr's head, and the pain abated somewhat. "Thank you, *Carl*."

"I'll add it to your bonding," Alfgeir said. "As the saying goes, 'A worker is worth his wages, and the wages must be worth his work.'"

Danr touched the brim of the hat. It was old and battered and too small for him, and he had the feeling Alfgeir would add the price of a brand-new hat to his bonding. But he only said, "Yes, *Carl* Oxbreeder."

"Go wash up," Alfgeir said. "And then I want you to run an errand."

Danr blinked. An errand? That was unusual. Errands were choice, easy jobs that granted a chance to leave the farm for a bit. Danr was never chosen to run errands. He always did heavy or smelly work, like cutting stone or dragging trees or spreading manure on the fields.

"Yes, *Carl*," he said, letting himself feel a little excited. Maybe today wouldn't turn out so bad after all. He trotted across the farm toward the main well.

Alfgeir's farm sprawled at the foothill bottoms of the Iron Mountains, meaning no one lived above them and there was plenty of free pasture in the hills for cows and sheep while Alfgeir's family and thralls farmed the flatter land below. Because Alfgeir was wealthy, his long, L-shaped thatched hall stood apart from the stables, unlike poorer farmers who attached animal housing to their homes for the added warmth. There was even a separate hall for the servants and thralls across a courtyard paved with mountain stones. Danr, however, lived in the stable, which was an enormous longhouse shaped like a giant log sunk into the ground. The building was less than three years old—the original had burned down two summers ago. Fortunately Danr had managed to get most of the cattle out, and only six had died. This hadn't stopped Alfgeir from blaming Danr for the entire incident and adding the cost of the lost cows and a new stable to Danr's debts. It didn't matter to Alfgeir that the new stable was almost twice as large as the old or that Danr had done the work of five men during the construction—Alfgeir said Danr's debt was for the full cost of a new stable. It seemed to Danr that his debt should have been for the cost of rebuilding the original and Alfgeir should have shouldered the difference for a bigger one. But Danr kept quiet. He could have taken his case to the earl—even a thrall had rights—but then he thought of facing all those staring eyes in the public arena. And how likely was it that the earl would rule in favor of a troll? So Danr had silently accepted the additional debt and with it, the burden of anger whenever he thought about the new stable walls.

The farm's well was equipped with a windlass and an enormous bucket that only Danr could lift when it was full.

He hauled it dripping from the depths and simply poured it over himself, repeating until the water ran clear. His ragged clothes were the only ones he owned, and he went barefoot even in winter, so he had nothing to change into. At least he would dry soon enough in the hurtful spring sunshine.

Hunger rumbled in Danr's belly. He sighed. He was almost always hungry, and whenever he ate more than a grown man, Alfgeir added the difference to his bonding, which meant Danr had to do extra work to have it removed, which in turn made him hungrier. It was a spiral he didn't know how to break. Perhaps today he could slip away during the errand and go fishing. A salmon or even a trout, spit and roasted over a little fire, would go a long way in quelling the eternal emptiness inside him.

A shrill whistle caught his attention. Alfgeir was waving to him from one of the paddocks near the stable. Danr clapped the ill-fit hat back on his head and lumbered over. A young bull, barely into adolescence, was tied in the paddock.

"Take this animal to Orvandel the fletcher," Alfgeir said. "He lives on the outskirts of Skyford, and I owe him a debt. If you hurry, you can make it to his house and back before dark."

Danr eyed Alfgeir uneasily. A chance to go into the city was definitely a choice errand, something Alfgeir's sons would fight over. Why was Alfgeir sending Danr? The offer rang false.

"Are you sure you don't want to send Norbert, *Carl* Oxbreeder?" he temporized. "Or Tager? They might—"

"I didn't ask your opinion, Trollboy," Alfgeir said in a deceptively even voice. "I gave you an order."

He turned on his heel and stalked away.

Danr looked after him for a moment, then shrugged and lifted the handle on the gate. The bull lowed at him. On closer inspection Danr realized it was not a bull but a steer,

newly castrated. The animal was brown and just came up to
Danr's waist. Bones showed through skin, and Danr recognized it—the animal had recently recovered from a winter
illness. This was repayment for a debt? The steer bawled
again, and Danr reached out with a big hand to scratch the
places where its horns would one day grow. It closed its eyes
contentedly. Oh well. This wasn't his decision, and Alfgeir
had handed him a chance to escape the farm for a few hours
on a fine spring day. Why question it? Danr took up the
steer's rope, and a few minutes later, they were both on the
rutted road that led toward the city of Skyford.

The farm receded behind him, and the steer seemed content to follow without being coaxed or hauled. Trees lined the
roads, forming boundaries between farms. Men and boys followed herds of cows around the fields, and their voices mingled with birdsong. Green grass had already filled the space
between the ruts in the old road, and it was soft under Danr's
feet. A good mood crept quietly over him, like a dog that had
been kicked away but still wanted to please. Maybe one day
Norbert would trip over his own feet and fall into a pile of
manure, and Danr would be there to see it. Norbert would
push himself upright, brown cow shit staining his beard, and
everyone around him, including Danr, would enjoy a good,
long laugh. Then Danr could dump cold water from the well
over him, again and again and again. How would Norbert like
that?

Danr had fallen so deep into fantasy that he was completely unprepared for the hooded figure that rose out of the
undergrowth beside the road. The steer bellowed in alarm and
tried to flee, but Danr tightened his grip on the rope and the
steer jerked to a halt, almost twisting its head to the ground.
Danr didn't budge. The figure's clothes were little more than
rags and were bundled in awkward layers. It stepped out onto

the road, a basket in one hand. A bit more gladness grew in Danr's heart, and he grinned a greeting.

"Aisa," he said. "I haven't seen you in days. You scared my steer."

"Apologies." Although the sun was quite warm, the low voice that drifted from the hood was muffled by multiple layers of scarf. "I was gathering greens and saw you coming down the road."

"I'm taking this steer to Orvandel the fletcher in Sky-ford," Danr told her proudly. "Alfgeir owes him a debt. Walk with me?"

"For a bit." Aisa's words carried an accent, exotic and ex-citing, though she had never said where she came from. All Danr really knew about her was that she was a couple of years older than he was, she had been a slave to the elves in Alf-hame for something like two years, and now she was a slave to a man named Farek. Well, he knew that, and that seeing her always brought a little flutter to his heart, even though she never went anywhere without all her clothes wrapped around her. The most Danr had ever seen was a pair of brown eyes above a heavy scarf. It was enough.

"How does Mistress Frida treat you?" Danr asked as they walked.

"As she always has," Aisa replied, and changed the sub-ject. "I came down to warn you."

Danr halted so quickly the steer bumped into him from behind. A little ball of tension turned cold in his stomach. "Warn me? Of what?"

"News just reached the village that the farm of the Noss brothers was attacked last night. House and stable were destroyed, and both Oscar and Olaf are dead."

Danr swallowed. The village lay between Alfgeir's farm and Skyford. Like Alfgeir, Oscar and Olaf Noss ran a farm that butted up against mountain wilderness. Every year they talked about expanding, but they never did, and their talk had become a running joke in the village.

"Why do you need to warn me?" he asked, though he had a feeling he knew the answer.

"It is rumored," Aisa said slowly, "that someone found enormous tracks among the ruined buildings. Troll tracks."

Chapter Two

A cold finger ran down Danr's spine, bump by bump. "By the Nine," he whispered.

"You know who they will blame," Aisa said.

His hand tightened around the halter rope. Oh, he knew. He knew down in the place where his guts coiled inside his belly. He also knew the only good way to Skyford took him through the village and past a hundred hard and angry eyes. True, he could leave the road, but that would send him tramping through freshly planted fields and earn him more anger.

Maybe he should just go back to Alfgeir's farm. But no—Alfgeir had made it clear that he was to take the steer to Orvandel in Skyford, and Alfgeir would be Vik-all furious if Danr returned, errand uncompleted. No matter what he did, someone was going to be angry at him. The Nine were laughing while they pegged his tenders to a wall. It seemed to be his lot in life.

With a heavy sigh, he wrapped the rope around his knuckles, straightened his back, and tromped resolutely forward. It was what you did, even when it hurt.

"What are you doing?" Aisa hurried to catch up. "Trolls

have not come down to the village in living memory. They all believe that you have somehow brought them down upon us."

"Yes, and?" he growled. "I should at least get my work done in the bargain."

"They may come after you. They *will* come after you."

"And they'll throw things, I suppose, but I have a thick skin."

"The skin around your body is thick," Aisa said, falling in beside him, "but what about the skin around your heart?"

There was nothing to say to that, so Danr trudged on in silence, every step taking him closer to the village. His earlier fine mood was a wreck. After a moment, Aisa reached over and gave his forearm a little squeeze. Her fingers left a warm print on his skin. He didn't slow down, but he felt a little better. A lot better. Aisa could do that for him, and she seemed completely unaware of how incredible this small power was for him. She made his life bearable, even happy, though he couldn't find it in himself to tell her. A troll simply didn't have the words.

Farek had bought Aisa from a slave dealer who trucked with the elves from Alfhame in the southeast. Something about the elves forced humans to adore their masters. Human slaves needed their elven masters the way a drunk needed ale, and the worst punishment a slave could endure was to be sold away from the keg.

Aisa had never said what awful thing she had done that made her owner decide to punish her with exile, and Danr, sensing the pain involved, had never asked. He could never cause Aisa pain.

Everyone in the village, however, knew exactly why Farek had bought Aisa, and everyone knew what he did with her in his stable at night, and everyone knew that Farek's wife, Frida, hated him for it. Frida couldn't do much to Farek, so her red and cruel anger found the next best target—Aisa herself. Danr knew without being told that Aisa wrapped herself up to hide the bruises, and the thought of those bruises made Danr angrier than anything Norbert might do, and he had to work hard indeed to keep his temper to himself whenever he saw Farek in the village. It was one of many reasons he kept to himself as much as possible.

They crested a slight rise, and the outer ring of village houses came into view. They were similar to Alfgeir's—long, rounded structures half-buried in the ground as if huddling for warmth, their wattle-and-daub walls covered in a blanket of whitewash. Every door had a tree carved or painted on it, some expertly, some crudely. The village was too small to have a name. Ordinary gossip got around quick, while bad gossip rushed fast enough to break its own neck. If Aisa knew about the troll tracks in the Nosses' flattened house, everyone knew. More tension tightened Danr's stomach and his breathing came faster. Aisa gave his arm another soft squeeze and left the road. He knew why. Being seen with him would give Frida another excuse to reach for her birch rod, and there was no reason for both of them to suffer. The road felt empty with her gone.

He held his head high as he took the steer through the outer ring of houses. The road widened and dropped into ankle-deep mud that sucked cold at his feet. The usual chickens and pigs rooted in the byways between the houses, and dogs barked at each other over fences about whatever it was dogs barked about. All the doors stood open to the fresh air and sunshine. A hammer clanked steadily against metal in Hagbart's smithy, creating a little echo against the throb of the sunshine ache in Danr's head, and the heavy smell of wood smoke hung beneath the painfully bright sky. Kinderlings, too young to work yet, chased each other up and down the main street, laughing as they ran. Adults walked, scurried, or bustled about their daily chores—until they saw

Danr, anyway. Wherever he and the steer went, everything stopped. Bearded men in tunics and careworn women in dresses gathered in clumps, openly staring and whispering behind their hands. Danr knew all of them by name, but they acted as if he were a stranger. His face grew hot, but he walked on as if he hadn't noticed all those staring eyes. Elsa Haug, a thin woman wrapped in a blue shawl, snatched up her baby daughter and slammed her door.

Dozens of eyes followed him, and dozens of voices whispered about him. He caught words and phrases here and there.

". . . monster . . ."

". . . Noss brothers . . ."

". . . filthy slut of a mother couldn't keep her legs together, even for a . . ."

". . . his fault the trolls attacked . . ."

". . . half-blood . . ."

". . . the earl should just run him out of . . ."

He felt exposed and naked, and his skin shriveled against his body. The steer squelched through the muddy street behind him with unhappy hooves. Like Danr, it sensed tension in the air, and its eyes rolled. More than once it balked. If Danr had been human, with a human's strength, he wouldn't have been able to move it, but he forged ahead with a half troll's strength, and the steer had no choice but to follow.

Something cold and soft splattered the back of his head beneath his hat. Reflexively he spun. Several knots of people stood at a safe distance behind him with grim faces. Danr smelled cow manure, felt it ooze around his ears. Anger boiled away his fear, and his fingernails plowed furrows into his palms.

"Who threw that?" he shouted without thinking.

The people stared back. Then a young man—Egil Carlsson—spat in his direction.

"A piece of shit for a piece of shit," he growled.

Danr's muscles bunched and rolled like boulders beneath his patchwork tunic. Manure dripped a slimy trail down his back. The monster inside pushed him to make a step toward Egil Carlsson. Egil stiffened, and the villagers around him came quietly alert. That was when Danr noticed several of them carried axes, pitchforks, and carving knives. He wondered how many of them he could crush with a single blow.

"Don't give them the satisfaction or an excuse."

He stared at the people for a long moment, hands trembling. They stared back. It would be so easy to teach them a few manners, show them that he didn't deserve this. The monster made fists.

And after you beat them black and bloody, what then? he thought. *Will you change their minds? And how long before the earl comes with his archers and his swordsmen? Mother was right. Never show the monster.*

The villagers stood there, half-expectant, half-fearful. Egil stood resolute, and skinny Elsa Haug opened her door a crack. Then Danr deliberately turned and trudged away. His heart pounded and his back prickled, waiting for the next blow. Would it be more cow shit? Maybe it would be a rock, or even a knife. Ahead of him, the road leading out to the other side of the village lay empty. Everyone in the village was behind him. Vik's balls, he wanted to run, bolt for the open spaces, and leave the stupid steer behind. But he kept steady steps.

Danr passed another rounded white house, then another, and then he was at the village edge. No blows, no more turds. When the road faded into a pair of ruts with grass growing between them, he breathed a heavy sigh and glanced over his shoulder. The village lay behind him in a haze of smoke that clung to the thatching. Chickens squawked a long way off, and a flock of geese honked in someone's garden. No sign of an angry mob.

Danr left the road to find a stream, tied the steer to a tree, and plunged his head into crisp, cold water. He scrubbed and scrubbed and scrubbed until his ears were raw and he felt clean again. Then he rinsed out his tunic. A brown smear ran downstream. He sat back on his haunches, feeling abruptly tired. Errand or no errand, right then Danr wanted nothing more than a hot meal and his bed in the stable. Alone. But he pulled on his damp tunic, untied the steer, and continued up the road.

The hard sun dried his clothes, and eventually he felt warm again. The tension faded, and he felt a little relief, as if he had passed some kind of test, though the sun headache was returning. Well, considering what had happened at the Noss Farm, maybe it was best that he disappeared for a few hours. In the meantime, no reason he couldn't enjoy a little solitude.

The farms around the village faded into hilly woodland. Trees loomed over the road, cutting off the sunshine and easing Danr's headache. He remembered walking through the woods like this with his mother, Halldora, when he was little. They gathered berries and set traps for rabbits. And Mother told stories, fantastic stories of the Stane—trolls, dwarves, and giants—and of the Fae—elves, sprites, and fairies—and the Kin—humans, orcs, and merfolk. She spun stories of the Nine, the gods who watched over Ashkame, the Great Tree whose roots and branches twisted through every part of the world. She told him about Fell and Belinna, the twin god and goddess, and their eternal battles with the Stane, of the way Fell's iron axe, Thresher, flew from his hand like a steel whirlwind to slice off a giant's head. Danr always pretended *he* wielded Thresher, swinging branches at trees or boulders for the satisfying *thwack*.

Sometimes Mother sat on the ground and let Danr crawl into her lap, even though he was almost as tall as she was. She smelled of sweetgrass and sweat, and now those smells made him think of her. He remembered reaching up to touch the small ragged pouch that always hung around her neck. It fascinated him because Mother never took it off, not even to sleep or bathe.

"Is it magic?" he had asked.

"Of course not. The Kin lost their magic a thousand years ago when the Stane destroyed the Iron Axe and sundered the world. The Stane lost most of their power. Only the Fae kept theirs. Humans and orcs and merfolk haven't had magic in a long, long time."

Danr reached out to touch the pouch. "If this isn't magic, what is it?"

"Truth." She pushed his hand away. "That's the most potent kind of magic. Never forget that, my son."

And that was all she would say.

Other times, the village women came to the stable to have their fortunes read. Mother was awful at reading fortunes. The problem wasn't that her predictions never came true—the problem was that they *always* came true. Danr knew because he scrunched up in a cow stall whenever she did it so he could listen. When Lorta, wife to Hagbart the smith, came during her third month of pregnancy to ask if her child would be a boy or girl, Mother touched the pouch at her throat and said Lorta would miscarry within two weeks. Lorta ran away in horrified tears, and who could blame her? But in ten days, Hagbart the smith was digging a tiny grave. When Henreth Ravsdottr came to ask if her intended fiancé, Jens, was cheating on her with another woman, Mother touched the pouch and told her Jens was not—he was cheating on her with Henreth's older brother, Kell. That had been a day.

Mother always told the truth. Always. It frightened people as much as it fascinated them. Danr himself learned early on not to ask questions he didn't want the answers to. *No one likes the truth* was one of Mother's favorite sayings.

But now Mother was gone, dead of coughing sickness the

winter after Danr turned eleven. True, she worked in the house, but she lived in the stables, and they were rotten cold in winter. Danr begged Alfgeir and his wife, Gisla, to let his mother sleep by their big, warm fire instead of near the stable's tiny, damp one, but although Alfgeir and Gisla would eat Halldora's cooking and let her clean their house, they wouldn't let her share their pristine hearth, no, they wouldn't.

"A woman who beds an animal and whelps an animal must sleep with animals," Gisla snapped.

Mother's fever rose higher and higher while her cough grew weaker and weaker. Danr didn't know what to do. He finally coaxed one of the cows to lie beside her for warmth and pressed her shivering body against its fur while icy drafts stole in through the stable door and circled her pallet like hungry wolves. He couldn't keep them away, no matter how strong he was. The other cows calmly chewed their cud, unaware of the dying woman and the terrified boy in the stall next to theirs. Danr prayed to Fell and Belinna, to Grick, queen of gods and lady of the hearth, and even to Olar, the king of gods himself, pleading with them to spare his mother's life. He begged with all the fervor a boy could bring up. But just before dawn, Halldora shuddered once and went still.

Danr didn't cry when he wrapped her body in old rags and amulets to Halza that he carved himself. He didn't cry when he built her funeral pyre in the northern pasture. He didn't cry when no one, not even Alfgeir, came to help him hold the torch to the wood or watch the flames blaze to the sky. But when Danr came back to the stable and lay down in his stall, alone with the cows, then he cried.

Chains clanked, startling Danr out of the memories. Ahead of him on the road, a fierce-looking man in a black cloak rode a black horse. He led a line of humans cuffed to a long beam with bronze shackles on their feet. Another man in black rode behind them. Above the second man hovered a glowing figure whose shape seemed to twist. A sprite—one of the Fae come to oversee the slavers.

Fear settled over Danr. Even the monster inside him cowered. Swallowing, he pulled the steer several paces off the road to let the procession pass. A thousand years ago, just before the Sundering had cracked the continent, a number of the Kin had gone to war against the Fae—and lost. Now, more than ten centuries later, the Fae were still extracting tribute. Except they didn't dare take it from the warlike orcs, who would leap at the chance to make more war on the Fae, and they couldn't take it from the merfolk, who merely dove under the sea to avoid paying. And so the Fae took payment from the humans. With no magic of their own, and with the kingdom of Balsia scattered and broken and unable to stand up to a united Alfhame, there was no way for the humans to stop them.

And it was worse. The Fae had an appetite for slaves that ran beyond the numbers negotiated for tribute. They bought yet more, every human slave they could get their hands on, and many a human became rich selling his own kind to the slavers of Alfhame.

No one knew how the Fae chose their tributes, but if the slavers descended on your house in their raven-black cloaks and knocked bony fingers on your door, there was nothing you could do, no, there wasn't. Whispers persisted that it was the worst luck to be on the streets when the slavers arrived. At least Danr was a troll, and immune to slavers. Probably. Possibly. Danr's hands were cold and he could feel the chains around his own wrists.

The sad procession clanked by. Exposed and frightened, Danr kept his eyes down. He desperately wanted to abandon the calf and run, but that would only call attention to himself. Besides, if the Fae chose him, he would have to go, and that would be that. No human could resist the Fae glamour, and the law forbade resistance in any case. Danr's heart beat fast and he tried to tell himself that the Fae didn't take Stane back to Alfhame, but how did anyone know that for sure?

Bronze clanked. Someone choked back a sob. Danr told himself not to look, not to see, but the more he tried, the harder it became, and finally he couldn't help peering up under the brim of his hat.

He stared at his own self. A second Danr was standing at the edge of the road, jaw jutting pugnaciously forward. Danr yelped and scrambled backward. The second Danr gave a high-pitched giggle that raised the hair on the back of Danr's arms.

"Stane!" it laughed. "The bane of Lumenhame!"

The second Danr leaped into the air and twisted back into the glowing form of the sprite who had been following the second slaver. Terror swept Danr. The second slaver snapped the reins on his horse but made no other acknowledgment. Danr wanted to run, but his feet wouldn't go. He looked at the slave train while the sprite giggled at him again.

The train was nearly past, and the people wore expressions of fright or resignation or simple sadness. A boy no more than thirteen or fourteen years old met Danr's eyes with his own, and he felt the boy's pain and fear until the chains yanked him forward. He wanted to help, but what could he do? He saw slaves every day. Aisa was a slave. They were part of the world. That didn't make it right or fair, but he of all people knew the world didn't run fair. Still, why had the Nine given him so much strength if he wasn't supposed to use it?

Still panting, Danr forced his gaze down again, but the image of the boy's blue eyes stayed with him.

The slaver bringing up the rear halted his horse. "You there!"

Danr's heart stopped in his chest, and his bowels loosened. The Fae wouldn't be kind to a Stane in their midst, of that he had no doubt. But he forced himself to bring his head up. "My lord?"

Now the slaver caught sight of his face. "Vik's balls! Did your mother get beaten with an ugly club before she whelped you?"

Danr didn't answer. He had long ago learned that the only answer to taunts was simply to remain silent. The slaver laughed at his own joke, and it suddenly occurred to Danr that he could probably yank the man from his horse and break his traitorous neck before he even understood Danr was moving. The other slaver was only one human, far weaker than Danr, and the sprite was tiny. How hard would it be? The slaves would go free and Danr would be a hero.

Until the Fae missed the slave shipment. Until the Fae sent more slavers to this district and took more slaves as punishment. Until they used their magics to uncover who had broken the tithe law. And anyway, Danr wasn't any kind of hero. He was a troll and a thrall. He looked down again.

"Is this the road to Rolk's Fork?" the slaver continued.

Danr blinked. "Yes, my lord."

"How long to get there?"

"Two days."

"You're not as dumb as you look." He flipped a copper coin at Danr, who caught it without thinking. "Go whelp some children, boy. The elves always need strong backs."

He wheeled his horse and rode away. The last thing Danr saw was the boy trudging away under the shimmering sprite. Danr watched the train go, feeling relieved and also feeling guilty that he felt relieved. Someone always had it worse, didn't they? And he had done nothing to help. The Nine were cruel even when they were being kind. Danr turned and trudged in the opposite direction, hauling the steer.

The woods ended, and Danr now followed the road through another mile or two of carefully cultivated fields until he came to Skyford. The city was large, considerably larger than Danr's home village, and surrounded on three sides by a stone wall with a blocky keep that glared down from the center. That was where the earl lived. Skyford had spilled over the original walls generations ago, and a palisade of heavy logs scored a second wall some distance outside the stone one. The fourth side bordered a river that wound down from the mountains. Danr caught a ripe whiff of fish on the breeze as he approached town. Two other roads converged here to enter Skyford proper through a gap in the palisade. Oxcarts and wagons lumbered in and out, as did a number of people. Many of the latter turned to stare when Danr got close enough. Danr felt self-conscious again, but he made himself walk forward, the steer trailing behind. In the distance, he heard a woman weeping. No doubt she had lost someone to a slaver.

Danr had been to Skyford several times—it was the closest place to sell cattle and crops, and the Oxbreeder family drove a nice herd to the town every year for sale and slaughter. The Oxbreeders, wealthy and respected, usually visited the earl on these trips, but Danr wasn't allowed inside the keep. He stayed with the cattle, and where else?

When Danr arrived at the city gate, he noticed over a dozen people staring at him from oxcarts, the street, and doorways of nearby houses. All his life, people had stared and whispered, but he never really got used to it. He wanted to pull the stupid, too-small hat over his face and melt into the ground under all those eyes.

A young man barely sixteen stood guard at the gate. He watched the traffic in and out with a bored expression until he caught sight of Danr. The boredom fled his face and he gripped his spear more tightly. Danr sighed. Did the guard think Danr was going to attack him here under Rolk's own sun? The young man's expression hardened when Danr stopped, and his fingers grew white around the shaft of the spear. People stopped and stared, unabashed.

"Can you tell me," Danr said quietly, "where I can find Orvandel the fletcher? I'm supposed to deliver this steer to him."

"You can speak?" the guard blurted in surprise.

A tiny sting pierced Danr's heart at the guard's thoughtless insult. "Do you know where Orvandel lives?" he asked.

The young guard grabbed a child in a page's uniform by the arm and whispered something in his ear. The boy scuttled away.

"Sir?" Danr said. "If you don't know where the fletcher lives, I can—"

"F-follow the main road until you come to a crossing," the guard said. "His house is on the corner, the one closest to the river."

Danr nodded his thanks and led the steer into town. It must be nice to be a cow. Cows didn't care if anyone stared at them or whispered behind their backs. It didn't matter who led them or where they were going.

Skyford was prosperous, and the streets were paved with logs sawed in half lengthwise and laid bark-side down. It made for a bumpy road, but it also cut down on the mud. The houses were similarly built of logs, and many sat on heavy, shoulder-high stilts in case the river flooded. The areas beneath were used as pigpens or chicken coops. People crowded the byways, but everyone stared at Danr and made way for him. Usually when Danr came into Skyford, he was surrounded by a herd of cattle, and people took less notice of him, but today was different. Danr sped his steps, concentrating on his goal and trying to close his ears to the whispers that rose behind him like a flock of bats.

An arrow skewered the log at his feet so suddenly it seemed to have sprouted there. Danr jumped backward with a yelp and bumbled into the steer, who bawled. Laughter burst all around them. Danr scrambled to unsnarl himself as best he could and regain his balance beside the half-panicked steer.

"Playing with your lunch, Trollboy?" White Halli, the earl's son, sat on a roan horse a dozen yards away, a bow in his hands and a quiver on his back. He was twenty-two—six years older than Danr—and his white-blond hair gleamed like a sword in the spring sunlight. Halli was tall, though not as tall as Danr, with ice-blue eyes and a whipcord build of flat muscle. His rich blue tunic was dyed to match his leggings, and a blade hung from his belt. The two men who rode beside him bore swords as well, and axes hung from their saddles. Danr eyed them with wordless apprehension. White Halli was the last person he wanted to see right now. Automatically his eyes darted left and right, looking for a distraction or a place to run to. But he wasn't on home ground, and he saw no sanctuary. Even the laughing crowd was sidling away. Whatever entertainment Halli might create with the troll's boy wasn't worth the chance of being caught up in it.

"Take your hat off when you're in the presence of the earl's son," Halli snapped.

Danr removed his hat with one hand, the other still tightly clutching the steer's rope. The sun smacked his eyes and drove a spike of pain through his head.

"I heard you'd come to town," Halli continued. "You saved me the trouble of hunting you down."

"What for?" Danr asked, then added, "My lord."

"You know what for," Halli replied easily.

"No. I don't." Danr did, of course, but he wasn't going to allow Halli to get away with a silent accusation. A steady loathing for the man grew black and harsh behind his eyes and he let it show in his face, even if his words remained civil.

A year ago, to give Halli something to do, Earl Hunin had put Halli in charge of keeping order in Skyford. Now Halli patrolled, and the damp cells under the keep grew crowded. So far, crimes seemed to include walking the streets too late at night, public disturbance (which included singing in front of taverns), and owning a poorly shod horse. Rumors slid about like shadows, whispering that Halli was deliberately building up a source of conscripts for the army, even though Earl Hunin had no desire to make war against anyone.

In his patrols, Halli often came across Danr. Danr, who had accidentally stumbled across Halli going after his cousin Sigrid during the cattle fair five years ago and who had been called, shaking and stammering, into a private conference with the earl. Danr was a mere thrall, so his word meant little, and Halli had simply called Sigrid a liar. It had ended with Halli's marriage to a pliable merchant's daughter while Sigrid had been sent south, far away from her family. The sickness of Halli's presence made Danr feel cold and slimy at the same time.

"You'll have to tell me, my lord, what I'm accused of," Danr said.

Halli pretended not to notice. "How like the Stane. Not half a brain among your entire race."

As before, Danr didn't respond. He merely stood there in his patchwork clothes, holding the steer's rope. Halli wanted an audience, but Danr wasn't going to play to one. Fortunately for Danr, the people on the street kept their heads down and went about their business, refusing to be drawn into Halli's street theatrics.

"The Noss brothers, you idiot!" Halli finally shouted. "You killed them and smashed their house last night."

"Are you sure this is true?" The monster inside Danr snapped, but Danr kept his voice even and quiet, though the mix of dislike and anger pushed more words out of him. "Or does the earl merely want to ask me questions about it? I'm sure the son of Earl Hunin wouldn't want to be wrong and look foolish in public. Especially after he failed to persuade the slavers from taking his people."

Halli's face went hard. The slavers had hit Skyford badly. Not only that, but if Halli made a charge too quickly and turned out to be wrong, he would look the goose in front of his father. Danr had twisted Halli's investigation around and put him on the defensive.

Good, Danr thought.

"What do you know about the attack on the Noss brothers?" Halli asked quickly.

Danr spread his hands. "Nothing, my lord. I was at home asleep. I'm sure my master, the wealthy farmer Alfgeir Oxbreeder, who I believe dined with your father just a month ago, will tell you that I was at work until after sunset, and then I was asleep in the stable."

"With the other animals," Halli spat.

It would be so easy to leap at the horse, break its neck with a single blow, bring Halli down with a crunch of bone and spurt of blood. Danr started to make a fist. Halli smiled.

"Keep the monster inside," Mother said, *"where it's safe."*

He forced his fingers to the pouch at his throat and remained silent.

"Who can swear that you were in the stable all night?" Halli demanded.

"No one," Danr said. "But you can be sure, my lord, that if I had killed someone and smashed their house while everyone was asleep, I would also have taken care to find someone who would swear that I was a thousand miles away when it happened."

One of the other men on horseback snorted at that. Halli glared at him, and the man turned the snort into a cough. The steer at the other end of Danr's rope lowed in counterpoint.

"Of course you were alone," Halli said. "No one would spend the night with a troll. Except your mother."

"We'll have to ask your cousin Sigrid what that's like," the monster snapped before Danr could stop it.

Halli's expression went stiff as a corpse. A ripple went through the few people who were watching the exchange. The men who rode with Halli edged their hands toward their sword hilts.

Danr bit the inside of his cheek. The loathing drained out of him, replaced by the more familiar chill of fear. He had gone too far.

And then White Halli burst into laughter. The harsh sound of it bounced against the houses and was eaten up by the silence on the street. Halli swung a fist and thumped one of his men on the shoulder. The man also laughed, too loudly. The second hurried to join in.

"Empty words from the half-blood," Halli said. "You may go, Trollboy. But don't go far." With that, he cantered off, his two companions rushing to follow.

Danr's legs shook like sickened tree trunks beneath him. He wanted desperately to sit down, but there was nowhere to sit. The other people moved about as if nothing had happened, but news of the exchange would fly about Skyford faster than black ravens, and these events would come back to punch Danr later. Why hadn't he just kept his mouth shut?

Feeling more than a little nauseated, he put his hat back on and continued on his way. At the first crossroad he came to, he caught a glimmer of river water through the forest of houses. The house on the corner closest to it—Orvandel's house—was a tidy structure made of stacked logs and surrounded by a neat vegetable garden. Thick thatch covered the roof, and the Great Tree on the front door was an elaborate painting in bright colors. Pigs and chickens poked about beneath the house's platform, and a goat was tethered to one side. The home of a prosperous craftsman.

The front door stood open, and a gray-haired man sat in the threshold. A bundle of long, pale sticks lay on either side of him. The man ran a long, curved knife over a stick, carefully smoothing away imperfections. Orvandel the fletcher, making arrows. At Danr's approach, he blinked, then set aside his tools and trotted down the short flight of steps that led to ground level.

"I know who you are," he said. "You're a thrall of Alfgeir Oxbreeder."

Danr nodded, a little startled that Orvandel didn't seem to notice or care that Danr wasn't human. He stood aside so Orvandel could see the steer. "He told me to deliver this to you because he owes a debt."

Orvandel looked at the steer, and his face darkened. The change in his expression was abrupt, and Danr stepped back in alarm. Orvandel spat angrily at the ground, and the spittle landed on one of the animal's hooves. The steer chewed a mouthful of cud, uncaring.

"Bastard!" Orvandel growled. "That son of a bitch owes me two bulls or one cow. This scrawny bag of bones doesn't nearly pay off what he owes me."

Danr remained silent. There was nothing to say. Orvandel's revelation didn't surprise him. In Danr's experience, Alfgeir spent more time counting his herds than caring for them.

"Tether that . . . that *thing* next to the goat," Orvandel finally said. "And I guess you'd better come inside."

This *did* surprise Danr, with all the power of a boulder dropping from the sky. He had never been invited into anyone's house before. He stayed in the cattle paddock on the annual trips to Skyford, and in the village no one ever allowed him to cross a threshold. Danr slowly tied the steer to the goat's tether stake and climbed the wooden steps with great hesitation. Orvandel had already gone inside. Danr paused nervously at the doorway. Everything beyond was dark, though he could hear voices in the gloom, and he realized he had no idea how people behaved inside houses. What should he do? Bow? Offer to shake hands? Stand by the door with his hat off? Maybe he should just tell Orvandel he'd stay outside. But no—that would be rejecting Orvandel's offer of hospitality, an unthinkably rude act. Moving carefully to avoid the pile of half-made arrows, Danr took a deep breath and stepped inside.

Chapter Three

His eyes took a few moments to adjust, but once they did, Danr stared in awe. Orvandel's house reflected his wealth. A long table ran the length of the main room, and freshly woven straw mats covered the floor. Beyond the table lay a stone-lined fire pit, where coals glowed red in the dim light. Freestanding screens partitioned off pieces of the room for private tasks. Tapestries hung from the walls, and the remaining exposed wood was elaborately carved in stylized leaves and animals, with an enormous tree looming over all. The interior smelled heavily of wood smoke and baking bread. What would it be like to call this place home?

A plump woman with silvering hair was adding wood to the fire. Three young men sat at the table behind piles of feathers. They were sorting them by size and type, a job that couldn't be done outdoors, where a random breeze could undo an hour's work in an instant.

"These are my sons," Orvandel said, gesturing at the young men. "Karsten and Almer. The one on the end there is my apprentice, Talfi. A foster son. Are you hungry from your trip?"

Danr's mouth went dry. It was hard to form words. No

one had ever formally introduced him to anyone, let alone offered him food. He started to refuse the latter offer, then decided it might be rude.

"A bit hungry," he stammered, and remembered to snatch off his hat. "Yes."

"Ruta!" Orvandel boomed. "Food for our guest!"

"You needn't bellow," Ruta clucked. "I'm standing here, oh mighty fletcher."

"My wife, Ruta," Orvandel said unnecessarily. "She's the real one in charge."

"And right you are to remember it."

Orvandel gave her a fond smile. "Have a seat, young man. What did you say your name was?"

Danr glanced uneasily around the house, feeling like a cow in a palace. Orvandel and Ruta seemed to accept who . . . or maybe *what* . . . he was without a qualm, but Karsten and Almer kept uneasy eyes on him as they sorted through their feathers. Talfi, seated by himself at the end of the table, stared unabashedly. Danr finally perched on the edge of the bench that ran the length of the table.

Orvandel was looking at him expectantly, waiting for an answer to his question. Danr swallowed. Back at the village, everyone knew who he was and Danr had never had to introduce himself. For the first time in his life, he had a choice about which name he could use. Except the only person who had ever said Danr's name aloud had been his mother, and he kept that name to himself, hoarding it like a wyrm's treasure. If no one knew what it was, no one would be able to steal it or twist it into something cruel. Unfortunately keeping silent about his true name left him with a single alternative.

"My name is . . . I'm Trollboy," he said gruffly, forcing himself to say the hated nickname. "From Alfgeir's farm."

"Alfgeir," Orvandel spat. "The bastard is a miser, a cheat,

and a scoundrel. Thinks he can get away with giving me a half-grown steer instead of two full-grown cows."

"What?" Ruta said, spinning to face her husband in outrage. "That . . . that . . ."

"My feelings exactly," Orvandel said.

Ruta muttered angrily to the wooden platter she was preparing, and Danr found himself ready to run, even though he knew she wasn't angry at him. She snatched a drinking horn from a shelf near the hearth, plunged it into an open barrel of beer to fill it, and came around the fire toward Danr. Talfi jumped to his feet.

"I'll bring it to him, Auntie," he said, taking platter and horn before she could object. Talfi came around the table, passing Karsten and Almer as he did so. Almer gave Talfi a heavy look and pointedly leaned away from him. Talfi didn't seem to notice. He carefully placed the platter and horn before Danr. The little feet that held the drinking horn upright were made of silver. The platter held three rolls stuffed by meat, half a cold chicken, and a chunk of sweet bread topped with sliced apples. Danr hadn't realized how empty his stomach was until he saw the food. He started in, taking care to eat with small bites. Mother had taught him to eat nicely; at least he could do that.

Talfi, meanwhile, plunked down on the bench beside him. Danr tensed again, wondering what Talfi was up to.

"Your name is Trollboy?" he asked. "Really?"

The question startled him. "No," he replied, his mouth full. He remembered his manners and swallowed. "That's just what everyone calls me."

"Because you're a troll?"

"Talfi," Orvandel said warningly.

"Sorry," Talfi said, but didn't look it.

"I'm half troll," Danr said. "My mother was human."

"Huh," Talfi said. "You must be pretty strong, then."

Danr shot him a sideways glance. Talfi looked to be a little older than Danr, maybe seventeen, though his beard hadn't begun to grow. His rich brown hair had a slight curl to it, and his features were sharply handsome. His eyes were as wide and blue as the sky. What would it be like to be blessed with such looks?

"I get by," Danr said.

"What are you going to do about the steer, Father?" Karsten asked. He was blond, wiry, and fully bearded.

Orvandel grimaced. "I'll have to send it back with . . . er, Trollboy here. You know, I wouldn't put it past that thief Alfgeir to have sent Trollboy to intimidate me into accepting that scrawny beast as payment."

Danr blinked and put down the drinking horn with a click. Sure, that would explain why Alfgeir had chosen Danr for the errand instead of one of his own sons. That made more sense than sending Danr away from the farm to quiet any unrest about the destruction of the Noss Farm.

"I won't have it." Orvandel's face was set. "Young man, you tell your master that his offer is unacceptable and that I want the two milk cows he promised."

"Yes, sir," Danr said.

"In fact," Orvandel said, stroking his beard, "I think it might be best to send one of my own sons with you. He can bring the cows back, make sure Alfgeir doesn't try to cheat me again."

"I'll go, Uncle," Talfi said quickly. "If we leave now, we can get to Alfgeir's by dusk and I can come back first thing in the morning. Is that all right, Trollboy?"

Surprised at being asked, Danr simply nodded.

"No need," Orvandel said. "Our guest should get a good night's sleep first."

A pang tightened Danr's stomach. The simple hospitality of a bench and a meal he could handle, but spending the night? The traps and pitfalls of guest etiquette lay scattered before him like a set of hunting snares. A wrong word, a mistake at the table, a fart at a bad moment, and for all he knew, he could cause a feud that lasted generations. The very idea made Danr's hands shake. His mind raced, looking for a way out, and after a moment, it found one.

"Thank you, *Carl* Orvandel," Danr said carefully. "But *Carl* Alfgeir's orders were clear. I return tonight."

"Not surprising," Orvandel snorted. "The man would squeeze pine chips for the pitch. I can imagine how he treats those who work for him. Talfi, you'd better get ready."

But Talfi was already pulling a brown cloak over his blue tunic. "I'm ready now."

"A moment." Ruta was at the pantry shelves, filling a sack. "I don't trust that man or his thin-titted wife to feed you properly. Take this."

Talfi fetched the bag. As he passed the table where Almer and Karsten were sorting feathers, Almer leaned over to his brother and muttered something. Karsten snorted, and a puff of feathers floated away from him. Talfi ignored this. Danr, now standing near the door, cocked his head. What in Vik's name was this about?

Talfi joined Danr in the rectangle of sunshine cast by the open doorway. Ashkame, the painted tree, gleamed green and brown. "I'll return tomorrow, Uncle."

Danr remembered his manners again. "My thanks for the hospitality, *Carl* Orvandel."

Orvandel waved a hand at this, and Danr exited the house, stepping carefully over the pile of half-finished arrows on the front stairs. In the garden, he untied the young steer and led it out to the street. Talfi fell into step beside him. Overhead the sun continued to burn, and the headache ground back into Danr's skull, despite his hat.

"I've never been to your village," Talfi said. "What's it like?"

"Small," Danr replied.

"What's its name?"

"I don't think it has one," Danr admitted, feeling oddly ashamed. What did he care if the village had a name or not? But for some reason, he felt a need to impress Talfi.

They walked down the muddy, wooden street. The cut logs were rough under Danr's callused feet. People continued to stare, but not as obviously, probably because Danr was with Talfi, and staring at Talfi would be rude. No one cared about being rude to a half-blood.

"Orvandel is your uncle?" Danr asked, more to fill the silence than anything else.

"No," Talfi said, a little uneasily. "He's just very kind and tells everyone I'm a foster son, so I call him that."

"How did you come to live with him? Are you really fostering with him or did your parents die, too?" The moment the insensitive words left Danr's mouth, he wished he could snatch them back. Danr was an idiot, and rude besides.

But Talfi didn't seem to notice. "I, uh . . . I don't actually know what happened to my parents."

"You don't?" Danr said, his surprise clear. Then he kicked himself again. A monster asking monstrous questions, that was all he was.

Talfi, however, didn't seem to notice. "Nope," was all he said. They reached the edge of the village and went through the crowded gate, still garnering stares. "I mean, I'm almost certain my parents *are* dead. Otherwise I'd be living with them. The rest is . . . strange."

"You're walking down a road with a troll and a cow," Danr said, "and you worry about strange?"

That got a laugh from Talfi. Talfi's laugh was a bright, clear sound, and Danr abruptly realized that this was one of the few times he had heard laughter that wasn't directed at him. It made him want to laugh himself, though he didn't.

"You're right," Talfi said, grinning. "So I'll tell you—one strange person to another." He paused, his gaze sliding into the distance. Red-brown cows grazed in a meadow near the road, and the breeze carried the scent of manure. Danr waited expectantly.

Talfi took a deep breath. "The strange part is, I don't remember."

Danr raised thick eyebrows. "You don't remember what?"

"Anything." Talfi sighed and bunched his hands underneath his brown cloak. "I have no memories at all."

"None?"

"My earliest memory is of looking at the Skyford gate. I was wearing a ragged tunic and only one shoe and I was hungry." Talfi was twisting the cloak now. "That was three years ago. I still have no idea who I am or where I came from."

"Huh." Danr tried to imagine this, but the idea of not having any memories failed him. "Do you know how to do . . . things?"

"Yeah. I can ride a horse. I can read. I can even make arrows. Someone must have taught me, but I don't remember learning any of it." He paused, and a raven coasted overhead with a low croak. "My skill as a fletcher was how I persuaded Uncle Orvandel to take me in, but I told him that I was an orphan with no master."

"Huh," Danr said again. "Have you tried to find your memory again?"

Talfi spread his hands beneath his brown cloak. "A little. One time Uncle Orvandel sent me to Meltown to buy feathers, so I was able to ask after myself—that was a strange business—but no one knew me there, either."

The sun continued to shine overhead, but the hard rays were blunted by the kindly shade cast by the trees that lined the road, and Danr scarcely needed his hat. The steer followed placidly, and Danr wondered if it was mystified about their trip to Skyford and back. Probably not. Cows leaned toward bland and idiotic. As long as they had enough to eat and other cows to moo at, they were happy. Sometimes Danr envied them that.

"It doesn't seem to bother you very much," Danr said. "Living without memories."

"What should I do, mope? I'll figure something eventually." Talfi dug around in the sack Ruta had given him and came up with a chicken leg. "Have something to eat."

Danr accepted it. "Thank you. It feels like I'm always hungry."

Talfi grinned. "I'll bet you eat like a . . . like a . . ."

"Troll?"

"I was going to say *giant*." Talfi sniffed.

"Sure you were," Danr said, and realized he was grinning, too.

"Anyway, I don't talk about my memory problems." Talfi took out a chicken leg for himself. "Not even with Uncle Orvandel. People would think it odd."

"That I understand." A cold idea stole over Danr as he finished off the chicken leg. He narrowed his eyes. "If you don't talk much about your memory, then why are you talking about it with me?"

Talfi cocked his head. "I don't know. In your way, you're as strange as I am, so that makes you easy to talk to. It feels good to say it aloud." He raised the half-eaten chicken leg to the sky like a tiny sword and shouted, "My name is Talfi and I have no memories! Fuck to the Nine! Fuck to the entire damn world!"

Now Danr halted. Behind him, the steer halted as well. "You aren't trying to play me for a fool, are you?"

Talfi brought the chicken leg down. "No. It's truth."

"Because sometimes people think a stupid troll will believe anything," Danr continued. "That he's as stupid as he looks."

"Oh." Talfi gnawed the meat with a thoughtful expression. "Do people think you're a monster?"

"Don't you?" Danr countered, and braced himself for the answer. But in response, Talfi only shrugged.

"I don't know you very well," was all he said. "Do you *want* to be a monster?"

"I don't have much of a choice."

"Liar," Talfi said cheerfully. He tossed the bone away.

The monster rumbled. Danr rounded on Talfi, teeth bared. "You think I'd be like this if I had a choice?"

To Danr's surprise, however, Talfi didn't shrink back. "Everyone has choices. Are you cruel to animals?"

"What?" Danr said, feeling suddenly off balance. "No!"

"Do you scare children? Eat people? Steal? Wreck things on purpose?"

"No!"

Talfi spread his hands. "That's everything on my monster list. Doesn't sound like you qualify."

A breeze stirred the leaves overhead. Danr licked his lips, still off balance. He could hardly believe he was standing on an ordinary road having this extraordinary conversation. He had never talked like this in his life, not even to his mother or Aisa. But something about Talfi made him want to talk, say whatever came to mind. And Talfi was right—it felt good to say things aloud. Did this mean he truly had a friend? Danr wasn't sure. How long did you have to know someone before he became a friend?

A cow from a nearby pasture bawled, and Danr's little steer bawled back. "You changed the subject," Danr said.

"I did?"

"You were talking about not remembering anything, and somehow the talk came back to me."

"Oh yeah." Talfi laughed again. "Funny, that. There is something else."

Danr started walking again. The steer followed. "What's that?"

"Wait." Talfi flung up a hand and Danr stopped near a small boulder. The steer yanked at the rope, but Danr held fast. "Do you hear that?"

Danr listened. All he heard was the gentle sighing of the spring wind. A half-uprooted ash tree leaned a little dangerously in their direction, adding extra shade to the road. Behind them, the steer bawled and tried to pull away.

"I don't hear anything except the stupid cow," Danr said.

"That's just it," Talfi whispered. "What happened to the forest noises?"

Unease slipped quietly over Danr. Talfi was right. No birds sang, no small animals rustled in the bushes, no squirrels chattered in the trees. The young steer bawled again, and Danr wished it would shut—

A massive green blur exploded out of the undergrowth. Danr caught an impression of flat eyes and sharp teeth. He felt a sharp jerk on the rope, and the steer's bellow turned into a bloody wail. The enormous serpent, a wyrm, snapped once, twice, and the steer was gone. The creature raised its head and a red tongue thicker than Danr's arm flickered in the air only a yard from Danr's head. The wyrm's head was taller than Danr himself, and its jaws were wide enough for him to walk right inside. Green scales glittered along a thick and muscular body that disappeared into the undergrowth. The wyrm reared back its head and stared down at Danr with hard black eyes. Danr stared back, so surprised he didn't even feel fear. The wyrm's tongue flickered again. Then he heard Talfi's breath coming in frightened gasps beside him. The surprise broke, and terror slammed through him. His heart jerked so hard it nearly burst through his ribs. The wyrm's head moved hypnotically back and forth, as if it were trying to decide which of them to eat next. Thick trees hemmed in the road, limiting escape.

"I'll distract it," Talfi said in a harsh whisper. "You do something."

"Do what?" Danr whispered back.

But Talfi was already moving. He fled down the tree-lined road. The wyrm hissed and lunged past Danr to snap at Talfi. Its jaws slammed shut with a terrible *clop*. Talfi, however, leaped nimbly out of range. For the second time that day, Danr gaped in awe. Talfi all but flew down the road, his feet moving so fast Danr could hardly see them. The wyrm gave chase. It snapped at Talfi, trying to swallow him as it had swallowed the steer. Talfi darted aside. The left side of the road followed a low embankment, and Talfi ran up the short slope, kicked off the side, and leaped onto the wyrm's back. The wyrm instantly twisted around on itself, striking at its own spine. Talfi leaped over its head, hit the ground, and ran back toward Danr at blinding speed.

"Quick!" Talfi shouted. "Do it!"

Do what? Danr thought desperately. Talfi thundered toward him, the wyrm barreling right behind him. Danr's eye fell on the thigh-high boulder near which he had stopped. Without thinking, he squatted and wrapped his arms around the rock. His arms bulged and his legs burned. Sweat sprang up on his forehead and trickled down his hatband, but the boulder moved. Gritting his teeth, Danr lifted the rock above his head and straightened just as Talfi shot past him, the wyrm in hot pursuit. Danr flung the boulder as hard as he could. It caught the wyrm in the side of the head with a meaty *thunk*. Instantly the creature stopped its forward lunge. Its body lashed and squirmed, and its head rolled from side to side. Danr barely leaped out of the way in time. He crawled up the embankment to a safe distance. Warm red blood spattered the road.

"Come on!" Talfi shouted. "We have to get out of here!"

Danr swallowed. The bloody end of the cow's rope was still looped around his wrist, a reminder that the wyrm could just as easily have killed Danr himself—or Talfi. The monster wasn't dead. It could still go after someone else, someone who couldn't bash its head with a rock.

The wyrm continued to squirm. Danr jumped back down to the road. One of the snake's coils rushed at him like an emerald avalanche. He saw it coming but couldn't move fast enough. Danr braced himself against the coming pain. The coil crashed into him, knocking him back against the embankment. Hot agony throbbed through his chest and shoulders, and he groaned beneath the fire. Every nerve screamed with it.

"What are you doing?" Talfi yelled. He was standing several yards away, braced to run. "Let's go! Now!"

The wyrm shook its head as if to clear it, and it stopped squirming. It rounded on Danr and hissed with anger. One of its eyes was missing, and Danr saw the impression his rock had made in its head. Blood oozed around the wound. Danr smelled it, a heavy, coppery miasma in the air. He had done that, he realized in wonder, and what a strange thing to think at the moment of his own death. He panted, still hurting. The wyrm reared back, gathering itself to strike.

"Run!" Talfi shouted.

The wyrm lunged, but Danr was already moving through the hurt. The creature's teeth clashed together so close to his back that he felt the concussion. Just ahead of him was the leaning ash tree. Danr pounded down the road, his bare feet slapping earth. Behind him the snake's cold scales rushed over ruts and gravel. Instinct told him to dodge, and he leaped to the right. The wyrm's teeth closed on his sleeve. Its tongue flashed out and flickered over Danr's face. Danr tore free and ran. He was almost to the tree.

Something hard closed over his left leg, engulfing it to the knee. Danr fell flat on the road. New pain snapped sharp and hard through his left shin. Vik! The wyrm had him. He tried to twist around so he could hit, kick, bite, anything. But the wyrm held him too tightly. It dragged Danr backward, his fingers leaving furrows in the ground.

And then Talfi was there. In a flash he was standing next to the wyrm's wounded head. He balled up a fist and punched the creature where Danr's boulder had dented its skull. The wyrm hissed in pain and released Danr, who rolled to his feet, ignoring the white-hot agony in his leg. The wyrm rounded on Talfi, but he was already running up the road, faster than a rabbit with a winter dog behind. They both passed under the leaning tree.

"Do something!" Talfi shrieked. "Hurry!"

Danr loped to the leaning trunk and reached up to dig his fingers into the wood. "Bring it back this way!" he bellowed. *Please, great Fell, grant me the strength!*

Talfi shot a glance over his shoulder. The wyrm rushed behind him, gaining ground with every turn of its coils. Talfi jumped sideways, hit a boulder, and pushed off in a new direction. He pelted back toward Danr. Confused, the wyrm halted, then looped back on itself to follow. Danr pressed his teeth together and pulled downward. For a dreadful moment he felt nothing. Then the tree moved, just a little. He pulled harder. The monster in him exulted. Roots cracked and earth shifted. Talfi shot past him, fear etched on his face. The wyrm's head passed under the tree, and Danr *heaved*.

The tree came crashing down. Limbs cracked and leaves flew in all directions. The heavy tree slammed into the wyrm's neck, pinning it to the road. It hissed again and lashed with its tail. The ash shifted.

"That tree won't hold it forever," Talfi panted beside him. Danr, however, hadn't stopped moving. He ran to the boulder he had used once, heaved it to his shoulder, and loped back to the wyrm. It was already partway free of the ash tree. Danr got as close as he dared and threw the rock with all his strength. It struck the wyrm square in its original wound. A horrible hiss rent the air, and Talfi put his hands over his ears. The wyrm's coils flung the ash tree aside as if it were a twig. It crashed against the embankment by the side of the road. Danr tensed to do something. Maybe he could get to the rock again.

But the wyrm was in its death throes. The lashing and thrashing grew weaker. At last the wyrm shuddered hard. It exhaled a foul-smelling stench, then lay still.

All the strength left Danr's body. He sank shaking to the ground. His leg and his chest burned with pain. He was panting, and he stared down at his enormous, callused hands in disbelief. Bits of brown bark clung to them. He focused on this detail. It made the entire incident real, somehow— more real than even the wyrm's corpse itself. The wyrm was too big to take in, but bits of bark he could understand. Had he really pulled down a tree? How strong was he, anyway? He had never actually tested himself. Not since that one day when he had . . . not since that one day.

A hand landed on his shoulder. "Are you all right?" Talfi asked.

Danr blinked up at him. The only person who had ever asked him that was his mother. "My leg hurts."

Talfi knelt to examine it. The cloth had torn where the wyrm's teeth had grabbed him, exposing bloody skin. He pulled the cloth aside and Danr sucked in a breath against the cutting pain.

"It doesn't look bad," Talfi said. "But I think we should wash it. Can you walk?"

In answer, Danr got unsteadily to his feet. Behind Talfi, the wyrm's enormous body lay motionless beside the tree on the road. The roadway would be impassible to wagons and cattle until someone removed the corpse. Danr decided someone else could handle that detail.

A thread of smoke curled up from the wyrm's half-open mouth. It smelled of rotten meat. The entire corpse abruptly burst into green flame with a *whoosh* and a blast of heat that bowled Talfi and Danr backward. Both of them scooted backward crabwise, eyes round with fright. Roasting heat licked at their faces and chests and shins.

"Vik!" Talfi swore.

In seconds, the wyrm's corpse collapsed into ash. Even the bones cracked and blacked into dry soot. The emerald flames died down and vanished, leaving behind on the charred ground a half skeleton of delicate charcoal that was already blowing away in the wind.

"Grick's tits," Danr breathed. "Let's get away from here."

"I saw a stream near the edge of the woods," Talfi said, and the two of them hurried away. Talfi threw occasional glances over his shoulder at the blackened ground.

"You just . . . killed it," he said. "I don't think I've ever been more scared in my entire life, but you ran up and smashed it with that rock. It was the bravest thing I ever saw."

"I was terrified," Danr admitted. "But I didn't want it to hurt anyone else."

They found the stream and Danr rolled up his trouser leg to wash. His skin was naturally swarthy, and the new bruises turned it even darker. The bleeding remained minor, and the pain was already fading, though Danr suspected he'd ache in the morning. They also splashed water on their hot faces and dusted the ash from their clothes.

Danr and Talfi continued on their way back to the village, discussing the attack all the way. Neither of them had any idea where the wyrm had come from, though both of them had heard stories of the orcs riding such creatures in the lands of Xaron far, far to the east, and Danr's mother had told tales of wyrms living wild in the northern mountains. Why one of them would come so far south was a mystery. Danr remembered Oscar and Olaf Noss and the troll tracks found at their ravaged farm. Were the incidents connected? He thought about saying something to Talfi, then clamped his lips shut. Their friendship was too new, too tentative for Danr to remind him that trolls were monsters.

They arrived at the village near sunset. The spring air was cooling, and Talfi pulled his cloak tighter around himself as they squished through dark streets filled with spring mud. The village looked deserted. Light glowed through cracks around closed doors, but no people were in evidence. This struck Danr as odd. At this time of day most people were inside eating or getting ready for bed, but there was almost always *someone* about. White Halli's men didn't patrol here.

Even as he completed this thought, a man carrying a lantern emerged from one house. He glanced up and down the street, but his lantern prevented him from seeing anything outside the circle of yellow light. He scurried to a neighboring house, knocked softly, and slipped inside.

"What's going on?" Talfi asked, voice low.

"I don't know," Danr admitted. Cold pricked his spine. "Let's hurry."

A small side track outside the village led to Alfgeir's farm. Danr turned down it and fought a rising sense of dread. Alfgeir wouldn't take the news of the steer's loss well. Somehow, Danr was sure, he would find a way to blame everything on Danr.

Alfgeir didn't disappoint.

"Why didn't you kill the wyrm *before* it ate my steer?" he demanded.

Danr looked down at his feet. His leg ached. They were standing in the dooryard of Alfgeir's hall. Night had fallen, and the air was sharp with a spring frost. Alfgeir crossed his arms and leaned against the doorpost.

"Can you answer?" he demanded. "Or are you mute as well as stupid?"

Alfgeir's scorn and anger filled the dooryard, pressing Danr to the ground. Danr's face grew hot, and he felt small enough to crawl under one of the pebbles near his foot. He was acutely aware of Talfi standing nearby, and his embarrassment increased. Talfi hadn't even been his friend for a day and already he had seen Alfgeir treating him like the thrall he was. Even Vik's cold realm would be better than this.

"Excuse me, *Carl*," Talfi said. "I'm not sure you heard us. My friend here *killed* a giant wyrm. All by himself."

"If it's true." Alfgeir sniffed. "Very convenient that this sudden wyrm ate the steer and then vanished into thin air."

Talfi bristled. "He saved our lives, and you're worried about a scrawny steer that wasn't worth half the debt you owe Master Orvandel?"

"That fine animal was *everything* I owed Orvandel, young man." Alfgeir speared a finger at Talfi's chest. "And you'd best remember to keep silent around your elders. As the saying goes, 'A child must be obedient, quick, and *quiet*.'"

"You owe my uncle two milk cows, and I'm not to go back without them."

"Then you'll not go back," Alfgeir snapped. "I wouldn't send him a half-dead dog."

With that, he slammed the door. Danr stared at it as the horror of Alfgeir's affront crept over him. It wasn't just his words—Alfgeir had failed to ask Talfi in or offer hospitality for the night. The insult was worse than spitting in Talfi's face. Danr forced himself to turn and face his friend.

Talfi drawled, "I can see why you enjoy working for him."

"You can stay with me," Danr said slowly. "I don't have much to offer, but—"

"I'm sure it'll be better than anything Alfgeir has," Talfi said. "Lead the way."

They trod in silence across the courtyard to the stable, and Danr entered ahead of Talfi. The familiar sounds and smells of sleepy cattle met him, and the air puffed a little warmer against his face. Straw rustled underfoot. Feeling a little more relaxed, Danr headed down the rows of stalls.

"How can you see in here?" Talfi called from the doorway.

Danr stopped. His night-sensitive eyes had no trouble with near darkness, but he had forgotten that Talfi had no such advantage. "Just a moment," he called back, and hurried down to his own stall, where he scrounged up a candle stump. He blew on the dim coals banked on his tiny stone hearth until he could light the wick and guide Talfi in. Danr's face burned as he realized his new friend was going to see how he lived among the animals, but there was nothing for it. He had offered hospitality, and the offer remained in force for as long as Talfi wanted to stay. Talfi, however, took a seat on the ground next to the open hearth as if everything were perfectly normal. Danr built up the fire as high as he dared. Cattle snorted and lowed softly around them. Talfi rooted through the food sack.

"Looks like Aunt Ruta was right about Alfgeir," he said, producing several stuffed rolls and half a smoked salmon. "But thanks to her, we don't need him."

A metallic gleam at Talfi's neck caught Danr's eye. Eager for a topic of conversation to fill the silence, Danr pointed to it. "What's that?"

Talfi paused, and his hand went to his neck. "Oh. That. It's . . . it's . . ."

Sudden insight flicked over Danr. "You said there was something else strange about you just before the wyrm attacked us. Is that what it is?"

"Yeah."

He looked reluctant, his eyes large in the light of the little fire. Danr felt uncomfortable. "You don't have to talk about it if you don't—"

"No, no," Talfi interrupted. "I was going to. It just felt odd for a moment. It's nothing foolish or shocking. I don't even know why I dislike talking about it." Talfi reached under his tunic and came up with a thin copper chain. A small silver amulet dangled from it. "I was wearing this when I arrived in Skyford, but I don't know where it came from. My belly was empty and this would have gotten me enough money for a few meals at least, but when I tried to take it off, I felt . . . afraid."

"Afraid?" Danr leaned over to look at the amulet. One side showed a leafless tree with its roots and branches wrapped around three spheres. It was the symbol of the universe, of the Nine Gods, and of the Nine People. The other side showed a double-bladed axe crossed over a shield. The amulet was badly worn around the edges and was clearly much older than the copper chain.

"Actually I was terrified." Talfi ran a finger around the amulet's edge. His eyes took on a distant look. "The idea of giving it away just about sent me to my knees. Even now, it feels weird admitting to you that I have it, and you saved my life. At any rate, I kept it and went hungry until I could beg some bread at Uncle Orvandel's door. He had his fletching materials out, and I showed him what I could do, so he gave me work."

"It's very old," Danr observed without reaching for it.

"Sometimes . . ." Talfi continued to trace the worn edge of the amulet, and his face turned darker, unhappy, and yet fascinated, like someone who couldn't stop poking at an old wound that still hurt. "Sometimes, when I feel its edges, I get . . . shadows. A battle. Metal clashing. Screams. Blood. A lot of blood. And water. Like I'm swimming or drowning or both."

Danr didn't know what to say to this, so he simply said, "Oh."

"Yeah." Talfi's eyes were glazing over. "So much blood. And sometimes I see a man with red hair and green eyes. He talks to me, but I can't hear what he's saying."

"It sounds like someone put a glamour on you," Danr said. "Maybe one of the Fae."

Talfi's face cleared and he dropped the amulet back under his tunic. "I'm cursed."

"Do you think so?"

"Vik's balls, who knows? I don't know what being cursed feels like." He sighed. "I want to find out what's wrong with me."

Something clicked in Danr's head again. "That's why you were so eager to come here," he said.

"Nothing to learn in Skyford," Talfi admitted. "What do I have to lose by nosing about here? I . . ." He hesitated. "I don't suppose you know any trollwives. The ones who can still do magic?"

Danr felt bad for him. "No. My father was a troll, but I never met him, or any other Stane. I'm sorry."

Talfi shook his head and put a smile on his face. "At least we have Aunt Ruta's good food."

They made a party out of it, eating and talking late into the night while shadows danced to the music of the flames. Danr hadn't known how hungry he was for companionship until he had it, and the company was more filling than any meat or drink.

"What do you want for yourself?" Talfi asked over the bones of the salmon.

Danr's head was a little muzzy from the late hour and a full belly. "Want?"

"Yeah. Want. One day, when your bonding runs out, you'll be free. What do you want to do when that day comes?"

"I don't know if I'll ever be free." Danr leaned back in the straw and stared at the ceiling. "*Carl* Oxbreeder keeps finding ways to add time to my bonding. He does it on purpose to keep me here."

"You can't think that way," Talfi insisted. "Trolls are supposed to live a long time, longer than humans. Eventually he'll run out of excuses, and you'll be free."

Danr shifted on the prickly straw. That was one of the thoughts that sometimes kept him awake at night, that he might live a long life under Alfgeir's thumb, and when Alfgeir died, he would pass like an heirloom to Norbert. He didn't often dare think about being free, no, he didn't. But Talfi's presence let him bend a few rules.

"I'll never be free," Danr said. "It's impossible."

"You aren't a slave. When your bonding is up, you walk away. That's the law. Why won't you be free?"

Danr looked at the stable wall, and for a moment it seemed he could look through it to Alfgeir's house, where Norbert was sitting at his father's hearth, probably drinking from a horn with silver feet and massaging his left arm.

Monster. The word echoed in his head.

"When I was six or seven, Norbert and I were playing. Vik's gate, I don't even remember what." Danr sighed. "Norbert lost, and he got mad. He called me names—troll's bastard, stony Stane. A kid's chant. I got angry."

Even now, the memory dredged up a mixture of anger and a child distress, and Danr's fists clenched.

"What happened next?" Talfi asked.

Danr stared into the fire. "He called my mother a troll's slut."

"Uh-oh."

"Yeah. The monster inside me came out then." Danr closed his eyes, remembering the awful words, the screams, the crunch of bone. "I yelled, but it came out more like a roar. I grabbed Norbert by the arm and swung him around and slammed him into the ground. Both Alfgeir and my mother heard and came running. I slammed Norbert into the ground again, and a third time before Mother was able to pull me off him. Norbert's arm was both dislocated and broken. More than ten years later, it still hurts him."

"Wow."

"Yeah. Alfgeir was all for turning me over to the earl for hanging, but Mother begged him not to. She said I'd be his thrall like she was, and that I'd never show the monster again. I haven't, either. She saw to that."

What he didn't say was how often Mother had used that little incident to remind him how close the monster was. *"You have to keep the monster half caged in,"* she told him over and over. *"Others don't deserve to die over a few words—and neither do you."*

And so he had kept the monster half inside him, always inside. But people always saw the outside. The half-blood.

"Alfgeir and Norbert still remember," Danr continued. "Norbert makes my life as bad as anything Lady Halza can dream up, and Alfgeir adds to my bonding every chance he gets. I'll never be free."

"Huh." Talfi rubbed his nose. "Still, he can't really keep you forever. Even Alfgeir has to die one day. Or maybe you'll just walk away."

Danr was still trying to imagine what it would be like to walk away and was coming up empty. You couldn't just walk away from what you owed. The Nine would get you for it, in the end. But he didn't say that aloud.

They talked more. Danr wished the night could go on forever. In the end, however, fatigue forced both of them to roll themselves up in the ragged old blankets Danr had scavenged over the years. Danr, however, dozed only restlessly. In dreams, he was looking for both Talfi and his mother through muddy village streets. The mud pulled at his feet, and darkness lay thick around him. Even his trollish eyes could barely make out shapes. His mother's voice echoed somewhere ahead.

"Don't be a monster!" she cried. *"See the truth instead."*

A hand landed on Danr's shoulder and he jerked awake. In the dim light of the dying fire, he saw a hooded figure in a ragged scarf leaning over him. Aisa.

"What—?" Danr gasped. On the other side of the fire, Talfi sat up, his brown hair mussed from sleep.

"You must hurry," Aisa said. "Quickly!"

Danr came fully awake. "What's wrong?"

"The villagers are coming," she hissed. "They want your blood."

Chapter Four

Danr scrambled to his feet, heart already pounding, and flung his ragged cloak over his shoulders. Talfi did the same, though his cloak was new and unpatched. Cattle shifted nervously in the stalls. Aisa crept to the stable door and pushed it open a crack.

"I see torches coming up the road," she reported. "They are nearly here. A very efficient mob."

Danr peered outside. A half-moon shed plenty of light, and to Danr's eyes, the farmyard was nearly bright as day. A line of yellow lights bobbed toward the main gate. Alfgeir's house was between the road and the stable, and Danr wondered if the villagers would stop there first or come straight for him. Fear pushed bile up the back of his tongue.

"Do they really want to kill?" Talfi whispered.

Aisa spread her hands. "My mistress, Frida, sounded very angry, and she was the one who laid blame. The other men gathered to listen, and they were happy to become angry as well. Now they come with pitchforks and scythes and whips."

The blood drained from Danr's face. His mind raced in little circles, seeking a solution. He could run for the mountains. But they were inhabited by monsters even worse than the wyrm he and Talfi had killed. He could sneak away and head south, farther into Balsia. But everywhere he went, people would recognize a half-troll monster.

He could stay and fight.

Danr swallowed, remembering Norbert and the way bone had grated against flesh under his hand. *Don't show the monster,* Mother's voice murmured inside his head. Monsters were evil, terrors, and whenever he thought about fighting, he saw his mother's disappointed, fear-filled eyes. But if he ran away, what would happen to Talfi? He had given Talfi hospitality, and that made it Danr's duty to defend him from harm.

"We should run from this place," Aisa murmured behind her veil of scarves, and Danr very much wanted to follow her advice. He wanted to run with Aisa somewhere safe, where just the two of them could spend time together, without worrying that his master or her owner would make demands or threats. Where the world was peaceful, and they might share an actual meal and have a conversation like normal people. He wanted to be normal with *her.*

Instead he sighed. "I don't see how we can run." With a deep breath, he shoved the stable door open and strode outside, gathering the night in a pitchy cloak. The crowd of torches flickered in the dooryard. Danr stomped toward them, jaw set. His heart beat like a fast drum, and fear sang a shrill tune in his ears, but he kept moving. A hand plucked at his arm.

"What are you doing?" Aisa hissed. Talfi stood beside her, looking frightened. "This way!"

Danr shook her off, though his mouth was dry as sand. "Now that I've killed a wyrm, it's time to face a mob."

A few more steps took him within hearing of the crowd. The men had stopped at Alfgeir's hall. Danr picked out individual faces in the torchlight: Anders the thatcher, and Mikkel the pig farmer, and Henrik the butcher, and Soren the farmer, who had lost his father to frostbite last winter. And all the others he knew. They weren't friends, but he had known them all his life. Now they were calling for his death. Anders carried a length of heavy rope.

Danr was not surprised to see White Halli in the lead, torch in one hand, sword in the other. Golden firelight gleamed on the silver blade. Danr *was* surprised to see Rudin standing beside Halli. Rudin was Halli's son, barely four years old. Before Danr could react further, Alfgeir's door opened and the man himself stepped into the chilly night air, beard a-thistle with indignation. Norbert followed.

"What's happening here?" Alfgeir demanded. "What do you want?"

"We've come for the monster who killed the Noss brothers," Halli said. "Trollboy and his kin—" Halli spat. "—destroyed their house and crushed their bones."

"I did no such thing." Danr moved into the circle of torches. The men in the crowd, perhaps a dozen in all, tightened their grips on their makeshift weapons. One or two stepped back, but the rest held their ground. The light hurt Danr's eyes, but he refused to blink. Instead he folded his arms over his broad chest. "Why are you causing trouble, Halli?"

"Did your pet witch warn you we were coming, Trollboy?" Halli said.

Danr just stared at him, unmoving despite the tat-tat-tat of his heart. The word *witch* was filled with a danger all its own, and Halli was attaching it to Aisa. Witches were beaten, branded, and burned or beheaded. He thought of Aisa's head rolling away from a bloody axe, and all his words shriveled away. Halli noted the silence with glee.

"Dumb as a rock." Halli turned to his son. "Take a long look, Rudin, and remember this day. The Stane are monsters, and monsters deserve to be exterminated." He raised his voice. "Men, let's—"

"Touch one hair on his head, Halli," Alfgeir said, "and I'll take it straight to your father."

Halli and the men stared in astonishment. So did Danr.

"Trollboy here does the work of ten men around my farm," Alfgeir continued. "He's stupid, he has no manners, and he's filthy most of the time, but he isn't a murderer."

Halli blinked. No one, least of all Danr, had expected Alfgeir to stand up for Danr. An air of uncertainty stole over the men. Several torches wavered. Norbert and Alfgeir's two other sons, all heavily muscled from years of work in the fields, looked stonily over their father's shoulders. Norbert rubbed his arm but remained silent.

"Papa?" Rudin asked, tugging at Halli's tunic. "Are you going to kill the Stane monster?"

"We found troll tracks in the wreckage," Halli said, trying to rally. "It couldn't be anyone else."

"How do you know what troll tracks look like," Alfgeir asked reasonably, "when no one here has ever seen a troll?"

"The tracks definitely weren't human!" Halli shot back. "And only a troll could have—"

"Trollboy's feet are human." Alfgeir pointed. "Look."

Every eye in the crowd went to Danr's feet. Danr wanted to clench his toes in embarrassment, but forced himself to remain still. His feet were large and the toes splayed outward, but they were indeed human. Danr realized he himself had no idea what troll feet looked like. Several men in the crowd began to mutter and the small crowd shifted about, losing cohesion.

"Trollboy killed a giant wyrm on the road to Skyford today," Alfgeir continued. "Go see the burn marks for yourself. Perhaps many creatures are coming down from the mountains. Only Olar knows why, but it has nothing to do with my farm or my thralls."

"Trollboy consorts with witches. His mother and that slave girl. Now he's bringing the monsters down on us," Halli said, though his words lacked conviction. Danr still flinched at the word *witch*. "The Stane are coming down here because he is one of them."

"Strange they should wait sixteen years to come visit," Alfgeir drawled.

"Who knows why the Stane do anything?" Halli retorted, though it was clear he had lost the support of the crowd.

"My slave girl is a good healer," added Farek, belying his wife's angry words. "I wouldn't count her a witch, exactly. Your Lordship. She cost a pretty penny."

"She knows things," Halli said darkly. "Foreign things. Mark me, Farek—she'll bring darkness on us."

"And what's that to do with Trollboy?" Alfgeir put in.

Rudin looked up at his father, confused. "When are you going to kill the monster, Papa?" he piped up.

"Gisla!" Alfgeir shouted. The door opened, and Alfgeir's wife appeared. Like Alfgeir, she was middle-aged and running toward plump. Her dark brown braids hung loose behind her, down for the night. "It's a chill night. Have the boys roll out a barrel of ale for our guests. As the saying goes, 'Ale is proof the Nine want us to love life!' "

A little cheer went up from the men, and they gathered around the door. Danr stepped backward until he was out of the circle of torchlight. As Gisla served up brimming horns of ale in the dooryard, he turned to head back to the stable. Alfgeir caught him up.

"Are you all right?" he demanded.

"Yes, *Carl* Oxbreeder," Danr said. "Thank you for . . . for supporting me."

"If I were you, I'd avoid that slave girl Aisa. You know what people say about her, for all that she brings healing. As the saying goes, 'A bad friend hurts more than a good enemy.'"

Danr remained silent. Nothing he could say would change Alfgeir's opinion, so he didn't waste words.

"You still have six years and four months left on your bond, Trollboy," Alfgeir said. "If they killed you, I'd be out all that labor. And speaking of which, I'm adding seven months to your bond—six for saving your life, and one for that barrel of ale."

"A barrel of ale isn't worth a month's labor," Danr protested, forgetting himself. "It's three days at most."

Alfgeir gave him an icy stare. "Do you want to challenge it before the earl, Trollboy?"

"I . . ." For a moment, Danr wanted to say he would. Alfgeir was unashamedly breaking any number of laws. The earl would have to listen.

To a troll. To a monster.

Danr—Trollboy—hung his head. "I don't," he said.

Alfgeir snorted and strode back to the impromptu party. Danr watched him go, hatred mingling with despair. He would never be free of his bonding. He would never be free of his monstrous stigma. He would never be free.

Danr trudged back to the stables. When he pushed open the door, he found Talfi and Aisa waiting for him.

"They didn't hurt me," he said heavily.

"We heard," Talfi said flatly. "Friend, you really need to go to the earl about Alfgeir."

"The earl won't listen to someone like me," Danr said quietly, repeating his earlier thoughts. "And even if he did, what would it get me? Once my bond ends, I have nowhere to go. I don't own land, and no one will hire a monster."

"Didn't we already talk about this?" Talfi asked.

"You are no monster," Aisa said at the same time. Her

tone was sharp. Startled, Danr looked from one to the other, and it occurred to him that he was now entertaining two people in his—for lack of a better word—home. A slow flush crept over him, and he wished he had something better to offer them than the leftovers from the food Talfi's foster mother had given him. Aisa was good and kind, and he was filled with a sudden desire to sit with her, put his arm around her, and feel her softness against him.

"Whatever you might tell me," he said gruffly, "*they* see me as inhuman, and it's what they think that counts."

Talfi looked ready to object, then closed his mouth instead. Aisa just looked at him over her scarf. Not for the first time, he wished—even ached—to know her face.

"Talfi told me of the injury to your leg," Aisa said, changing the subject. "May I see?"

Glad of the distraction, Danr drew his torn trouser leg up. Aisa leaned over it with the candle, and her closeness sent a small shiver over him.

"The cuts have scabbed over well," she said. "I see no sign of infection, but that may not come for two or three days. Talfi, do you have strong ale in your bag?"

Talfi handed over a clay bottle, and Aisa poured it over Danr's leg. He winced as ants of pain scurried across his skin. From a pouch at her waist, Aisa took several dried leaves, mixed them with more ale, and applied them to some of the wounds.

"This will deaden pain and help block infection," she said. "If you were anyone else, I would tell you to keep this leg warm for the next day or so, but I doubt Alfgeir will allow this. So I will only say that you should exercise care that you do not strain yourself. If it hurts, stop what you are doing."

"I heal fast," Danr said gruffly. "You don't have to worry."

"Hmm." Aisa sat back on her heels and pulled his trouser leg down. "You are welcome."

Danr flushed. "Thank you," he blurted. "I know you usually charge for . . . I mean, I don't have any money . . . that is, I don't . . ."

She held up a hand. "I will take my payment in the form of three extra guesses today."

"Guesses?" Talfi said.

"Oh . . . uh . . ." The flush deepened. This was the first time anyone else had ever heard of the name game, and he wasn't sure what Talfi would think.

"Is it Magnus?"

"Er . . . no."

"What are you doing?" Talfi asked.

"Perhaps Klaus?"

Danr chewed a thumbnail, both pleased and embarrassed by her attentions. "No."

"Is it Hudl Knopfenstropfer?"

A small smile snuck across his face. "Afraid not."

"What the Vik?" Talfi demanded.

"He won't tell me his true name, so I am guessing," Aisa said. "Perhaps you can help."

Light dawned on Talfi's face. "Oh! I want to know, too. Is it Fred?"

"You don't get to play," Danr said shortly.

"Hmm. So, what now?" Talfi asked, to Danr's relief.

"The village is holding a funeral for the Noss brothers tomorrow," Aisa said. "At noon."

"I should probably stay away from that," Danr said.

"You should not," Talfi replied emphatically. "You should stand up front, show everyone you're not afraid to be there. You certainly bought the right with that keg of ale."

That took Danr by surprise. "I don't know . . ."

"I'll go, too," Talfi said. "As an emissary from Skyford, or something." He leaned back on his cloak, and straw crackled beneath him. "I'm in no hurry to return home."

"Why not?" Danr asked without thinking how rude the words might sound. He flushed again, wishing he could take them back.

Talfi, however, didn't seem to take offense. "I hate sorting feathers," he said, a little too casually. Danr cocked his head. There was something else that Talfi wasn't saying, but Danr decided not to press for details—he still didn't know all the rules for keeping friends.

Sounds of revelry continued in the dooryard beyond the stable. Aisa got to her feet.

"I should go before Frida misses me," she said, heading for the door. She left a sad, empty space near Danr's tiny hearth.

"Aisa," he called in his gruff voice before he could stop himself. A slight draft from the half-open door made the candle flame dance like a tiny demon. "Uh . . . thank you for helping with my leg. And for warning me about the villagers."

She nodded once and vanished into the darkness outside. Danr stared after her for a long time, not noticing Talfi's thoughtful look.

Aisa pulled her ragged scarf more tightly across her face and shivered as she hurried up the dark, muddy road. This place was always cold. *She* was always cold. Even in summer, when the men stripped off their shirts and women sweated over cook fires, Aisa felt cold. She wore three ragged dresses, bound her hands in rags, and drew a hood across her hair, but still the cold crept in, biting her bones and gnawing her ribs. Only one thing could make her warm again, a thing she loathed even as she yearned for it during every waking moment.

The village streets were deserted, though she could just hear in the distance thin shouts of laughter from Alfgeir's farm. Alfgeir's wife was still serving ale to the men. Aisa shivered. Farek, her master and owner, was among them. It was through him that Aisa had learned of White Halli's plan to kill . . . *him*.

The plan had fallen apart, but Farek was likely to come home drunk, and the possibility filled Aisa with dread.

Like Alfgeir, Farek was a farmer, though his lands butted up against the village, and his house stood at the edge of town. A split-rail fence surrounded the yard, and Aisa slipped quietly through the gate. The moon hung overhead, shedding accusatory silver light over Aisa's ragged form. Her hands ached with chill. Mistress Frida had gone to a neighbor's house so the two of them could commiserate over the foolishness of their men, and she had left Aisa in charge of the two children, but they were long asleep, and Aisa felt it more important that *he* should know of the plot against him.

Aisa hurried across the frostbitten yard, her mouth set tight beneath her scarf. Mistress Frida's beatings hurt, and leaving the young ones alone would rate a long one. Aisa reached the front door of Farek's round house and, heart pounding, lifted the latch. It made a small clatter, and the hinges creaked enough to make her hand shake. Aisa crept into the house like a rabbit sneaking into a guarded garden. A cold draft followed her in. The house's interior was dark except for a few coals glowing red like wyrm's eyes on the fire some way ahead of her. Aisa listened. Soft breathing emanated from one of the wide benches that lined the walls. Twelve-year-old Abjorn, wrapped in warm blankets, was still asleep. The crib that held baby Helga was also quiet. No sign of Mistress Frida. With a relieved sigh, Aisa picked her way through the long, narrow main room, remembering to skirt the table. Smells of smoke, dried meat, and diapers that needed changing assailed her. Aisa should probably clean Helga up, but she put it off. Right now she needed a moment to herself. Aisa reached the open hearth just past the table and sat down. It was her allotted sleeping place. She kept it clean as best she could, but some bit of dirt or ash always hung about the spot—and her. The tripod hung empty over the coals like the skeleton of a spider. In the morning it would be her duty to fill a kettle with water and hang it to heat for washing. She would be tired from lack of sleep, but at least *he*—Hamzu—had been warned.

Aisa wrapped her arms around her shins and rested her chin on her knees, a shapeless bundle in the darkness. This spot was warm, more or less, and she could think about something besides the constant cold and never-ending hunger. She turned up the pleasurable thought that Hamzu would live, which drew from her a small, satisfied smile. Everyone called him *Trollboy*, but Aisa refused to use this demeaning nickname. Difficulty was, he had never told her his real name, so privately she called him *Hamzu*, which meant *strong* or *steadfast* in her mother tongue, and then refused to tell him.

Aisa had felt a kinship with Hamzu from the day she first arrived at this place. Both of them were outcasts, both of them unwillingly served masters who treated them with indifference at best, cruelty at worst. And he was handsome, though he thought himself ugly. Unfortunately she did find his size and easy strength intimidating. Frightening, even. But his liquid eyes and his voice were kind and gentle. Unlike those of other men.

Aisa's first master had been her father, of course. He had been a poor excuse for one. The priests of Rolk, who ruled the green valleys and desert plains of Irbsa and taught the sun god's wisdom, required a father to love his daughter, protect her, keep her safe. But Aisa's father, Bahir, had loved dice far more than his children, and his debts kept his two sons working as laborers, but Aisa, a daughter, could earn nothing. When Aisa's mother fell ill with a terrible, wasting disease, there had been little money for physicians, and Aisa had been forced to learn how to ease her mother's pain using plants and herbs she could gather for herself. Aisa's skill grew quickly, but not quickly enough to keep up with her mother's fading strength, and in the end, she had died, leaving Aisa, now ten years old, to run the house in her place.

Once Aisa reached marriageable age, thoughts of paying dowry and wedding weighed heavily on Father's mind. Just after Aisa's fifteenth birthday, Father wordlessly took Aisa down to the market and handed her over to a man in a purple turban. Only when Aisa saw the silver fall into her father's hands did she fully comprehend what was happening—Father had sold her into slavery. No dowry to pay, no wedding to hold, and the silver would mean a long night over the dice cups.

Aisa had been too shocked to resist the heavy shackles clapped around her wrists. Two days later, the man in the purple turban took Aisa and a dozen other slaves aboard a ship intent on crossing the Iron Sea, the small ocean that separated Irbsa from Balsia. Aisa huddled on deck, sick as an elephant in an earthquake.

The weather grew colder and wetter the farther east they went. Aisa eventually became accustomed to the waves, but not to the water. She longed for the warmth of the desert, for familiar smells of sandalwood and spices, for familiar sounds of good music and calls to prayer, and she silently begged Rolk to give her the strength to cast herself over the side and let her chains carry her to the bottom. But Rolk withheld his strength, and the ship sailed on.

Once, a group of merfolk, easily twenty of them, hauled themselves dripping over the gunwale to perch there. The men were sleek and flat-muscled. Tattoos of cobalt blue and scarlet red made intricate designs on their arms and faces. The women were also muscular and bare-breasted, and their tattoos were no less intricate. Their tails gleamed a rainbow of jewels in the sunlight. All of them bore weapons—double-headed spears and thin swords. The other slaves yelled in fear, as did the man in the purple turban, but Aisa stared. And stared. She couldn't break away from them. She had heard of the merfolk, one of the three Kin races, but they never visited the deserts of Irbsa. In person, they were terrible but at the same time alluring for reasons Aisa couldn't explain, even to herself. The tattoos gave the men a dangerous air that Aisa found both appealing and confusing at the same time. And they all went naked. It took a great deal of power for a woman to appear bare-breasted in public, more power than Aisa had thought a woman could have. Somehow it felt . . . right.

The captain, who also showed no fear, greeted the merfolk in a language Aisa didn't understand. A merman responded. The captain handed over a sack, and one of the mermaids counted the coins within. Aisa continued to stare.

One of the merwomen noticed Aisa's gaze and said something to one of the other women. Her voice was low and musical. Both women laughed, and one of them gestured at Aisa to approach. Aisa could not have refused even if she had wished it. One of the merwomen touched Aisa's face, tracing a design with her finger. Aisa gasped at the sensation, as if the touch had woken her from a dream.

"You have no face," the mermaid said. "They stole it. Such a shame."

Meanwhile, the other mermaid satisfied herself that the amount was correct. She barked a command, and the entire lot of merfolk dove into the water without another word.

"What was that for?" the man in the purple turban asked.

"Toll," replied the captain. "It is expensive to go this way, but it cuts more than two weeks off our trip, and we can more easily go around the maelstroms that spawn in the middle of the Iron Sea."

Aisa looked over the gunwale, aching to see the merfolk again, but all she saw was endless ocean.

One day, the ship arrived at a city like none Aisa had ever

known. At first she thought it was a forest of the biggest trees she had ever seen growing right up to the edge of the ocean, where docks and piers poked into the water like strange fingers. Then she realized that houses of wood and vine hung cunningly among the leaves, as if they had grown there instead of being built, and a system of balconies, bridges, ladders, and staircases writhed in a confusing lattice. People swarmed the docks as well as tree branches and the ground beneath, but they were definitely not human. Waist-high, knobby-limbed creatures with wide faces, sail ears, and skin the color of oak bark scampered out to help haul the ship closer to the quay. They brought with them a damp, earthy smell. Amid the treetops flitted smaller, shimmering beings. Different colors coruscated over them. They moved in ways alien and strange. Aisa couldn't quite make out what shape they were; her eyes twisted whenever she looked at one for too long. Both the dull fairies and the chaotic sprites were of the Fae, creatures who might live four or five centuries.

The man in the purple turban refused to make eye contact with the sprite who came to buy the slaves, and the negotiations went quickly. In no time at all, a group of knobby fairies were hauling the slaves off the ship and into the city. Aisa felt small and frightened beneath the tall trees and the swinging walkways. Carefully trimmed ferns and shrubs and flowers made gardens everywhere, and generously wide dirt paths wove among them. Strange sounds surrounded her at every turn. The fairies chattered and gibbered. Feet clumped and thudded on wooden planks. Glowing sprites fluttered. Smells of exquisite cooking and herbs and sea salt mingled everywhere, with none of the heavy scents of garbage, waste, or other refuse Aisa associated with a city. After some time, Aisa noticed humans as well. They moved about the city, looking relaxed and cheerful. Not one looked unhappy. The sight should have reassured

Aisa, but it only unnerved her. Who could be happy as a slave? Her stomach roiled. She wanted to tear the shackles from her hands and use them to choke the fairies and smash the sprites from the air.

There was no more buying or selling that Aisa saw. One of the little brown fairies took her shackles in hand as if she were a horse and led her and six of the other new slaves to a river barge run by more chattering fairies. She spent two weeks on board as it traveled north upriver. This trip was much smoother. No one tried to talk to her, for which she was grateful.

At last the barge came to a halt in another city, one almost exactly like the one they had left, except this town straddled the river at the edge of an enormous sapphire lake. The air was warm and cloying, and bright birds sang strange songs in the treetops. Bridges arced gracefully across the gentle water. At the urging of the fairies, Aisa and the other slaves disembarked from the barge and clambered down the sides to a wooden dock that smelled of cedar and made Aisa terribly homesick. Did her two brothers even know what had happened to her?

A hand touched Aisa's shoulder, and she looked up into the face of the most beautiful man she had ever seen. His golden hair all but shimmered with Rolk's glory, and his ocean blue eyes cut through bone to her very heart. He had a long, straight nose and fine blond eyebrows that Aisa ached to touch. His rich blue tunic was heavy silk embroidered with silver thread, and he wore a short bronze dagger at his belt. A hunger woke within her, and he leaned down to kiss her forehead. The rest of the world simply went away. Sound and light and scent all vanished. There was only him and the soft caress of his lips on her forehead. Aisa's knees wobbled, and she thought she might faint. She smelled cinnamon. Warmth flooded her, light and fine and delicious. She could walk across frigid mountains and never feel the slightest chill. Thoughts of the merfolk evaporated.

"I am Lord Vamath," he said. "I am king here, and you belong to me."

"You belong to me," Aisa repeated, dazed.

Vamath gave one short laugh, and Aisa would have clawed her way through a mountain to hear a second. "Indeed."

"Indeed," Aisa echoed.

"You are a little parrot, then." Vamath fitted a silver collar around her throat, and the touch of his fingers made her feel warm and happy again.

"A little parrot?" Aisa asked.

"Exactly." He smiled like the sun. "Come along now, Little Parrot. You have work."

He took Aisa to his house, a palace that occupied three entire trees. Rooms and suites connected by an intricate system of indoor-outdoor staircases festooned the enormous trunk and ran along the branches. The fact that Vamath, her master, was the elven king himself did not impress Aisa in the slightest. She only wanted to please him so he would speak to her or even touch her again. Her duties were difficult—hauling water up long staircases and scrubbing floors and heating baths and cutting wood—but thoughts of Vamath kept a quiet smile on her face, and she barely noticed how her muscles ached or the way blisters broke on her hands.

One afternoon he stole up behind her while she was making up his bed. The silken sheets hissed under her fingertips as she smoothed them into place, and abruptly Lord Vamath was there. He stroked her neck. The delightful warmth returned, and she didn't want to move.

"Little Parrot," he murmured. "How lovely you are."

He pushed her forward onto the bed and thrust her knees open with his own. A wrench tore Aisa in two, and she wanted to scream and cry and fight and run. But she also hungered beyond hunger for Vamath's touch, longed and yearned for it. Vamath stroked her hair, whispered delights in his beautiful voice while her hands clutched the sheets. When he was spent, he pulled away quickly and left. Aisa knelt by the bed, feeling both ecstatic and nauseated at the same time.

After that, she understood everything. The elven beauty, the glamour, was a drug worse than the opium some of her countrymen smoked back in Irbsa. Aisa wanted the elven king the way a lifelong drinker wanted wine, and it mattered not one bit that she hated him as well. A word from him made her happy for hours, and a touch thrilled her for a week. And when he took her a second time, she felt the gladness for a month even as she wanted to plunge a dagger into his back. The thought of leaving him, of trying to escape, made her ill.

In the end, she hadn't escaped. It had been far worse. One of the other slaves, a young man named Gell, had somehow held himself apart from the elven glamour and wanted to escape. Aisa had used her hatred of the king to force herself into performing a small task—she distracted a fairy with a bit of talk while Gell slipped away, and then lied about Gell's whereabouts when he came up missing. But Gell had been caught, and under torture, he had revealed Aisa's part in his escape just before the sprite scoured his brain out of his skull.

Aisa's deeds had rated a punishment far worse: sale into exile, away from warmth and light, to a Balsian man who kept her as a servant and a concubine while the cold hunger for her former owner kept her shivering at a dirty hearth.

Aisa let the heat of the coals bake into her bones, pushing the ever-present chill aside, if only for the moment. At least she didn't have to worry about becoming heavy with Hunin's child. Something about the elves stole fertility from humans of both sexes. It was why the Fae needed a continuous supply of human slaves. Aisa felt both relief that she would bear no child to Farek and sorrow that she would never have a baby of her own. Always she was pulled in two.

A sharp kick to the ribs wrenched her to wakefulness. Aisa gasped at the pain and rolled reflexively away. Frida stood over her, foot drawn back for another kick. Aisa scrambled upright. She had dozed off without noticing, and now it was morning.

"Get to work, lazy slut," Frida snapped. "The fire's almost out, the baby needs to be changed, and the children will want breakfast."

"Yes, lady." Still smarting from the kick, Aisa stirred up the fire, added sticks and logs, then lifted Helga from the crib and set to work.

Farek's house, like most farmhouses, was L-shaped, with a heavy curtain of hides dividing the long arm of the L from the short arm. The animals lived in the short arm, and the hearth sat at the juncture of the two arms. Wide benches for both sitting and sleeping lined the walls, and a long table near the hearth was used for preparing food and eating. Foodstuffs, clothes, and tools were stored up in the rafters and in boxes and chests under the benches.

Farek snored from his bench. Frida shook Abjorn awake and sent him into the stable to milk the cow and clean out the stalls as he did every morning before breakfast. Aisa unwrapped her hands, cleaned baby Helga, wrung the urine out of the dirty diaper into the wastebucket, and tossed the cloth into a second bucket. Later, she would take the urine to Helmut the tanner for sale and bring the diapers down to the river for washing. The infant woke and cried just as Aisa was tying on a dry cloth, so she silently handed her to Frida to nurse. Frida opened the front of her blouse while Aisa poured fresh water into the kettle and hung it over the fire. Frida watched her with hard blue eyes. She was pretty enough, with thick blond

hair she wore in a braid coiled at the back of her head, but
Aisa did her best to stay out of reach.

Abjorn emerged from the stables just as Aisa was slicing
old bread, cheese, and sausage for the breakfast table. Helga
crawled around under the table, and Frida, who had already
washed, was putting together flour, water, and scraps from
yesterday's rising to make new bread. Farek awoke with a
groan. Aisa shot him a nervous look, then reminded herself
that he wasn't likely to come for her the morning after he'd
been drinking.

"You have a cat on you from all the ale, Farek," Frida
observed harshly. "Wash up. Breakfast is ready."

Aisa poured warm water into a washbasin, set it on the
bench beside Farek, and edged out of reach, just in case.
Farek groaned again, then washed his hands and face, blew
his nose into the bowl, and left it for Aisa to empty. She
waited to one side until he put his boots on and staggered to
the table. He didn't even look her way, for which Aisa was
grateful. The family sat at the table, Farek at the head, Frida
at the foot, and Abjorn in between. Helga continued to crawl
around the floor, babbling to herself. Aisa's stomach growled.
She would eat the remains of the family's breakfast while she
cleaned the kitchen.

"Funeral for the Noss brothers is today," Farek muttered
over his bread. "At noon."

"Will there be a feasting?" Frida asked. "They have no
relatives around here to give one."

Farek wiped his mouth on his sleeve. "Their sister's
family came in from Skyford, so there'll be a proper
service—and a feasting."

"Hmm." Frida jerked her chin at Aisa. "You, girl, are not
to attend. I won't have people thinking my husband's slave is
part of our family."

Frida was being deliberately unkind. Missing a feasting,

even for a funeral, was a cruel punishment for anyone, especially after a long, hard winter of near isolation. But Aisa felt a small swell of anticipation. If the family went to a funeral and feasting, she wouldn't have to cook all day. Even supper would be cold leftovers. Aisa would also have some time to herself while the family was gone. Most of her herb stocks were low from the long winter, and she was still eager to go out and gather more, now that the leaves were green again. It was what she had been doing when she met Danr on the road. But if Frida knew any of this, she would force Aisa to go with the family, so Aisa put an expression of disappointment on her face.

"Yes, mistress," she murmured.

Frida snapped her fingers at Aisa. "Find my red dress, girl. Get a damp cloth to take the wrinkles out, and do the same for Abjorn's good shirt. Move!"

A frantically busy morning passed with speed, and Aisa soon had the house to herself. Frida gave Aisa a great deal of make-work to be done while they were gone, but Aisa knew from experience that none of it mattered. If things went well at the feasting, Frida would come home in a good mood and she would forget all about Aisa's work. If things went poorly, she would arrive in a temper, ready to take it out on Aisa, and it wouldn't matter if Aisa had lined the hearth with gold.

With the family safely away, Aisa took up a basket and headed outside. The basket was her secret, her hope, and she hid it in plain sight.

Aisa was known through the village as someone with a healer's touch. She knew no magic, but colicky babies dropped off to sleep under her hands, wounds she tended avoided infection, and fevers cooled themselves the moment she entered a house. Caring for her mother had given her an extensive knowledge, and she had learned more during her time with the elves: vervain for headaches and womanly cramps, marigold for sensitive nipples after breast-feeding, black-and-blue cohosh for muscle spasms, birch for painfully dry skin, and so many more. Most women knew at least something of healing herbs, of course, but Aisa came from a foreign land and had lived among the Fae, which gave her additional mystique, which she wore close about her like the rags and scarves. The mystique also meant people feared and mistrusted her, but that somehow made her more effective, as if coming from a foreign land granted her access to secrets no one else could understand, and the villagers asked for her often.

Aisa clutched the basket close and crept around the side of the house, making for the fields and forests beyond. She needed to refill it so she could keep earning money, for although she was a talented healer, Aisa did nothing for free. Every visit she made cost something. Those who owned coins had to give them up. Those who owned none had to give her some object of value, no matter how small or silly. If there was nothing else, she accepted food to keep her belly full and her limbs strong. Twice a year, when she was by law granted a day to herself, Aisa walked to Skyford with her treasures, where she sold every one for hard coins. Frida had wanted to take a percentage at first, but the earl's law said that a slave could keep entire anything he or she earned, as long as the money came from outside the borders of the master's holding. Farek allowed it because renown as a healer increased Aisa's value. And so her small silver hoard was growing.

When she had enough, she would run away.

Not back to Alfhame and the elves. That path was closed to her forever more, and she did not truly wish to return there in any case. Not back to her homeland of Irbsa, where she would be nothing but property and where Rolk had abandoned her pleas for help. No, when Aisa had enough money, she would travel to the South Sea, where she would

heal the sick and use her earnings to buy a small boat so she
could sail out onto sun-drenched water and speak with the
bare-breasted merwomen until their language danced on her
tongue like thin, sweet wine. And then she would tattoo her
forehead and cheeks with intricate designs of red-and-blue
power. Once she had her face again, she would rip the rags
away and fling them into the sea forevermore.

Aisa shifted the basket. The Farek house was one of several that made up a rough circle of homes around the village
center, where the funeral and feasting were being held. Aisa
would have to creep past the service in order to get to the
woods outside the village. Already a gathering of people
was speaking in hushed, respectful tones. One group Aisa
didn't recognize, and she assumed they were family to the
Noss brothers, in from out of town. Automatically she
looked for Farek and Frida but didn't see them. However,
she did catch sight of Hamzu, tall and strong, hovering at
the edge of the crowd. Her heart made a small flutter, like
the wings of a small bird, and she longed to stand beside
him with his protective hand on her shoulder. Near him was
the handsome young man Talfi, the one from Skyford. Aisa
had mixed feelings about Talfi. Hamzu seemed to have
befriended him, and that was a fine thing, but likable as
Talfi was, something about him made Aisa's eyes narrow
and put an itch in her wrapped fingertips.

On a pair of tables in the center of the village circle were
the bodies of the Noss brothers. They were tightly wrapped
in white cloth, with flowers and small branches tucked in.
From the branches hung amulets and small cloth pouches,
which would be burned along with the bodies outside the
village after the priest invoked the nine names of Vik, the
god of the underworld. The amulets and pouches were vi-
tally important. Without them, the Noss brothers would
have nothing with which to bribe Halza, Vik's cold and

merciless wife who brought ice and winter every year, and she would banish them to the frigid depths of Eishame before they even reached Vik for judgment.

The priest of Olar was also someone Aisa didn't recognize. He looked barely old enough to be away from his mother. He didn't even have a beard. His red robe was threadbare, and he wore no gold pectoral. Clearly, the temple at Skyford hadn't seen fit to send their best to the funeral of a pair of rural farmers. An older man standing among the Noss was glaring at the young priest, and Aisa had the feeling Skyford would soon be hearing about this. She felt somewhat insulted herself, for all that these weren't her people. It did not seem right to send these young men off to Vik on the words of someone who looked like an acolyte.

As Aisa reached the edge of the circle of houses, the young priest rang a brass bell to start the death ritual. He intoned something, and the family and several villager women set up a wail and cry, howls of mourning to show respect for the dead and frighten away evil spirits. Aisa hated that sound—it always made her think of her mother. She was turning her back to slip away when she realized the wails had turned into true shrieks of terror.

CHAPTER FIVE

"I can't believe I let you talk me into this," Danr said out of the side of his mouth.

"If you don't come," Talfi murmured back, "it's like saying you're not one of them."

"But I'm not." Danr jerked his head. "Look there—White Halli."

The man in question was in the thickest part of the crowd, his two blocky guardsmen standing on either side of him. Halli's silver-blond hair caught the sunlight as he spoke in low voices to the grieving Noss family, who had arrived from out of town. Once he looked up and met Danr's eye. The glint in his gaze sent a chill over Danr's skin.

"He's going to speak," Danr said, "and he's going to say something bad about trolls to get everyone angry at me. You watch."

"Just shut up and enjoy the funeral."

In the center of the village circle, the crowd of mourners was trying to edge away from Danr and his ragged hat. The trouble was, that meant they had to edge toward the two corpses lying wrapped on the trestles, so the entire situation created something of a ripple that washed back and forth.

Danr stood like a rock, holding his head up and trying to pretend he had nothing to do with it. Then the young red-robed priest rang his bell, and everyone settled down.

"We call upon Olar, King of Birds, to bless this place, and we call upon Grick, Queen of Grain, to make this a holy stead," the skinny priest intoned in a surprisingly deep voice. "We bless our brother Lars Noss and our brother Nils Noss and pray that the Nine watch over them on their journey to Vik's realm. We—"

One of the wrapped corpses quietly sat up. The priest's voice died with a wet gurgle. For a moment, no one moved. The second corpse sat up in a soft rustle of bandages. And yet the brothers' bodies still lay behind on the table. Frozen by surprise and a strange fascination, Danr stared. He couldn't understand what he was seeing. Tiny sounds whimpered in the crowd. Danr came to realize that the creatures sitting upright on the table were spirits wrapped in ragged bandages of their own, and they were climbing out of their bodies. Their gray translucent flesh rippled like pond water in the sunlight. Horror crawled cold over Danr. Still no one moved.

A woman screamed, "A witch! A witch called them up!"

The sound shattered the crowd's startled freeze. More screams broke out, and everyone stampeded in a hundred diverse directions. Danr's feet felt staked to the ground. The villagers streamed around him like minnows around a rock. The two guards cleared a way for White Halli, who ran with wild eyes. More cries of "witch!" followed. Dread fascination forced Danr's gaze toward the two ruined bodies that were clambering off the trestle tables. It occurred to him that he should be afraid, or at least disturbed, but compared to a thirty-foot wyrm, a pair of broken spirits didn't seem much of a threat. Either that or he had gone so far past fear that he had come out the other side. The cold spirits clambered down from the boards, leaving their shells behind.

"Draugr," said Talfi, who hadn't run away, either, though he had edged behind Danr.

"What do you suppose they want?" Danr whispered. He forced himself to remain where he was despite the chill fear trickling over him now. Fear was unpleasant, but you pushed through it, like everything else. What else was there to do? He tugged nervously at the brim of his hat.

In a voice that came from the bottom of a well, both *draugr* said, *"Release!"*

Now Danr did step back. He trod on Talfi's instep, and Talfi yelped.

"Release!" the two draugr repeated, though neither of them moved farther away from the corpses on the trestle table.

"What do you mean?" Danr tried to call at them, though the words came out as more of a hoarse grunt.

"Release!"

"You're supposed to go to Vik's realm," Talfi said. "Leave!"

"Release!"

Danr took another step back, ready to run but not sure he should. The *draugr* that had been Nils Noss lurched forward while his corpse lay on the bier behind. Cold nausea made an icy pit in Danr's stomach and he tried not to think how that leg had been damaged. Still, the *draugr* didn't seem interested in moving. Danr chewed his lip. He felt he should do something but didn't know what. Ghosts came to priests, not farmers and thralls.

"Release!"

Danr glanced around the village circle, his mouth dry. Talfi's face was white. The *draugr* hadn't attacked or screamed or called curses upon him or anyone else. All they had done was demand release. And they hadn't moved more than a few feet from their wrapped bodies. They couldn't stay here in the middle of the village. The more Danr thought about it, the more wrong it felt. If spirits were to haunt the world, they should skirt the edges of dark places and give the living a chance to avoid them, not stand in the center of a busy village where they would frighten children and disrupt daily life. Someone should do something about it. And there was no one else around.

Before he could think more about what he was doing, Danr strode past the *draugr* to the table they guarded. He reached under the table with both arms and lifted it, cold corpses and all. Talfi clapped both hands to his head.

"What are you *doing*?" he yelled.

Danr ignored him. Move fast, move forward, don't think. The table and its sad burden were a hardly noticeable weight.

A chilly voice whispered wet in his ear, *"Release!"* Ice clenched Danr's bowels, but he kept moving. He moved down the road, past the circle of houses.

"Release!" The voices were sleet on a north wind, and his back prickled, waiting for pain or worse. The dreadful sweet, rotting smell of the corpses mingled with the soft scent of drying flowers woven into the bandages. One of the bodies shifted on the table as he jogged, but nothing touched Danr, though his entire skin crawled cold. He came to a grove of ash trees a short distance outside town. In its shade he set the table. The *draugr* drifted over to hover near the bodies. To Danr's eyes, the ghosts looked more sad than scary now.

"Release!" they whispered.

"I'm sorry," he said to them. "I can't help you. But I'll ask the priest."

He backed away. The ghosts showed no interest in following. A hand touched his shoulder, and Danr whirled. It was only Talfi.

"What in Vik's name are you doing?" his friend demanded. "They could have killed you! Or worse!"

"Worse than what they're going through?" Danr said. "Come on. We should get back."

"Trolls, wyrms, *draugr*," Talfi muttered as they went. "What's next? Giants? Gods?"

Back at the village, they rounded a corner of one of the houses—it belonged to Anders the thatcher, one of the men who had tried to hang him last night—and suddenly the enormity of what he had done crashed over Danr. His knees weakened, and he leaned against the house wall. Stiff thatching brushed his head as he blew out a heavy breath. One part of his mind was aware of the irony—he had found shelter at the house of a man who had wanted to kill him. A small flock of chickens pecked and clucked amid the stilts under the house, unaware that their owner had only last night tried to stretch the neck of a sixteen-year-old thrall.

"Huh. I thought you were brave when you faced down the wyrm," Talfi said. "That was . . . I have no words."

Danr shrugged. "Maybe trolls are too stupid to be afraid."

"That sounds about right, monster," said Anders behind them.

Talfi rounded on him. One of the chickens fled in an explosion of feathers. "Who the hell are you?"

"This is my house." Anders, a stocky, brown-haired man, looked pale and unhappy. "Two *draugr* and a troll at my home in one day. Now there's talk of witches. I'm cursed."

"Because everything centers on you," Talfi said before Danr could respond. "You've a healthy mind, *Carl* This-Is-My-House." In the distance came more shouts and screams. Some kind of fuss was going on where Danr couldn't see, though his vision had never been strong in sunlight, even with his hat on. "I didn't think *draugr* came out in the daytime."

"Neither do trolls," Anders pointed out.

Danr hunched over and pulled himself down to Anders's

level. The man looked a lot smaller in the day, alone, with
empty hands. Danr wanted to say something to Anders about
last night, how the man had come for him with a long, heavy
rope fitted for a troll's neck. The monster inside grumbled.
Danr's fists clenched, and Anders backed up a step. One flick
of the monster's finger. One poke with his fist . . .

Keep the monster inside, Mother's voice murmured in
his ear. *Don't give him the satisfaction.*

Danr forced himself to relax his hands, and he touched
the pouch at his throat. The splinters inside pricked his fingertips with further reminders. "What do you think the spirits want?" he asked instead.

"We'll find out soon enough." Anders summoned up
some courage of his own and snuck a glance at the empty
village circle. "By the Nine! The *draugr* have gone! And the
corpses, too! The witch must have magicked them away."

"What witch? What do you mean we'll find out what the
spirits want?" Danr asked.

"White Halli caught the witch who summoned them."

Cold blood sliced Danr's veins. He knew the answer, but
still he had to ask the awful question. "Who's the witch?"

The words hit him like stones from a hundred slings.
"That slave girl. Everyone knows her healing powers can
call up the dead." Anders was still peering around the
corner. "Halli blundered right into her when he was running
away from the spirits. He grabbed her and dragged her to
Farek's house for beating until she tells us how to—"

Danr rushed past Anders, leaving the startled Talfi behind. Heart in his mouth, he bolted across the empty village
circle to Farek's house. The fuss he had heard earlier was
coming from behind it. Panic nipped at his ribs. He tore
around the rear corner to the sheltered courtyard made by
the L shape of the stable and main house. A smelly pigpen
stood to one side, and more chickens perched on the railing,

creating a strange audience. In the center of a crowd of people were White Halli and his two guards. Halli was raising a thin rod, one that would flay skin and slice meat. Aisa huddled at Halli's feet. Two stripes tore open the rags across her ribs and made terrible red marks on her exposed brown back. It felt as if his own flesh lay scored.

Hot anger slammed through Danr. His control snapped and the monster exploded forth. For the first time in more than ten years, a roar burst from his throat and shook the house walls. The people, men and women both, screamed just as they had for the *draugr* and scrambled to get out of the way, but not fast enough. Danr lumbered forward, sweeping them out of the way with his oak tree arms. They tumbled aside like ninepins. Aisa looked up.

Do not show them the monster, said his mother's desperate voice. *Do not—*

Danr ignored her. He barreled straight for White Halli. The guards had the presence of mind to draw their swords. Danr knocked the first man's weapon arm aside with a wet snap of bone. The sword spun into the pigpen and the man screamed in pain. Danr punched the second man in his leathery breastplate with the heel of his hand. The man arced backward into a group of people and went down in a tangle of arms and legs. Halli tried to draw his own sword, but Danr grabbed him by the throat and lifted him bodily off the ground. Unshaven skin scratched Danr's hand and he smelled both herring and fear on Halli's breath. Halli clutched at Danr's arm with both hands, but his whole strength was nothing compared to half a troll. Aisa crawled several paces away, and the sight of her on hands and knees only enraged Danr further.

"Keep back," Danr snarled at the first guard, who was trying to draw a knife despite his broken arm, "or I'll snap his neck."

"Drop me, half-blood," Halli growled.

Do not show them the monster, Mother begged. The crowd had withdrawn to a safe distance but hadn't fled entirely. A tiny bit of control stole back. Danr thought of Norbert's arm. He spoke.

"Tell them she's not a witch, Halli," he said. "Tell them now."

Halli managed a choked laugh. "Walk away now, Trollboy, and you'll only lose one ball instead of both."

Do not, Mother said.

Danr wavered. Even if Halli recanted his accusation, the rumors would persist. Eventually someone would accuse her again. And Danr was in trouble for laying hands on the son of an earl.

Aisa got unsteadily to her feet and tried to gather her rags about her, but they were cut in the back, revealing red welts on brown skin. A hot snake of anger twisted inside Danr, and he nearly snapped Halli's neck right then. He squeezed a little tighter. Halli's eyes bulged. Then Aisa's eyes met his, and she gave a quick shake of her head.

That did it. He couldn't show the monster to Aisa. Slowly, with trembling hand, he lowered Halli to the ground and released him. Halli grimaced and massaged his neck, his white-blond hair shining silver in the sunlight.

"Better," he rasped, and straightened. "And you have to pay for that, Trollboy."

Danr set his jaw hard and stared at nothing. He didn't care. He wouldn't care. As long as Aisa was safe, nothing else mattered.

"In fact," Halli continued, "I'll give you a choice of punishment. I'll even show you mercy. Would you like that, Trollboy?"

Danr kept his gaze on the horizon. His chest heaved. He didn't want to look down and see Aisa, bleeding in the mud. He was afraid he would lose control again.

Halli's voice grew harsh. "Answer me, thrall. Would you like that? Would you like me to show you mercy?"

The crowd stared, every eye round and hard. Danr's face burned. Halli was setting a trap, he knew that, but there was only one answer he could give, so he gave it. "Yes, my lord."

"Very well. Listen carefully, if there's a brain in that stone skull of yours." Halli crossed his arms. "You can become my personal thrall for life. Or you can be freed of your bond forever—if you first beat the witch bloody and make her confess."

A murmur went through the crowd that hemmed them in. Still on the ground a few paces away, Aisa gave a gasp behind the scarf covering her face. Halli put the cane in Trollboy's hand with a small smile.

"Go ahead, Trollboy," Halli said. "Make her bleed until she confesses, and I'll release you from Alfgeir Oxbreeder. I swear before all these witnesses, you'll be a thrall no more."

Aisa's dark eyes met Danr's again. She was trapped, and they both knew it. Anyone accused of witchcraft took nine strokes with a cane. If that didn't bring a confession, the accused was caned to death. But anyone who did confess was branded on face and hands, and hanged from an ash tree. Or beheaded.

He's already killed me, said Aisa's eyes. *Take your freedom from it.*

A long future stretched ahead of Danr, flat and bleak. He stared at Halli, and Halli stared back. Aisa begged with her eyes. *Get it over with,* they said silently. *Better you than him.*

Danr snapped the cane. The crowd rippled.

"You're a coward, Halli," Danr said. "She's no witch. Those pigs have more honor than you."

"A pig would know." Halli made a great show of sighing and gestured to his two guards. The second was only now getting to his feet after Danr had knocked him across the yard. The first was still cradling his arm. "Take the witch to Skyford keep for caning and execution. Then draw up a bill of sale from the earl for this new thrall of mine."

The second guard yanked Aisa to her feet, and Danr's mouth fell open. "What are you doing?" he shouted.

"Making the choice you refused," Halli said reasonably. "For attacking me, you will be my thrall for life. And for the heinous crime of witchcraft, this slave bitch is—"

Danr exploded like an angry volcano. He punched Halli in the stomach, and Halli folded around Danr's fist with an "oof." Danr brought his hand up and cracked Halli on the underside of the jaw. Every insult, every slight, every taunt, every jeer boiled out of him. The monster bellowed his fantastic rage and smashed Halli in the shoulder, slammed him to the ground, kicked him in the ribs. He felt the impact of every hit beneath his hands and feet. He heard the crunch of bone. A lifetime of wrath and injustice boiled around him in a dreadful thundercloud as the punches and kicks fell like hail. Halli dropped to the ground, bleeding and bruised. Danr was only vaguely aware of the crowd around him. He punched Halli hard in the temple. Halli stiffened and went limp. Danr raised both his hands, boulder-hard and mountain-heavy, high above his head. His fists hung there for a moment—

Don't! said his mother.

Aisa cried out, and Danr brought them both down toward White Halli's skull.

Pain exploded behind Danr's left ear. All his muscles went limp and he staggered. The second guard swung the shovel again. Danr dully watched it coming. Another explosion of pain, and the world slid into darkness.

The trial was short. Danr stood in a circle of spears thrust point-down into the ground with iron shackles weighing down his wrists and ankles. Outside the circle on a small

platform stood Halli's father, Earl Hunin. Like Halli, he was
tall and blond, but his hairline had receded, and his blue eyes
were watery. A silver coronet circled his brow, and he wore a
heavy blue tunic embroidered with silver eagles. Danr's eyes
traced the eagle designs. The morning's anger had evaporated, replaced by a leaden resignation that weighed him
down more than the shackles. How much would the villagers
laugh when Trollboy's head rolled across the grass?

How much would Aisa cry?

He tried to picture Aisa weeping over his corpse, but the
image wouldn't come. She had disappeared during the con-
fusion of his attack on Halli and his arrest afterward. She
would never guess his name now. No one would. He was
seized with a desire to shout his name aloud so everyone
would at least know that much about him, but he kept quiet.

Danr had crippled a man. He had intended to kill him.

Halli was propped up in a bed a few paces behind his
father, the earl. He wore a splint on his left leg and right arm.
His face was a purple mess. But the worst was his eyes. One
was swollen and shut. The other was open and glassy. It saw
nothing. Halli didn't respond to anything: not food, not drink,
not even the voice of his son, Rudin. The little boy sat on the
edge of the bed with Halli's hand in his own. The healer in
Skytown had said the blow to Halli's temple had driven away
his wits, and it was doubtful they would ever return.

Now that the haze of anger had cleared, the awful
memory of what Danr had done clung to him like the blood
that still stained his tunic. He felt ready to throw up at any
moment. It wasn't fair that he felt this way. Halli was, in his
own way, a bigger monster than Danr. He had bullied Danr
all his life, tortured his own cousin Sigrid, thrown dozens
and dozens of innocent men into prison, and worst of all,
tried to put Aisa to the witch's cane and rope. But now Halli's little boy hovered like one of the *draugr* at the edge of

Halli's sickbed, and with that came the heavy knowledge that it was because of Danr's own self. The chains he wore felt light in comparison.

On Earl Hunin's left was a priest to Urko, the god who had been cut in half by the Stane as a traitor during their war with the Nine Gods. Mother had told Danr a number of stories about how half of Urko lived with the Nine, and half of him with the Stane, and how both sides thought he spied for the other. Strangely his sacrifice came to associate him with law and justice, as someone who could weigh both sides of every argument, and his priests attended major trials as advisers, witnesses, and occasionally judges. Danr didn't know this priest, but he recognized the strange hooded robe—left half black, right half white. The priest kept an elaborate walking stick at his right side, a symbol of Ashkame, the Great Tree. His face was hidden by the hood, and Danr couldn't read the man's expression, or even tell if he were looking at Danr at all.

Talfi stood at the forefront of the crowd of villagers. His expression was at once angry and helpless. Danr hated appearing in front of his only friend in shackles like an animal. Alfgeir watched from the back with a stony expression. No matter how this went, he was losing Danr as a thrall.

The rest of the villagers were gathered around as well, their faces ranging from angry to curious to frightened. Few were actually sorry that Danr had beaten White Halli into a stupor, but a trial was a show, and no one wanted to miss a moment. They were on a meadow some distance outside of the village, well away from the two *draugr* hovering in the ash grove and the one behind the pigpen. Neither of the ghosts showed any signs of moving. After the trial, the priest of Urko would try to drive them out. Whispers floated around the village that they wanted revenge for their deaths, and the execution of that troll boy might send the *draugr* away, especially the one that had once been White Halli. Danr pulled into himself at the thought. His head ached, both from the blows he had taken and from being out in the sun for so long without his hat. At least Aisa was safe.

"We've heard the evidence," said Hunin. His face was a stone, but his eyes were red, and he refused to look in Danr's direction. His fingers twitched, and he stank of sweat even from this distance.

The priest intoned, "The Nine find it inappropriate for the father to pass sentence when his son is the victim."

"There is no one else," Hunin snapped.

"It still must be noted."

"Noted, then." Hunin's voice was level as a grave. "The normal sentence for . . . injury is for the earl to decide how much the victim has . . . " Here, Hunin's voice quavered. ". . . has lost. The criminal must pay that amount to the family, or labor for them until the debt is paid."

Danr swallowed. The debt for White Halli would be high, probably more than Danr could ever work off in a single lifetime. He would be a thrall to Earl Hunin for the rest of his life. The thought of spending years—decades—in the keep under the thumb of a man who probably wanted him dead made his jaw tight and his heart pound at the back of his throat. The earl might order him beaten every day, or branded with hot irons, or sliced with thin knives.

"However," the earl continued, "the law also demands that injured party's wishes be considered in the sentence. As the injured party, I wish to see this troll's head and hands nailed to my doorpost."

Danr swayed dizzily and bitter bile piled up behind his tongue.

"Deliberately executing one of the Stane could be seen as an act of war, my brother," said the priest.

"They executed two of ours!" Hunin shot back. "Three now! My son . . ." His voice broke again. "My son is all but dead because of that stone filth up the mountain. Why shouldn't we go to war? We could take the land they've held for centuries and selfishly refused to let us use. We Kin could become a more powerful presence in Balsia."

Danr's ears pricked up. It sounded like an old argument between brothers, though it was the first time Danr had ever heard of it. Something more was going on here, something he had never seen or understood. Danr felt abruptly small and stupid, like a *hnefatfl* piece who didn't even know it was in a game. Was it possible Hunin was using Danr only as an excuse to go to war against the Stane? Was his grief nothing more than theatrics?

"The Noss brothers tried to farm land that butts up close to the trolls," the priest replied from beneath his bicolored hood. "The priesthood can't condone going to war over a few hectares of disputed land."

"And over my *son*!"

"The defendant was brave!" Talfi called out. "He defeated a wyrm! He took the first two *draugr* out of the village! He stood up to White Halli's false accusations! No one else has done such things!"

On the bed, White Halli stirred. His good leg quivered and he turned his head just a little. Danr started to say something, but Rudin also noticed the change. Hope dawned on his face. The boy grabbed Halli's hand again and mouthed, *Papa*. Halli's remaining eye blinked once, then fixed in the distance again. Rudin hung his head. Danr's words died.

"These actions do not excuse crimes!" Hunin barked, not noticing the exchange behind him. "The troll boy deserves only death!"

"Tread carefully, brother," said the priest. "Choosing death only leads to more death. How many other fathers will grieve for their lost sons if you make the wrong decision?"

Rudin spoke from the bed. His face was hard, more adult than a little boy's should have been. "If a half-blood thrall hurt my papa," he said, "he should die. It is only fair."

The crowd followed this argument with hungry attention. The last few days had provided more entertainment than the past ten years. Danr stood in his shackles with sunlight pain squeezing his head and waited. Sixteen years as a thrall was all the life he was going to get. The earl closed his eyes for a long moment and the entire crowd stopped breathing.

"The penalty for a man who lays hands on nobility is to become a thrall for the victim's family," Hunin said. "However, given that Trollboy is not a man, we must impose a stiffer penalty. I call for his death."

"Thank you, Grandfather," Rudin said.

The words dropped on Danr's head like stones. Talfi's face went white. Not a murmur stirred the crowd.

"Still," Hunin continued, "even a father's love is no excuse to increase tensions with the Stane. Therefore, our sentence is exile. Trollboy, you are no longer a member of this community and you no longer enjoy the earl's protection. Beginning at sundown, any man who lays eyes on you may do to you as he wishes. So be it."

"So be it!" The priest rapped his walking stick on the side of the platform.

Confused babble rushed through the crowd. Danr stood thunderstruck in the circle of spears. Exile. He was an exile. Exile was for men who murdered their parents or raped children, men whose necks weren't worth an axe stroke. Exile meant he had no family, no tribe, no people. He wasn't even a person.

Because you showed the monster, said his mother's sad

voice in his ear, and that was even worse. Automatically he tried to touch the pouch at his throat, but the shackles held his wrists low and prevented it.

"My lord!" Talfi shouted above the noise. "This isn't fair! You can't mean—"

But the earl had already stepped down from the platform to mount his horse. He rode away without another word. Rudin watched him go from White Halli's bed.

"You could appeal to the priests," Talfi said in the stable. "Maybe they could get the sentence reversed. Or maybe you could—"

Danr steadfastly ignored Talfi's flow of words and shoved his other tunic into his sack, along with a few candle stubs, a knife, a chipped axe no one wanted, and some flint and steel. Outside, the western mountains were already casting purple shadows over Alfgeir's farm, and he had no doubt White Halli and his men were waiting for the last of the sun to disappear, oh yes, they were.

". . . and you can have the rest of the food from my aunt," Talfi continued, handing it to him. "Do you want me to have Uncle Orvandel send word to Father Nikolas in the monastery at Rolk's Fork? Everyone respects Uncle Orvandel, and the priests might . . ."

The cows made their familiar lowing. One kicked in its stall, another familiar sound. Smells of straw and manure and thatching surrounded Danr, and he stared down at the pile of blackened stones that had made up his tiny hearth for years. The wide, flat one he kept to one side was perfect for heating a bowl of soup or a cup of beer. It was the first thing he had brought to the stable after his mother died. This place was a stable, where he had been a thrall and where people had made fun of him or shunned him, but it was his life. In a few minutes, he would lose it forever.

The worst was that Aisa hadn't come. She was in hiding somewhere, had to be, until the talk of her supposed witch-craft died down. It wasn't safe for her to come and see him off. He knew that. But the disappointment created by her absence still stung, as though she was saying he wasn't worth the effort, even after he had stood up for her.

Nothing for it but to keep moving, as he always did. No direction to move but forward. He picked up the sack and interrupted Talfi's river of words.

"I need to go now." His voice sounded thick and heavy in his own throat. "Thank you for . . . for staying with me, Talfi."

"You saved my life." Talfi followed him out the stable door into the darkening courtyard. The sun hadn't quite set, but the air was already chilly. "I couldn't—"

Alfgeir Oxbreeder was waiting for them on the stones, his face wooden. "I suppose this is good-bye, Trollboy. You're not an exile yet, so I can give you this." He handed Danr a loaf of bread. One side was burned. "It's not much, but as the saying goes, 'Crumbs are still bread.' "

Danr thought about refusing it, then took it anyway. Later, if he became hungry, pride would seem foolish. "Thank you, *Carl* Oxbreeder." *Thank you for the crumbs.*

"You were a hard worker who did the work of three, and sometimes ten," Alfgeir finished. "But what can you expect when someone like you strikes down the son of an earl?"

It seemed as if the remark should have made Danr angry again, but he was too tired. Instead he stuffed the burned bread into his sack. Alfgeir walked back to his warm house with the air of a man who had turned out a stray dog. In the far distance, hoofbeats galloped up the road. Halli's men, no doubt, coming to look for the exile. Danr glanced around, hoping one more time to see a figure wrapped in rags slip out of the shadows. But he saw nothing.

"Where are you going?" Talfi asked.

"To the mountains." Danr jerked his head to the northwest. "Maybe I can find my father's family, whoever they are. Maybe . . ."

He trailed off, but Talfi understood. "You think you can find a home with them."

It wasn't until Talfi said it aloud that Danr realized how much he'd been thinking it, hoping it. With his mother gone and his status as a thrall officially ended, he had no ties here. This place had never been his home; these folk had never been his people. But the trolls . . . they would see him differently. They would accept him for who he was. They would have to.

"I'm glad you were my friend, Talfi," he said. "Even if it was only for two days."

Talfi hugged him, the first embrace Danr had experienced since his mother's death. Danr hugged him gingerly in return, and tears pricked the back of his eyes. "We're still friends," Talfi said. "Always and forever."

The hoofbeats grew louder. Talfi turned aside and wiped at his eye. "Shit."

Danr picked up his sack and gave one final glance around. Still no Aisa. With the hoofbeats growing ever louder, he trotted away. The soft half-moon and the two stars that made up Urko's halves gave his troll's eyes more than enough light to see, and he had no need of a hat. He leaped the fence and loped across the far pasture toward the mountains.

CHAPTER SIX

The fire crackled and snapped like a tiny trapped demon. Danr fed it another stick and scooted his toes a little closer to the heat. Shadows capered across the huge trees around him, twisting around the smell of smoke. Darkness normally held no terrors for Danr, but he was more than an hour away from the village in the foothills of the Iron Mountains—Stane territory. Even the earth was unfamiliar. House-sized boulders thrust upward like the bones of giants, and gullies traced paths through the hills like their veins. Nothing was level, either. Even now, Danr sat on a slant. A few paces away, a creek rushed down the hill with a sound like chattering teeth. He clasped his knees and tried to keep his nerves under control.

Only a fool lit a fire at night in the foothills or the mountains. Flames attracted attention from the Stane. The strange thing was that Danr had been following the ghost of a trail through these foothills, and just at the time he decided to rest, he had come across a ring of stones that had clearly encircled a fire, though years ago. Had the Stane made the trail? And did the Stane start fires of their own?

He blew out a breath and scanned the shadows. Perhaps

now the Stane would come. Danr *wanted* them to come. Sort of. If the humans wouldn't take a half troll, perhaps the trolls would take a half human. And perhaps . . . perhaps they would know something about his father.

Danr touched the pouch at his throat. Mother never once talked about Danr's father. Her face grew tight and unhappy whenever he brought the subject up. When he asked who his father was, she only said, "He was a troll who betrayed me." Once, when he had pressed too much, she had actually slapped him and run out of the stable with her hands over her mouth. He had stopped asking after that, but he hadn't stopped wondering. That she had been raped was a given, he supposed, and it made him feel both sad and guilty to think that he was the result of his mother's fear and pain. Should he be angry at his father about that? Probably, but he didn't even know his father, didn't even have a good mental picture of him. In Danr's mind, his father was a tall, bulky creature with a shadowy face and big arms. He had hurt Mother, and that should make him angry, but if he hadn't hurt her, Danr wouldn't even exist to *be* angry. A part of him got hot and red as a blacksmith's forge when he thought about his mother getting hurt, but another part of him was secretly glad to be alive, and then a third part threaded him with guilt for finding some kind of good in his mother's pain.

If he could go back and stop his father from . . . attacking his mother, would he do it, even if it meant he would never be born? Danr poked at the fire with chilly hands while night's shadows tried to devour the light. It seemed an unfair question to ask, and it hurt him deep in his gut to think his mother might look at him and see pain every day. It was easier just not to think about it.

A footstep rustled in the shadowy trees. Then another, and another. Danr's mouth went dry and he came quietly alert. He backed away from the fire and looked away from it so his eyes could better see in darkness. A troll. His first time seeing one of his people. Fear and excitement tightened his stomach. Maybe the noise was just an animal. The chances of a troll happening to find his tiny fire were—

Aisa stepped into the circle of firelight. Her ragged clothes and scarf were wrapped tightly around her, and she carried a pack on her back. Danr stared, dumbfounded. Then delight poured through him like soft starlight and he ran forward to snatch her into a hug. She shied away with a small sound, and Danr stopped before he actually touched her. His arms fell limp at his sides. Even now, he remained an oaf who forgot himself.

"Aisa!" he said instead. "What are you doing here?"

"I have been trying to catch up with you." She set the pack down with wrapped hands. "If you had not lit that fire, I would have lost you forever."

He suppressed an urge to caper like the shadows on the trees. The sight of her filled him with such gladness, he could hardly speak. "But *why*? When you didn't come to see me off, I thought—"

"That I wanted nothing more to do with the man who stood up for me and had saved my life? Huh!" She leaned toward him and lightly tapped the back of his hand. Her touch burned his skin. "How little you think of me."

Abashed, Danr sank to the ground. "I'm sorry. I didn't—"

"You! I am joking." She sat across the fire from him and settled her rags about her. Above the scarf, her eyes were actually merry in the yellow light, and she stretched her arms out to the fire. "The heat feels good. I could not be angry at you, my friend and savior. Never at you. You were exiled because of me, and now I am joining you."

"Oh." Danr scratched his head. It had been a long, difficult day, and he was having a hard time following the conversation. "But you weren't exiled. Or did they did do something after I left?"

"No, silly one. Evil spirits pollute the village, and everyone thinks *witch* when they see me. How could I stay?" Aisa shook the pack, which clinked. "I have silver coins, and I was planning to run to the ocean one day." Her lovely eyes grew distant. "It appears that day has come."

"I'm not going to the ocean," Danr protested, even as an inner voice told him to shut up. "I'm looking for the Stane."

"Huh. I appear to have run in the wrong direction. Whatever will I do?"

"Er . . . you could . . . oh." He shook his head, feeling stupid. "That was another joke."

"He can learn. That delights me no end." She met his eyes for a long moment over the flames, and tiny fireflies fluttered in Danr's chest. "I must thank you, deeply, for what you did. You gave up everything for me, and I can never repay that."

Danr flushed. "I . . . you're . . . that is . . ."

" 'You're welcome' will probably suffice."

"Uh . . . you're welcome." This was idiotic—Aisa was his friend, and he was braying like a startled donkey around her. The *draugr* had surprised him less. Gathering his wits, he asked, "How did you get away?"

"Simple enough. I have kept this pack hidden for a long time. Your trial distracted everyone, so I snatched it and hid near your farm until I saw you leave. I thought you would go down the road, which is why I was so far behind you."

"You'll be marked for death if you return. Runaway slaves are—"

"I will *die* before I return there!" Aisa spat the words like a wounded snake. "That man will never touch me again."

Her response startled Danr. He didn't want her to get

angry and leave. He retreated and spread his hands placatingly. "Of course, of course."

"As long as we understand that," Aisa growled behind her scarf. There was a long, awkward pause. The creek behind them clattered its toothy chatter. Then Aisa sighed. "I am sorry. You are the last person who should see my anger."

Danr let out a silent, relieved breath. She was going to stay, and that single thought thrilled him to the marrow. He said, "You don't have to explain anger to me, Aisa. Anger is my oldest friend."

"Thank you for that." Aisa sighed again and looked at him. "I would like to ask you a question."

"Anything." The shadows didn't seem so threatening now; the fire had become warm and friendly.

"What is that pouch at your throat? I have never seen you without it."

Danr's fingers automatically went up to it. "This? It was my mother's. She said it contained the truth, though actually it has two wooden splinters inside. I never understood what she meant by that."

"Hmm." Aisa looked thoughtfully at him. "When my mas—when Farek first brought me to the village, I met his mother. She was kind to me, and when she saw I knew something of healing, she showed me more of the local plants, ones I did not yet know. Frida resented that, and she resented the way Farek . . . came to me at night."

"I'm sorry," Danr said, and meant it. The thought of Farek touching Aisa, hurting her, made him angry all over again, but he also wanted to hold Aisa and tell her it wouldn't happen anymore.

"Farek's mother told me some stories of your people. Trolls, she said, work with stone and are born with stone splinters in their eyes. This is why trolls have weak eyesight and why they cannot see truth."

"Truth." Danr touched his own eye. "How much truth can we live with?"

"People rarely wish to know the truth," Aisa agreed, and she reminded Danr of his mother right then. For a bad moment, he missed his mother with an ache that went all the way down to his toenails, and he would have chopped off his left foot to talk to her again, just for a moment.

"Speaking of truth," Aisa said, "I will take my three guesses now."

Danr blinked at her. "Guesses?"

"Your name. Is it Torbert?"

It seemed strange to be playing this game under these circumstances, in a forest so far away from home and both of them exiles, but the old ritual was comforting. Danr smiled, feeling the anger retreat. Aisa could do that, and it gave him a warm feeling. "No," he said.

"Is it Jan?"

"Sorry."

"Is it—"

A huge figure emerged silently from the trees behind Aisa. It was a troll, two heads taller than Danr, heavily muscled. Its—his—skin was as swarthy as Danr's, but his ears were larger and more pointed. His lower jaw jutted forward, and his lower fangs were as long and thick as fingers. His nose was little more than a button in the center of a craggy face, and shaggy black hair topped his head. More black wiry hair covered his arms and legs. He wore a leather tunic and trousers, and his feet were bare. At his belt was sheathed a stone knife, and over his shoulder he carried an enormous club with spikes in it.

Danr didn't remember leaping the fire. One moment Aisa was guessing his name; the next Danr was standing between her and the troll. Aisa's final guess died in her throat and she made a strangled sound.

"Who are you?" Danr demanded in his gruff voice. "What do you want?"

The troll's voice was equally gruff. "You trespass on troll land. I have a right to kill you."

He swung the club with startling speed. Danr shoved Aisa one way even as he dodged another. The club smashed the ground. Danr felt the shock through his bones, and the flames danced.

"Wait!" Danr put up his hands in fear and supplication. "I'm troll!"

"Liar!" The club rushed at Danr's head. He ducked under it and stumbled backward. His foot came down in cold water—the creek. Behind the troll, Aisa pulled a burning brand from the fire.

"It's true!" Danr shouted. "My mother was human, but—"

Anger twisted the troll's face, and he swung again. Danr tripped and fell sideways into the freezing water. The club hit the creek. Water exploded in all directions.

"My father was troll!" Danr sputtered on his back in the creek. Stones dug into his skin. He felt exposed and vulnerable. Danr was used to being the strong one, but compared to the troll, he was small and weak, and the troll intended to see him dead. He raised his club again.

Aisa hit the troll in the side with the flaming brand. He whirled, plucked it from her with a hand the size of a cow's head, and flicked it into the water, where it extinguished with a hiss. The troll turned back to the creek. Danr tried to get to his feet, but the rocks in the creek bed slipped under him. The club rushed down at Danr's head, but he caught the troll's wrist in both his hands and pushed back. The troll's muscles bulged, and a terrible weight came down on Danr's arms. Two spikes on the club edged toward Danr's face.

"I'm troll!" Danr panted. "Stane!"

"Does he look like me?" Aisa shouted behind them.

"Hmf." The troll's face poked into Danr's line of sight. The club quivered a moment longer. The troll's eyes narrowed over his jutting jaw, and the weight left Danr. "I see something of the troll in your face, little one. Under all that human."

Danr sat up and rubbed his burning wrists. "My thanks."

"Your girl, however," the troll continued, "she is—"

"Leave her alone!" Danr scrambled partway to his feet. "She's a . . . powerful witch."

"That is correct," Aisa said evenly. "But I will not use my magic on you if you guide us to the other trolls."

"Hmf," snorted the troll again, and Danr couldn't tell if he believed her or not. However, he offered a hand and hauled Danr dripping from the creek with easy strength. Danr swallowed. The troll had given in fairly easily, considering that he was winning and that Aisa had offered no proof she was a witch of any stripe. Was there more going on here than he knew?

Danr shook himself out over the fire. Aisa stared defiantly up at the troll, who was nearly twice as tall as she was. Danr admired her courage. His own heart pounded fair to break his ribs, and his knees were weak as bread dough. Still, he forced himself to stand straight.

"My name is Kech," the troll said, pronouncing the name with a guttural *ch* at the end. "Yours?"

"I'm . . ." Danr glanced at Aisa. "I'm called Trollboy. Can you take me under the mountain?" He hurried to add before Kech could comment, "I want to meet my people."

"Your people?" Kech leaned on his club, looking incredulous. "What right have you to call us your people, little one?"

Now Danr felt a spark of anger. He blew on it and made it bigger. Anger was better than fear, yes, it was. "My father was a troll. The Nine have declared I have family right. Or are the Stane as godless as the Kin claim they are?"

Kech met Danr's eyes for a long moment. They were

large and brown, like Danr's. Danr made himself stand straight and let his anger show, even if he had to look up to do it. And then, to Danr's surprise, Kech looked away. What was going on?

"Very well," he said with a resigned air. "But if you are not troll, little one, you will die."

Without another word, he turned and stomped away. It took Danr a moment to understand he was meant to follow. He caught up Aisa's hand and ran after Kech, leaving the fire behind. Only at the last second did Aisa snatch up her pack and Danr's sack.

"Don't lose me," Aisa said. "In the dark, I would vanish forever."

Her wrapped hand was small and cold in his damp one. Under other circumstances, Danr would have marveled at the fact that he was holding her this way, but his mind was more fully occupied. Kech set a fast pace in the dark on the rocky, tilted hillside, and Danr had to thread his way around a number of obstacles in the dark while ensuring that he didn't lose Aisa. Bushes and low branches slapped his face and scored his arms. Kech crunched his way through the forest, not seeming to notice or care whether Danr was keeping up or not, and Danr refused to make himself look weak by calling out for him to check his pace. Twice, however, Aisa stumbled and fell, and Danr finally picked her up, packs and all, and hurried forward. She didn't protest, but put her arms around his neck. She smelled of dried herbs and wood smoke, and for a moment Danr wanted more than anything to run with her, keep his arms around her, until the sun came up and he dropped in his tracks.

At last they arrived at a place where no trees grew. The hill became the mountain now, and slabs of stone rose to the starry sky. The two stars that made up Urko were still far apart, but moving steadily toward each other. An outcrop of rock jutted out like a great fist punching its way out of the mountainside. Kech leaned on his club next to the outcrop. Danr set Aisa down.

"Only a troll can open this door, little one," Kech grunted. "It is heavy, but a full-grown troll like me opens it on the first try. So try. And if you fail, I will roast both you and your spae-wife."

Uncertainly Danr checked the outcropping in the chilly starlight. His troll's eyes picked out a door carved into the stone, done so cleverly that its outline appeared as nothing more than ordinary cracks and crevices. When he looked closer, he saw more cracks that ran together to form an abstract Great Tree. The workmanship was nothing like anything back at the village or even Skyford. Danr touched the tree, then felt around and found rough places, hidden handles where he could insert his hands.

Everyone always said that you're a troll, he thought. *Time to prove it.*

He heaved. The muscles on his back bunched. His arms stretched. The seams on his tunic popped. His breath burned in his lungs. But the door didn't move. Danr was finally forced to step back, panting.

Kech shook his head with a snort like a bull's. "Try again, little one. My oldest son opens the door on his second try."

You can do this, he told himself. *You* have *to do this.*

Danr braced himself and *heaved.* He felt pain as bones bent and joints cracked. Sweat ran hot down his face. His hands and fingers screamed outrage at him. The door shifted.

Come on, he thought. *Come on!*

He hauled again but couldn't get full purchase. Danr lost his grip and staggered backward, chest heaving. Dreadful pain pulled at his muscles.

Kech laughed. "Once more. I am sure even my younger son could open the door on his third try. And if you fail this time"—he casually smashed a large rock with his club. It cracked into rubble—"your fat will sizzle on my spit and your witch's skull will hold my ale."

Aisa made no reaction to this. She stood still as a ragged statue, her wrapped hands clasped before her. Watching him. Counting on him. Danr gritted his teeth, grabbed the hidden handles, and pulled. The door didn't budge. Danr set his feet and continued to haul on the door. His back and arms burned like lava, and he felt his strength giving way. The door stubbornly refused to move. Kech leaned on his club and shot a glance at Aisa. Aisa remained stock-still. A small breeze fluttered the end of her scarf, a scarf that Kech had originally intended to soak in her blood. Her eyes met Danr's, and she nodded. She wasn't afraid because she was certain he could do it. Her confidence in him lent him new strength. The monster in him bellowed to the sky and *heaved*.

The door shifted again. Danr ignored his screaming body and continued to pull. The door ground open one inch, then another, and another. At last it came free of the hidden doorsill and Danr flipped it aside. It crashed against the side of the mountain. Danr collapsed on hands and knees to the stones, laboring for every breath. He had done it!

There, Mother! he thought. *A use for the monster.*

After a long moment, Kech hauled him upright. "You are at least part troll," he said grudgingly. "Stay close behind me, then."

"What . . . about . . . Aisa?" Danr panted. "We can't . . . leave her . . . here."

"I do not mind waiting," Aisa said. "Even for several days. But what if another troll comes? It might try to devour me."

"It?" Kech echoed. "Do you think we are *things*, girl? Monsters?"

Aisa said, "You murder human victims. That certainly makes you monstrous, if not monsters."

"What are you talking about, girl?"

"You—or one of your kind—killed two men from our village. That started everything."

"Ah. Them." Kech twirled his club. "Yes. I killed them. But only because they attacked me first. I came down out of the mountain for the first time in years and found them on Stane land. They attacked me with pitchforks, then ran back to their house to loose arrows at me. Look here." He held out an arm that showed two healing puncture marks. "They tried to kill me, so I broke their house and killed them."

"That is horrifying," Aisa replied. "You are strong and powerful. You did not need to—"

Danr forced himself to his feet and stood between them, his aching arms outstretched. "We don't *need* to fight. Again. But we do need to protect Aisa from other trolls. She's my friend."

"Hmm. Since she is your friend." Kech drew his stone knife. "But a friend should keep a civil tongue." He pierced his thumb, drawing a dark bead of blood. Before Aisa could react, he smeared it across her forehead. Aisa gasped and put up a hand.

"Leave it," Kech ordered. "Other Stane will smell it and know not to harm you. Come."

A long, tall tunnel gaped behind the open door. Kech strode down it without looking back. Aisa came up beside Danr and put a small hand on his shoulder.

"Thanks be to Rolk," she murmured. "You should be proud of yourself."

Inwardly, Danr glowed at her praise. Outwardly, he glanced at the watery half-moon. "The trolls favor Kalina. Perhaps we should thank her instead."

Together, they headed down the dark tunnel behind Kech. Some kind of fungus glowed green on the walls, providing enough faint light for Danr to find his way, though

Aisa had to stay close beside him. Danr's arms and shoulders still burned from opening the door, and he wondered how much he would hurt after he slept.

A *boom* made them both jump. The door had shut itself behind them.

Chapter Seven

Danr followed Kech down the wide, echoing tunnel. Water dripped, and it smelled of ancient stone and growing mold and chilly air. Aisa's breath came harsh beside him. He knew she was frightened, and he wanted to reassure her, but he didn't know how, or if it was even possible. Best to keep moving forward.

He lost track of time and distance, and his sack was growing heavy in his hand, though it didn't weigh more than a few pounds. At last, the tunnel opened into . . . Danr blinked and drew in a breath. Aisa gasped and moved closer to him. The space before them was so huge that Danr couldn't see it as a space. The ceiling was lost in murk and shadow so high a hawk could have flown it without realizing it was underground. Danr couldn't tell if there was a far wall, it was so far away. The floor lay many, many stories below, and it glowed faintly. This great space swallowed up sound as if it had never existed.

In the distance were cheerful yellow lights, some fixed in place, others moving about like fireflies. Some were up high, others down low. As if he were listening to a noise that abruptly became a symphony, Danr came to understand this was a great city, but unlike a human city built on the ground, this one was built on walls and floors and even hanging from gigantic stalactites that dripped from the ceiling or climbing up the stalagmites that rose from the floor.

He inhaled, trying to get some sense of the place, a feeling of rightness or belonging. This was where his father had come from, half his heritage, his strong and powerful Stane side, and the very stones would welcome him for the lost son he was. Or maybe he should feel anger and pain and fear. These were the people—well, one of them, anyway—who had hurt his mother. Vik! Why did everything have to be so complicated?

To his disappointment, he felt nothing except the vast, swallowing emptiness. Well, he didn't *really* expect anything from stones. Once he arrived in the town proper and met some trolls, he would feel more at home. Or more anger. He hoped for the at-home feeling. It would be nice. After all, only one troll had hurt his mother. The others hadn't done anything.

But that was part of the problem, wasn't it? The other trolls hadn't done anything. Hadn't they known he existed? Hadn't they known he was a thrall, trapped among humans and forced to work for a thieving miser? Why hadn't they come for him? Or at least asked after him? Now he was here, hoping for strength and a home from a people who hadn't really done a thing for him except give him a father who had ignored him. He squared his shoulders. Well, maybe now it was time to find out. In any case, he had a heritage to reclaim, right?

A rough staircase carved from the rock led downward, though the risers were made for people with much longer legs than Danr or Aisa. Kech strode easily down the steps, while Danr and Aisa struggled. The final stair didn't quite reach the cavern floor, which was thick with a noisome mixture of bat droppings, water, and mud. The pungent smell made Danr's eyes water. Long insects skittered through the mix. From all this sprang growths of mushrooms—gold and green and scarlet shot with purple veins. Some were as small as toads; others pushed toward the cavern ceiling like trees. Most of them glowed, sending up just enough soft, eerie light to see by.

The staircase ended at a wide wooden walkway that hung ten or fifteen feet above the floor. Kech strode along the boards while Danr and Aisa cautiously followed. As they drew closer to the city, the walkway split in a dozen directions. Ladders ran up to balconies and platforms. Staircases appeared, zigzagging or twisting into the dim light. It all made a confusing, many-tiered maze. Houses of stone, clay, and brick clung to the walls or balanced on stilts and platforms. They varied in style and construction. Some were well built and tidy, others slapped together and falling apart. Many had no roofs. It took Danr a moment to realize that underground houses didn't need to shelter the inhabitants from sun and rain. Each house, however, did have a door with a tree carved or painted on it, though these trees emphasized the roots more than the trunks or branches. Danr kept waiting for a feeling of familiarity, a sense that he knew this place in his blood, but everything felt strange and foreign.

They encountered other trolls. Trolls tromped, hustled, or strolled about the walkways, staircases, and ladders on business of their own, troll men, troll women, and troll children. All of them were built like Kech—two heads taller than Danr, heavy shoulders, swarthy skin, large eyes, long arms, thick hair on head and body. The trolls wore dark clothing, much of it in poor shape, and they all went barefoot. None wore a hat, and Danr stuffed his own in his sack. It was nice not to need it. A crowd of voices echoed in a booming babble against the stones and mushrooms as the trolls talked, called, and shouted. A troll woman argued with a troll man over a basket of dried fish. A group of trolls laughed and drank from enormous clay mugs at a clump of tables while two other trolls refilled them from great brown pitchers. Two troll children chased each other down a ladder and up a staircase, ignoring the old trollwife who shouted something at them from a balcony above. It was so loud and raucous. This shouldn't have surprised Danr—did he suppose trolls did nothing but crouch in dark caves all day and night?—but he had a hard time taking it all in and couldn't help staring. He hadn't realized how hungry he had been for trollish company, to look around and see people like himself. But these people didn't much look like him. All of them were taller and stronger than Danr, and he felt small and naked, knowing they could break him in half with little effort. Was this how the people in the village felt around him?

Kech threaded through the enormous town with Danr and Aisa in his wake. The trolls stared at Danr and Aisa and muttered as they passed, but made no move to stop or molest them. A troll woman abruptly stormed up to Aisa with hands outstretched, as if to snatch her up. Danr tensed and Aisa looked ready to run. At the last moment, however, the troll woman sniffed the air near Aisa's head so hard Aisa's face scarf fluttered. Then she stomped away. Aisa touched the smear of dark blood on her forehead, and Danr let out a breath he hadn't realized he was holding. Kech only shrugged.

A lumpy ball rolled up to Danr's feet. Danr automatically picked it up, and a child who was more than half Danr's height dashed up to him. The child saw Danr and stared at him.

Danr held out the ball to her. "Hello."

"Monster!" The child backed away and fled. Danr set the ball down with a sigh. One thing remained perfectly familiar no matter where he went.

Kech eventually brought them to a large, multistoried house that twisted around a mountainous stalactite at the edge of town. Beyond the house, an enormous lake spread across the cavern floor. Kech slammed the door open.

"Pyk!" he boomed. "I'm home! And I'm hungry!" He stomped inside, dragging his club after him and leaving Danr and Aisa standing uncertainly on the threshold.

From inside the house, a gruff female voice shouted, "You're always hungry! It'll be ready when it's ready, and you can keep your mouth shut about it until then!"

Kech poked his head outside. "I suppose I have no choice but to offer you a place to spend the day. Come inside."

The world had turned upside down, indeed it had. Only yesterday, Orvandel the fletcher had flummoxed Danr with an offer of hospitality in the world above, and now a troll was doing the same in the world below. Danr edged toward the house with Aisa clinging to his shadow. She had guts, he had to admit. He doubted *he* would have braved a troll's house if he were fully human. The more he learned about her, the more incredible she became. Danr took a breath and crossed the threshold.

His first impression was that Kech's house wasn't that much different from Orvandel's. A table flanked by wide sleeping benches ran the length of the main room, and a blazing hearth sat at the back. A haze of meaty smoke stung Danr's nose. The house had no roof, but the stone walls were so high it didn't matter. Just as in Orvandel's house, cloth screens stood about to direct the hearth's heat or grant a little privacy. Hooked tools and clawed implements hung from the walls, along with mesh bags of mushrooms and other lumps Danr couldn't identify. Kech was just hanging his great club on one wall.

A spit with a haunch of . . . something on it straddled the fire. Turning the spit was a troll boy who looked to be maybe

eighteen, though Danr supposed he could be eight hundred—
what did Danr know of the age of trolls? Juice sizzled on the
coals. A tall, tall trollwife with black braids piled on her
head was lifting the lid of an iron pot as big as a tub, though
in her clawed hands, the pot looked normal-sized, and the
strangeness of it twisted Danr's eyes. Her lower jaw jutted
forward, and her ivory fangs gleamed in the firelight.

"I brought company, Pyk," said Kech, and his expression
was uncertain. "They'll be eating with us."

Pyk saw Danr and Aisa. The pot lid crashed onto the pot.
The boy gaped.

"Humans!" Pyk spat. "Get them out of my house, Kech!"

"Manners," Kech replied, though his face looked as if a
ghost had reached inside his trousers. "Hospitality."

The boy stopped turning the spit. Danr swallowed, feeling
the mouse caught between a hawk and a cat. Aisa touched the
blood on her forehead. Pyk folded her arms across an enormous chest and deliberately turned her back. Danr became all
too aware of the open door behind him and of other trolls passing by in the street. Many of them slowed when they caught
sight of Danr and Aisa in Kech's doorway, and they grumbled
at each other behind their hands. An icy finger slid down
Danr's back. What would happen to him and Aisa if they were
left alone in Kech's stable or put out of the house entirely? A
passing trollwife glared stones at Danr. He stepped away from
the door, doubting the night would pass peacefully.

"Why would you offer hospitality to humans?" Pyk growled.
"They're a danger, and filthy to boot."

"I begin to see why humans and trolls rarely visit one another," Aisa murmured in a voice so low only Danr heard it.
He kept his face neutral, but inside he squirmed with embarrassment, not only because he was watching a group of
strangers argue, but also because they were insulting him and
Aisa. It seemed a great joke. Trolls were more similar to

humans than he had expected. Their houses were different, but still houses. They wore clothes as humans did. They spoke the same language, though they sounded as though they gargled their words instead of keeping them in the front of their mouths as the villagers did. They practiced hospitality. But they also could be rude and cruel, just like Alfgeir and White Halli. Why should he have expected anything else?

"I promised, Pyk." Now Kech pulled himself more upright. "That should be the end of it."

Pyk snatched up a long-handled spoon. "They can stay in the stable. That's hospitality enough."

"Now, Pyk—"

A hand slammed onto the table. Danr jumped, and Aisa squeaked. The hand, easily as big as Danr's head, was twisted as ivy and lumpy as old oatmeal. Black claws extended from the fingertips. The hand's arm extended into shadow behind the table.

"Hospitality enough?" grated an ancient voice. "Hospitality *enough*?"

"Mother." Kech hurried over to grasp the arm and help the owner to its feet. From the shadows emerged a trollwife clinging to life like an iron oak at the top of a worn cliff. The muscles on her arms and legs were bags of sand, and her face looked more eroded than wrinkled. Worn, scraggly teeth poked upward from her thrusting jaw, and one of the fangs was broken. She kept a fringed blanket wrapped around her simple dress, and her feet made sliding sounds on the floor as Kech helped her into the dim light of the fire. Danr's tongue dried up in his head and his bowels quivered. Aisa's hand stole into his. All trollwives had power, but the old ones . . . the old ones could challenge the war gods Fell and Belinna themselves.

"Whoever heard of hospitality enough, Pyk?" the trollwife croaked. "You shame your husband, and you shame me!"

Now that she was upright, she pushed Kech's helping

hand away with irritation and shuffled toward Danr and Aisa like a slow avalanche. In that moment, he wanted very much to be back in Alfgeir's familiar stable, away from this strange and dreadful place. He would have taken daily beatings, even let the earl cut off his fingers.

Aisa's wrapped hand turned within his. Danr stole a glance at her. Her face above her scarf was pale, and she was weaving in place. She was terrified. Once again, the thought that Aisa was frightened pushed Danr forward with an invisible hand.

"Good evening, Grandmother," he said, and his voice quavered only a little.

The trollwife poked at the pouch at Danr's throat with one claw. He tried not to flinch. "I see what you have there, boy," she said. "How much do you know of truth?"

That question caught Danr off guard. "Truth?"

"Aye." The trollwife fished about beneath her blanket and extended a closed fist. She opened it. On the palm lay two flinty splinters. "These are mine. Fell out when I talked back to a certain giant and she smacked me a good one."

Danr clutched his own pouch. The wooden splinters inside pricked his fingers. "My mother gave these to me."

The trollwife grinned. It was a terrible thing to see, the jaws of a cave gnashing on old stones. "Your mother told fortunes, didn't she? And her fortunes always came true. And people hated her for it."

"How did you know that, Grandmother?" Danr breathed.

"I see truth, boy. Day is coming. You and your friend will accept our hospitality and eat. Then we will pay our respects before the dawn breaks."

"Our respects?" Danr repeated. "I don't understand."

"Of course you don't. If you did, we wouldn't have to pay respects. My name is Bund, but you will keep calling me Grandmother. Now sit! Eat!"

Danr and Aisa traded glances and obeyed. The wide benches that ran the length of the table were so tall that neither Danr's nor Aisa's feet touched the floor, and Aisa barely saw the top of the planks. Pyk unceremoniously dropped stone dishes in front of them containing food Danr didn't recognize in the slightest. A platter held slices of something that steamed in brown gravy. An enormous bowl contained a dark soup. A round loaf looked like bread. The foods smelled . . . different. Earthy and meaty all at once. After some examination, Danr realized they were all made from mushrooms. Timidly, he tried some of the slices in gravy. They tasted something like goat. The loaf had a heavy texture that left peat on his tongue. It wasn't unpleasant, but not anything he was used to, either. Aisa was clearly forcing herself to eat while the old trollwife ate heartily. Pyk held herself apart and kept the boy distant as well. Kech hung between the two groups, clearly wishing he was elsewhere. Silence hung heavy with the smoke.

At last, they finished. "We go," the trollwife said. "Quickly, now. The Three won't wait."

Kech dropped the knife he was holding. "The Three?"

"That's impossible," Pyk said. "We can't Twist there."

"*You* can't," the trollwife replied, amiably picking up an enormous twisted walking stick and getting to her feet. "But the *draugr* and the chain have changed everything. That was the entire point, yes?"

"The chain?" Danr said.

"The Three are *giants*," Kech blurted. "You can't bring humans there!"

"You have good reason to know your statement isn't true, son."

At those words, Kech slammed his mouth shut and shot Pyk a guilty look that Danr didn't understand.

"But perhaps we should ask," Bund continued. She turned

to Danr and Aisa. "Do you want to accept further hospitality from Kech and Pyk and spend the day? Or do you want to pay your kind respects to the Three?"

"Three what?" Aisa said, speaking for the first time.

"Stane. Giants older than even I am. They'll tell you what you need to know. If they like you."

"And if they don't?" Danr replied.

"Pyk doesn't like you." Bund pointed to her with the stick. It was carved with runes. "What do you think your day here will be like if you stay?"

Pyk and the still unnamed boy were staring at them now with undisguised contempt. Kech stood a distance away, his lower jaw jutting even farther forward than normal. Danr didn't need to consider long.

"Thank you for your offer of hospitality," he said to them, "but I think we'll pay our respects."

"Indeed," Aisa added.

Out on the streets and walkways, Danr noticed a clear difference now that Bund the trollwife took the lead. The other trolls snatched themselves out of her way, indeed they did. Some of them even bowed or touched their foreheads. Bund leaned on her heavy walking stick, but this hardly slowed her down. She moved with the momentum of a falling tree. Danr and Aisa followed, feeling like very strange ducklings behind their mother.

"Is it far, Grandmother?" Aisa asked after a time. "I only ask out of general interest."

"Very far," Bund groused. "Too far to walk. Or ride. Or fly."

Confused, Danr said, "How will we get there?"

"You will Twist through the roots of Ashkame. I will show you." Bund had reached a walkway that ended at the cave wall covered with a thick carpet of tiny mushrooms that didn't glow. The wall stretched up, up into darkness like the cloak of a god, and the dim light of the fungi below the walkway did almost nothing to light it. Even Danr's trollish eyes could barely see.

"Here we are." Bund thumped her stick twice against the cave wall, and from the echoing darkness flew thousands of points of light like summoned fireflies. They settled on the runes carved into Bund's walking stick, making them glow with a soft silver light. In the new brightness, Danr made out the mouth of a tunnel just tall enough for someone like Kech to squeeze through. Something about the opening made Danr think of a throat.

"If you think I intend to pay respects to anyone who lives in there," Aisa said, "you may wish to think harder."

Bund ignored her. "Did your mother tell you of the Iron Axe and the Great Tree, boy?"

"Of course," Danr said. "She was a wonderful storyteller."

"Hmm. Did she ever tell it like this?" Bund rapped her stick against the top of the tunnel. The mushrooms below glowed brighter, throwing velvety shadows up onto the cracks and contours above. The shadows, however, contained richness and texture, like sand made of dark jewels. Parts of the shade were so deep that the light in between cast by the mushrooms seemed dazzlingly bright in comparison.

And then, with a sound like a giant grinding diamonds between her teeth, the stones above the tunnel moved. They pulled and twisted, revealing shifting sand and even gleaming gems of a thousand sizes and colors. A soft musical tone rang through the cavern, and the hair rose on Danr's neck and arms. Aisa gasped. The rocks moved, manipulating the gems and shadows to create on the rock face an enormous leafless tree. The bark shimmered with a thousand dark colors. Branches stretched up to the ceiling, and roots stretched down to the floor. The tree was symmetrical at top and bottom—each branch that went up had an identical root that went down, and a simple line of emeralds symbolizing the earth bisected the tree sideways in the middle of the trunk. The branches wrapped around a ball of golden sand, and the roots wrapped around an identical ball of blue shadow, and the center of the trunk bulged around a ball of green mushrooms.

Danr let out a long breath. He had seen Ashkame, the Great Tree, thousands of times, carved or painted or embroidered on doors and ships and cloaks, but never had he seen anything like this. The shadows deepened and dimmed, making Ashkame appear to wave in an unseen breeze above while the roots writhed through the earth below.

Bund brandished her walking stick, and darkness swallowed the tree. "Long ago, it was only Grick and Olar. They lay together at the beginning of time, and Grick became heavy with child."

The shadow and stones moved again, forming a new picture. Grick, large-breasted and big-bellied, squatted near a fire. Olar, heavy-muscled and long-bearded, helped keep her upright while she panted in labor. Both of them had a definite trollish air to their faces, with jaws thrust forward and fangs thrusting up.

"Grick gave birth to four seeds. From the first three sprang Rolk the Sun, Kalina the Moon, and Bosha the Sea. From the husks rose Vik, lord of the underworld. The fourth seed, however, remained dormant. Grick planted it and watered it with her own milk and menstrual blood, and a thousand years later, it sprouted and grew into the Great Tree we call Ashkame."

The huge cave wall told Bund's story in moving pictures of shadow, gems, and stone. Danr and Aisa stared in awe.

"Ashkame, the Great Tree, twisted her roots through the entire universe and discovered Gloomenhame, the lower world where the gods went to live. Ashkame's trunk gave birth to

Twixthame, where mortals now live. And her branches grew into Lumenhame, the upper world where evil lies."

"Er . . . your pardon," Aisa said softly.

Bund's gaze swept over her, and the Great Tree froze. "Girl?"

"I believe the stories say Gloomenhame is where evil lies, and Lumenhame is the home of the gods."

Danr, who had been thinking much the same thing but hadn't had the courage to say so aloud, nodded in an attempt at solidarity. He was still a little stunned at the sight of a naked ten-foot-tall goddess giving birth to four seeds.

"When you have the magic stick," Bund sniffed, "you can tell the story the way *you* want. Now, where was I?"

"Lumenhame, the world of evil," Danr said.

"Yes. Good. Hmm." She waved the stick, and the tree's leaves twisted again. "Rolk bedded Kalina—" Here the image shifted to a trollish sun god and an equally trollish moon goddess clutching each other in a wild embrace, and Danr didn't know whether to be embarrassed or fascinated. "—and she gave birth to three beautiful daughters: Nu, Ta, and Pendra. Then Bosha gathered clay from the bottom of the sea. The rich, dark clay became the Stane. The fine, smooth clay became the Kin. And the soft, weak clay became the Fae."

"Perhaps the Fae tell this part differently," Aisa observed.

Bund ignored her magnificently. "Rolk breathed light into one each of the Stane, Kin, and Fae, and they became giants, merfolk, and sprites. Kalina breathed silver into a Stane, Kin, and Fae, and they became trolls, humans, and elves. Then Vik breathed earth into the final Stane, Kin, and Fae, who became dwarves, orcs, and fairies.

"Nu, Ta, and Pendra decided these Nine People needed tending, and they became the gardeners who tend Ashkame and plow the paths of our lives in her bark. They also gave the Nine People the gift of magic. To the Fae, they granted the magic of the Mind: glamours and thoughts and illusions. To the Kin, they granted the power of the Shape: shifting and melding and merging. And to the Stane, they granted the most powerful magic of all—the magic of the Hand: crafting and carving and rune-making. Because of their superior power, the Stane ruled the three worlds for a thousand years."

"Wait!" Danr said. "This wasn't part of the stories I knew. The three Kin races have no magic, and the Stane never ruled anything."

"The Kin leave that part out," Bund said, "though it is truth. The Stane ruled wisely and well but became corrupt in their—our—power. We enslaved the Fae, stole their lands, pushed them to the edges of their branches. At last they had had enough and forged an alliance with some of the Kin so they could make war against us."

A great battlefield as seen from a dizzying height appeared on the wall. Armies of people and animals moved below. Among the elves and humans and fairies, thousands of lean, long-haired people rode slithering wyrms into battle, and Danr realized they were orcs, Kin he had heard of but never seen. Male and female soldiers with heavily tattooed faces in scaled mail carried spears and curved swords. Aisa put a hand to her face and leaned forward for a closer look.

"Are those merfolk?" she breathed. "They walk on land!"

"The Kin power of the Shape was strong in those days," Bund replied. "But even that power couldn't stand up to the Iron Axe."

A gleaming double-bladed axe swirled into being on the wall; then the design dispersed back into a battlefield again. The blue Stane army rushed forward and smashed into the golden Fae, destroying them. The red Kin were divided.

Some fought alongside the Stane, and others fought along-side the Fae.

"The giants captured the power of Death and created the Axe for the Stane army. It was the most powerful weapon in the world. It slaughtered entire regiments, leveled entire armies, until a traitor to the Stane came forward, a dwarf who believed the Stane had become corrupt and evil. He stole the Axe and delivered it to the elven king. The battle turned."

Now the golden soldiers slaughtered the blue ones—and plenty of red ones. The field ran scarlet with blood, and Danr thought he heard screams, though the stones remained silent, and the only sound was dripping water and the squeak of bats.

"Rather than leave the Iron Axe in the hands of the Fae, the Stane decided to destroy it. They crafted a knife and used powerful runes to twist the Great Tree's live-giving magic through the blade into a single Kin, a human. They split his chest and used living power of Ashkame to destroy the Axe of Death. This sundered the Axe into three pieces, and took most of the continent with it. The land dropped straight down, and the ocean rushed in. Few survived."

Fire and water flooded the battlefield. Danr looked away from the scene, unwilling to watch so much death.

"I crossed that ocean on a slave ship," Aisa murmured. "I did not know it was a graveyard as well."

"The pieces of the Axe were lost," Bund finished, "and the Stane had stolen so much magic from the Nine People that even after a thousand years, it has never fully returned to them. The Fae tried to repair the world. They regrew the forests. They showed the Kin how to farm. They pushed the Stane deep underground. But now the Fae have become cor-rupt in their own power. They enslave the Kin and steal land from the Stane. The cycle repeats. It is time for the tree to tip and bring her roots up to the sky."

Bund rapped her stick on the cave floor, and the stones went utterly dark.

"That was delightful," Aisa said. "I especially enjoyed the part where thousands of humans were slaughtered by two uncaring armies."

"How did you do that?" Danr put in. "You just told us the Stane have very little magic left. But this—"

"You are less intelligent than you let on, boy," Bund said. "Did you think I was idly showing off? That I was wasting time and magic just to tell you a little story? You need to *think*." She rapped his shin with the heavy stick, and Danr yelped. "I used magic to show you how Ashkame's branches and roots twist through the entire universe, through all three worlds, so you would understand that those with the proper magics can twist with them."

"Meaning you can use magic," Aisa said. "This cannot be possible, with nearly all the magic gone."

Danr remembered the heated conversation Bund and Pyk had shared back at Kech's house. "This has to do with the *draugr*," Danr said sharply. "And that chain you mentioned earlier."

"Perhaps the boy is more intelligent than we knew. But now it's time to pay your respects to the Three. They'll tell you what you need to know." Bund raised her stick, and more fireflies rushed to the runes. They glowed silver once again. With the tip of the stick, she sketched lines of light and shadow that hung in the air before the mouth of the tunnel. The design looped back on itself, twisting in ways that made Danr's eyes ache in his head. When she was done, Bund was panting with the effort, and she leaned heavily on the glowing walking stick with clawed hands. "Go now. When you wish to return, call my name three times."

"Why us?" Danr asked suddenly. "Why are you doing this for us?"

"To us," Aisa corrected.

"Hmm." Bund flicked one claw toward the pouch at Danr's throat. "Because you can see truth, boy. Or you will soon. The Tree needs to tip again, and it will tip around the five of you."

"Five?" Danr said.

"He can count." Bund poked at their backsides with the stick. "Go on. Twisting is almost never fatal."

"Almost?" Aisa squeaked.

"Nothing valuable comes without risk. Go!" And she shoved them into the design of light and shade.

Chapter Eight

Dreadful light smashed through Aisa's skull. Her feet left the ground, and for a moment the world turned upside down. Nausea split her stomach. For a terrible moment, she lost her body and was no longer herself. She had branches and roots that twisted through not just three worlds, or three dozen, or even three million, but a countless infinity of worlds. Aisa was connected with every tiny piece of everything everywhere. Even the eternal hunger for elves receded. She was losing herself.

And then a tiny particle, a seed of time and place, grew and blossomed nearby. Greedily, she snatched at it, felt it strengthen under her hand. She yanked at it. With a vicious wrench, she landed hard on a hard stone floor. A thud, and Hamzu, the strong one, landed beside her. They both lay there a moment, breathing hard. Hamzu sat up first and helped Aisa to her feet with his immense, gentle strength. The cave swayed and settled.

"Are you all right?" Hamzu asked in his gruff voice, and not for the first time Aisa wished she knew his real name, even if Hamzu suited him better than Trollboy.

"I am not at all all right," she said, secretly gratified that his first question came for her welfare. "But I believe I will adjust. Where are we?"

They were standing at the end of a long, high tunnel lit by the ever-present mushrooms. It was as if Bund had shoved them into her tunnel and they had emerged from this one. Perhaps, Aisa considered, they had.

Ahead of them, far distant, echoed the sound of female voices raised in argument. Hamzu gave Aisa a glance. "The Three?" he asked.

"Seems likely." Her mouth was dry despite the dampness of the tunnel. "Perhaps we should find out."

Hamzu tapped the wall behind them. It remained unmoving beneath his fingers. "Do you think it'll work, calling Bund three times to get back?"

Aisa had to try twice before she could answer. "I am unsure. But since we cannot now go back, the best we can do is go forward."

He snorted. "Go forward. That's usually my philosophy."

"Is it?" Aisa was aware she was blithering, talking about nothing to cover her unease. "Then it would appear we are both intelligent, sharp-witted people, except for one thing."

"What?"

"We are neither of us actually moving forward."

Hamzu snorted again, and together they set out down the tall tunnel. As they walked, the gnawing desire for elven company returned full bore. It tugged at Aisa, drilled through her bones. This cold and brutal place felt empty without the shining light of the Fae, and she longed for her lord's tantalizing fingers on her skin. She did her best to push the feeling aside. Hamzu was there. Tall and strong and gentle. Except when he had roared to life and crushed the monster White Halli. That day would live forever branded on her mind.

Aisa had been half waiting for the word *witch* to fly from someone's mouth like a poisonous wasp and sting her. Healer women always seemed more susceptible to such accusations. More than once, she had almost given up healing entirely for fear of it. But not only did healing give her a sense of purpose; it also let her build a road to freedom, coin by coin, and she kept at it despite the risk. And when White Halli's inevitable accusation came, Aisa had known then that she was a dead woman. She would be either beaten to death as an accused witch, or executed as a confessed one.

And then . . . then Hamzu was there, standing between her and White Halli's beating stick. In that moment, she had seen her chance to do some real good. If Hamzu wielded the cane as White Halli ordered, he could kill her in one painless blow, and Hamzu himself would go free in the bargain. Her death could buy his liberty.

But it hadn't happened that way. Hamzu had given up his life for her instead. The event left her at a loss. No one had ever done such a thing for her. Not her father, not her brothers, certainly King Vamath, her former elven owner. When Aisa looked at Hamzu, she felt she might fly apart or shout for joy or dive into the deepest ocean. Instead of doing any of these things, she wrapped herself deeper in her scarves and followed him underground, despite trolls and tunnels, mushrooms and magic. She would follow him until she had the chance to learn if she would do the same thing for him that he had done for her.

The tunnel sloped sharply downward, and they made their way slowly to avoid falling. Great stone teeth hung down from the ceiling, and equally great stone spikes thrust up from the floor. Aisa pulled her rags tighter around her, trying to drive the ever-present cold hunger away. There were no bats or worms here, just dripping water, a few glowing mushrooms, and Hamzu's soft breath in the darkness. And the squabbling. It grew louder, and Aisa was eventually able to make out three distinct voices.

"It's my turn," one voice cried.

"It's not," contradicted another. "It's mine."

"You're both wrong," snapped a third. "It's still *mine*."

Aisa and Hamzu crept around a pile of rocks and found the entrance to a cave. Cautiously they slipped closer to peer inside. What Aisa saw made her heart pound. Three gigantic women, taller even than Kech, sat on the floor around a fire that was small to them but would have been a bonfire to anyone else. Their clothes hung in black tatters, and so many wrinkles creased their faces that Aisa could barely make out any features. Aisa exchanged a nervous glance with Hamzu. Their eye sockets were black and empty, and they had no ears. Skulls and other bones littered the floor. The Three.

The woman closest to Aisa snatched something from one of the others and clapped her hand to her face. When she took her hand away, her left eye socket was no longer empty. A single glittering eye looked around the cave.

"Give that back!" the second woman howled, revealing dark, toothless gums.

"You have the ear," the first replied, peering at the fire, then at her clawed hands.

"Only because she stole it from *me*," the third snapped. Her lone yellow tooth gleamed in the dim light.

A chill crawled over Aisa. She knew the story of the three mountain women who shared a single eye, ear, and tooth, and who ate the flesh of those who entered their cave, but she'd had no idea the women were real or that they were the ones Bund was sending them to see.

Hamzu was watching the women. They passed the eye, ear, and tooth among themselves with dazzling speed, bickering all the while. Aisa's teeth chattered, and not just from cold.

"They'll tell you what you need to know," said the memory of Bund's voice. Aisa knew in an instant what they needed to do, and she also saw that Hamzu hadn't yet come

to the same conclusion. She gnawed her lip. People often treated Hamzu like an idiot, but she had long ago realized that he was far from stupid. He just took his time in making up his mind, and he moved with a deliberation that the less observant mistook for imbecility. However, in this particular case, they had no time for deliberation. The longer they stayed, the greater the chance the giant women might notice them and their bones would join the ones on the cave floor.

Aisa straightened one of her scarves and forced herself to focus past the cold, past the hunger, focus on the eye as it passed from hand to hand. Eventually it came to the woman closest to her hiding place. Before she could lose her nerve, Aisa launched herself toward the giant as she passed the eye to her sister. With speed she didn't know she possessed, Aisa snatched it from the giant's hand and dashed back to the boulder again. It was bright green, and felt cool and heavy against her palm.

"What have you done?" Hamzu whispered in horror.

"What you would have done if you had thought a moment longer," she whispered back. Her fingers barely encompassed the eye, and she tightened them around it.

A blackness swept out of the orb and wrapped itself around her in a warm, velvet cloak. Aisa nearly cried out, but then the aching cold and the awful hunger vanished as if they had never been. Delicious, heavenly warmth filled her like soft truth. Her stomach was full, and even her fingertips felt warm. The eye wriggled against her hand like a fish.

"Where is it?" the first giant screeched. "Give me the eye!"

"I did," the second cried.

"You lie!"

Aisa gripped the eye and took a breath. "I have it!"

The first two women continued shouting at each other, but the third, who had the ear, turned her face toward Hamzu and Aisa.

"Sisters!" she snapped. "We have a visitor."

The other two instantly fell silent, and Aisa understood that without the ear, the sisters could hear each other, but nothing else.

"Who's there?" the third sister asked.

Aisa swallowed despite the wonderful warmth. Even empty, the giant's black eye sockets seemed to be looking straight at her and Hamzu, and their hiding place was only a few paces away, within easy reach of a giant's arm.

"I—we—have come to pay our respects and to learn what we need to know," Aisa said, her voice shaking slightly.

"What did it say?" the first sister demanded.

"Tell us!" shrieked the second. "Tell us quickly!"

"There are two. They seek knowledge," the third replied. "And the female has our eye."

The two deaf sisters immediately set up a howl of dismay. "Give it back!" "Thief!" "Give back our eye!"

Aisa took her time and replied carefully, despite her pounding heart. "If you answer my questions, I will hand over the eye. If you lie or try to trick me, I will squeeze your eye until it breaks."

The third sister relayed her words and the trio whispered briefly among themselves.

"Do you know what you're doing?" Hamzu murmured.

"No," Aisa replied. "So be ready."

"I'm not going anywhere." His strong, steadfast presence made her feel a little better.

"We agree," the third giant said at last. "But we will only answer three questions from you."

"Agreed," Aisa said.

"Ask!"

"How can I free myself of my hunger for my elven lord?" Aisa blurted out, then blinked. She hadn't meant to ask that. Her face grew hot. Hamzu stood next to her, his jaw strong, his face impassive. He knew of her constant desire. Everyone in the village did. That made it no less embarrassing to talk about.

The question bounced around the cavern and spun back to Aisa herself. The Three cackled among themselves.

"See the truth," said the third. The eye pulsed in Aisa's hand and a burst of warmth rushed over Aisa, and abruptly she *knew* the answer, like truth that lived down in her long bones, like an answer she had always known and was just now remembering:

She had to seek out the Iron Axe, and the quest for it would break her hunger.

The new memory made her legs go weak, and she grabbed for Hamzu's arm with her free hand. He gasped at her touch, and she knew that he understood the same truth she did.

"This is not possible," Aisa said aloud. "Bund said the Iron Axe was destroyed a thousand years ago."

"That is not a question," said the third giant.

"All right. Where is the Iron Axe?"

Again, the question bounced around the cavern and spun back to Aisa herself while the Three cackled. "See the truth!"

The eye pulsed warm and dark, and a new memory poured heavily through Aisa. Except this time, there was no great revelation. She already knew that the Iron Axe had been destroyed a thousand years ago. Aisa sighed.

"A foolish question," mocked the third giant. "Ask your last question."

Aisa gave herself a mental kick. "Why are the spirits of the dead hanging about instead of going to the underworld?"

"Good one," Hamzu breathed in her ear, and she shivered.

"See the truth!"

The heavy eye pulsed a third time, and a third time truth came to her, but the new memory landed with the force of a blow. She staggered against the cold rock:

The Stane had chained up Death itself, and without Death, no one could truly die.

Hamzu shared this truth with her, and his mouth fell open. Even his great strength seemed to drain away. Death itself was chained up? How could anyone do such a thing? *Why* would anyone do such a thing? This question was on Aisa's lips when the third giant interrupted.

"The eye has spoken to you," she said. "Give it back!"

"I'm hungry," said the second giant.

"I'm thirsty," said the first.

Aisa's fingers tightened around the eye. Its warmth kept Aisa so calm, so free of the terrible elven hunger. She couldn't possibly give it up now. Hadn't she earned a respite after all these years of cold and hunger? And what did these women who lived in a dark cave need of an eye?

But no. She had made a bargain with these giants, and she must live up to it. With a trembling hand, she dropped the bright green eye into Hamzu's startled palm.

The awful hunger returned, slammed into her like an icy hammer, and sent her to her knees. Hamzu inhaled sharply as the eye's dark warmth swept over him, and she longed to trade places with him, take even a scrap of the eye's gift.

The Three set up a howl. "You gave your word!" the third one screamed. "You promised to return the eye!"

Aisa pulled herself to her feet. "I promised to hand it over," she gasped. "I never said to whom I would hand it. Our bargain is complete, and I offer my respectful thanks. If you want your eye back, I suggest you bargain with my friend."

The Three howled again, and the stones trembled. Aisa clapped her hands over her ears at the awful noise. Hamzu finally got hold of himself and held the eye high over his head. It was much smaller in his hand.

"I offer the same bargain," he bellowed. "Three questions for your eye."

The Three fell silent, leaving only the drip of water in the quiet. "He smells familiar," whispered the third to the second. "He smells delicious."

"We should answer. It will be amusing."

"Very well," said the third. "But the person to whom you hand the eye must be me."

"Agreed."

"Then ask!"

Aisa let herself sag against the rocks and slide to the chilly floor. The hunger was all the worse now for the few moments when the eye had removed it from her. She huddled in her rags and watched Hamzu wield the eye.

"Who is my father?" he asked. The question spun around the cave. Hamzu stiffened, then staggered under new knowledge. Was that how she had looked when the eye answered for her? Timidly, she reached out and touched his shin as the giants cackled. Aisa didn't feel the warmth of truth, but she did share in the knowledge:

Hamzu's father was Kech the troll.

"Oh," she said.

"Yes," said the third giant through her gums.

"It makes sense," Hamzu murmured. "He said he was sure his youngest son could open the door on the third try, and I did. Bund told me to call her Grandmother because that's what she is. Kech wanders the forest outside the mountain. That was how he found my mother." He held up the eye again. "Did Kech rape—"

Aisa saw what was coming. She pulled herself upright and clapped a hand over Hamzu's mouth before he could finish the question. "Don't!"

His half-finished sentence spun around the cavern and

died in the dark. The third giant shifted on the cavern floor. "Ask!" she growled.

"I'm still hungry," said the second.

"I'm still thirsty," said the first, and this time they turned their heads toward Hamzu and Aisa. The second giant felt around the floor with a huge, clawed hand. "He smells familiar."

"Ask after the nature of their relationship," Aisa hissed. "You'll learn more. Quickly! Bargain or no bargain, I think they're losing patience."

"What kind of relationship did my father and mother have?" Hamzu asked in a shaky voice.

Because her hand was still on him, she felt the memory drill into Hamzu. This time she caught a little flash of the past, of Kech the troll and a pretty young woman sharing a fire out in the forest. Their arms went round each other, and they kissed. The embrace became more intimate. Hamzu leaned against a boulder. He was sweating.

"My mother . . . she was in love with him."

"But they couldn't stay together," Aisa said softly. "Kech was married. And a troll."

"That ring of stones I found in the forest was where they . . . it was where I was . . ."

"Do you have a third question?" cackled the giant.

Hamzu straightened and held out the pouch he wore around his neck. "Why did my mother wear these splinters around her neck?"

This time there was no pulse from the eye. Instead the third giant repeated the question to her sisters, and all three went into harsh gales of laughter. Hamzu's face went red and his arms trembled. Aisa recognized the signs of his anger.

"Stop laughing at me!" Hamzu snarled, and he squeezed the eye. It made a squelching sound.

The giant sisters ceased laughing and clapped their hands to their eye sockets, shrieking in pain.

"Please!" the third sister begged. "Please don't hurt our only eye!"

To Aisa's relief, Hamzu relaxed his grip, looking ashamed.

"I'm sorry," he mumbled. "I don't mean to be a monster."

The third sister brought her hands down, then cocked her head. Her empty eye sockets came around, and a chill went down Aisa's spine. The sister seemed to be staring at them, and Aisa had the feeling that, eye or no eye, she knew exactly where they were.

"We were not laughing at you," the giant said. "We were laughing at your question. It's a very simple one, but it would be easier to show you the answer than to tell you."

"Show me?" Hamzu asked suspiciously.

"Yes."

Hamzu considered this. "No tricks? You won't hurt me?"

"No tricks, no harm. The Three swear on the roots of Ashkame. Come closer, child, and I will show you."

"I don't think—" Aisa said.

"They swore," Hamzu replied, and sidled closer. The sister felt around until her fingers brushed his chest. She laid one huge, gnarled hand on his shoulder. Aisa tensed, though she had no idea what she might do if the sister tried to hurt him.

"Here is your answer," the sister said. Her other hand smacked the back of his head.

Hamzu reeled and went to hands and knees on the cold stone floor. The third sister snatched the eye from Hamzu's limp hand and popped it into one socket. Aisa sprinted over to him and tried to help him to his feet, but he was too heavy.

"You said no tricks," Aisa snapped. "You said no harm."

"Does it harm a newborn baby to have its bottom slapped?" the sister countered. "Look at the floor in front of you, boy."

Hamzu looked down. With shaking fingers, he picked up two splinters from the cave floor. One was stone; the other was wood.

"Stane work with stone. Kin work with wood," the giant said. "You are half-blood, so you were born with both kinds in each eye. You lost two splinters from one eye, but your mother lost one splinter from two, twice the trouble to her, my half-blood boy. She wore her splinters around her neck to remind her of a past, an innocence, she had lost. Did you never wonder why she stayed in a village where everyone hated her? Why she didn't leave to seek a better future?"

"She was a thrall," Hamzu said, clutching the new splinters to his chest.

"That didn't prevent *you* from leaving." The giant stared down at them with her gleaming green eye. Her single wrinkled ear twitched once. "Your mother knew no one anywhere would accept her as long as she had borne the bastard son of a troll, so she stayed where she was. She thought she could make her way up in the world by trading the truth for money, but people don't like the truth. Not even the truth-teller does."

"Truth-teller?" Hamzu said.

"The smallest tribe in the world." The giant grinned with gray gums. "With nothing to cloud your vision, you will see the truth wherever you turn your true eye, boy, and that is a powerful thing. But those splinters did more than keep truth out, boy—they kept your truth in."

"I don't understand." Hamzu looked more confused than ever.

"You will," the giant said, "the next time someone asks you a direct question."

Now all three giants creaked to their feet like redwoods in a storm. Aisa backed up a fearful step.

"I'm hungry," said the first giant.

"I'm thirsty," said the second.

"Run!" said the third.

They ran. The Three came after them with thunderous footsteps. Aisa and Hamzu made it to the tunnel moments ahead of them.

"Grandmother Bund!" shouted Aisa.

An enormous hand came down the tunnel, pushing air ahead of it. Aisa felt its grasping breath on her back.

"Grandmother Bund!" shouted Aisa a second time.

Hamzu snatched her up and dove at the end of the tunnel. The hand reached toward them from behind as the rocky wall rushed at them from the front.

"Grandmother Bund!" shouted Aisa a third time.

They struck the wall. The universe Twisted both of them, and they were gone.

Chapter Nine

Danr pushed himself upright. The cold stones spun beneath him, and he threw up. Bile burned his throat and tongue. He crouched a long moment on hands and knees, the steam from the vomit curling around his chest. Nasty stuff.

"I hate Twisting," he muttered. "I'd rather spend a week in a cougar's den." This had to be the world's strangest day.

"Where are we?" gasped Aisa. She was kneeling next to him. "This is not the place from which we started."

"No, honey. It's where everyone ends."

The new voice yanked Danr to his feet. He found himself crouching between Aisa and the speaker, his hands partly curled into fists, and a part of him wondered how often this was going to happen. "Who are you?"

They were in yet another cave, or so Danr thought at first. The floor was stone, but the walls were made of earth and the ceiling . . . the ceiling was a mass of tree roots thick as his waist and thin as his finger. This cave was much smaller, not even as large as the house of Orvandel the fletcher, and the winding tree roots gave the impression of a thatching. Soft beams of sunlight worked their way down through the

roots, granting enough light to see by but not enough to hurt
Danr's eyes. It was all strangely cozy.

A simple door made of stone, wood, and . . . glass? . . .
took up part of one wall, and sitting on a rocking chair next
to the door was a plump, motherly-looking woman in a red
dress and a white shawl. Her graying black hair was pinned
up in braids, but Danr couldn't quite make out her face. Either the shadows got in the way or his eyes were blurry from
the nausea, he wasn't sure. Was she troll or human or . . .
something else? A clicking sound came from her lap. She
was knitting. On a table next to her stood two lit candles,
one silver and one gold.

"You know who I am, honey," she said to Danr. "You just
refuse to see the truth."

Danr backed up a step and bumped into Aisa. Roots
brushed the top of his head, and the back of his skull ached
where the giant woman had smacked him. His right eye
stung. Clenched in his fist were the two needle-sized splinters, one wood and one stone, that she had knocked out of
him. Everything was happening so fast he couldn't keep up.
His father was Kech the troll, he wasn't the product of a rape
as he'd thought all his life, he'd been conceived during an
illicit love affair between his parents, and his mother's
splinters . . .

He looked down at his own splinters, still in his hand,
and blinked hard. His left eye, the one that had lost its splinters, came open first, and he saw the knitting woman through
that eye only. His knees went weak. When one eye was still
shut, he saw the woman . . . differently. He couldn't quite
explain it. She hadn't changed in any way. But he *saw* more.
The dress was red as blood. The knitting needles were of
shiny human bone. Her knitting was a thousand, million,
billion strands all inextricably woven together. The rocking
chair was carved from a single piece of Ashkame itself. A

chain, fine as a silken thread, wound nine times around her neck and vanished into the roots of the roof. This woman was Death.

"Now you see," said Death. "So like your mother."

Danr opened his other eye, and the woman returned to . . . not normal, but something like it. The truth stopped slapping him in the face. Still, Danr's legs trembled and he started to kneel before her.

"Don't, if you please." Death continued rocking and knitting. "Though if you're very brave, you may kiss my cheek."

Danr wondered how brave he could be. Cautiously he leaned in and pecked her on the cheek. Her skin was cool and soft, and she smelled of dry daffodils.

"What is happening?" Aisa demanded. "Who is this?"

"This is Death," Danr said, still a little bewildered.

"Is it?" Aisa came around Danr for a better look. "Hmm! How strange. The Three frightened me. My master terrorized me. But Death . . . does not. Why is that?"

"Most people don't fear me, honey. They fear what comes just before me. And what comes after."

"What *does* come after?" Aisa asked.

"At the moment, nothing." Death paused in her knitting to pull at the thin thread around her neck. The roots overhead shuddered in sympathy, and Danr flinched. "Everyone enters that door, and sooner than they think. Even the Nine will troop through it eventually. On that day, I'll set down my needles, blow out these two candles, and follow them. But as long as the Stane's chain binds me, nothing at all can enter that door, and that's the truth."

"Who made the chain?" Aisa asked.

"The dwarves, of course." Death's needles dipped in and out of her knitting. "They can make anything, if they have the right materials. It took the power of all the giants under the mountain to put it on me. More than a few vanished through that door during the fight. Vik was dancing in his drawers, I can tell you. He doesn't get many giants on his side."

A dreadful thought struck Danr. "How did *we* get here? Are we going to . . . ?"

Death laughed. "You haven't been paying attention, honey. No one can really die right now. Their *draugr* hang about begging for release."

"Then how *did* we get here?" Aisa persisted.

"I have some power still." She leaned forward, though the thready chain brought her up short like a dog coming to the end of its leash. "Listen, dear, the Stane have the world's biggest tiger by the tail, and that's a problem. You help me, you help the world. You in?"

"Where's my mother?" Danr asked suddenly. "Is she on the other side of that door?"

"Sweetie, everyone asks that question. Vesha, queen of the Stane, lost her daughter two years ago, and even *she* asked that question. I'll give you the same answer I gave her: you'll have to wait and see."

"How do we help you?" Aisa said.

"Break this chain."

Without thinking, Danr reached out to grab the thread, intending to snap it. Death clicked a hand around his wrist. Her grip was cool and bony. "No. Hand me that rock, will you?"

Mystified, Danr obeyed. The rock was the size of a small melon. Death held it over the thin chain and dropped it. With a soft feather of sound, the rock fell through the chain. It landed on the ground, split into two neat pieces. Danr sucked in his breath and stepped back.

"Mustn't touch," Death agreed.

"How long have you been chained like this?" Danr asked, brown eyes wide.

"Not long." The knitting needles clicked and clicked. "And yet long enough. It happened just a few days before those foolish Noss brothers attacked Kech. In your little village, only those two have died—or tried to. In the bigger worlds, hundreds and hundreds have tried to die. Time grows short, dear."

"How do we cut this chain, then?" Aisa said.

"Didn't you pay attention to the Three? Find the Iron Axe."

A thunderous *boom* crashed through the cave and made Danr's bones throb. Aisa spun.

"What—?" Danr asked.

"Nearly time for you to go," said Death. "Anytime you want to see me, I'll be here. And not for the reason you're thinking."

Danr's gaze darted about the little cave, looking for the source of the noise. "But how do we find the Axe?"

"And don't answer us in nonsense and riddles," Aisa put in. "It wastes everyone's time."

Death said, "This chain clouds my vision, so I can't say for sure."

"I knew it," Aisa muttered wearily.

"But the old stories told true when they said the Axe was split into three pieces—the head, the haft, and the power. The haft was last seen among the orcs in Xaron. The Fae keep the head in their court at Palana as a souvenir."

"No," Aisa whispered.

Another *boom* rumbled through the cave. It sounded like a giant's footstep. Danr tried to look in all directions at once. "What *is* that?"

"Bund is calling. I can't keep you here forever." Death's needles clicked and clacked.

"Where is the Axe's power, then?" Danr demanded.

Death shook her head. "I'm afraid I can't help you, sweetie. Even I haven't seen it in a thousand years. But I think if you put the first two pieces together, they'll tell you where to find the third. And you're under a time limit. The Axe can only be assembled when Urko, the split god, comes together. You'll know by the two stars that represent him. They will come together in twenty-seven days—nine times three. How fitting is that?"

"Twenty-seven days!" Danr gasped. "That's no time at all! Not even a month!"

"Then you'd better get moving."

To Danr's shock, Aisa flung herself at Death's feet. She begged in a tone that wrenched his heart, "Great lady, can you cure me?"

Death paused in her knitting and put a gentle hand under her chin to raise it. "I can, dear child, but only once, and not in the way you want me to. I'm sorry."

Aisa swallowed hard, nodded, and rose.

"How will we find you once we have this Axe?" Danr asked around the lump in his throat.

"That won't be a problem. I'd start looking for the haft in Xaron, if I were you. Remember—you have to find the pieces before the stars merge in twenty-seven days. And that's twenty-seven days from the time you arrive back under the mountain. Time is a bit different here, you see. If you miss the moment, it'll be another hundred years before another one comes along, so move quickly! And watch for the helpful traitor, dear."

"What does *that* mean?" Aisa said.

"You'll know when the time comes. Go!" A third *boom*, and a pattern of light and dark ribbons appeared against the wall opposite the door. Danr's gorge rose as the pattern swallowed them.

"There you are, boy," Bund grumped, and set her cane down. It made a very small *boom* that nonetheless echoed against the stones. "I'd begun to think you'd gotten lost, and believe me, you don't want to get lost in a Twisting."

Danr dragged himself to his feet and helped Aisa up. This time he managed it without vomiting. Twenty-seven days. They had twenty-seven days to find the Iron Axe, or Death would be chained for another hundred years. How was he supposed to do that? Xaron was months away on foot and weeks away by horseback.

Aisa, meanwhile, was staring at the ends of her long, ragged scarf. The trailing ends had been severed as if by a sharp knife. Thin tendrils of smoke curled from the wool. Danr blinked in dismay.

"What happened?" Aisa whispered.

"Hmm," Bund said. "One of the little risks of Twisting, especially if the spell is interrupted—or you change direction unexpectedly."

Next to Bund was another trollwife, a younger one who stood taller and straighter. Her dark dress was cut from more luxurious fabric and her lower teeth gleamed in the mushroom light. "I'm not happy about this, Bund," she said. "They could have been killed. And there's that other matter."

"They needed to pay respects, and that's the truth," Bund replied blandly. "Even if they've been gone longer than I thought."

Danr's head barely reached the other trollwife's chest, though after the Three, she didn't seem nearly so large.

"Who—?" he began, but then he closed his right eye so he only saw through his left, the one that had lost the splinters. To his surprise, the trollwife . . . changed. She became regal, powerful, someone who owned everything around her, and who had a family connection to Bund—Danr could see they had the same eyes, the same jaw, the same hands and knees. But the trollwife also carried a heavy load, one that threatened to crush her. All these ideas slipped into place like grains of sand forming a picture. Danr had never met a queen before, but he did know he was supposed to bow, so he did.

"Your Highness," he said. Aisa, hearing the term, quickly curtseyed.

The queen looked at him sharply. "How did you know who I was?"

"It was obvious, lady," he said, "once I looked. I also know you and Grandmother Bund are sisters."

Bund burst out laughing and thumped her stick on the stony floor. "Wonderful, boy! Welcome to the family of truth-tellers! We're not popular, but we get the word out. This is my sister, Vesha. The queen."

"We spoke to Death," Danr said quietly. "I don't like what she told us."

Queen Vesha sighed, and Danr remembered her daughter had died. "I was afraid of that when I heard Bund had Twisted you away and you didn't come back for all that time."

"All that time?" Aisa said. "What do you mean? It hasn't even been an hour."

"Then you did see Death," Bund said. "Time goes funny when the truly old ones play with it."

"How long have we been gone?" Danr demanded.

"I've come down here to bang against the wall to try and bring you back every night, and I've done it . . . " She paused to count on her gnarled fingers. ". . . fourteen times, so that would make it two weeks."

Danr staggered. Only a few days ago, he had been living his ordinary farmer's life. Now he was trucking with trolls, dealing with Death, and mucking with magic. The power in this place staggered him.

"I need to sit," he muttered, and sank to the damp cavern floor.

"Hungry?" Bund produced a melon-sized chunk of what smelled like smoked mushroom and a bottle of water. "Eat! You're too thin for a troll."

"A word, sister, while the humans rest." Vesha took Bund

a ways up the cavern, where queen and trollwife conversed in low voices. Aisa sat beside Danr. He tore a chunk of the mushroom. It had the taste and consistency of smoky cheese. The water in the bottle was sweet and tasted of a spice Danr couldn't name.

Aisa accepted some of the food as well, and they chewed in companionable silence for a moment. Danr drank from the bottle again. How strange it was. For a long time, Aisa, with her exotic accent and the ragged scarves across her face, had been the strangest thing he'd known and it had been all he could do to say more than two sentences to her at once. Now, in comparison, she was the most normal. Was that the way it worked? Perhaps normal and abnormal, exotic and mundane only existed in relation to each other. Someone who saw one-eyed giants and tremendous trolls on a regular basis wouldn't look twice at a girl who hid her face in scarves. He rubbed his chin. The people in Skyford and the village mistrusted Danr because he was part troll. But was that only because they never saw the Stane?

Aisa yawned behind her scarf, then caught herself. "I am sorry. It has been a long time since I last slept."

"Hmm." He hugged his knees to his chest, feeling suddenly tense and strange. Everything was loose and chaotic, and he wanted something more familiar, more solid. Strangely he missed Alfgeir's stable. It was stupid—who could miss living in a stable? And that place had never been a home to him, not really. Still, he missed the simple straw and the stones of his hearth and the sweet swell of the cows as they exhaled at night. Most of all, he missed the sound of his mother singing as she combed her hair. She would have walked through that door, past Death and her knitting needles. Danr had stood in her very tracks and not realized it until just now. An unexpected bubble of grief grew inside him. "How do you do it, Aisa?"

"Do what?"

"How do you take all this?" Danr made a general gesture at the darkness and the two enormous troll women deep in conversation. "Two days ago, I was shoveling manure out of a stable and helping a calf that had fallen down a well. Today, I talked to Death. How many people *do* that?"

"All of them, eventually."

"You know what I mean. And I promised her I'd find . . ." He shot Bund and Vesha a glance and lowered his voice ". . . the Iron Axe. How should I? Vik's balls, I was born on a farm. I'm not a . . . not a . . ." He stammered to a halt.

"Are you trying to say *hero*?" Aisa asked.

"I can't do it." He gave her a puzzled look. "The words won't come."

"You cannot lie, truth-teller. You know very well that only a hero would have saved me from White Halli."

His face grew hot. "*You* were heroic. I still can't believe how you grabbed that eye. Where did you find the courage?"

"The same place you found the courage to stand up to White Halli and to kiss Death on the cheek." Her dark eyes danced over her scarf and made his heart flutter. "Courage is the ability to do what you must, and heroism is simply courage on behalf of someone else. You are brave and a hero."

The flush continued, and his heart swelled to hear Aisa say such things about him. "It's just . . . it's all turned upside down."

"I know something of worlds that turn upside down," Aisa said solemnly.

She wasn't looking for sympathy. He could hear that in her voice. So he only said, "Do you know what the most incredible thing I've seen here is?"

"Hmm. With that question, I must guess that it isn't Death or giants who share an eye. Is it the glowing mushrooms? Or perhaps a cave so large it could encompass Valorhame itself?"

Danr shook his head. "It's learning my father loved my mother." He ran a hand over his face. The world was indeed tipping. All his life he had thought himself the product of violence and fear. All his life he had been the victim of both. It was just now catching up with him that he had been conceived in love, and the idea made his breath catch in his chest. He was just like other people. He wanted to jump and shout, and he wanted to tell someone, anyone. Everyone.

Aisa sat beside him, still gnawing on a mushroom, solid and at ease. In fact, she seemed far calmer than he had ever seen her. It felt good and fine and comfortable to have her beside him, and he wanted to put his arm around her to keep her with him.

She noticed him looking at her in the dim glow. "What is it?"

His face grew hot and he took another sip of water, even though he wasn't thirsty, trying to keep the answer to himself. But she had asked, and the truth wouldn't stay inside him. His mouth moved by itself. "I'm glad you're here, Aisa. I want you to be here always."

Aisa gave him a look. "You saved me. I told you I will follow you until that debt is repaid."

"I don't want you to follow me," he said. "I want you to walk next to me."

Before Aisa could answer, Vesha returned with Bund behind her. "We should leave this place," she said. "Come, if you please."

The four of them followed the stony path back toward the underground city. Mushrooms glowed and water dripped. The strange, rhythmic sound pulsed at Danr's ears. It grew louder as they walked, and his blood stirred. His hands felt hot.

"What is that sound?" he asked at last.

"You'll see soon enough," Bund replied.

"Why did you do it? What gives you the right to chain Death?" Danr blurted out. This was a queen he was addressing, but he couldn't seem to stop himself.

"Power," Vesha said.

"I don't understand," Aisa said.

"Once we reach the city," Vesha replied, "your friend here will explain."

"I will?" Danr said in surprise. They were nearing the city as he spoke, and the sound was louder, pounding and booming, echoing off the stones.

"You won't be able to help it, truth-teller," Vesha said. "Look now. What do you see?"

They rounded the last bend in the path and entered the great cavern proper. It had changed. Spread out across the dark floor were hundreds and hundreds of lights. Dark figures loomed among them, and Danr finally realized the lights were piles of mushrooms and small fires. They were at the edge of the great camp, and Queen Vesha led them fearlessly through it. Trolls pounded drums the size of wine casks—the source of the thrumming that had stirred Danr up. Even now, he felt his heart beating in time with each booming thud. They walked through the camp, passing gigantic shelters of fur and cloth and stone so high Danr had to lean back to see the tops. He gaped in awe. Trolls tromped about, hauling armor and carrying clanking weapons—maces, clubs, and even swords—too big for any human to lift. They passed forges where short, twisted men with beards that went down to their toes pounded metal with hammers nearly as tall as they were in time with troll drums. Dwarves. And through it all stomped the giants. Danr could do nothing but gape. They were tall, so very tall. Taller than even the greatest ash trees. Some had two heads, or three. One had a dozen. Male and female alike, their skin was blue or red or tinged with green. The cavern floor shook with their every step. It was like watching thunder take solid form. They smelled of moss and wet stone and old hair. Some wore armor, some wore rags, some went naked. Danr could do nothing but stare up and gape, both thrilled and awed. This was something no Kin had seen in a thousand years.

Dwarves and trolls bowed hastily to the queen as she passed, though the giants took no notice of her, perhaps because their heads were so far off the ground they couldn't see her, or perhaps giants didn't bow to anyone. Danr didn't spare a lot of thought for this—it was difficult enough to fathom that he was looking at giants. And dwarves, too. The heat from their forges made Danr sweat while they pounded out intricate designs in metal. And through it all pounded the drums, drums, drums.

"What is happening?" Aisa asked in a hushed voice.

"The drums summon everyone for war, girl," Bund said. "Always war."

Danr's hands itched again, and he felt a rising need to hit something, to bite and crush and smash. It was the drums, he realized. The rhythms sang to him and created a strange excitement. He tried to push it down, but it wouldn't go.

"War?" Aisa echoed. "But what for?"

"I told you your friend would explain," Bund said. "And right about now."

They were skirting the edge of the great camp and had arrived in the troll city proper. It was exactly as Danr had remembered it—bustling and busy with huge trolls of all sizes and ages lumbering about their business as the group of four passed by. When people caught sight of the queen, they stopped and bowed until she waved them away. The incredible houses climbed the walls and stalagmites. Staircases twisted in all directions. Children played, adults worked. But when Danr closed his right eye, the city . . . changed. The trolls were thinner than they should be, their clothes shabbier. How had he missed the worn spots, the pinched expressions, the too-small loaves, the half-full flagons, the wilting mushrooms? Many of the houses looked tired, ready to tip over, and they showed cracks Danr hadn't noticed before. Dirt and mud were everywhere, and the sharp smell of rot and waste hung in the air. He should have noticed all this before, but he hadn't. Was it magic that showed him such secrets, or was he simply seeing what everyone could see if only they would just look? He didn't know. Perhaps it was both.

A troll *draugr* drifted through the wall of a nearby house. *"Release!"* it begged. Bund and Vesha didn't react. Aisa flinched. Danr's left eye told him the *draugr* was a troll man who had died of old age, but who would have lived many more years if he'd had better food.

"What do you see, boy?" Bund asked.

"You're all dying," he said. "In less than a hundred years, you'll all be as dead as that *draugr* over there."

Aisa put a hand over her mouth.

"Indeed," Vesha said gravely. "The Fae drove us underground after the Sundering. They warded the doors shut, and here we've lived ever since. After a millennium, we've pried open one door—"

"The Great Door," Danr said.

"Yes. Our family has been working on those wards for nearly three hundred years, and we finally broke them twenty years ago."

"When my—when Kech first started to explore the mountain," Danr said.

"My nephew has long had a fascination for the world above," Vesha agreed. "He was instrumental in helping the Trollwife Council to break that ward. When that happened, other great spells slowly began to unravel. Some of the great beasts that live in the mountains felt the change. They've become braver and have begun visiting the occupied lands again. But that's a mere side effect."

"What are you trying to do, exactly?" Aisa's voice was flat.

"Our civilization can't survive forever on what we grow or hunt in the caves. We *must* reclaim the land above, or we'll starve. We are going above, come the Nine, come the Fae, come Death herself."

"Now *I* need to sit for a moment," Bund said, and lowered herself onto an enormous stone bench outside what Danr assumed was a tavern. Trolls passed on the byway, but fewer of them now. Day was coming, and it was nearly time for bed, though the camp drums pounded without cease. Weariness pulled at Danr's bones, and he realized he'd been up all day and all night. Aisa's eyes looked tired, and he wordlessly helped her up to the bench as well. Her feet swung above the ground. Beside her, Bund tapped her stick on the ground. The runes were dark now, and Danr remembered the lights that had flown into them. A cold truth struck him.

"So, new truth-teller," Bund said, "what do you see now?"

His eyes pricked with the pressure of words piling up behind them. Damn it, he didn't want to speak. He was in control of his mind, of his tongue. But the truth came out anyway, and helplessly he heard himself say, "The troll-wives have chained up Death to force the spirits of the dead to remain in this world, and they use their power to open the other doors. You're using the *draugr*. You feel bad, you feel guilty, but it doesn't stop you. It doesn't even slow you down. It's filth, even for a queen."

In that moment, he understood why so many people had hated his mother. *No one likes the truth,* she had said. He stared at the ground, waiting for angry words or blows from Vesha.

But none came. She only said, "The true filth is that our children starve. The food Pyk and Bund gave you is the richest we have. We have to get out. In one month, perhaps two, enough Stane and Kin will have died to give us the power to open all the doors."

"Such a terrible thing!" Aisa whispered from the bench. "You steal power from the dead!" Then she added, "Your Highness."

"I don't justify myself to you." Vesha's voice was solid, but Danr saw the way her jaw worked back and forth. "We have discussed it for centuries and found nothing better. Either we use the dead, or we join them."

"What would your daughter say?" Danr asked without thinking.

Now Vesha did grow angry. "You forget your place, human child. Do you think I haven't considered what it would be like to see my own daughter's *draugr* staring at me every day? Do you think I haven't considered how many of my own people I've chained up along with Death herself?"

"I've never thought about your feelings." The dreadful words, the required answer, tripped out of Danr's mouth. He tried to add that he was sorry, but those words stuck in his throat. He tried again, but still the words wouldn't come. Baffled, he looked at Vesha, then at Bund.

Bund cackled from the bench. "You're a truth-teller now, boy."

"I don't understand," Danr said. "What does that mean?"

"Without splinters to hold back the truth, you can't lie. You can't even make false apologies, boy. But be thankful. Unlike some of us, you can still choose to see the soft, kind world you saw before. Keep both eyes open, and you'll be able to see the lies. You only have one mouth, though, and it will forever speak the hard truth."

Danr touched the pouch at his throat. No lies ever again, not even small social fibs. He swallowed hard.

"The elves won't like what you're doing," Aisa said, still whispering. "They won't like it at all."

"It always comes down to war, dear," Bund said. "Just as it did a thousand years ago. The Tree tips."

"With humans caught in the middle," Danr spat.

"What do you care of humans?" Vesha said. "Have they treated you well? Did they give you a home?"

"As much as the trolls have," Danr shot back truthfully.

"Yes." Bund heaved herself off the bench and continued down the street toward Kech's house. "The half human is at home in all worlds and in none. The truth is always difficult."

Vesha followed with a sigh. "I get very tired of hearing about your truths, sister."

They reached Kech's door, and the carving of the tree and its tangled roots seemed to stare at Danr. Something occurred to him that made his breath catch.

"If you two are sisters," he said, "and Kech—my father—is Grandmother Bund's son, that would make me . . ."

"A prince," Bund agreed, and moved to push the door open. "For all the good it will do you."

"Wait." Danr put up an arm to stop her, though it was like trying to push aside a giant oak root. "Let me?"

Bund gave him a look but obligingly backed up a step. Danr knocked sharply. A moment later, Kech himself opened the door. Danr closed his right eye. It made Kech look different, just like all the other trolls. He was losing weight, and a strange fear hung about his features. Kech's face and eyes also looked more familiar—Danr saw similar features every time he looked into reflecting water. How could he have missed them before?

"What do you want?" Kech growled.

"I want to talk to you. Father."

Kech's face went pale. "I am not your father."

Danr's first instinct was to shrink away from Kech's tone. Why did Danr want to talk to Kech anyway? Kech hadn't been a real father, and Danr didn't want him to become one. But then Danr paused. Why should Kech get away with this particular lie when they both knew the truth?

The truth gives me power over him, Danr realized. *He's terrified I'll tell his wife. Or the community. Imagine—he loved a human monster.*

Armed with the truth, Danr said, "Do you want me to request entrance as a guest, or demand it as a son?"

Kech drew himself up in outrage for one moment more, and Danr lost his nerve. He opened his mouth to say he didn't mean it, that it didn't matter. But that was a lie, and it caught in his throat. In the tiny silence that followed, Kech deflated like a leaky bladder. He looked much smaller, there in his own doorway, no obstacle at all.

"Don't tell her," he whispered. "Please."

"She already knows, son," Bund said. "Any wife worth her salt does."

"It's not the same as saying it aloud," Kech said sadly.

"What's my brother's name?" Danr asked.

At this, Kech looked surprised. "Torth."

"Is he going to war?" Danr asked. "Are you?"

"We're both moving down to the camp tomorrow," Kech said. "We'll command troops."

"Will I?" Danr asked.

Kech had no answer. Wordlessly, Danr pushed past him and stepped through the door.

To Danr's left eye, the inside of Kech's house had also become worse. Smoke hovered so thick it made Danr cough. The mushrooms and meat hanging from the ceiling were going rancid, and they dripped gooey ichor. Danr remembered that he had eaten from those foodstuffs, and his stomach oozed.

On the tables lay pieces of armor, dented and blemished with rust. A heavy mace, old and dusty, leaned against one wall.

"So it's you." Pyk sniffed. She was banking the fire for the night. Day. "What do you want?"

"I just wanted to see how things had changed here," Danr was forced to reply.

Torth, who was laying out enormous, moth-eaten blankets on the table benches for bedtime, glanced up. Danr saw the resemblance between his own face and his half brother's. Aisa, Bund, and Vesha came in behind him. At the sight of Vesha, both Pyk and Torth straightened, then bowed.

"It's all right," Vesha said. "This isn't a formal visit."

Pyk licked her lips. Danr closed his right eye and understood how trapped she was. She knew the truth about Danr's origins, and she knew how everyone around her would react if they knew—officially—that her husband, prince or not, had lain with a human monster. She might be able to exit the marriage with her head held high, but she would still have to exit the marriage. What would the repercussions be? As an outsider, Danr didn't know, but he could see Pyk didn't think they'd be a night of games.

"Will . . . will you be staying the day?" Pyk asked.

Danr looked around the dank, smelly house, at his father, who stood to one side trying not to wring his hands, and at his grandmother. She gave him a grim smile.

"No," he said finally, and Kech gave a small sigh. "We were just seeing Grandmother Bund home after paying our respects to the Three."

"Such a nice boy," Bund murmured.

Danr looked at her a little more closely. There were heavy lines on her face and he could see an overwhelming tiredness dragging at her, as if the earth itself were pulling on her body. Bund noticed his gaze.

"What is it?" she asked sharply. "What do you see?"

Danr hesitated. The awful truth pricked his eyes. He didn't want to say it. He bit his lip until the blood ran, but he felt his jaw move on its own. Aisa put a hand on his arm.

"Go on," Bund said. "I want to know."

"You're dying," Danr answered softly. "I can see it. You won't last longer than the new moon."

"Ridiculous," Kech snapped. "You're not going to die, Mother. He doesn't know what he's talking about."

The old trollwife looked at Kech with fond sadness in her eyes. "Yes, he does. I've known myself for a long time. My *draugr* will haunt these walls until the coming war ends and Death is set free. My penance, I suppose."

Kech swallowed once, then abruptly whirled on Danr. With a start, Danr recognized the look on his face as one people often gave his mother after she read a fortune.

"Why did you have to come back here?" Kech shouted. "Leave us alone! Get out of my house!"

Without a word, Danr grabbed Aisa's hand and fled.

Chapter Ten

Danr and Aisa sat in the mouth of the tunnel that led back to the surface. The soft mushroom glow crawled over the walls and stones. A pair of bats circled him for a moment, then fled squeaking into the dark. The drums faded in the distance, a faint memory. Aisa hugged her knees to her chest, understanding that this wasn't a time for words. The entire world pressed down above him like a giant's hand.

His hand stole up to the pouch and its newly expanded collection of splinters. His mother could see the truth. That was what had allowed her to read fortunes—and why people had disliked her so much. No one liked the truth. Now he had become like her. A cold feeling crept through his bowels. Was he doomed to the same sort of life, with people fearing and fleeing him? Then he suppressed a snort. Honestly it wouldn't be much of a change.

And he had spoken to Death herself. Vik, what in nine types of hell was that? She had all but commanded him to find the Iron Axe and cut the chain that bound her, which felt foolish on the face of it—what sane person would hare off to find a destroyed weapon in order to free Death, and in just twenty-seven days? Just the memory turned his hands cold. He glanced sideways at Aisa. At least he didn't have to do it on his own.

"What are you thinking about?" Aisa said at last.

"Right now?" Danr shifted on the cave floor. "Right now I'm thinking how glad I am not to be alone. It's too much."

She nodded. "I am glad I can be here. I am glad you saved my life so you can continue to be in mine."

He looked at her half-hidden face in the mushroom glow, and a wave of affection made his throat thick as winter syrup. Danr couldn't imagine life without her, and when had he ever told her that? "Aisa, I—"

"I wish you hadn't run." Vesha strode out of the darkness toward them. Startled, both Danr and Aisa bolted to their feet, the moment gone. "I have more to say to you."

Danr thought about the dark power she drew like ink from a well. It made worms crawl over his skin. But she was a queen, one who towered over him, and he bowed low to her.

"Highness," he said. "If I may ask, I thought a queen traveled with attendants. I haven't seen you with any."

She looked down at him without answering. Danr closed his right eye and saw the empty space around her, a space he now knew was usually filled with other trolls. Other troll-wives. Powerful trollwives. A faint tremor shivered the cave floor under his bare feet.

"Oh, damn," he said.

"What?" Aisa asked. "What do you see?"

"Her attendants are other trollwives. They aren't with her because they're all busy. They're opening the doors."

"We need all the doors, including the larger ones for the giants," Vesha said. "The single door we managed to pry open is too small by itself to release an entire army, and you saw how difficult it is to use. That is thanks to Fae magic. But in a few weeks, we Stane will be free of our prison. The doors will open easily for everyone, and our people will stream down the mountains." She paused. "It is more than food, you know. I have lived all my life under these mountains. Never once have I set foot above. I want to do that. I want to have the choice to walk among the trees above all night, if I choose. So should my people. We are held prisoners down here, and this is wrong. I—we—must walk free above. I dream of it for my people and myself."

"And once the doors are open and you can walk around, you can let Death go," Danr breathed. "All this will end."

Vesha shook her head. "The moment the Fae learn of this, they'll declare war on us. In our state of weakness, they'll crush us. We'll need power from the *draugr* to fight back."

"Then what do you want me for?" Danr demanded.

"The Fae may have locked up the Stane," Vesha said, "but they prey upon the Kin. They take humans as slaves. They war with the orcs. They exact tribute from the merfolk. All so that the Kin remain soft and weak."

"If this is how trolls use flattery," Aisa said, "our people are less alike than we knew."

"You can help end it faster," Vesha continued as if she hadn't spoken. "Be the emissary between our peoples. Build an alliance between Stane and Kin, help us release the harsh grip of the Fae on both our people, and Death's release will come even faster."

"It will at that," Danr said sadly.

"The Tree tips," Vesha said. "The question is whether you let it smash you down, or make it lift you up."

"Why me?" Danr said. "I'm nobody. The humans don't even like me. Neither do the Stane."

"The Three like you," Vesha countered. "Only they can make a truth-teller, and if they do it more than once in a generation, I have yet to hear of it."

"Why didn't they do it for me?" Aisa asked. "I stole their eye in the first place."

Vesha grinned, and her lower fangs gleamed. "Would you want them to make you a truth-teller?"

Aisa remained silent.

Something occurred to Danr. "How did my mother become a truth-teller?"

Here Vesha looked uncomfortable. "Kech took her to see the Three, obviously. They couldn't Twist, so they must have gone the long way."

"Why would he do that?"

"You'll have to ask your father," Vesha said.

He smells familiar. Danr remembered how the Three had laughed at his questions, and now he understood why. His parents had stood before them just as he had. Something else came to him then. Whenever he had asked who his father was, Mother always said, "He was a troll who betrayed me." Those words, the only ones he'd known, were branded on his brain. The one time he had pushed for more, she had slapped him and run away with her hands over her mouth. He knew it now—she had fled before her truth-teller's compulsion had forced the words out of her. She hadn't wanted him to know his father was Kech or that she had loved him. Why? And what had she meant when she had said Kech had betrayed her? The questions swirled around his head like a flock of bats, making him dizzy and uncertain. He wanted to run back to the house, ask Kech, demand more answers, but his father's angry face loomed in his memory. The thought of facing that made Danr cringe, and he set the idea aside. For now.

"You still haven't explained why you want my friend to be your emissary," Aisa said, "and not your nephew Kech, who seems to enjoy visiting the upper world."

"Your 'friend' is still a prince," Vesha said. "And he doesn't have the Stane's . . . problem."

"Sunlight," Danr breathed. "It causes you even more pain than it does me."

"Indeed." Vesha sat on a boulder with surprising grace for a woman of her great height and bulk. "The Stane can't go about in the day. At one time the trollwives could cast spells that blunted the sun's power, but those are beyond us now. We need someone who can move freely in both daylight and darkness. Someone of royal blood. Someone trustworthy, who won't lie to us or for us. You."

Danr thought a long moment. He knew Vesha was telling the truth, and again he saw the heavy load she carried. She knew that Death wouldn't look too kindly on the queen if—when—the chain was broken, and she was willing to accept the dreadful consequences if it meant freeing her people. To her, this appalling choice gave her people their only chance to survive. The question was whether or not Danr wanted to be a part of it.

I am a part of it, he thought. *Whether I want to be or not. The Tree tips.*

"I'll do it," he said aloud.

"Hmm," Aisa said behind her scarf.

Vesha let out a long, heavy sigh on her boulder. "You have no idea how much that relieves me, truth-teller. Take these." From her upper arm, she took a heavy band of woven gold. The metal was so pure and soft the band didn't need a clasp, but was instead bent open and shut. The intricate weave looped hypnotically around itself in a fascinating, unending pattern. "This armband will prove you are my nephew and that you speak for the Stane. Does Skyford still exist?"

"It does," Danr said slowly.

"You'll have to talk to the earl there, then," Vesha said. "Many of our doors open near Skyford, and we'll need his goodwill to use it as a staging area to launch an attack at Alfhame."

"Uh . . . I'm not on the best of terms with Earl Hunin," Danr told her. "He's the one who exiled me."

Vesha brushed this aside with a wave of her huge hand. "You still *know* him. No one down here does. Besides, you are no longer an exile with no people. You're a prince of the Stane, and you speak with my authority. Act like it, and people will treat you accordingly. Take this."

From her pocket, she took a small stone chest inlaid with more eye-twisting designs of purest gold. It didn't even cover the palm of her hand, though it took Danr two hands to hold it. He was expecting a weight, but it rested lightly in his hands. "It contains gifts of friendship for the earl or anyone else who wants to ally with us. You may decide how to distribute them, as befits a prince who speaks for the queen."

"It doesn't seem much," Aisa said.

"It will suffice," Vesha replied tightly. "I know it won't be easy, but you will have to convince him that you have the authority and that allying with us is in his best interest. If the humans don't become allies, we'll be forced to treat them as enemies, and thousands and thousands of them will die before we attack Alfhame."

"Why would he care if other Kin live or die?" Aisa asked sharply. "They have been nothing but cruel to him. To us."

Vesha nodded. "An excellent question. Do you care, truth-teller?"

Danr thought, and only for a split second. He remembered how cruel Alfgeir and his family had been, how they had caused his mother's death and virtually enslaved him. He remembered the terrible things Farek and White Halli had done to Aisa. But he also remembered the little boy dragged away by the slavers and the grief of White Halli's son, Rudin, and the kindness of Orvandel and the friendship of Talfi. The actions of one person, or even a group of people, did not mean everyone deserved punishment. He thought of White Halli's eyes, the eyes that Danr himself had drained of thought, and a lump of guilt rose in his throat. Maybe he could do something to balance that now.

"I do care," he said. "I'll do my best to represent the Stane, Lady Aunt."

"And what is your name?" Vesha asked. "Bund never said."

Danr could feel Aisa's eyes on him in the near darkness. Vesha's direct question brought the prick of words back, but this time it felt different. It took him a moment to understand that there was more than one answer, and this time he could chose between them. "It seems that down here I'm known as truth-teller, so it'll have to do."

She gave him a look. "Very well, Truth-Teller. Go now, and serve us all."

"Is it Kael?"

"No."

"Is it Luewe?"

"Sorry."

"Is it Barhof von Schickelmeister?"

"Oh, I hope not."

It was late afternoon, and they were just now emerging, grubby and hungry, from the woods at the edge of Alfgeir's farm. Danr had discovered the Great Door opened easily from the inside. He had let it boom shut behind Aisa, and the two of them had slept most of the day away, Aisa curled up in a patch of warm sunlight, Danr in dappled shade with his hat over his face. Now smoke drifted from the thatching of Alfgeir's house in the distance, and a herd of Alfgeir's cows bumbled slowly down to the bottom of the pasture, ready to be brought in for the night. The cows' familiar lowing and the smell of manure on the cooling spring air pulled Danr forward, and for a confused moment, he was ready to bring the herd in.

"That's not your duty," said Aisa, reading his expression. "You're an emissary, not a cowherd."

Danr shifted his bag and touched the heavy twist of gold at his throat. What had been an armband for Vesha was a neck torc for Danr. "It feels like I've been gone for both a day and a decade."

They trotted down the hill, past the lowing cows, and into the farmyard proper. Because of the two weeks they had lost to Death and the Three, it was now close to summer, and the air had become warm. Puffs of cloud obscured the late sun and blunted its golden blade, though Danr clapped his hat firmly on his head anyway. It felt strange to feel soft breezes move against his face after being in the still underground for so long. Danr closed his right eye and saw Alfgeir's farm was different. Danr shouldn't have been surprised, but he was. The fences weren't as heavy and well built as he remembered, the cows not as sleek and plump. Some of the latter had been carefully daubed with red dye. Danr chewed the inside of his cheek. People had been buying sacrificial cattle for the Nine from Alfgeir for years just because of their reddish color. Why hadn't they noticed the fakery? Why hadn't he?

"I have a question for the truth-teller," Aisa said as they reached the bottom of the hill. "Why were you able to avoid answering what your name is just now?"

Danr blinked. "I . . . don't know. I didn't have to tell Aunt Vesha, either. Maybe it's the way you gave the question. You asked if my name was Luewe, and I said it wasn't. That's the truth."

"So I could simply ask you directly what your true name is, couldn't I?"

The thought horrified him. She—or anyone else—could drag his true name, the one thing that belonged to him and only to him, out into the open and expose it for anyone to see.

Only his mother knew that name, and it was his greatest treasure. Sharing it was more frightening than stripping naked in the village square. "Don't!" he begged. "You can't!"

Aisa read his distress. "It bothers you that much, does it?"

"Yes." He was almost panting now.

"Hmm. Then our game continues."

Danr's knees were still weak with relief when they approached the farm proper. Like the rest of the property, Alfgeir's house was in poorer condition than Danr remembered. Even from a distance, Danr saw thin spots in the thatching. Just as Danr and Aisa reached the half-finished well, Alfgeir and Norbert emerged from the stable a few paces away. Alfgeir was carrying a pitchfork.

Alfgeir gasped and dropped the pitchfork. "What—" he squeaked, then cleared his throat and tried again. "What are you doing here? It's been weeks."

"We bring glad tidings," Aisa said, "of joy and comfort."

"You're an exile," Norbert said. "Nobody. We can kill you where you stand, bastard, filthy troll."

His words were hammers, and Danr felt them slam into him with an old, accustomed weight. The old accustomed anger came with it, along with his mother's voice: *Don't show the monster.* Automatically, he hunched in, pulled himself down under the weight of all these words. He was indeed nobody. A bastard son of—

No. *No!* He had opened the Great Door by himself. He had talked to a trollwife and faced the Three. He was a prince, an emissary of the Stane, a truth-teller. And he knew. His. Father.

Danr drew himself upright and saw, really *saw*, how tall he was. And then he noticed something. Alfgeir and Norbert were different somehow, even though they hadn't really *changed*. Not like the trolls. Danr gave them a long look through his left eye. Norbert stepped back and rubbed his arm where Danr had broken it as he always did, but there was no stiffness there, nothing to cause him pain. Truth dawned. All these years, Norbert had been exaggerating. Faking. How long had Danr felt bad about Norbert's arm, and how many times had Norbert used false phantom pain to guilt Danr into extra work? A weight lifted from Danr's back. He stood straighter and met Norbert's eyes, letting him know the truth.

"Don't call me filth," Danr said. "Or a bastard. You have no right to those words."

Norbert's mouth fell open and he looked away, face flushed.

Alfgeir, meanwhile, pulled into himself, not letting any part of himself get too far away from his body. He kept his fine clothes close about him, and his fingers never strayed far from the money pouch at his waist. A stingy man.

And something occurred to Danr.

"You, Oxbreeder," he growled, "you owe me money."

Alfgeir clutched at his belt pouch and fell back a step. "I owe you nothing, exile. As they say—"

"'Poverty does not force a man to steal,'" Danr interrupted, "'and wealth does not keep him from it.' You stole from me, *Carl* Oxbreeder. In your own words, I did the work of three men, sometimes ten, but got less than the pay of one boy." He stepped toward Alfgeir, who retreated. "You stole money from me, Oxbreeder, and I will have it."

"Oh my." Aisa leaned against the wall of the house. "If only I had a snack."

"I needn't pay an outcast anything," Alfgeir said, but he was plainly nervous.

Danr picked up Alfgeir's pitchfork and effortlessly snapped the handle in two. "Eleven years' pay."

"I don't have it," Alfgeir temporized. But his face told Danr he was lying.

The monster growled again. Danr could so easily encircle

Alfgeir's neck with one hand. He could so easily squeeze until Alfgeir's eyes bulged.

Be gentle, be kind, said his mother's voice in his head. *They expect you to be mindless and violent. Do not give them the satisfaction of being right.* Danr remembered White Halli and took a deep breath.

"Don't lie to me, Alfgeir," he said softly. "Other people may think you're generous, but I know better. You so generously let my mother bond herself to you in return for food and shelter, and then you made her live in a stable and eat scraps. You so generously let her cough up her lungs with the animals when your warm fire could have saved her. You so generously worked her son like a beast until he was exiled for defending an innocent. And you will now so generously give me eleven years of silver."

"I don't have it," Alfgeir repeated, more stubbornly this time.

With a roar, Danr grabbed the front of Alfgeir's tunic, hauled him up to eye level—

—and stared. Alfgeir had splinters, one in each eye. Wooden splinters. Just as the Three had said.

A strange sound started low in Danr's belly, then abruptly exploded from his throat. The sound swelled and echoed off the mountains high above Alfgeir's farm. Danr was laughing.

Trolls worked with stone, he thought, but humans worked with wood. Each group saw beauty in itself and ugliness in the other because the splinters clouded their vision. He had known that, the Three had as much as told him that, but now he could *see* it, and it was . . . funny. Foolish and funny, both at once.

"I wish I understood the joke," Aisa said. "It would be a fine thing to laugh so."

Alfgeir, meanwhile, mistook Danr's mirth for something more sinister and squirmed in desperation. "I can pay! I can pay!" he squeaked.

Danr laughed again and opened his hand. Alfgeir hit the ground and scurried into the house.

"Some food wouldn't go amiss, either," Aisa called after him while Norbert gaped.

He returned moments later with most of a ham, a loaf of dark bread, and a clay jar. The latter clinked.

"Father!" Norbert gasped. "You owe him nothing! He's a filthy beast! His mother was a troll's slut!"

Aisa gasped. Danr turned like a mountain noticing a mouse. "Say that again, Norbert. Like you mean it."

"Are you going to break my arm again, beast?" Norbert said, though his face was pale.

"The one you've been lying about all this time? The one that doesn't pain you one bit? The one that gets you out of work when it suits you?" Danr reached out and grabbed Norbert's shoulder. "This arm?"

"Spread tales," Norbert said through clenched teeth. "No one will believe you, or see you as anything but a monster."

The queen's torc lay heavy around Danr's neck. He took a grip on the monster inside him. "We used to be friends, Norbert. We could be again. This"—he shook Norbert's shoulder slightly—"could be the embrace of a brother, or the grip of an enemy. You decide."

There was a beat, a quick pause. Danr saw Norbert consider, but only for a second.

"I was never friends with the son of a troll's slut," he snarled. "Never!"

Danr sighed, truly sad. "As you like." He gave Norbert a slight shove. Norbert backpedaled with a yelp and dropped straight into the half-finished well. A muffled squelch and another yelp reported him hitting bottom.

"The day is filled with surprises." Aisa sidled up to Alfgeir and took the food and the jar from his numb fingers. "The prince ambassador is thrilled to receive your tribute,

Carl Oxbreeder. We shall consider it the beginning of good-will between our people."

"Tribute?" Alfgeir echoed dumbly. "Prince?"

"Indeed, sir. The great one who stands before you is the nephew of Queen Vesha of the Stane, Lady of the Underworld, Ruler of the Cavern Kingdom, Commander of the Dark Armies."

And she did something that Danr didn't see, but which made Alfgeir yip and sketch a little bow.

"As you were," Danr said before Alfgeir could recover. "We will consider your offering when the rest of the giants, trolls, and dwarves begin to arrive, *Carl* Oxbreeder."

"Help!" Norbert shouted faintly from the bottom of the well. By now, Alfgeir's wife and other sons were watching from the farmhouse door.

"The . . . rest?" Alfgeir repeated.

"Yes. My people are coming. All of them. They wish to speak to the Kin in kindness and friendship. Many of the doors aren't far from your farm, so you'll see a whole lot of them—us—very soon."

Algeir looked desperately about, as if the trees beyond the pasture might sprout heads and walk toward his farm. "Oh. Er . . ."

"Good day, *Carl* Oxbreeder," Aisa said brightly. "We will probably never meet again, and that is a fine thing."

Aisa put food and silver in Danr's sack. Together, they left the farm and strode down the road toward the village. Danr felt eyes on him as he and Aisa walked in warm spring air, but no one followed. Clouds skittered across the sun, and a breeze muttered in the ash trees. When they were a safe distance away, Danr's legs gave way. He dropped to the side of the road like a young tree and let out a heavy breath.

"I can't believe I did that!" he puffed. "Hoo!"

Aisa stood beside him. Even seated on the ground, he

was nearly as tall as she was standing. "You mustn't do that, Hamzu. You are a prince now, and must always act it."

He blinked. "What did you call me? Hamzu?"

"Oh!" She put a wrapped hand to her mouth, or the place where it would be, if Danr could see it for the scarves. "I spoke by mistake!"

"It's the name you made for me!"

"Now, that is unfair," she protested. "I haven't forced your name from you!"

"I like it," he said softly. "Thank you, Aisa."

"I . . ." Her eyes softened. "You are welcome. It means 'strong one.' Hamzu."

His eyes held hers for a moment. He had to look up just a little, and that disconcerted him almost as much as her quiet brown gaze did. He wanted to touch her, take her rag-bound hand. His heart beat at the back of his throat, and he even reached forward a little. But then he took a small moment to peer at her through his left eye, something he hadn't done with her before.

Knowledge rushed over Danr as his vision pierced the rags and scarves that wrapped Aisa's body, and he saw her as she really was. Hungry, always hungry for the touch and voice of her former elven owner, and more hunger for something else, a longing for something he couldn't name or understand. That something was near the water. The ocean. A soft thrill touched Danr. Aisa was free now and could go wherever she liked. But instead of running to the ocean to fulfill that longing, she had followed Danr underground. True, she had said she was in his debt for saving his life, but hadn't that been repaid when she stole the eye from the Three for him?

Tenderness made his heart swell, and he wanted more than anything to wrap his arms around her and make her feel safe. He was about to reach for her, was just doing so, in fact, when Aisa drew back a tiny bit and Danr saw one more thing: fear. Deep, overwhelming fear. Aisa was frightened. Danr froze. He hadn't done anything to scare her, had he?

And then he remembered how Aisa had been . . . hurt. By both elves and men. It occurred to him that Aisa didn't really see him as a man, and she would be truly frightened by him if he reached out to her as one. Clearly she saw him as nothing more than a friend, a strange, half-troll friend. A monster. Something in him died, and with difficulty, he dropped his hand.

But then he thought, maybe if they stayed together long enough, she could overcome that fear and see him as something besides just a friend. The idea gave him hope.

"Well, we should move along," he said gruffly, and got to his feet. "Princes can't afford to waste time. Want some ham?"

Aisa finished backing up a step. "I . . . would. Thank you."

"I seem to be collecting names," he said as they walked, more to fill the silence than anything else. "Trollboy. Truth-Teller. Hamzu. Prince Ambassador."

Aisa munched a bit of ham with some bread. "An ambassador who cannot lie. This could be awkward."

Rather than deal with the village, they decided to skirt the place entirely, not caring if they walked through a field or not. They did pass the grove where Danr had set the table and the two corpses of the Noss brothers. Someone had gathered the courage to burn the table, leaving the brothers' lumpy black remains behind. The *draugr* drifted toward Danr, reaching with their ragged bandaged arms. Their voices were ice on the breeze.

"Release!"

Danr felt no fear this time. He closed his right eye and saw them for what they were—frightened spirits caught halfway between worlds. A thin silver thread ran away from each *draugr* and vanished toward the mountains in the distance.

Danr tightened his lips. He felt sickened at the thought of hundreds, perhaps thousands, of people who had died all over the world in the last few days and were now unable to pass through Death's door. Worse, still more would die in the days to come.

"I'll help you," he told them. "I promise."

The two *draugr* faded back to the grove.

"How will you help?" Aisa asked as they walked away. "By becoming an emissary and speeding up the upcoming war with the Fae, or by finding the Iron Axe and releasing Death?"

"I haven't decided yet," Danr admitted. He looked about at the gathering spring evening. The trees were fully green, and yellow flowers poked shyly through new grass. "It doesn't feel like war is coming."

"In a few weeks, all this may be burned and dead," Aisa said. "War, like that wrym you fought, can come from no-where."

"Does the grass die now?" Danr wondered aloud. "Do animals and birds?"

"I do not know that such things are important," Aisa said. "We have twenty-six days left to find the Iron Axe, but we are also required to talk to a man who nearly had your head cut off for the beating you gave his son."

Danr winced at the reminder. Aisa continued her way up the road without breaking stride. He pulled his hat down more firmly on his head and trotted after her. "Do you ever feel guilt, Aisa?"

"For what? The pain of a man who intended to see me dead? Who took me into my former master's stable and used me because it amused him? Who put dozens of innocent men in prison to make himself look good to his father? Guilt? Pah!" She spat. "I should feel more guilt when a wasp is crushed by a horse."

"Guilt devours you, Aisa," Danr said seriously. "More painfully than the wasp."

"Then it's good I feel none. How much longer to Skyford?"

The road and the gate outside Skyford were all but deserted, but spread out on the far side of the river, well past the city, were dozens of flickering fires, like fireflies fastened to the ground. The smell of smoke was heavier than usual. For a moment, he was back underground.

"What's going on?" Danr said, shading his eyes. He could just make out men moving among the fires. Tents were pitched in neat rows. "Another army camp?"

"I doubt we'll find the answers up here on this hill," Aisa said.

They arrived at the Skyford gate just as the soldier manning it was closing up for the night. It was the same young man who had let Danr in before, and he recognized Danr. He jerked his pike toward Danr's chest. "You're an exile. And the earl has put a price on your head."

"I doubt you'll collect it with a pig poker," Aisa observed.

Danr pulled himself up. Now that he was among humans again, this was an impressive sight. The guard looked up at him with an open mouth. The pike quivered. Danr casually plucked it from the boy's hands with meaty fingers and tapped the gleaming gold torc at his neck with the iron blade.

"As this torc proclaims, I am Prince Truth-Teller, nephew to Queen Vesha, Lady of the Dark Lands, Commander of the Stane Armies, and Merciful Ruler of the Mountain Roots. And I require an escort to the earl in his keep."

The guard still wavered. Danr handed him three silver coins from the jar in his bag. It was more than the guard made in a month. That decided the matter.

"Sir!" the young guard said, and bowed. "It would be an honor to escort you."

"I think we've learned our first lesson in diplomacy," Aisa murmured as he led them through the darkening streets.

"What's your name, guard?" Danr asked, ignoring her. He was trying to think.

"Filo," the guard said. "Son of Egil."

Danr looked at Filo through his left eye only. Filo changed. There was fear in his posture, but also hunger and a need to please. Danr thought a moment and handed him the pike.

"I'll need some help while I'm here, Filo Egilson," Danr said. "You seem to be . . . alert and on top of your duties. It will pay well. Are you for it?"

"Er . . . thank you, my lord." His suspicion seemed to be wavering. "But I'm in the earl's guard, and I can't become a personal—"

"I'm not looking for a guard. I need eyes and ears around Skyford. I'll pay for all the bits of information you and a few trustworthy friends can bring me, no matter how small." He gave Filo two more coins. "I know you're the right person for the job."

Filo looked at the coins and nodded hard. "Yes, sir, my lord! I'm your man, my lord!"

"Excellent, Filo, son of Egil." Danr gave him a grin. "You're a smart man."

"Lesson two," Aisa said.

Filo marched ahead of them, his pike held high. Danr made a mental note—five pieces of silver and a need to please went a long way. How much further would silver take him? And how much easier would his life have been, Stane blood or not, if he had been born into a rich family? It was another truth: money had more power than blood.

"Make way for the prince!" Filo boomed. "Make way for the emissary prince!"

And how strange it felt to hear those words!

Almost everyone had gone indoors for the night, but the

few people left on the wooden walkways turned to stare. Danr thought about the previous time he'd come to Skyford, when everyone had stared at him, but this time it was different. They stared out of a certain awe instead of contempt. Was it possible they didn't recognize Trollboy the exile? Danr kept his back straight and pulled himself to his full height. He tried to walk as White Halli did, as if everyone around him didn't exist. Aisa came behind in his wake like an attendant.

Skyford had also changed. The city stank as much as the troll caverns had. The heavy, nasty smell of rotting fish clogged the air. Pigs rooted for food in the mud between the cramped houses, and manure piles lay everywhere. Danr forced himself not to wrinkle his nose. The squalor had always been there. He just hadn't noticed it before.

"Release!" A *draugr* Danr didn't recognize drifted between two houses. Filo flinched and dodged around it.

"Are there a lot of them?" Danr asked.

"Ever since the Noss brothers died," Filo said. "Everyone who dies just . . . stays. No one knows why."

"Is that an army camped north of the city?" Aisa asked.

"The earl offered amnesty to any prisoner who joined up," Filo said, and Aisa shot Danr a look. "Even more soldiers are coming. The earl is calling in favors from all over Balsia, and he's hiring mercenaries. Anyone who can fight is welcome in his army. Even women."

"Fight for what?"

"That he hasn't said," Filo replied. "The earl gives a lot of speeches, though. He says humans need to unite under Balsia, and the three races of the Kin need to unite as a people if we want to claim our true place in the world. He wants to be king."

"Hmm," Aisa said. "There has never been a king among the Kin. Here we have earls, and tribes among my people follow their *calipha*. I don't know what the merfolk and the orcs do, but there's no Kin king."

"Maybe it's time, then," Filo said. "Ever since his son was made an idiot—begging your pardon, my lord—Hunin has given a lot of speeches, and when he speaks, even the stones listen. He would make a good king."

"Speeches don't make a king," Aisa observed.

"No. But a king sure makes speeches."

They were passing the street by the river at that moment, and Danr said, "Wait!" Without waiting for a response, he dashed over to a familiar house, the one that belonged to Orvandel the fletcher, where he rapped sharply on the door. A moment later, a startled Orvandel opened it.

"Trollboy!" he gasped. "What in the world—?"

"I'm sorry to break in on you," Danr said as Filo and Aisa hurried to catch up. "Is Talfi here?"

In answer, a fleet form slammed into Danr and he found himself in a fierce hug, though Talfi's head barely reached Danr's chest. "I can't believe it!" Talfi shouted. "I thought I'd never see you again!"

Danr gingerly returned the embrace while Filo and Aisa looked on. In the house beyond, Orvandel's wife, Ruta, and his two sons stared.

"It's good to see you, Talfi," Danr said, and meant it. "So much has happened. We went under the mountain and met my grandmother. She's a trollwife, and my aunt is their queen."

"You're a prince?" Talfi blinked. "Wow! That's what the torc is for. That'll play well when the earl finds out."

"I'm glad you're well," Orvandel said. "You know, more than one person around here thinks White Halli got what he deserved and your so-called trial was a farce."

Danr raised his eyebrows. "Really? Why didn't anyone speak at the trial, then?"

"Too scared of the earl," Orvandel said frankly. "And of

all these spirits floating about. But we shouldn't stand here talking in the doorway. Come in! You must be starving!"

Danr couldn't put into words how wonderful it was to hear such friendly talk, how fine a thing it was to know someone out there would tell him to share a roof and food and simple conversation. He thought about the giants and their great clubs, and for a moment he saw one crush Orvandel's house like a quail's egg. A lump came to his throat. He couldn't let that happen. Not ever.

"Your offer of hospitality means a great deal, sir," Danr said softly, "but I'm here as an emissary from the Stane. We have to talk to the earl right away. I just came to make sure Talfi was all right."

"I'm more than all right." Talfi was pulling on a cloak. "If this involves trollwives, I'm going with you."

Chapter Eleven

The great hall of the keep wasn't quite as great as Danr was expecting. The low ceiling beams, blackened by centuries of smoke, almost brushed Danr's head, and the rushes on the floor hadn't been changed in quite some time. The long table that ran the length of the room was a scarred survivor of too many feasts, the tapestries on the walls needed cleaning, and a thin fire burned on a hearth that hadn't been swept. Aisa and Talfi, however, looked about in awe, and Danr wondered if they saw the same room he did.

A door banged open, and Earl Hunin strode into the room with two guards close on his heels. Behind them came little Rudin, White Halli's son. More guilt lumped in Danr's throat at the sight of the boy. Rudin would live without a father in his life because of Danr.

Behind Rudin came Hunin's brother, the priest, still robed in his vestments of half black and half white. He carried his stick, and Danr was reminded of Bund's cane.

However, Danr's main attention went to Earl Hunin. The man was different, even to Danr's normal eye. At the trial, he had seemed tired and unhappy. Now he moved with purpose and power. His white-blond hair, so like his son's, gleamed in the firelight, and his very presence pressed against the walls and beams. On his left hand he wore a ring of black iron, a sign of mourning. Hunin apparently had decided to act as if his son had died. A bad sign.

"So it's true." Hunin's face was red and he was clearly trying to keep his ire in check. Danr found himself feeling small and wanting to flinch. "The exile Stane who destroyed my son has the audacity to enter my keep and demand an audience."

"My lord." Danr wasn't sure if he was supposed to bow or not. He was a prince now, and didn't a prince outrank an earl? Still, he had nothing to gain by making the man angrier than he already was. So Danr bowed, and he felt Hunin's anger heavy on his back. "I've returned. Not as an exile, but as a prince of the Stane. And an emissary. I am . . . I'm . . ."

Danr floundered. He should be using language that sang, words that rang off the walls, demands that made the trees pay attention. His voice should thunder in the mountains. But none of those things happened. He wasn't worth any of that.

You're nothing but a farmer's . . . a farmer's . . .

He paused again. He couldn't complete the thought—that he was a mere farmer's thrall. Was it true that a truth-teller couldn't even lie to himself?

"All right, listen," he said. The words tumbled out, hard and cold as truth. "I'm here on behalf of Queen Vesha of the Stane. They're as desperate as a hundred cats in a washtub, and they've figured out how to claw their way out from under the mountain. In a few weeks, the doors will open and an entire countryful of dwarves and giants and trolls will boil out. The Fae will become upset about that, and you know they'll declare war. You also know that Balsia stands between the Stane and the Fae, and the Fae won't give a pile of pig shit that all these Kin are in their way. Queen Vesha"—he touched the gold torc at his throat—"is offering an alliance with you and any other humans who want in."

"Huh," Talfi said.

"That was . . . forthright," Aisa murmured.

"My mother had the same problem," Danr murmured back. "The truth is never pretty."

"You crushed my son," Hunin said in a voice as cold and sharp as a snowflake, "and only the prospect of war with the Stane kept me from taking your head."

Danr ducked his head beneath a stab of guilt, but at least Hunin hadn't asked a direct question, so Danr could make a more careful answer. "I did hurt your son. You're also the earl, and by now you must have heard a lot of stories about what really happened that day. You know what led up to the fight, and you know that I hurt Halli to stop him from killing someone else unfairly. I wish I could have done everything differently, and that's the truth. But now we have something bigger to worry about. An avalanche of the Stane are coming with Queen Vesha at the head. You need to decide whether you and your army want to join it or stand in its way."

"Words." Hunin's voice remained cold, and he gestured with his black iron ring. "How do I know these words that float in the air before me are true? How do I know the worthless exile isn't lying to save his own worthless skin?"

He had asked a direct question, and Danr had to answer. "I've been made into a truth-teller just like my mother, my lord, and I can't lie any more than you can bear to tell your brother here that you still feel guilty about those things the two of you used to do together in the stables when you were boys."

Here both Hunin and the priest flushed identical shades of angry red. Danr winced internally and hurried on. "You know I wouldn't come back to face my own death over a lie.

I have nothing to gain. Not only that, but I wear the queen's torc, and I bring you the queen's treasure."

With a desperate prayer to the Bird King, Olar, that Vesha wasn't having some awful joke at his expense, Danr took the carved stone box from his sack, set it on the table, and opened it.

It was empty. Danr's heart sank.

"Is this meant to be an insult?" Hunin demanded, still upset over the stable remark.

"No." Danr studied the box, trying to force his thoughts into some kind of speed. He wished for Talfi's quick mind or Aisa's quick tongue, but he had neither. Perhaps the box itself was the gift? No. Mere stone and iron, no matter how prettily carved, didn't rate a gift to a future king.

Aisa leaned over for a better look, and her shadow fell across the box. Shadow. The carvings on the box reminded Danr of the shadowy patterns Bund had woven for the Twist. And then he had it.

"For you, my lord," he said, and plunged his hand into the box. On his hand and wrist, he felt a strange *wrench*, exactly like the one he had felt when Bund shoved him into the Twist—the box was a Twist put into solid form. Then he touched something cool and smooth. Danr yanked out his hand and a gleaming pile of gold and silver coins clattered on the wood. Talfi and Aisa gave identical gasps. Danr himself was mightily impressed. The pile made the little jar of silver Alfgeir had handed over look moth-eaten and poor. The box itself was no less impressive. It was Twisting Danr's hand into some sort of treasure vault back under the mountain. Danr wondered if he had snatched something at random or if Vesha had chosen the coins in advance for effect. Hunin, however, remained impassive. Danr decided to see what would happen if he tried again.

"And more!" He plunged his hand into the box and came

up with a pair of goblets made of beaten gold and set with sea green emeralds. The handles of each were formed into breathtaking figures of Fell and Belinna, the gods of love and beauty, harvest and war. Danr had never seen anything so rich or beautiful in his life.

"Those look nice," said Rudin. "I want to drink from one."

Hunin looked more interested, but not entirely won over.

"The Stane offer gifts of friendship to the earl." Danr reached into the box a third time and pulled forth a human skull. It had been gilded, and the gold shone like fire. Jewels encrusted it—glowing diamonds lined the eye sockets, red rubies made scarlet stubble on the jaw, pale pearls fitted across each tooth, purple amethyst rounded the ears. It was enormously heavy, and Danr almost dropped it at the unexpected weight.

Before Hunin could react, the priest rushed forward, black and white robes rustling. His face showed utter shock. "Bal himself," he whispered in a trembling voice. He placed both hands on the table on either side of the skull and kissed the top. "His skull has been lost since the Sundering. It's said he walked with the Fates, Nu, Ta, and Pendra, themselves."

"The Fates weren't kind to him if they allowed that to happen to his skull," Aisa murmured.

For once, Danr recovered quickly. "Now it has returned. As a gesture of goodwill from the Stane."

Hunin finally looked impressed, but still wary.

The priest straightened and gave Danr a serious look, apparently for the first time. "You must tell me. Are the *draugr* plaguing the Stane as well as the Kin?"

Danr couldn't lie. "Of course they are."

"What do the Stane know of it?"

He tried to hold the words back but found he couldn't. "The Stane are the cause. They've chained Death herself and are draining power from the *draugr* to open doors under the mountain."

Behind him, he heard Talfi draw in a breath, a sound echoed by the priest. Rudin fiddled with the buttons on his cloak.

"Why would they do that?" the priest asked.

"They need to escape from under the mountain at any price," Danr said in truth.

Hunin went white, and Danr wanted to run away from such anger. "This is . . . an abomination! The Stane are feeding off the dead. No amount of gifting can—"

Danr tried to reverse the damage with more truth. "It's the only way out for them—for us—my lord. The Fae have imprisoned the Stane underground, just like they've enslaved the Kin. If we do nothing, we'll starve in less than a year. We want to end the Fae threat. If you help us, the threat will end faster. The Fae slavers will stop coming sooner, Death will be released sooner, everything will end sooner."

Hunin's lips were tight. "Balsia and the Kin have been fractured for centuries. I have an army of my own, drawn from many places in Balsia, and I am swelling our ranks more and more. We have strength, we have power, we have *ourselves*. The Kin will take our rightful place in the world, whether the Stane and the Fae wish it or not."

His voice echoed off the ceiling and walls and the table, thundered against Danr's bones, and Danr understood now what Filo meant when he said even the stones listened to Hunin speak. Talfi and Aisa were staring, rapt. It was frightening. Danr closed his right eye, expecting to see some kind of magic or perhaps a hollow shell of speeches and an emptiness inside. Instead Hunin's own power slapped him hard. His son's permanent injury at the hands of a Stane had created a change in him, given him a desire—a *need*—to change the rest of the world. In Danr's eye, Hunin had become a great sword, one that could cut in either of two directions.

"What do you intend, my lord?" Danr asked.

"I will unite Balsia under a single king," Hunin thundered. "We will throw off the yoke of the Fae."

"Then let us help you," Danr said.

Hunin leaned toward him, and it took all Danr's will not to lean back. "A Stane. Destroyed. My. Son."

"I'm Kin, too," Danr replied quietly. "Can you blame all Kin for my actions, too? A king—a true king—should put aside his own problems and think of what's best for all his people."

"The half-blood has a point, Hunin," said the priest in a gentle tone Danr hadn't heard from him before. "We have strength, the Stane have wealth. Perhaps we should combine the two."

Danr held his breath and closed his right eye. Through his left, he saw Hunin perched on an edge. He could go in either of two directions. And then he tipped, just a little, toward Danr. Danr's heart beat fast. Hunin opened his mouth to speak—

—and Rudin interrupted. "Is this the troll who hurt Papa? I miss him. I'm scared he'll die and the trolls will eat his ghost."

At the sound of his grandson's voice, Hunin tipped back again. His face went hard, and he touched the black iron on his finger. Danr knew he had decided against him, would never, ever side with him, but didn't want to say so just yet.

"Indeed," Hunin said. "Dark Emissary, you will have my answer after I have had time to consider. My headman will show you where to sleep."

He had lost. Cursing silently, Danr made a rough bow and withdrew from the hall. The headman, a short man who ran toward plump, met them in the foyer and with few words showed them to a room with a table, a pair of benches for beds, and even a window. A brass brazier provided heat. When the headman had shut the door, Danr leaned against the stone wall and blew out a hard breath. "Shit."

"Do princes swear?" Aisa asked beside him.

"This one does."

"It didn't go too bad," Talfi pointed out. "He didn't say no."

"He won't say yes. Not ever. I saw it." Danr paced the small stone floor. A candle burned on the table, and Filo lit a second. "Damn it! We were so close! It makes no sense that he'd say no."

"Emotion," said Aisa, "rarely makes sense."

"It was his grandson," Danr sighed. "The earl was ready to side with us until Rudin spoke up. A few wrong words from a child are going to create a war."

"Humans against Stane," Talfi mused. "Won't the fight be one-sided? The Stane can't even fight in daylight."

"But at night, they'll rip the Kin to pieces. You didn't see how many Stane were down there, or how big those giants were," Danr said. "If the Stane come out and the Kin aren't already their friends, it'll be really, really bad."

"Why do you care so much?" Talfi asked suddenly. "We humans weren't very good to you. It seems like you'd join the Stane."

"Do you *want* me to?" Danr asked.

"I'm just wondering. I mean, you could just walk away. That torc around your neck and the treasure in that box would set you forever. Why not do it?"

Suddenly Danr had had enough. Enough poking and prodding. Enough questions and demands. Enough curiosity and stares. Angry words piled up and burst. "Because I'm not a monster!" he snarled. "Because someone in this whole Vikshit of a world has to do the right thing for once! Because I learned that people like Orvandel and Aisa and you, Talfi, are worth more than a pretty piece of metal!" He pulled the torc off his neck and flung it away. It clattered and clanged. He turned his back on them then, not wanting them to see the unexpected tears that welled in his eyes.

A long moment of silence followed. Then a wrapped hand touched his shoulder. Aisa. "There is more to it, my Hamzu. If you were only worried about me and Orvandel and Talfi, you would simply warn us so we could flee."

"It's not . . . it's . . . not . . ." The falsehood, the lie that it was nothing, wouldn't come. He hardened his jaw in an effort not to speak and swiped at his eyes instead. The rough stone wall rose hard before him.

"Only secrets have power," Aisa said softly. "When you say things aloud, you vanquish them. Tell us, your friends, and become strong."

Secrets bubbled black and powerful inside him. He didn't want to vomit them out. The taste would be more than he could bear. But Aisa's careful, patient presence pulled them forth. He stared down at his hands. "I *destroyed* him, Aisa. I let the monster out and I took his life. He's not dead, but he may as well be. I heard his bones break, I felt his blood on my skin, I heard him scream. And I liked it. I *wanted* him to die. Hunin and Rudin used to have a son and a father. Now they have nothing but a sack of meat. It's all my fault."

"It isn't," Aisa said. "If you hadn't done exactly what you did, I would be dead and my *draugr* would be haunting that road. And you had nothing to do with Death's chain."

"I know that in my head. But not here." He touched his heart. "So. At the very least I can balance out what I did to White Halli. Either I can help end the upcoming war sooner so the Stane can release Death, or I can find the Iron Axe and cut Death's chains. Then I'll be free of White Halli. And maybe . . . maybe I can find a real home."

Another pause. Then Aisa's hand tightened on his arm. "I am sorry, Hamzu."

"For what?"

"I was a . . . poor friend on the road. I said I didn't feel guilt, and that was cruel of me. I should have understood what you were saying."

"Don't be sorry, Aisa. Never be sorry." He wanted to embrace her, hold her close, but the memory of her fear held him in check. Instead he forced a small smile. "Now you know why I'm forging this alliance. And why I have to find the Axe."

"Er . . . my lord?" It was Filo. He held out Danr's torc before him. "May I say something?"

"Oh." Danr had all but forgotten the young man was there. That was a little embarrassing. He took the torc back and bent it around his neck. "What are you thinking, Filo?"

"You wanted information, my lord?"

Danr came alert and turned to him, as did Aisa and Talfi. Filo shifted, now uneasy at being the center of attention. He licked his lips and glanced around, as if the earl might leap through a wall at him.

"Filo," Danr said, a little surprised at how easily he was taking up authority, "just spit it out."

He coughed. "Not long after your trial, a number of riders galloped out of Skyford. I wasn't on duty that day, but my friend Munor was. He said he heard they were headed for Xaron. A delegation to talk to the orcs."

Aisa and Talfi traded looks. "Why would Hunin send men to the orcs?" Talfi said.

The news came with a weight. Danr sat heavily on one of the table benches. It creaked beneath him. "To negotiate an alliance with them."

"If the orcs ally with Hunin and his army," Aisa said, "the earl has no need to join the Stane. He will happily fight against them instead."

"Why isn't he just joining with the Stane right now?" Talfi said. "The Stane are powerful and united and ready to welcome him as an ally. I'm not a king or an earl, but it seems stupid to turn down an offer like that."

"I don't know," Danr said. "Every time it looked like he was ready to accept it, something happened to tip him back. He's angry enough at the Stane—at me—to raise an army and start a war. Maybe his plan is to ally himself with the orcs and the merfolk, destroy the Stane, and use the plunder to attack the Fae. The Stane are still a little weak, and he might be able to do it, if he has enough friends."

"The Fae would enjoy that," Talfi said. "Watching Kin and Stane destroy each other."

"Does Hunin have any hope of an alliance with the orcs?" Aisa said. "Or the merfolk?"

"He sent a lot of gifts, too," Filo said. "Gold from the mines and silk from northern Balsia and a whole herd of those special warhorses he breeds."

Suddenly the objects Danr had pulled from the box seemed a lot less impressive.

"We're up a river of shit and paddling with our hands," Talfi said. "Hunin's men left days ago. We can't stop them— or beat them to Xaron."

"Beat them to Xaron?" Danr said.

"Yeah." Talfi dropped onto the bed. "Orcs *live* for fighting, right? That's got to be why Hunin is rushing over there now—the orcs will probably ally themselves with whoever offers first, just for the chance to go to war. If *we* got there first, we could probably persuade the orcs to side with the Stane. But Hunin has that head start—and they have horses."

"How do you know so much about orcs?" Aisa asked narrowly.

Talfi considered this. "No idea. I just . . . know."

"It would be fascinating to learn what else you know."

Danr, meanwhile, stared out the window for a long moment. The two stars that made up Urko were closer together. He looked at them with just his left eye, and instantly he could see how far apart they were. They would touch in less than twenty-six days. And Death had said to start looking for the Axe among the orcs. Danr caught up his sack and strode for the door. Aisa followed him with her eyes. "Where—?" she began.

"Xaron." Danr put his hand on the door and sighed. Keep moving forward. Sometimes that was all you could do. "But first we need to ask my grandmother if she can Twist us one more time."

"You realize that if Vesha finds out I'm sending you to Xaron, she'll have my head, sister or not," Bund groused. "It'll take a lot of power to Twist you to Xaron, and stealing it will delay opening the doors by three or four more days. She also wants an alliance with the humans here in Skyford, not the orcs east in Xaron."

"What can she do to you?" Danr said. "You're dying."

"Well. The truth-teller comes into his power. And it hurts." Bund rapped her walking stick on the stone wall above the tunnel, the one that had created the shadow pictures before. The fireflies rushed from all over the cavern to land on it, making the runes glow blue and white. Talfi stared in wonder and awe, the smear of Danr's blood still fresh on his forehead protecting him from the trolls' hunger.

"You *are* a trollwife," he said. "With magic and everything."

"Not everything. I wouldn't have the space to keep it all."

And Danr remembered how Talfi had first visited him in the hopes of meeting a trollwife so he could learn why he had lost his memory. Before Danr could say anything to stop him, Talfi blurted out, "Can you tell me what's wrong with me?"

"Of course," Bund replied. "You're stupid. You run off at the mouth, and when you fell in love with your foster brother, you told him about it. Stupid."

The words thundered through Danr with lightning shock, made all the worse for how unexpectedly they came. He almost staggered. Talfi? Talfi was *regi*? Danr's skin tightened. *Regi* were men who liked to be . . . touched by other men. The word wasn't very nice, even as a joke, and *rassregi* was a deadly insult. Danr's mind went back to all the times they had walked and talked together. Since they'd met, Talfi had hugged Danr and slept near his hearth in the stable. He had made frank and forthright overtures at friendship when no one else had. Did it mean he thought Danr was interested in him? Did he think Danr himself was . . . ? The thought made Danr's stomach clench.

"Vik!" Talfi turned bright red, a fact that was visible even in the dim mushroom light. "That wasn't what I—"

"Did I mention something you wanted to keep hidden, little Kin boy? Tsk." Bund tapped her stick against the wall again, and the shadows twisted. In the background, the war drums pounded at Danr's head and body. His head spun and he couldn't sort out how he felt. The drums made him want to roar and stomp and crunch. Or was that the news that his friend, his only friend, wanted things that only a woman should want?

"Dear me. We seem to have discombobulated the truth-teller." Bund waved her cane, and the glowing runes drew at the shadows around the wall like a breeze pushing sand. "Tit for tat, I suppose. A big tit."

"You enjoy congress with men?" Aisa said to Talfi. "Why, for Rolk's sake?"

"I just do." Talfi stared at the ground. "So what?"

Aisa shifted her pack. "You may have my share. I, for one, would be perfectly happy if a man never touched me like a woman again."

It took Danr a moment to understand what Aisa had just said. It made a second shock that overshadowed the first. A hot knife and then a cold icicle speared his heart, one after the other, and he forced himself to stay upright. Of course. It wasn't just him Aisa feared—Aisa didn't desire men at all. Vik's balls. Why hadn't he understood it before? After everything she'd been through, Aisa connected a man's caress with pain. How could he have hoped that Aisa might one day overcome fear and return his feelings? All the secret fantasies he'd ever had about Aisa, of touching her, kissing her, loving her, came rushing out of the dark corners of his mind to taunt him like cruel children. He'd been a fool. More than a fool—a blockhead. A blockheaded troll with no brain. And to think he had almost told her how he felt on the road to Skyford only this afternoon. His blood chilled at the close call. He had given up everything for her, nearly killed a man, been forced into exile, because of kind, sarcastic, quick-witted Aisa. And she would never, ever feel the same way about him as he did about her. Her own words showed it. Thank Rolk he had kept his mouth shut.

For a wild moment, he thought about looking at her with his true eye a second time. Almost instantly he shrank away from the idea. The first time had filled him with pain. This time he already knew the truth, and more truth would only make things worse.

"You look like an ox licked the back of your head," Talfi said. "Are you all right?"

"No." Danr couldn't lie. He sat on a rock. "I'm not."

"Shit." Talfi kicked a stone while Bund continued to twist shadows. "Look, I'm sorry I didn't say anything. It's not something you tell around, you know? It's true—I fell for Orvandel's son, Almer. He was . . . well, I thought I loved him. And I thought maybe he might feel something for me. I was completely wrong. It was bad, but at least he didn't tell Orvandel."

Danr had a hard time finding words. Both admissions were hitting him hard here in the soft darkness. Although it was Aisa's that had punched him the hardest, Talfi assumed it was his. Danr's heart dragged. If Aisa didn't want a man to touch her, he wouldn't—couldn't—push the issue. He would have to put all such thoughts aside. How difficult could it be? A sickening lurch in his chest told him it would be difficult as every hell in Vik's realm. Damn it. Why had he, a monster, let himself even hope?

And then there was Talfi. . . .

The shadows twisted and reeled on the wall. The magic was taking a long time because, Bund had said, they were going all the way to Xaron, and such a powerful spell took time to cast. Apparently it took a great deal of strength. Bund's massive body was sweating, and her breath was coming short. Danr barely noticed. He clutched his sack to his chest. The stone chest lay heavy within.

"Are you angry at me?" Talfi asked in a small voice Danr had never heard from him before.

"I don't know," Danr replied shortly. Truthfully. The words spilled out of him. "I don't know what to say. I never knew a man who liked to be fucked." And Talfi's face fell.

"Hamzu—" Aisa began.

"Spell's done," Bund interrupted. The awful pattern of light and shadow twisted across the wall. Bund was panting and leaning on her stick. "The orcs have no cities, so I'm . . . sending you to the center of Xaron . . . near the Great Wyrm River. You should find—"

"Bund!" Vesha was striding up the stony path toward them in a fury. Three enormous trolls with equally enormous clubs stomped behind her. "By the Nine, what do you think you're doing?"

"That's . . . your signal . . . to go," Bund gasped.

Her tone startled Danr out of his interior world, and he

looked at her for the first time since the spell had begun. Her face was a sickly green in the pale mushroom light, and sweat darkened her ancient dress. Her tongue hung gray and dry from one side of her mouth. A pang went through him, and he closed his right eye.

Bund's life force had all but left her. The spell was draining her dry, and she had nothing left to replenish herself with. The moment Danr and the others stepped through the Twist, she would let it close and her body would drop dead. Only her *draugr* would remain.

"No!" he whispered.

"Stop!" Vesha boomed. She and the trolls were only a few yards away.

"Now!" Bund managed. "Or it'll be . . . for nothing. Take my blessing and go!"

"Quickly!" Aisa tightened her grip on her pack and dove through the pattern. Talfi licked his lips and followed. Both of them vanished. The trolls rushed forward, brandishing their clubs. Danr locked his gaze with the dying Bund.

"Good-bye, Grandmother," he said hoarsely. "I wish—"

"Why die in bed when I can die with a Twist?" she snapped. "Go, you fool!"

Danr jumped backward into the Twist just as the first troll swung his club.

Chapter Twelve

The Twist was by far the worst Danr had encountered. He was a minnow in a whirlpool, a twig in a hurricane, a pebble in an avalanche. Every direction was up; all directions were down. He touched the entire world, felt his roots and branches ripping, tearing, snapping. White-hot pain sliced through him, and he smelled burning flesh. A scream tore itself from his throat. He reached out for something—anything— and landed hard on solid ground. The smell of dry hay tickled his nose, and stiff stalks crunched beneath him. He was lying faceup on a grassy plain, though an enormous circle of it had been scorched to bare earth around him. Sunlight from a diamond sky slammed painfully into his eyes. Somehow he'd kept hold of his sack. He groaned, partly from the pain and partly from new sorrow.

Grandmother Bund was dead. He had seen it coming seconds before he fled the cavern. The Twisting that had sent him here—to Xaron?—had killed her. The sorrow intensified, clotting like bad milk. Two hot tears came to his eyes. He had only known her for a day, but he had felt a kinship with her. She was his grandmother. For the first time, he'd actually had a grandmother. Now she had left him.

Anger made him dig fingers into the ashy ground. Anger. That was it, wasn't it? She had left him, and he was angry at her for it. She had given up her life to Twist him here ahead of Hunin's men without telling him it would happen. If she had said something, he would have looked for another way. Yes, she was already near death, but how could she—

Talfi's scream yanked him upright. It was a dreadful, high-pitched sound. Danr scrambled to his feet, ignoring the pain in his head and his joints. The grassy plain, rumpled with low hills covered in green grass and multicolored flowers, spread in all directions. Some distance behind him, a stony river cut through the plain. All this Danr took in with a glance. His main attention went to Talfi. He lay curled around himself several paces away inside the scorched circle. His scream was the most frightening thing Danr had ever heard. Danr bolted toward him and dropped to the ground.

"What's wrong, Talfi?" he gasped.

Talfi didn't answer. He just screamed and screamed. Then Danr saw his leg. The right one was just . . . gone. Severed neatly halfway above his knee. Fleshy smoke curled up from the meat, and Danr saw the yellow bone with a pink center. Blood gushed over the grass. Danr stared in helpless horror. He had no idea what to—

And then Aisa was there. Her pack was already off her back, and she had a leather thong in her hands. Swiftly she used a twig to knot it around Talfi's leg just above the wound. The bleeding slowed. Talfi stopped screaming, but he was panting like a frightened dog.

"There is a bowl in my pack," she snapped at Danr. "Get me water. And wood for a fire. Now!"

Danr scrambled to the river. When he returned with the dripping bowl and several pieces of driftwood, Aisa had laid out a number of small clay jars and bundles of dried herbs. The bottom of Talfi's leg was covered in rags that seeped red.

"Build a fire," Aisa told him. "He will need the heat. Talfi, concentrate on my voice. You will not die here. I will not let you."

Talfi groaned. The silver amulet gleamed at his throat. "My leg. What happened to my leg?"

"You lost it in the Twist. The wound was partly cauterized, which prevented you from bleeding to death before I could tie you off. However, your skin is clammy, your heartbeat has weakened, and you are not breathing properly," Aisa said. "This puts you in more danger. You must take deep breaths and try to remain calm. Hamzu, where is that fire?"

Danr had already built a small fire. The grass gave him plenty of tinder. He struck iron on flint and blew the sparks to life. For once something went right, and flames blazed up quickly.

"My leg," Talfi whispered. "I can't feel it, but everything hurts."

"Drink this." Aisa opened a jar and sprinkled powder into the bowl. "It will ease the pain and help you regain the water you lost."

She helped him sit up to drink while Danr clenched his hands helplessly. "More water," Aisa said, handing him the bowl. "I need to heat it this time."

Danr hustled back to the river. Water rushed over large stones and made white foam. This was a shallow place, probably a good ford. He dipped up more water. The image of Talfi's awful wound crowded his mind, and his gorge rose. Before he could stop it, he vomited into the river. Bile burned his throat. Quickly he rinsed his mouth and refilled the bowl. It occurred to him that it was daytime. When they had left Skyford, it was coming close to night. Bund's Twisting must have played with time as well as space, as Death's had. He remembered how Aisa had lost the end of her scarf that time. The same thing must have happened to Talfi's leg.

Talfi. Help Talfi. Grik's tits, he couldn't let Talfi die. *Aisa* couldn't let Talfi die. But how would he get on with a missing leg?

That was a worry for later. Right now Aisa needed more water. Danr turned—

—and found himself face-to-face with a wyrm.

Icy fear washed over Danr, and water from the bowl slopped over his hands. The wyrm wasn't quite as large as the one he had killed outside Skyford, but it was big enough. Emerald scales glittered in the sun. It ran out a long tongue that lapped the air inches from Danr's face, and he smelled a strange, heavy scent. Danr saw his own reflection in the wyrm's golden eyes. His feet were frozen to the ground.

"What are you doing here, Stane?"

For a moment, Danr thought the wyrm had spoken. The wyrm shifted then, and Danr saw that the creature had saddle and rider. It was a woman, tall and lean. Her smooth skin had a faintly green cast to it, and her eyes were the same gold as her wyrm's. She wore both armor and boots that looked woven out of long strips of leather. Her auburn hair was bound in braids and wrapped around her head. The reins to a strange bridle that controlled the wyrm hung loosely in the woman's left hand. In her right, she held a long, wicked spear. It made a striking picture.

Danr gaped, trying to recover. He had heard of orcs; he had encountered wyrms. Never had he thought of the two together. Until a few days ago, he had never gone farther than Skyford, where he himself had been the most exotic creature. Now he walked among giants, trolls, dwarves, and, apparently, wyrms with orc riders. While his friend lay dying. Urgency propelled him forward.

"Talfi!" he said. "I have to help my friend."

He started to move around the orc and the wyrm, but the

orc's spear pricked his chest and the wyrm turned its head to follow him. "How did you come here, Stane?"

Now Danr began to get angry. Talfi was half-dead, and this woman was standing in his way. Danr, who had more than a head of height on the orc and only had to raise his head a little to look her in the eye even from her vantage point on the wyrm's back, nearly snatched the spear, intending to break it like Alfgeir's pitchfork. One punch and the orc would go down. Now that anger had overtaken surprise, he realized how much smaller the wyrm was than the one Danr had killed, and Danr was fairly certain he could fight it. But Talfi was hurt, and Danr couldn't see Aisa. For all he knew, she was a prisoner of another orc, or a dozen. He closed his right eye and looked at the orc. Her muscles were relaxed, but she was ready to move in an instant. She was only a year or two older than Danr, but a number of scars crawled over her arms and legs. She was used to fighting but wasn't ready to fight at the moment. Her questions came out of curiosity than fear or anger.

"I traveled here by magic," Danr said levelly, ignoring the spear. "My friend was hurt. I need to help him. Do you have medicine or a water bucket?"

The orc moved the spear aside. "I do not. But my nest mates are with your friend. Help him, and then we will talk."

Nest mates? Danr put that aside for later and hurried around the wyrm, which stretched out more than the length of four horses. In the scorched area stood or knelt eight other orcs. They had apparently dismounted from their own wyrms, which formed an enormous crowd several paces away. Their armor matched the first orc's, and like the first orc, they were tall and lean, though half of them were male. Some were dark-haired; some were fair. One had red hair. The women all wore sets of tight braids coiled around their heads. All of them had golden eyes like their wyrms. Danr chewed his lip, nervous all over again. How had he not heard them coming? He arrived at the circle, where Aisa continued to tend Talfi. She seemed to be ignoring the orcs, but Danr could see the tension in her movements. The fire was already dying down. It needed tending.

"Er . . . greetings," Danr said, setting the bowl by the fire to heat. "I'm Hamzu. This is Aisa and Talfi. We're from Balsia, and we've had an accident."

"Where is his leg?" said a male orc with dark hair that clashed with his golden eyes. "I see it nowhere."

"I don't know," Danr said. "The magic that brought us here hurt him. If you're willing to help us, we need more wood for the fire and more water."

"And rags," Aisa murmured, "for fresh bandages."

Talfi's breathing was quick and his eyes were shut. Danr couldn't tell if he was unconscious or asleep from whatever Aisa had given him. His skin looked like wax. The bandage was still leaking blood. Danr's stomach twisted at the sight. Was this some kind of punishment from the Nine for being a *regi*? Belinna, the goddess of love and war, wasn't kind to men who spurned her favors. Had she arranged this? It had happened moments after Talfi confessed. As a punishment, it seemed awfully harsh. Danr's jaw tightened. He was trying to help the gods, help Death herself. If the Nine wanted him to succeed, they had a strange way of showing it.

Two of the orcs built up the fire with more driftwood from the river. They built it higher and higher, and the smoke climbed a gray pillar into the sky. The other orcs stood about with their arms folded, apparently content to do nothing but wait and watch while Aisa tended Talfi. Several paces away from the heat of the fire, the first orc, the auburn-haired woman Danr had encountered at the river, held out a long, lean arm.

"I am Kalessa from the Eighth Nest, daughter of Hess and Xanda," she said. Her spear lay across her back, along with her shield. A short bronze sword was sheathed at her hip. The great wyrm she'd been riding slithered down to the river for a drink. It made almost no noise as it slipped over the grass, and Danr understood how Kalessa had appeared behind him so suddenly. He held out his arm to her as she had done for him.

"Hamzu," he said, "son of Halldora and Kech. Er . . . Emissary Prince of the Stane, nephew of Vesha, Queen Under the Mountain."

He was expecting a handshake. Kalessa clasped Danr's forearm instead—or she tried. Danr's arm was much larger than an orc's fingers could encompass, though her grip was strong. Her golden eyes met his brown ones pointedly, and for a moment, Danr's breath caught. She was beautiful, and his body tightened at her touch. Then Danr understood that she was greeting him, and he engulfed Kalessa's forearm with his own hand.

"I feel deeply about your friend," Kalessa said. "May Grick smile on him that his pain be light and his passage quick."

"Er . . . thank you." So many strange images pulled at the edges of Danr's vision. A woman in woven armor. A dozen orcs. The saddled wyrms and their unblinking eyes. Aisa bent over Talfi's pale form. And the bonfire that climbed higher and higher. One of the orcs tossed something on it that gave the smoke a greenish cast and a sweet smell.

"I have never met one of the Stane," Kalessa said. "Or the Kin. You said magic brought you here. What has happened?"

Danr forced himself to snatch his scattered thoughts together. He was an emissary and needed to act like one. But it was damn hard with Talfi lying over there. He felt helpless and stupid. And guilty. It was his fault. He shouldn't have told Talfi he could come.

But he had, and now they were here in Xaron, and Danr had to persuade the orcs to join with the Stane against the Fae, and it looked as though Kalessa was the place to start. If Kalessa had never seen Kin before, it was a good bet he had arrived ahead of Hunin's men. Danr touched the torc around his neck and then the pouch at his throat to make himself concentrate. The truthful answer to her question was already pushing its way out of his throat.

"The Stane are coming out from under the Iron Mountains," he said. "The Fae will declare war on them the moment they do, and the Kin lands of Balsia will become the battleground. I'm here to ask the orcs to fight beside the Stane." He glanced at Kalessa and the other orcs with just his left eye, gathered a bit of information about them, and quickly added, "For the glory of the Kin! You can fight beside giants and destroy the Fae. Bards will sing your name forever!"

"Is this true, then?" Kalessa cracked her knuckles. "Our shamans have seen auguries that whisper of a great coming war, and now you arrive with a truer word of one."

"I hate to bring bad news," Danr said. "I don't—"

"Bad?" Kalessa drew her sword and slapped the flat against her forearm. "This is wonderful news! The Nine bless us with a chance for glory!"

"Ah. Of course." Danr pulled himself straighter and deepened his voice. "The Stane are ready to stand beside you as we fight our way into Valorhame!"

"You present well," Kalessa said. "Your words are powerful. You bring good news, and you are tall and strong and handsome. You should speak to my father. He is chieftain of the Eighth Nest."

"Thank you." He was handsome? A hot flush crawled up his face. She must be mocking him. But no—he could see she wasn't lying. Handsome. No one had ever called him that before. This beautiful woman really thought—?

"The others in my nest will arrive soon," Kalessa continued. "The wyrm smoke summons them. Come now. You should speak with your friend."

As they turned toward Talfi, Kalessa's wyrm returned from the river, its face dripping. It slid up behind her and delicately flicked its tongue over her head. Kalessa turned and pointed to the other wyrms, which were coiled about one another in an emerald mountain. "Go!"

The wyrm bumped her shoulder with its nose. Kalessa pointed and gave the order again. The wyrm wiped its golden eyes with its tongue and scurried off in a huff. Now that it wasn't threatening him, Danr was able to watch it move. It was easily large enough to carry four, and it flowed across the ground like an emerald river. The power and speed made Danr's heart thump.

"Wyrms," Kalessa sighed. "So touchy. But no better steed, yes?"

"Yes," Danr said, still staring.

"Ah." She reached up to clap him on the shoulder. "You admire the wyrms. Very good. We will make you an honorary orc, Master Stane."

"My mother was human," Danr said, "so I'm part Kin, too."

"Yes? Even better. Come now—your friend needs you."

Aisa had already been forced to change Talfi's bandages. The old ones lay in a scarlet pile. The new ones, however, seemed to be less bloody, even to Danr's unpracticed eye.

The small crowd of orcs let them through, and Danr knelt next to Aisa. "The next night and day will prove whether he lives or dies," she said tightly. "If his *draugr* doesn't rise before tomorrow evening, he should live."

"But without my leg," Talfi gasped. Danr jumped. Talfi's eyes were still shut.

"You'll be fine," Danr said gruffly. "Death is my friend, remember? She won't take you now."

"Not while she's chained up, she won't." Talfi managed a sound that barely resembled a laugh. "Don't let me wander as a *draugr* when I die. Please! Do something so I don't."

"You're not going to die," Danr said around the lump in his throat. "You see? I said so, and I can't tell a lie."

"Only because you don't know if it's the truth or not." Talfi coughed and winced. "All Nine, it hurts."

"Here." Aisa held a cup to his lips and helped him rise slightly. "You need to drink all of this, then sleep."

Talfi obeyed and lay back down. His breathing evened out a little and he seemed to sleep. The orcs watched, perfectly patient. Danr drew Aisa aside. "What are his chances?"

"Surprisingly good," Aisa replied from within her scarves. "The wound was absolutely clean, and he should experience no infection. With time, he can recover from the blood he lost. The danger is that his body has received a terrible shock. But his mind is strong, and if I enjoyed gambling, I would bet on his recovery."

Relief flooded Danr like warm water, but it was tainted with disappointment. "Talfi will never run again," he said. "He was the fastest runner I ever saw, and now . . ."

"Yes," Aisa agreed. "I can do much, but I cannot regrow a limb."

"You did save his life. Thank Grick for that." For a moment, he wanted to hold Aisa close, feel her against him, let her know how much this meant to him. How much *she* meant to him. Instead he said, "And thank *you*, Aisa. You're a goddess, too."

"Not yet," she said with a flash of mischief that made his heart flicker. "But perhaps one day."

"My father comes." Kalessa pointed. In the far distance, the prairie grass was moving as if stirred by a great wind. Dozens of wyrms of many sizes and colors lunged into view, streaming across the hilly plain. Some were just large enough to allow a single rider. Others were so tall even Danr couldn't have seen over them, and they carried a dozen orcs each. The sun gleamed a rainbow off their scales, and their tongues lashed the air. Danr winced and shaded his eyes at their brightness, but the incredible sight rooted him to the ground. The wyrms barely made any noise as they rushed across the grass, but the orcs shouted and yipped and howled in a cacophony of sound that wove together like their armor. Even the children were shouting. Danr's heart beat at the back of his throat. He forced himself to stand straight, as a prince should, but it wasn't easy with an injured friend at his feet and a shouting mob of orcs rushing straight at him. A bloodred wyrm at the head of the formation slid up to Kalessa and Danr and halted. The orc on its back had the same auburn hair Kalessa did, but his was streaked with gray, and Danr's left eye showed he was trying to hide some stiffness as he leaped off the wyrm's back.

"Father!" Kalessa clasped him a great, crushing hug, which he returned without embarrassment. Danr shifted, a little uncomfortable but also envious. It would be a fine thing to grow up with a father who hugged. Even if it were an orc.

"Why did you burn the green smoke?" he boomed in a voice three times louder than was needed. "What is the emergency? Who are these people?"

"We were scouting and came across them," Kalessa said, equally loud, and Danr understood they were both speaking for the rest of the orcs, who had fallen silent on their great wyrms. "They bring great news—an alliance with the Stane and war with the Fae!"

An exultant cheer thundered through the silence. The orcs raised spears and swords to the sky or beat them against their shields. Wyrms rose and hissed their approval. Danr worked not to wince at the noise.

When it at last died down, Kalessa's father clapped Danr

on the shoulder. "It shames us all to admit that the Fae are stronger than our scattered tribes. It has been hundreds of years since we have heard from the Stane, and our irregular contact with the humans is far from a true alliance. With the Stane beside us, we could end these mere skirmishes against the Fae and declare the finest war in orcish history! What is your name?"

Danr shifted. He hadn't expected a reception quite like this. "I am Prince Hamzu, son of Kech and Halldora, Truth-Teller from Under the Mountain, Nephew to Queen Vesha of the Stane."

"And I am Hess, son of Nox and Vaxan, Chieftain of the Eighth Nest, Rider of the Scarlet Wyrm." Hess stepped back. "But where is your sword, if you are a prince?"

The orcs and their wyrms, meanwhile, had moved into a great circle around them, one that also encompassed Aisa, Talfi, and the fire, which continued to send up leafy green smoke. Danr suddenly felt less secure.

"My sword?" He touched the pouch at his throat. "Uh . . . we left in a hurry, and I didn't think to take one."

"Never mind. Kalessa!"

With a great grin, Kalessa tossed her sword at Danr, who caught it by the hilt without thinking. In his hand it was barely more than a large knife. "What—?"

"Those who want to negotiate with the orcs must prove their worth," he boomed. "Fight!"

He stabbed at Danr. Danr leaped back with a yelp.

"You think this is a game, boy?" Hess snapped. "The Stane insult the orcs by sending a hatchling!"

He flicked his blade at Danr's stomach. Danr only barely twisted aside. The orcs bellowed their disapproval. Hess was honestly trying to kill him. Blood and fear sang in Danr's ears. He had no idea how to use a sword, hadn't even held one until now. Danr tried a lunge, but Hess batted the attempt aside with contempt. Aisa clapped both her wrapped hands over her mouth.

"The orcs do not ally themselves with weaklings." Hess stabbed again. Danr closed his right eye, and the world seemed to slow. He saw the way Hess moved, how his muscles were still stiff, both from age and from riding the wyrm all day. In a moment, he saw which way the sword point was going. For once, his mind moved faster than its usual careful plod. He dropped the useless sword, stepped sideways on the burned grass, and let Hess's blade stab his side. Pain slashed his ribs, but Danr ignored it. Hess was now within his reach. Danr snatched at Hess's forearm with a meaty fist. Hess tried to fall back, but his movements were slowed by stiffness and the way his blade dug into Danr's flesh. Danr yanked upward, and Hess's feet left the ground. His sword spun away. Anger roared behind Danr's eyes. He flung the chieftain straight up into the air. Hess yowled in surprise and . . . fear? Danr caught him by the front of his woven armor as he fell and slammed him the rest of the way to the ground. Hess grunted and his head lolled. The orcs fell silent.

Panting with anger and pain, Danr slapped a hand around Hess's neck. Some of the monster came out. He wanted to feel the bones break, hear them crunch.

White Halli, he thought. *Remember White Halli.*

Danr forced the awful monster back and grunted, "Do you yield?"

"I . . ." Hess's face contorted. ". . . yield."

Danr released Hess, then held out an arm to haul the chieftain to his feet. Staggering only a little, Hess thumped his chest and raised his hand in salute. The gathering of orcs burst into more shouts. Aisa closed her eyes. Danr blew out a long breath and wondered how much time the orcs spent shouting. Then he realized he had just beaten an orc chieftain in single combat and all these people were cheering for *him*. Never in his life did he think he would hear such a thing. The cheering crested in a wave that lifted his heart and flung his soul to the clouds.

"The Nine," he whispered, and wished his mother could have been there. Perhaps here, among the orcs and their acceptance, he could find a home.

The cheering died down as Hess clapped Danr on the shoulder, and the pain in Danr's side bit him like a snake. Blood ran down his side.

"A true warrior," Hess said. "Fell himself would approve."

Aisa hurried over and pulled up Danr's tunic. Her concern made him a little warm. "This will require stitching," she said. "You were foolish. My heart nearly stopped when—"

"Now it is you, Lady Aisa," Hess interrupted.

Danr froze. Aisa stared up at Hess from the depths of her scarves and wrappings. "I could not have heard you correctly, Chieftain Hess," she said. "I am not trained to fight."

"That is a shame." Hess dropped a sword at Aisa's feet and gestured to Kalessa, who drew her own sword. "It will be difficult to prove yourself worthy."

"I'll fight in her place," Danr said instantly, his pain forgotten.

"You have fought today already." Hess gestured again. His wyrm flashed forward like scarlet lightning and plucked Danr out of the ring of burned grass by his collar before he could so much as blink. Danr kicked and swung his arms, but the wyrm held him high off the ground by the scruff of his neck and he couldn't connect with anything. Icy terror for Aisa poured over him.

"Aisa!" he shouted.

A few of the orcs started a rhythmic clap that spread through the crowd. Aisa picked up the sword, but even with both eyes open, Danr could see her fear. Kalessa moved in confidently, blade at the ready. Danr desperately struggled in the wyrm's grip but couldn't get free. It shook him once like a kitten, and the pain in his side forced him to fall still.

Kalessa lunged. Aisa abruptly dropped to her knees before Kalessa in the slave's posture. The sword fell to the burned grass.

"How should I fight you?" she said in a voice that carried through the crowd. "You may as well cut my throat now." And she lifted her chin.

The clapping stopped, and Kalessa hesitated. For a heart-stopping moment, Danr was sure Kalessa was going to drop her own sword and declare some kind of truce. Instead she gave a battle cry and stabbed at Aisa. Danr's heart shriveled in his chest.

But Aisa rolled away and flung something up at Kalessa's face. Black powder scattered through the air like angry dust motes. Kalessa coughed and went off balance, partly from surprise and partly from the powder. Aisa scooped up her own sword and stabbed at Kalessa with it. Danr wanted to cheer. But Kalessa recovered quickly and caught the blow on her blade. She held Aisa's sword, metal on metal, and stared at her across the X. For a tiny moment, Aisa stared defiantly back. A moment hung between them.

"Surrender," Kalessa hissed. "Your death will be quick, I promise."

Aisa kicked at Kalessa's ankle. The blow connected. Kalessa leaped back. Aisa threw the sword straight at the orc. It whirled in a deadly arc. Danr held his breath. Kalessa easily parried it with a clang. Aisa snatched up a stone and threw it. Kalessa dodged like a snake. Aisa threw another stone, and another. Kalessa dodged every one.

"I will not yield!" Aisa cried. "You may cut off my hands, and I will not yield. You may slit my throat and slice me in half, and I will. Not. Yield!"

She threw a final stone half the size of her head. It arced toward Kalessa's arm.

And then Kalessa deliberately thrust out her sword. The stone struck the blade and knocked it from Kalessa's unresisting grasp. The assembled orcs looked at one another and murmured in puzzlement. Danr swallowed hard, though it was hard to breathe now.

"I yield!" Kalessa announced. "And I further declare that this woman is my blood sister."

"Kalessa!" her father said. "What—?"

Before Hess could protest further, Kalessa regained her sword, slashed her palm with it, and held her hand out to Aisa. Aisa hesitated only a moment before slicing through the wrappings on her own hand and into the skin beneath. The two women clasped hands, and the orcs roared again. Danr went limp with relief, then *whuffed* hard as the wyrm unexpectedly dropped him to the ground. Hess helped haul him to his feet, though the gesture was more symbolic than helpful—Danr was a full head taller than the chieftain. Hess drew his sword and held it high next to Danr.

"We will summon a Council of Wyrms," Hess declared, "so that we may all discuss the coming war and who the orcs will join. But first—"

Hess strode over to the spot where Talfi lay near the fire. Talfi had managed to prop himself partway up on his elbows. His pupils were fully dilated from whatever Aisa had given him. At least, Danr noted, his pain seemed to have eased.

"What is your name, human?" Hess asked.

"T-Talfi," he managed.

"May Fell and Belinna guide your spirit, Talfi," he said. With a single stroke, Hess cut off Talfi's head.

Chapter Thirteen

When Danr came to himself, it was dark. A group of drums beat in the near distance, and stars burned steadily overhead. The air was cool now, but Danr was slick with sweat. He couldn't move, and his head ached. It took him a moment to work out that a wyrm had wrapped itself around him, gently but tightly. The scales were cool and unyielding as iron. Danr could draw breath, nothing more. He shook his head. The last thing he remembered was—

Talfi. Talfi was dead. Hess had cut his head off. Danr could still see the blood fountain from his neck, hear the awful thud of Talfi's lifeless head hitting the ground. Grief and despair crushed him, and if the wyrm hadn't held him upright, he would have fallen to his knees. Tears ran unchecked down his face. Talfi was dead. The orcs had killed him. How dared they call themselves Kin when they murdered a crippled man? And how could he create an alliance with creatures that were as cold-blooded as the wyrms they rode? They might slaughter the Stane as fast as look at them.

But these thoughts were nothing but a dodge from the main matter—that this was Danr's fault.

Danr had known little of orcs and less of their ways, and

he had definitely known how dangerous a long-range Twist could be, but he had allowed Talfi to come along anyway. If he had told Talfi to stay behind, Talfi wouldn't have lost his leg and none of this would have happened. But Danr had allowed it, and Talfi was dead. Worse, he had died thinking Danr disliked him, maybe even hated him, for being *regi*.

Danr's cheeks burned with shame and guilt. Talfi had been forced to reveal a secret that frightened and unnerved him, and what had Danr, his closest friend, done? Shunned him, shamed him. Danr himself knew what it was like to be despised for being born the way he was. How could he have turned around and done the same thing to the first real friend he'd ever had after Aisa? Now Talfi was dead. *Dead.* And Danr had no way to beg his forgiveness. The grief crushed him like the wyrm's coils.

"You are yourself again," Kalessa said. It was her wyrm that held him. "Fell's fever took you when your friend died. It took six orcs to pin you down so Slynd here could wrap you. My father was much impressed."

"You filth," Danr spat. "He was helpless. He hadn't done anything to you, and you killed him."

She cocked her head. "What a strange and cruel person you are."

"I'm cruel?" he said. "Vik's balls, what—"

"Your friend could never again ride or run or even walk. So cruel to condemn him to such a life. Instead he was dispatched by an honored chieftain and sent straight to Valorhame itself." She slapped her chest. "Most orcs would give their wyrms for such an honor."

Danr closed his eyes. Even without looking at the truth, he could see she meant every word. His gut felt filled with lead.

"Just let me down," he said woodenly.

"Has the madness left you?" she said. "Chax and Xentho will be aching for days."

"I'm . . . I can't say I'm fine, but I won't attack anyone."

Kalessa made a gesture. Her wyrm uncoiled and withdrew, recoiling itself a few yards away. Danr winced as his feet touched the ground and hot pain scored his side. His wound hadn't been attended. He grimaced. Maybe he should just leave it, let it fester as a penance for his foolishness.

"Hamzu!" Aisa hurried over. "You are yourself again. They would not let me—I was so worried."

"I'm sorry. Talfi—" Still grimacing, he started to sink to the ground, but she wouldn't let him, and somehow the support turned into an embrace. He knew she feared him and his strength, but for just this moment, he gave in and let himself hold her, and even though he was more than twice her size, it felt as if she was holding him. She was a rock, a mountain, even, and he was able to rest on her. It felt good to let someone else prop him up, and until this moment, he hadn't noticed how difficult it had been to keep himself upright on his own all this time. Only Aisa could do that. Tears welled up, and he couldn't hold them back.

"It will be all right," Aisa whispered into his chest. "It will."

"How can he be dead?" Danr choked. "He was my friend, and now he's dead."

"I know," was all she said, and it had to be enough. "I know. You must come to the fire so I can examine your side."

Danr pulled away and wiped at his eyes. The orcs had set up camp. Hide tents of many sizes and more fires had sprung up all around the river. The wyrms, unsaddled, curled together in hissing mountains. The drums throbbed a constant rhythm, though these didn't stir Danr up like the ones in the troll city. These drums were instead softer, quieter, calming.

"The comfort drums are to aid us through Talfi's death," Kalessa said as they came to the fireside. "He was a friend of my blood sister, which makes him a friend of the Eighth Nest."

Danr knew she meant well, but he wanted to hit her. Only the pain in his side kept him moving toward the fire instead of dropping to the ground beneath a black load of guilt and grief. Next to the hearth lay a sad little bundle covered in a red cloth. Talfi's body. The sight of it wrenched Danr's chest anew, and his jaw trembled. Orcs drummed nearby. Danr didn't want to show more tears to them, but he wasn't sure he could hold off, and he desperately wished Kalessa and her friends would go away.

"The orcs use red for mourning," Aisa explained quietly. "Sit here and let me examine you."

All three of them sat. The heat of the fire felt good. Aisa pulled up Danr's tunic, and he hissed at the fresh pain.

"This is not as bad as I had feared," she announced. "It just needs a few stitches. You do heal quickly."

She poured something alcoholic and burning over the wound—Danr had no idea where she'd gotten it—and set to work with a needle. Danr didn't feel the pricking, not with Talfi's corpse cooling a few feet away. The orcs drummed on.

"You were immensely brave, Prince Hamzu." Kalessa was seated cross-legged next to him, her auburn hair neatly braided across her head. Danr couldn't help noticing how striking she was, but he found her much less beautiful than before. "And my sister Aisa was equally brave. You acquitted well both Kin and Stane."

"I don't understand that," Danr said, more to take his mind off Talfi for a moment than anything else. "What did you do?"

"Aisa was brave and resourceful, even at the point of death. When I looked into her eyes, I saw a like spirit, even if she didn't know how to fight," Kalessa said. "Among our people, the bonds between sisters are the strongest of all, but

I was born with none, so I made Aisa my sister. I will defend her to my last breath, and she will do the same for me until Belinna takes us to Valorhame."

Danr closed his right eye. Kalessa was filled with truth. "How does Aisa feel about it?" he asked.

"Aisa never had a sister, either," said Aisa. "She finds the arrangement satisfactory, though she is unhappy about . . ." She paused and gulped air. ". . . Talfi's death."

"Yes." Kalessa's voice turned sad. "I wish there were some other way, friend Hamzu. Talfi could not ride a wyrm or run beside one, and we could not leave him behind to starve or be devoured by wild animals. That would be cruel indeed. Your friend died the moment he lost his leg. He just did not know it." She touched his shoulder. "I am very sorry."

New grief welled up and Danr worked his jaw back and forth while the orcs drummed and drummed. His head said Kalessa was right, but his heart shouted she was wrong, that they could have found another way.

"Done," Aisa said. "I will check this in a few days, but I think you have nothing to fear."

"Good, then." Kalessa rose as an orc dressed in an elaborately embroidered green cloak with the hood drawn approached them. "Now it is time, good Prince Hamzu."

Danr got stiffly to his feet, followed by Aisa. "Time for what?"

"You must give your friend to the fire." The hooded orc gestured toward Talfi's red-shrouded body. Her voice was female, but her face remained hidden and she wore emerald gloves. Ashkame, the sacred tree, was embroidered in gold thread across the back of her cloak. "We have built it up for you so his remains will burn quickly while we drum for his spirit."

"Oh." Already? Danr looked at the red bundle. It seemed too small to be Talfi. How could he put his best friend in the fire? It was that, or leave his body for wolves and vultures.

Except the orcs hadn't put any amulets or coins into the shroud. How would he bribe his way past icy Halza? Danr searched through his pockets, and came up with nothing. He touched his throat.

"Wait," he said.

The shaman waited, her emerald hands clasped within her sleeves. Danr unbent the heavy gold torc from around his neck, knelt, and slid the piece into Talfi's shroud. It was enough to bribe passage for a dozen earls past Halza. But it still felt paltry and small. Perhaps he could take something from Vesha's chest. He shook his head. The torc, troll-made coins, all the treasure from under the mountain, was nothing but gold, not worthy of someone like Talfi. Danr needed something more, something real.

Then he knew. With careful fingers, Danr removed the pouch that contained his and his mother's splinters and slipped it under the shroud into Talfi's cold hand. It was the most valuable thing he owned, and he could think of nothing better to give, no, he couldn't.

"I'm sorry I brought this on you," Danr whispered. "I'll do everything I can to make everything better. I'm sorry I called you a . . . what I did. I'm glad you were my friend." His voice choked over the last words.

Aisa came to stand beside him, and her eyes were wet over her scarf. "I should say a blessing," he muttered thickly, "but I don't know how."

"When my mother died," Aisa said, "I had no words for days and days. That is why priests speak for the dead."

He wished she would embrace him again, that he could hold her. But he remembered her fear and held back. The ache of loneliness, especially for Aisa, was the worst he could remember. And the drums droned on. Their rhythm shifted, readying themselves for Talfi's spirit.

His spirit.

A thought speared his mind and chilled his insides. Death was chained up. Everyone who died became a *draugr*, a spirit who haunted the earth. So where was Talfi's *draugr*? In his grief, Danr had entirely forgotten.

"This doesn't make sense," Danr whispered. "Where are you, Talfi?"

"I don't understand," Aisa said, confused.

And within the red shroud, Talfi sat up.

Danr shot backward, snatching Aisa with him. The drummers dropped their drums and fled. In no time at all, the circle around the fire was deserted, and screaming chaos spread through the camp. The fire danced as if nothing had happened. Even the emerald-cloaked shaman had vanished.

Kalessa, next to Danr and Aisa, had her sword out. Danr swallowed. This had to be Talfi's *draugr* manifesting a little late, that was all. Wasn't it? Except Danr couldn't see through Talfi, and it was clearly Talfi's body that was sitting up. This was not a spirit leaving the body behind. Danr's heart beat so fast his eyes hurt.

Talfi pulled the shroud away from his face and body. His hair was mussed and his face was a little pale, but he was still the handsome, sharp-faced young man Danr remembered. His head was back on his shoulders, no sign of the great sword cut, or any cut at all. Aisa put her hands to the scarf over her mouth and made a small sound. Talfi got unsteadily to his feet—both of them. His right leg was hale and whole, if bare. His leggings were still cut neatly at midthigh and his right foot was unshod. The gold torc fell out of the cloth and rolled away as Talfi gained his feet, and he stared down, confused, at the pouch of splinters in his hand.

"What creature is this?" Kalessa gasped.

Danr stood half in the circle of light, half in the dark. His mouth was dry as sand. He didn't know how to react to this, and his mind was stuck halfway between here and there, between life and death, grief and happiness. This had to be a trick. Who had done it, and how? But the other half of him hoped beyond breathless hope that it was indeed true, that Talfi had somehow come back from the dead. He stared, unable to move, unable even to breathe.

Talfi blinked, as if blinded by the firelight. He raised Danr's pouch to his face and sniffed hard, then closed his eyes and sniffed again. He cocked his head like a cat listening for something. Then he put the pouch around his neck over the silver amulet he customarily wore, the one that he had refused to sell even when he was starving.

Danr couldn't stand it anymore. "Talfi?" he called hoarsely. "Is it you?"

Talfi's head came up and he shaded his eyes. "Who's that?"

By now a number of orcs had recovered from their consternation and a small crowd of them stole back to the darkness just beyond the fire, most of them with swords or axes drawn, though they didn't get too close. The shaman was nowhere to be seen.

"It's me, Talfi." Danr cautiously stepped into the circle of light. "Do you see me?"

Talfi yelped when he saw Danr, and he backed away. Only at the last moment did he avoid backing into the fire. "The Nine! Who are you?"

Danr's chest constricted in iron bands. "It's me. Hamzu. Truth-Teller. Your friend."

"Don't hurt me," he said.

Orcish swords gleamed like grins in the darkness.

"I . . ." Danr hesitated. "I won't hurt you, Talfi. You're safe."

"Is that my name?" he asked. "Talfi?"

The direct question forced Danr to answer. "Of course. You don't remember?"

Talfi shook his head.

"What's the last thing you *do* remember?"

"I . . ." Talfi concentrated, though he kept his distance from Danr. If he noticed the orcs beyond the firelight, he gave no sign of it. "I don't remember anything."

Talfi's memory. He already had no idea what his life had been before he arrived in Skyford. Now something had happened—

—*he died, you idiot*—

—that took away the rest of it. Danr realized his mouth was hanging open. He shut it. "Do you remember me? Grandmother Bund? The trolls? Orvandel the fletcher? Your foster brother, Almer?"

"No," Talfi said. "Nothing."

"Talfi." Aisa entered the circle. "My name is Aisa. The magic that brought us here took your leg off. I tended you. Does this sound familiar?"

"No. Why are you all wrapped up? Is it winter?"

"You know what seasons are, and how to speak, and how to walk," Aisa said. "And you remember how to swear by the Nine. But you remember nothing about your own past."

"Not a thing. I suppose we're friends?"

At last relief rushed over Danr. Unable to help himself, he ran forward and crushed Talfi in an embrace. Talfi lived and breathed, and Danr wasn't going to let that go. But Talfi struggled within Danr's arms and made muffled cries for help until Danr set him down again.

"Sorry," Danr said. "It's just . . . Vik, you were my best friend and you were *dead*. You have to make at least one allowance."

Talfi blinked at him. "I was dead?"

"That orc there, the one who is trying to appear more brave than he is, only recently chopped off your head," Aisa said. "I watched it roll across the ground."

"Pardon?" said Hess from outside the circle.

"My head?" Talfi touched his head as if it might come off. "Orcs?"

It finally occurred to Danr to look at Talfi with his left eye only. It hadn't come to him to try it since he'd arrived in Skyford as a truth-teller. He shut his right eye—

—and Talfi vanished. Danr could see the ground and the fire right through the spot where he should be standing. Of Talfi himself there was no sign. Astonished, Danr opened both eyes. Talfi reappeared. Danr reached out to touch Talfi, but he ducked away.

"What's wrong with you?" he demanded. Danr backed up again, and a certain tension invaded the circle. He traded glances with Aisa, confused and upset, but also strangely thrilled. What should they do?

Kalessa raised her sword into the air. "The human warrior has conquered death! Celebrate his victory!"

And the orcs cheered.

The party went on until dawn. The orcs summoned up more drums, drink, a great deal of shouting, and a sinuous dance formed from the line of orcs that wound endlessly around the camp with Talfi at its head. Talfi accepted everything with a bemused sort of cheer that Danr recognized as his usual nature. That fascinated Danr in a grim sort of way. Talfi had no memory of his life before Hess killed him, but his personality remained the same, and how did that happen? Wasn't a person the sum of his memories?

But Talfi was a bundle of mysteries, one that Danr had been too busy to examine closely. He had told Danr that he had no memories before his time with Orvandel the fletcher. Now it seemed he couldn't even remember how to die.

Huh. Interesting way to think of it. Was Talfi's resurrection related to his memory loss? Or did it have something to do with Death being chained up? Or both? He wanted to ask Aisa about it, but she was talking to Kalessa near the fire amid a pile of food and drink, and Kalessa wasn't letting anyone get close during their "sister time."

In the meantime, the orcs continually asked Danr himself to relate the story of Talfi's death and resurrection between congratulations and back-poundings for winning his battle with Hess. They didn't seem to care in the slightest whether he was human or troll, Stane or Kin, and that was a strangely warm feeling, indeed it was, and now that Talfi wasn't dead after all, Danr's earlier mistrust and dislike for them was fading.

Surrounding the orcs was a great fence of wyrms. They tangled themselves into an enormous barrier that wove all the way around the camp. It was like watching a living version of certain carvings the Kin put on cups or tables, carvings of branches or serpents that wound around each other with no beginning or end. Danr wondered what would happen if anyone or anything tried to breach that fence.

Overhead near the waxing half-moon, the two stars that made up Urko were still drifting together. They were twenty-five days apart now. Twenty-four, if you didn't count today. Had Death known Danr would ask Grandmother Bund to Twist him to Xaron? Perhaps Death and Bund were talking about it right now. The thought made Danr reach for more drink.

After a couple of hours, he found himself drooping at one of the smaller fires with his stomach full and his head a little muzzy from the strange-tasting orcish ale. Unexpectedly, Aisa dropped down next to him.

"You look tired," she said. "Hess has a tent near his for you and Talfi to share. If you don't mind sleeping next to a *regi*, that is."

Danr sighed. "Not now, Aisa."

"The truth-teller has a difficult time seeing the truth within himself," she observed. "Have you ever looked at yourself with that new vision of yours?"

"I said not—no," he said, interrupting himself as the truth forced itself out of him.

"Did you look at Talfi when he came back? It might tell us something of how he did it or why it happened."

"I did." Danr realized that, tired or not, he was hungry to talk about it to someone. Around them, the celebration was winding down. The drums had stopped. Orcs were drifting off to their tents alone or in groups, their children long since asleep. Some curled up near the fires, content to drop off with the wyrms on guard.

"And what did you see?"

"Nothing at all. It was like he wasn't there." Danr shook his head. "I don't understand a thing. Maybe we should ask Death about it."

"Ha!" Aisa put a hand to her scarved mouth. "I suppose she might know the answer. And she wasn't at all frightening. Though I wonder if she appeared to us in a kindly aspect so we would help her."

"It would be difficult to help a skeleton dressed in black," Danr agreed, "especially if it waved a scythe at me."

"Everything has happened so quickly," she mused. "You stepped in when White Halli attacked me and set all this into motion. We both ran to the trolls and met your Stane family, and then your grandmother sent us to see the Three, and—what is it? What is wrong?"

He didn't want to answer right away, but her question tore the truth out of him. "My grandmother is dead," he choked. "The spell that Twisted us here killed her. My left eye saw it coming. It's the monster's fault she died."

"Oh." She touched his arm. Like a friend and not a lover.

That made him ache again, and for a moment he saw himself with her, sharing a table in a long house together, milking cows together, tending hearth and heart together. Sharing bodies together. His groin tightened a little, and he became uncomfortable.

"I'm so sorry, my strong one. I liked her, and it is unfair that she died so soon after you met her."

"Thank you." He sighed heavily. "I don't know why I'm so upset. I barely knew her. Vik, I barely knew the trolls. They abandoned me to the humans. Why should I care?"

"They are your past," Aisa said. "Even if you did not know them. It was not their fault they were not part of your life, after all. The Stane were unable to come down the mountain. Your mother could have taken you up to see them, I suppose, but she never did. Perhaps it was a mistake for her to keep you away from—"

"My mother did the best she could," Danr shot back with unexpected heat. "Everyone hated her because she told the truth and because she had me for a son. It wasn't her fault."

"Yes, of course," Aisa said. "I only meant—"

"I know what you meant," he snapped. "You're very clear."

Strain hung in the air between them like smoke. Danr knew he was tired, knew the drink and his tangled emotions pushed him into a snappish mood. He should apologize and say good night, but the monster inside wouldn't let him speak. Instead he stared at the fire, half hoping Talfi or one of the orcs would come by and say something to break the tension.

"Hamzu," Aisa said suddenly, "have you looked at *me* with your true eye?"

Damn it. "Yes," he was forced to answer.

She looked taken aback, and Danr's face burned. Now that she had asked him, he understood how she might see it—an invasion of her privacy, a way for someone else to burrow through the protective scarves she wrapped around herself. The tension grew tighter, like a net around a great fish.

Aisa pulled her rags closer. Her voice grew both soft and hard. "Why did you do this?"

Danr didn't want to answer this, either, but the words came. "I wanted to know what I would see."

"And what—"

"No!" Danr snapped up a hand to interrupt her. "Just no. You're going to ask what I saw. But, Aisa—the truth always comes out bad. Don't ask for it. Truth hurts."

"But still you *looked* at me," Aisa said. "Why do you think I wrap myself up, Hamzu?"

The words shot out of Danr like wasps from a hive. "Everyone knows it's to hide the bruises from Farek's rape and Frida's beatings, and because you're always cold."

"So I am," Aisa said in a flat voice. "Your country freezes me. But it is also because *this*"—she gestured at herself—"is all I have that belongs to me alone. *This* is the only thing I have that no one can see."

And he had violated it. He hadn't seen her body, but he had touched something much deeper than simple flesh. A sick feeling slid over him, mingling with the tension. But why should *he* be unhappy? Aisa had asked, and he had answered. It shouldn't be his fault that she asked for truth and became upset about the answer.

"My mother was right," he said. "No one likes the truth."

"It is not your place to decide if I will like the truth or not!" Aisa shot back. "It is wrong of you to keep these things from me. I am no longer a slave or a toy."

"And I'm not a troll's bastard to be kicked around, and insulted, and yanked from one end of the world to the other," Danr snarled. "I'm not your personal prophet who's forced to cough up answers when you demand them."

Aisa stared hard at him. "What. Did. You. See?"

And Danr had to answer. "Hunger. You want the elves in the worst way. You're afraid that if one stood here right now, you'd fall into his arms and weep for joy. I saw pain. You relive what Farek did to you at night and now you can't fully trust a man in the day. Not even me. I saw fear. You're afraid of me. You hope no man will ever touch you like a woman again. Not even me."

"Do you *want* to touch me that way?" Her words came out in a harsh whisper. "Do you want me in your bed?"

Now Danr fought. He clamped his mouth shut. He chewed his lips until salty blood flowed across his tongue. But truth pricked behind his eyes and pushed forward. He tried to scramble to his feet to run away, but the answer burst out before he could manage it.

"Yes," he gasped. "Just a moment ago I was thinking how I wanted you in my bed."

And then Aisa was gone, leaving an empty hole next to him at the fire. Danr slumped into himself and stared into the flames. His stomach was cold. Shit. Why did she have to ask him that? Why couldn't she have asked him something else, like how he felt about her or *why* he wanted her in his bed?

"Because I never stop thinking about you," he whispered to the dying fire.

But no—just like everyone else, she had to ask the foolish question, the one that got a bald-faced, painful answer, and like everyone else, she blamed Danr for what she herself had asked to hear.

Maybe he should run after and explain. She knew he couldn't lie. But even now his face burned with anger and shame. She had forced him to speak, pulled words out of him when she had known he wanted to remain silent. He felt violated and sick, as if icy Halza herself had run her hands over his soul.

And Aisa had said his mother had made a mistake in not bringing him to see the Stane. Aisa had no idea. Having a troll for a son had destroyed his mother's hope for a normal life, and being a truth-teller on top of it had only made things worse. Vik's balls, if Danr hadn't been born, she might have found a husband and lived her life in a warm house with human children on a prosperous farm. Instead she was doomed to cough her lungs out with animals in a stable. And Aisa claimed it was her fault for not taking Danr to see the other Stane?

He cut his eyes toward her. She was talking to Kalessa again with her back pointedly toward him. Well, fine. She could go off with her new blood sister, or whatever it was the orcs called it.

Talfi had forgotten him. Aisa spoke against his mother and all but called him a rapist. The victory he had felt earlier that day was burning to ash at his feet along with the fire.

"Ah! Here you are!" Hess hauled Danr to his feet despite the height difference between them. "I have sent night riders ahead of us to summon the other nests to a Council of Wyrms. It is a journey of nearly two weeks to the meeting place."

"Two weeks?"

"The wyrms are quick," Hess said, "but the herds slow us down."

"Herds," Danr repeated. He was tired and upset, and he was finding it hard to follow everything now, but he didn't feel he should say so.

"Herds, yes. The plains don't provide enough to feed ourselves and these ravenous beasts both." Hess gestured at the wyrm fence. "We rushed down here when we saw the wyrm smoke and left the herds behind with our herders, but tomorrow we will catch them up and leave for the council."

"Who is the council, sir?" Danr asked.

"Each nest chooses one man and one woman to sit on the Council of Wyrms. In the days before the Sundering, we orcs fought one another all the time over grazing lands and herds and eggs. After the Sundering, we created the council."

"What happens now?"

"We still fight over grazing lands and herds and eggs, but now the losers can complain to the council."

"Ah." The Sundering. The Axe. He kept getting distracted. The haft or the power was supposed to be in Xaron, while the elves kept the head in Palana, the capital city of Alfhame. "Sir, have you heard of the Iron Axe?"

Hess raised his eyebrows. "Of course! It was lost during the Sundering. What a weapon that would be!"

"I want to find it," Danr said, and explained, though since Hess hadn't actually asked about it, he was able to leave out the parts about Death and the Three. Instead he let Hess think Danr was only looking for it to ensure that the Kin could win the war against the Fae.

"Well!" Hess looked Danr up and down. Mostly up. "There's more and more and more to you, Prince Hamzu from under the mountain. This is a quest worthy of Fell himself, and your songs will speed across the grasslands long after you're gone."

"I don't want songs," Danr said. "Just the Axe. Do you know where the haft or the power might be?"

"Hmm. In the songs, this is the verse when the wise old man tells the young warrior where to find the weapon he seeks." Hess drummed his fingers on his thigh. "I must not be old or wise enough, because I have no idea."

Danr sighed. Of course not. When had anything been that simple?

"But perhaps someone at the council will know," Hess continued. "Many orcs there are much, much older than I." And before Danr could say more, Hess strode away.

Exhausted now, Danr turned his back on Aisa and the orcs and crawled into his tent, barely noticing that Talfi was already asleep inside.

Chapter Fourteen

It took a solid fortnight of riding to reach the Council of Wyrms meeting place. Danr had thought he was strong, but those two weeks nearly destroyed him. It wasn't the riding. It was Aisa.

Wyrm riding itself was a unique experience, both challenging and exhilarating. Danr had never been on the back of so much as a plow-horse, and he found the saddle, with its scent of leather and the strange smell of wyrm, intimidating. One orc held the wyrm's bridle for him while Hess himself showed Danr how to swing himself up into the seat. The saddle creaked, and Danr abruptly found himself high as a tree. The wyrm, which was easily long enough for three riders, dipped slightly under his weight, and Danr, feeling off balance, clutched at the saddle with both hands.

"Nix will not run off with you," Hess said. "He will follow wherever the nest goes. Hold yourself in place with knees and thighs. Here are the reins. It is much like a horse—pull gently in the direction you wish to go, and pull back to slow or stop."

And with those minimal instructions, they were off. Wyrms slithered ahead with both a forward and a side-to-side rocking

motion that made Danr a little dizzy until he adapted to it.
Then it became a little more fun. Once the nest got going and
Danr felt more sure of himself, he urged Nix to go faster, then
faster still, and the speed took his breath away. Wind rushed
past his ears, and the grass turned into a blur beneath his feet.
Faster and faster he flew across the green plain with the azure
sky above, and for a moment, the wind blew away Aisa and the
Iron Axe and Talfi's resurrection. He even managed to half
stand in the saddle, feeling tall and strong and fast with the
wyrm beneath him, flying breathlessly across the prairie. He
could run, slide, fly forever, never stop, leave all his troubles
behind him. He was light and air and glory all at once.

But then he felt Nix's movements change. The wyrm was
laboring, and his mouth was open, half panting. Guiltily
Danr reined him in. They had outpaced the nest, and he
slowed Nix to a bare crawl until first the scouts, and then the
main group caught up with them. The enormous herds of
sheep brought up the rear. The Eighth Nest consisted of
about three hundred orcs of all ages, and they flattened the
green prairie grass in a mile-wide swath wherever they
went. Hess gave him a silent nod of understanding and rode
past. Danr flushed a little and settled into a regular ride that
lasted days and days.

He learned a great deal during those days. Riding the
great wyrms wasn't a matter of simply clutching a saddle. It
involved balance and thigh muscles and shoulders. Unlike
the orcs, Danr was forced to use reins, which added even
more difficulty. The orcs gave him only cursory guidance—
they simply expected he could keep up. Danr had seen how
they treated people who couldn't keep up, so he did his best
to move ahead, even in the mornings, when his muscles
screamed and his bones begged him not to get into the saddle. After the first agonizing hour, however, his stiff body
warmed up and he was able to enjoy the ride again.

Talfi, another honored guest, had a wyrm as well. Most days, he and Danr rode side by side as the nest slithered forward, with scouts in the lead and the enormous herds of sheep bringing up the rear. Now that Danr had a chance to watch it at length, he found the prairie quite beautiful. A rumpled plain spread in all directions, covered with both emerald grass and carpets of sweet-smelling flowers—yellow roses and purple violets and sunny daisies and scarlet hyacinth and a rainbow of others Danr couldn't name. Few trees broke the landscape, but rich flocks of birds—geese and ducks and swans and pheasants and quail—rushed overhead, and the orcs brought them down with arrows and slings, letting them hang from saddles as they rode for later roasting. A relentless sun burned in the clear sky and threatened to crush Danr's head and eyes until one of the orcs, noticing his discomfort, gave him a wide hat of heavy felt. It was the thickest, finest hat Danr had ever owned, and it blocked the sun so well he barely noticed it was light out. He hadn't noticed how much sunlight headaches had been a part of his life until they stopped, and the difference lent a little exhilaration to balance out the body aches.

Anyway, it wasn't the aches that threatened to break him. Aisa avoided Danr with great proficiency. Wherever Danr was, Aisa simply was not. He suspected she had learned that skill as a slave. On the rare incidences he caught sight of her, she was with Kalessa. She rode daily beside Kalessa, also on a borrowed wyrm, and the two of them often ran ahead of the nest. Jealousy flared whenever he saw them together. He knew it was irrational, but he couldn't help it. And when he wasn't jealous, a strange mix of guilt and anger over his argument with Aisa's rejection pulled him down. She was angry at him for using his true eye on her, but he hadn't done it out of malice or cruelty. All right, he had been thoughtless, that much was true, but he would never hurt Aisa on purpose. And she had said bad things about his mother, the only person who had ever loved him, then forced—*forced*—him to speak when he had begged her to let him stay silent. How was that different from what he had done to her? She was being cruel and unfair in her own way, and the injustice of it simmered a slow anger in him.

At the same time, he felt the loss next to him where she usually walked, and he missed her voice and her sharp, sarcastic tongue with a pain that hurt more than sunlight. He lost weight, and it was difficult to crawl out of his tent every morning.

Talfi, on the other hand, thrived with a cheer that Danr half envied, half admired. He made several friends among the orcs, who still treated him with a certain amount of awe, and didn't seem overly bothered by his own death. Of course, he didn't remember it.

The orcs remained surprisingly busy while they rode, no matter how fast the wyrms went. They hunted birds and small animals, scouted for water and campsites, checked the herds, supervised children, and even performed small tasks such as darning clothes or repairing armor while in the saddle. In the evenings, they set up quick camps and went to bed. Hess said they were moving fast and spending more time traveling every day than normal. As a result of the long days, Danr didn't have much time to meet his orc hosts, and during the night, the two stars drifted closer and closer, eating away his time.

He did talk to Talfi while they rode. Talfi was hungry to know who he had been, and he pumped Danr for information. Danr told him everything he remembered about their friendship, how they had met at Orvandel's house, killed a wyrm on the road back to Alfgeir's farm, faced down a mob, and encountered the first *draugr* together. It all seemed so long ago, as if it had happened to different people.

For completeness' sake, he also told Talfi what had happened to him and Aisa under the mountain, how they had met the Three, and how Danr was trying to make alliances while finding the Iron Axe. But he avoided saying anything about Talfi being *regi*. Talfi didn't ask, and Danr couldn't bring himself to say the words. It was the strangest thing, knowing something about Talfi that Talfi himself didn't know, especially something as . . . as . . . well, Danr didn't know how to describe it. When Talfi had lost his leg, Danr suddenly found he didn't give a dead cat's whisker whether Talfi was *regi* or not—he only wanted his friend to live. And when Hess had killed Talfi, Danr's monstrous half had ripped free with an unexpected and terrifying power. Now, against all laws of nature, he had his friend back. Compared to that, a thing like who Talfi might love seemed as inconsequential as a mosquito to a warhorse. And yet . . .

A small bit of understanding crept over him. He was having trouble with this because this was outside the normal rules.

He snorted to himself. After a lifetime of living on a farm, he had killed a wyrm, visited mystic giants, become an emissary to trolls, argued with an earl, and Twisted halfway across the continent, but *this* was outside the normal rules?

Well, yes. It was. All the other things he had heard about in tales and stories. They were distant things that had come suddenly close, but at least he had known what they were. But *regi* men were only mentioned occasionally, and then with scorn and derision, as if they were monsters worse than the greatest wyrms. In the back of his mind, Danr had always known that trolls and giants and other such things existed, but it had never occurred to him that he might become friends with someone who was *regi*, let alone one who didn't actually know it yet. The stories gave you rules about

trolls and giants and even humans. But there were no rules
for *regi*, except that you were supposed to hate them, and no
matter how shocked he might be, Danr couldn't hate Talfi.
Not ever.

He found himself studying Talfi, trying to see if there
were any signs of it now that Talfi had no memory of himself. But what signs was he looking for? Feminine behavior?
A way of speaking? An unexplained desire to sew? Danr had
no idea. Maybe, now that Talfi had died and come back to
life, his desire for men had disappeared. Or maybe, now that
Talfi wasn't around human men anymore, he wouldn't notice he was *regi*. That brought another thought: did Talfi find
orcish men desirable? The thought sent a shudder over him.
On the other hand, Danr thought Kalessa was attractive. If
Danr thought orcs were good-looking, why shouldn't Talfi
think the same thing about humans? He sighed. It was all
very confusing. Much easier just to keep his mouth shut and
hope Talfi didn't ask.

Talfi also often touched Danr's pouch at his throat, and
Danr felt strange every time he did so. The pouch was the
only remnant Danr had of his mother, and seeing Talfi wear
it was like walking around naked while Talfi wore two
cloaks. Trouble was, he didn't know how—or if—he should
ask for it back. The pouch had been a grave gift, and no one
ever took a grave gift back.

He sighed again. Life back in Alfgeir's stable had been
dull and dirty, but at least it had been empty of stupid moral
problems.

"What was it like?" Danr asked one day as the nest
rushed across the prairie. The orcs spread out on their
wyrms in a great tapestry sliding across the grass ahead and
behind them. As he always did, Danr scanned for Aisa from
underneath his heavy felt hat, but he didn't see her, and the
lack made his chest tight.

"What was what like?" Talfi rode his wyrm with an easy skill, as if he were only remembering something he had learned long ago. Maybe he was.

"You know. To die and come back."

Talfi touched Danr's pouch—Danr twinged—and thought a moment. Then he shook his head. "I still don't remember. My first memory is of opening my eyes and seeing red cloth."

"That pouch," Danr said, trying to be delicate for once, "is special to you."

"Yeah." He lifted it to his nose and inhaled. "It's strange. When I touch it or smell it, I get . . . little images. Tiny memories that try to form, but don't quite. It's the same when I touch this." From under his shirt, he fished out the copper chain and the silver amulet with Ashkame on one side and the double-bladed axe on the other and ran his thumb around the perimeter. "Sometimes, when I feel its edges, I get . . . shadows. A battle. Metal clashing. Screams. Blood. A lot of blood. And water. Like I'm swimming or drowning or both. And sometimes I see a man with red hair and green eyes. He talks to me, but I can't hear what he's saying."

With a chill, Danr remembered their conversation on the road from Skyford, when Talfi had repeated those exact words.

"But when I touch this pouch, or smell it"—Talfi did both, and Danr wanted to snatch it from him—"it brings back other shadows. Big hands. A man with white hair. Feathers and arrows. And a stable with a tiny fire and smoked salmon. It's so close. Last night, I dreamed about them. I swear, I'm on the edge of remembering everything with this, somehow. But I'm not quite there."

Danr, who himself had been on the edge of asking for the pouch back, stopped his words. Maybe Talfi could get his memory back if he held on to the pouch. Maybe it smelled like Danr or maybe the pouch had hidden truth in it, or maybe it was something else. Danr guided his wyrm around a hillock, though the creature didn't really need guiding. "I see," he said instead.

"I'm kind of scared," Talfi confessed. "I don't know anything about myself except what you've told me, and you only knew me a few days. I don't know who my parents are or where I was born or how I got to . . . where was it? Skyford? Let alone how I came back to life."

Talfi's own wyrm ran its tongue out. Talfi asked abruptly, "Do you know where I came from?"

Danr shook his head. "I wish I did, Talfi. Now that Aisa's . . . well, you're the only friend I've got."

"Have I changed since I came back?"

"Except for the missing memories, you're exactly the same Talfi I knew," Danr said.

"Huh." He touched the pouch with his free hand. "Do you know where I got—"

"Talfi," Danr interrupted quickly, before he could finish a question Danr didn't want to answer, "how old are you?"

He shrugged. "It's kind of silly to ask. I don't—"

"Yeah, yeah. Dead, back to life." Danr shifted in the saddle and nodded to a pair of younger orcs who slithered past on wyrms of their own. "So, do you think this has happened more than once? When we first met, you told me your first memory was walking into Skyford. What if you died and returned back then, and—"

"And that's why I lost my memory," Talfi breathed. "Wow. Do you think something killed me on the way to Skyford?"

"I don't know what to think. But when you came back this time, your leg and your head had regrown." He thought a moment longer, letting the ideas move together like continents colliding. "What if . . . ," he said slowly, ". . . what if that healing helps with aging? What if you don't just heal missing heads—"

"I have more than one?" The joke, however, was a feeble one. Talfi had already seen Danr's point, but was reluctant to arrive at it himself, like a cat coming to the inescapable conclusion that the only way to cross the river involved a brisk swim.

"—but what if you also heal aging?" Danr finished. "You could have died and come back a dozen, a hundred, a thousand times, and each time you healed back to your original age. Vik, Talfi—*how old are you*?"

The wyrms slithered on, their odd gait both smooth and rocking at the same time. Behind them, a group of women burst into laughter. Talfi's fingers were white around the amulet and pouch at his throat.

"Maybe I only died that one time," he countered, but the argument was halfhearted.

"Do you really think that's true?" Danr said, voice low.

Talfi bit his lip, then shook his head. "I think I must be—"

"Ho, Talfi!" An orc, perhaps a year younger than Talfi, pulled his tiger-striped wyrm up beside them. His name was Jaxo, and he was Kalessa's brother. "Race me! If you dare." He flicked his wyrm's side with the ends of his reins and his wyrm bolted forward.

Talfi gave a mischievous grin. "Watch this!" He vaulted down from the saddle and sped away with the incredible speed Danr remembered from the day they fought the wyrm. Danr watched him go, wishing he could forget so easily.

Aisa dismounted the emerald wyrm and winced as her muscles protested. Kalessa leaped down beside her, supple as soft leather. Aisa sighed. Even the painkilling tea she brewed for herself every morning had minimal effect on riding a wyrm.

The elven hunger only made things worse. She had been hoping that the new climate of Xaron might mitigate it somewhat, but to her disappointment, the near-constant gnawing didn't abate in the slightest. Her first thought on waking every morning was of Lord Vamath's sweet and terrible touch, and her elven lord's face hovered over her when she went to sleep at night.

Alerted by Hess's fast-slithering scouts, the other nests were already arriving along with the Eighth at the council meeting place. This was at the southern edge of a network of rivers called Many Wyrms, a system of tributaries that twisted up to the warm waters of the northern ocean. Aisa had no idea how the orcs found the place—it all looked the same to her. Water and grass were plentiful for the herds, and the open space gave the wyrms room to stretch. Tents and shelters spread from horizon to horizon.

In the center of it all lay the one landmark that looked different: a crater large enough to swallow all of Skyford. Kalessa told her that a thousand years ago, the Sundering had flung up a chunk of rock. It had landed here, carving out this crater. The orcs had been using it as a central meeting place for centuries. Aisa had been expecting a dirt-filled hole, but the floor of the crater was as thick with grass and flowers as the rest of the prairie. On the north side of the crater stood an actual grove of ash trees, tall and thick and majestic. Kalessa said their seeds had been carried there by the Sundering, and the trees had sprouted the day the earth split. Far away, at the crater's very bottom, stood a great slab of a stone table, where, Aisa presumed, the Council of Wyrms actually met.

"We made good time," Kalessa said. The rest of the nest dismounted. As the nest who had called the meeting and who had brought with them the Great and Foolish Prince Hamzu, the Eighth Nest was allotted high-status camping space right next to the crater's edge, though what mechanism had decided this, Aisa could not determine.

"My legs will ache for years," Aisa admitted. Her knees were shaking, partly from the ride and partly from cold desire. She worked hard to push it away. It was all in her mind, she told herself. Elves were a horror who stole lives and bodies. But she couldn't help wanting them as well.

"Bah!" Kalessa, ignorant of Aisa's internal struggle, clapped her on the shoulder. "You are a fine rider, my sister. Soon you will command the wyrms without reins, and I will be there when you receive your egg and your saddle."

Aisa gave a small smile behind her scarf. Even after seven days together, she found it a little unnerving the way Kalessa so freely gave sisterly affection. During that awful duel, Aisa had nearly lost her water when Kalessa's sword came at her throat, and she had all but fainted with relief when Kalessa tossed the blade aside. She had taken Kalessa's offer of blood kinship without a second thought—a former slave's instinct for self-preservation. Only later in the tent they shared had she wondered if she had done the right thing. Aisa had no females in her family but her dead mother, and she didn't know how to react to a birth sister, let alone an instant sister. Kalessa, for her part, seemed unfazed.

"I saw it in your eyes," Kalessa said one day from wyrmback. "Your spirit is strong, and we are much alike, even if you are a human. So now we will learn how to be sisters, and our people will become strong together."

Aisa narrowed her eyes. "Is that why you did it? Was it some sort of ritual bonding for diplomacy?"

"Ha!" Kalessa snorted. "You have spent too much time with men. You think like them. Sometimes a woman does something because she knows it is right. Now you will spend time with me and let yourself be a woman again."

Aisa had to laugh, and it felt . . . good.

They had talked of many things while they rode together. Kalessa told of her life on the open plains, of the day she had watched her wyrm hatch, of helping her mother weave her first suit of armor, and Aisa had wondered if they had anything in common at all. But then Kalessa had spoken of the torture of growing up with five brothers and no sisters, of her secret love of swimming, of losing her aunt to coughing sickness, all things Aisa understood intimately. Shyly, Aisa mentioned how she had lost her own mother to the same disease, how she had spent days caring for her, to no avail, and Kalessa reached over from the saddle to hug her while their wyrms moved side by side.

"It is difficult to lose an elder woman," she had said, "and even more difficult when you have no other woman to talk about it with. Who else can truly understand how it feels?"

And here, Aisa had wept. Kalessa had wept with her, unashamed, and for the first time in her life, Aisa felt the release of shared pain. It even seemed to lessen the hunger, just a little.

It was, she decided, a fine thing to have a sister.

Several wyrms over, Danr climbed down from his own wyrm and stretched. He looked over in Aisa's direction, but she was already on the other side of Kalessa's wyrm, where Danr couldn't see. Whenever he turned his eyes—his *eye*—on her, she felt utterly exposed and naked, with Farek's or Vamath's cold hands roaming over her body. Worse yet, he didn't seem to understand what he had done, how badly he had violated her body and her trust. Hamzu had reached inside her with a cold, clawed hand and pawed over her very soul, and for that she couldn't forgive him. Even if she *could* forgive him, how did she know he wouldn't do it again? Any time he liked, he could close one eye and see her true self naked before him, and she wouldn't even know he had done it.

But even through the anger and betrayal, she kept expect-

ing to see him next to her, and the loss was as constant as
her hunger. He had effortlessly—and thoughtlessly—barged
through barriers she had thought impregnable, but she had also
done the same to him, hadn't she? In the privacy behind her
scarves, she could admit that forcing him to speak truth had
made her feel powerful, and she had done it, yes, to hurt him.
As he had hurt her. Did that make it right? She did not know,
and the ambiguity made her angry.

For a moment, she let herself think of living a life of her
own, perhaps in a small cottage at the seashore. People
would come to her for healing so she could earn her bread,
but some days they would find her cottage empty, because
on days when Rolk shone high and clear and the wind was
light, Aisa would row out onto the light waves to find the
merwomen. And swim with them.

"What is the nature of this argument you are having with
Prince Hamzu?" Kalessa asked, and not for the first time.
She reached under Slynd to loosen the saddle girth and he
expelled a heavy breath.

"There is no argument," Aisa replied as she always had
before.

"You humans," Kalessa said. "You hide behind your words,
but your bodies betray you. Why do you bother, when it is
obvious what is happening?"

"We just do," Aisa replied shortly. "Can I help with that,
sister?"

That evening, a procession formed, and a fight along with
it. Two orcs from each of the nine nests, one man and one
woman, dressed in glittering rainbow finery—bright feathers and singular scales, supple silks and flashing swords—
arrived at the crater's edge, ready to parade around the camp.
But as they lined up, Kalessa's parents, Hess and Xanda, who
represented the Eighth Nest, tried to take a place at the front
of the procession. The orc woman who represented the First

Nest shouted in outrage while everyone else gathered to watch.

"The Eighth Nest has no status!" the First Nest orc boomed. "Your herds are thin, your warriors are weak, and your victories are few!"

Here Kalessa looked both embarrassed and indignant. "He lies," she snarled, but only so Aisa could hear. "He was born into a Fourth Nest and married a woman of the Third Nest, then built an alliance with the Second, and stole two herds from the First. Before they could retaliate, their chieftain died, and he challenged the new, younger chief to single combat so his nest could become First. Now he acts like he's First as if he were born to it. Bah!" She spat.

Aisa shook her head, unable to follow this dizzying path through orcish politics. "Does it matter who goes first in the procession?"

"Of course! People will talk of this meeting for generations, and every bard will recount who went first to the table."

Hess and Xanda both slapped their wicker shields with their hands. Hess shouted, "We have with us the new emissary from the Stane, Prince Hamzu, Nephew of Queen Vesha, Emissary of the Dark Realms, and Confederate of the Kin Who Conquered Death. He has seen our worth and allied himself with our nest, and we demand promotion!"

This brought up a protest from the Second, Third, and Fourth Nests, and a great deal of shouting and shield-beating ensued. Unnerved, Aisa backed away, but Kalessa seemed unfazed. They were watching the argument near the boundary of the ash grove where the trees came up to the edge of the crater.

"Won't they kill each other?" Aisa whispered.

"Not unless someone draws a sword or says something about eggs." Kalessa was watching, absorbed with the rest of the crowd. Hamzu stood among the representatives, looking uncomfortable. Someone had made or lent him new clothes: a sun yellow shirt and black silk trousers and even a pair of brown boots inlaid with silver, probably the first piece of footwear he had ever worn in his life. The ridiculous felt hat was gone, and his dark hair had been washed and combed. He shifted from foot to foot next to Hess, trying to hide his uncertainty. Aisa almost felt sorry for him. Almost. Perhaps if he felt the same hungers she did, he would be more considerate.

"That Hamzu is the handsome one," Kalessa mused aloud while Hess argued with the chief of the First Nest. "His muscles. His eyes. A strong and striking warrior. He does lend us status, and they will have to let Mother and Father descend to the crater as something higher than mere Eighth."

"Hmm!" Aisa snorted. But even in her current unhappy mood, Aisa had to admit Kalessa was right. Hamzu was far better looking than anyone at the village had thought. Aisa had never understood how people could have called Hamzu ugly.

Well, that was untrue. She understood quite well. People saw what they wanted to, and when they saw Hamzu, they saw a troll instead of a person. Sometimes she wondered if those splinters the Three had knocked out really existed, or if the Three simply hit Hamzu so hard they changed his perspective. Perhaps they should have hit him harder.

As Kalessa predicted, the argument eventually settled. The Eighth Nest would not receive a promotion just yet, but for tonight only, its representatives and Hamzu would proceed beside the First into the crater.

The prairie sun was setting as the newly ordered procession paraded past shouting orcs—Aisa decided the orcs loved nothing so much as an excuse to shout—and trooped down the crater toward the stone table. Talfi, as the Kin who had cheated Death, was part of the procession as well, though

Aisa had no idea what he would lend to the council meeting. He knew little of events and remembered less. No one had even asked Aisa to attend. She had not wished to, not with Hamzu there, but she had been through everything Hamzu had been, and she should have been asked. It was another slight, and the more she thought about it, the angrier she became. Perhaps she should go down there anyway, force her way in, assert herself, and—

"Enough now." The emerald-cloaked shaman, the one who had been present at the fire, slid out of the thick shadows of the grove. "How foolish do you think we are, girl?"

Aisa jumped. Kalessa spun, hand on her sword, but when she saw who it was, she relaxed and bowed instead. "Shaman."

"You are not being ignored, girl. You merely have other responsibilities," the shaman said, and the voice that emerged from the hood was that of an old woman. The sound stirred Aisa's blood, but she couldn't say why. "Come now. Your sister, too."

Uncertain, Aisa glanced at Kalessa, who seemed just as nonplused.

"Honestly," the shaman said. "Do you think everything important happens only at the council? Quickly now—the Tree tips."

The words sent a pang through Aisa. They were the same words Bund and Vesha had used. Her breath left her. "Stop! What did you say?"

But the shaman had already withdrawn into the grove. Aisa ran after her, trailing scarves and rags. Kalessa, seeing her sister dash into shadow, didn't hesitate to follow. Branches plucked at Aisa and snatched at her clothes as she ran after the shaman through fading light. "Wait!" Aisa called. "What did you mean?"

But the shaman ignored her, and no matter how hard Aisa tried to catch up, she always remained a dozen steps behind. Several times she thought she had lost the shaman, only to see a glimpse of an emerald cloak disappear around a tree or through some undergrowth to her right or left. Kalessa remained with her, a silent orcish shadow.

Aisa's breath burned in her lungs. How big was this grove? Surely they must be coming to the other side by now. Or was the old woman twisting her in circles? Birds sang evening songs in the leaves, and the smell of moss and ferns rose around her. It was almost completely dark now, and Aisa could barely see. Only the sound of the shaman's footsteps ahead of her pulled her on. This was foolishness. She should—

There was a *wrench*, and Aisa's knees wobbled. Her gorge rose, and she only barely pulled her scarf aside in time to vomit. She was vaguely aware of Kalessa doing the same beside her.

"Vik's beard and balls!" Kalessa growled when the spasm passed. "What in nine hells was that?"

Aisa wiped her mouth with her sleeve, wincing at the sour taste. "We Twisted. The shaman took us somewhere else. Judging by how I feel, it was quite some distance."

"What is Twisting?" Kalessa got to her feet, sword drawn, and helped Aisa up.

"Stane magic. I didn't think orcs could use it. Where are we?"

Nothing much had changed. They were still in a grove of ash trees, though perhaps "forest" was a more accurate term. Wide spaces between the ancient trees were carpeted with short grass and low ferns. Twilight had fallen. Aisa saw no sign of the shaman. What had—

A thin, high scream rent the air. Aisa's heart jerked. Kalessa's sword leaped into her hand. Instinctively Aisa spent half a moment centering where the sound came from, and then she was running toward it with Kalessa beside her.

They dodged around a pair of trees and nearly stumbled over a brown mountain lion. Fear and shock constricted Aisa's chest. The lion was crouching over a little boy, its face dripping blood. It saw them coming and growled low.

"I have the lion," Kalessa whispered, her eyes on the beast.

"I have the boy," Aisa whispered back.

Kalessa shouted and waved her sword. The lion snarled with a sound like a woman screaming. Aisa's hands went cold, and her hair prickled beneath her scarves.

Kalessa jabbed at the lion. "Ha! Ha!"

The lion leaped aside with unnerving agility. Nothing that big should move so fast. It snarled and swiped at Kalessa. Kalessa danced aside.

The moment the little boy was free of the lion, Aisa darted to him. Blood stained the ferns, and her heart pounded at the back of her throat. How bad was it? She didn't even think about where the boy might have come from. Aisa rolled him over.

Golden hair spilled away from a bloody and beautiful face. The boy was an elf. Her hatred for his kind roared so intensely it made Aisa's jaw tighten and her hands clench. She wanted to see him dead at her feet. This child would grow up to become an elven lord, one who would enslave and rape and neuter thousands of humans over his long, long lifetime. Like a gleaming new adder sliding out of an egg-shell, the boy would cause endless pain and suffering. He wouldn't be able to help himself.

"What are you doing?" Kalessa cried. She was dancing backward, leaping away from the lion and circling. The lion snarled and spat.

Aisa forced herself to look at the boy's wounds. Two long gashes along his chest bled copiously. He would die without aid; that was certain. She could help him, however. Dried sphagnum moss to pack the smaller wound, stitching for the deeper one. He would live.

Or . . .

She could let him die. No one would know. Aisa need only say he was too far gone. Take Kalessa, run, let the lion feast on his flesh and the beetles chew his bones. This elf would hurt no one else.

The mountain lion swiped. Kalessa ducked under it and stabbed. Her sword went straight into the lion's chest. The lion roared like thunder, then choked. Blood gushed from its mouth.

But this was a *child*. Did he not have the right to make his own choices about his life? Perhaps he would grow up to be an exception. And when she looked at his pale little face, she knew she could not just leave him to die.

Swiftly she removed materials from her pack—and when had she brought that with her?—and set to work with moss and rags, sinew and needle. No water to boil anything, so she doused everything with sharp-smelling liquor.

Kalessa leaned over her shoulder. "How is—Vik's balls!"

"Yes." Aisa continued to work. "He must have wandered over the border. Either that, or—" Her mouth went dry. "—the Twist sent us to Alfhame. The country of the elves."

Kalessa worked her jaw back and forth at that. She said in a grim voice, "Where are his parents?"

"If I knew, I would not be working on him right now." She tied a final knot. "The lion?"

"Dead." Kalessa raised her sword to the tree branches. "Ha! A fine opponent! Mother and Father will be proud to hear of this!"

"Your sister is also proud," Aisa said. She rolled the elven boy into her arms and stood, a little unsteadily. Kalessa tried to help, but Aisa shook her head. "Your hands must be free in case that lion has a mate. We should find shelter for this boy."

"Where? I don't—" She halted and sniffed. "Do you smell that?"

Aisa checked. Wood smoke drifted on the air. "I do. This way."

The boy was light at first, but he became heavier. Tears ran down her face, but she moved ahead with grim determination.

It felt like years, but was only a few moments later that they saw a light ahead of them. Sprites, Aisa knew, sometimes fluttered through the forest, using their glowing forms to lure travelers into swamps or over cliffs, just for fun. Praying this wasn't the case, she kept her eyes on the light and continued on, trying to ignore the unconscious boy in her arms. Eventually they came to a stone house at the base of a large, multitrunked ash tree. It was unlike any of the rounded houses Aisa had seen among the northern Balsians, or the square, sandstone houses among the people of Irbsa, where Aisa had been born. It also looked nothing like anything the elves had ever created. The house was built from round fieldstones fitted together with mortar. Tight thatching provided the roof, and there were two large windows in front. Both had glass in them, something Aisa had only seen in enormously wealthy households. Warm yellow light shone through them.

Aisa hesitated, the boy still in her arms, but Kalessa strode fearlessly to the door. Before she could knock, however, it whipped open. More light spilled over Aisa and Kalessa, blinding Aisa. No one was there.

"Hello?" Kalessa said. She poked her head inside, then went in. Aisa hesitated and followed. The boy needed shelter; Aisa needed rest. That overrode any concerns.

The moment she crossed the threshold, the boy snapped awake. He squirmed and wriggled until the startled Aisa put him down. Before she could react further, the boy . . . changed. His build blurred like running water. He grew taller, and his build thickened. In seconds, he had vanished and standing between Aisa and Kalessa was the emerald-cloaked shaman, but she was taller and broader than before.

Kalessa's sword was ready. "What is happening? Who are you?"

"Shut the door before all the heat gets out," the shaman said. When Kalessa blinked, she added, "Honestly, child! If I wanted to hurt you, I would have done it already. Quickly! We have much to do, and the Tree is tipping as we speak."

Kalessa sheathed her sword and folded her arms. "I think this is your decision, my sister."

Aisa looked at the threshold and at Kalessa. Then she straightened her back, pushed the elven hunger aside, and shut the door.

Chapter Fifteen

The inside of the house was big. Too big. With pale wooden floors and thick-beamed ceilings and tables and chairs. Aisa stood timidly next to Kalessa in the kitchen, feeling like a mouse seeking crumbs while a cat slept in the corner. Lamps and candles occupied dozens of sconces, but they didn't actually burn. They simply glowed with a warm light. Intricately carved shelves held cooking utensils and fat sacks of foodstuffs. An upright loom stood against one wall, half covered in fine white cloth. In one corner was a trapdoor with a bucket next to it. Aisa drew her scarves more tightly about her, feeling tiny and ragged in this fine place.

A bright fire burned in a fireplace. Aisa hadn't seen a chimney since her time with the elves. Four large windows were set into each wall, in direct contradiction to the single pair Aisa had seen outside flanking the front door. Moreover, the scenes outside the windows didn't match. One window looked out into a forest covered with ice and snow, one looked out on a mountain covered in a spray of new flowers, one looked out on a plain of green grass under an azure sky, and one looked out at an oak tree robed in scarlet leaves.

"What sort of house is this?" Kalessa breathed.

"The sort that belongs to me." The shaman, now a full head taller than Aisa remembered, dropped into a stool next to the fireplace and stretched, reaching to the flames. Her hands reminded Aisa of Hamzu's—thick and heavy. The shaman's fingers, however, were tipped with black claws.

"Shape-shifter," Kalessa said flatly.

"No, child." The shaman's cloak pushed itself back, revealing a heavy, lined face that reminded Aisa of a walnut. It was framed with a mane of uncombed white hair. "Out there, you see what you expect to see. In here, illusions come to die."

"I did not expect to see an elven child," Aisa said.

"Child, if you didn't expect to see elves everywhere, you wouldn't be so hungry all the time." She rubbed her hands over the flames. "You had to pass a test before you could come here, and that was what your own mind conjured up. Don't blame me."

"I do not understand," Aisa said. "What test?"

"Some girls see an apple tree that begs to be harvested," she said. "Others find bread in the oven that asks to be taken out. You two find an elf and a lion. I can see you'll be difficult."

Aisa didn't know what to say to that. At least her hunger had faded back to its normal level, and she was able to manage it again. She changed the subject. "You look like Grandmother Bund. And you sound like her."

"If you like, if you like." She picked up a thick, heavy stick from the hearth and poked at the fire with it. "Over time, women with power merge with me, or I merge with them. We all become one. People have called me Bund and Percht and Berchta and even . . ."

". . . Grick?" Kalessa said, awed.

"If you like," she replied again. "But you can call me Old Aunt."

"Why are we here, great lady?" Kalessa asked.

"When the Tree tips, it can turn over and change the

world or crash to the ground and destroy it," Old Aunt said. "The two of you can help it turn. But not as you are, oh no."

"What does that mean?" Kalessa demanded.

"It means you have problems. I brought you here to get you past them." Old Aunt dropped her cloak to the floor behind her stool and from the recesses of her dress pulled a pipe, which she proceeded to fill from a wooden box on the hearth. Then she plucked a red coal from the fireplace with her bare fingers to light it. She grinned, showing sharp yellow teeth. "Or perhaps I'll devour you. I haven't decided yet. The Tree is still tipping."

Aisa forced herself to stay where she was, though her instincts were telling her to run for the door. "Tell me, Old Aunt—are all the great powers in the universe women? So far, I have met three giants, Death, a trollwife, and now you."

Old Aunt tossed the coal back into the fire and puffed on her pipe. "Why do you ask?"

"If women control everything," Aisa said, "they're doing a terrible job of it. They allow the men to kill and rape and steal and do anything else they please."

"Hmm." Old Aunt nodded. "Your question tells me much, young Aisa, and I will have an answer for you, but you will have to earn it."

Aisa sighed. "I have angered my elven master to earn exile. I stole the eye of the Three to earn knowledge. I fled my master to earn freedom. I followed a foolish troll into the underworld, and I healed a boy who came back from the dead. What else must I do to prove myself worthy?"

"You must clean," said Old Aunt.

Silence hung like an anvil in the air. "I do not believe I heard that answer correctly," Aisa said at last.

"Housework, girl. Every day, you will sweep my floors and wash my dishes and haul my water and cook my meals and dip my candles and brew my beer and do whatever else

I require. And when all those duties are done, girlie, you will take my feather beds outside and beat them until the feathers fly so thick and fast that snow falls in the parts of the world that need it. And when you're all done with that, I'll give you the answer you demand."

"And what must I do?" Kalessa asked. "If I cook and clean, you will find yourself thinner and dirtier than when I began."

"You will do housework of a different sort," Old Aunt replied with a sharp-fanged grin. "It will be easier to show you than tell you. And don't worry, girl, you'll get a nice reward, too."

"I want a *good* reward," Kalessa said. "Something I'd really want, not a sarcastic reward like pitch poured all over me."

"Yes, yes, yes." Old Aunt waved a hand. "Something nice. Do we have a bargain?"

Something occurred to Aisa. "How long will this go on?"

"That," Old Aunt said in a low voice, "will depend completely on you."

The work began that evening. Aisa cooked a rich supper of salmon roasted with mushrooms and new potatoes and strawberries with cream and bread pudding and plenty of mead to wash it down. Kalessa, divested of her woven armor, set to work sharpening an impressive set of knives on a whetstone while Old Aunt sat by the fire, puffing on her pipe. Aisa expected the sullen silence of the sort she had gotten from Frida in Farek's house, or the quiet of the sickroom punctuated with her dying mother's occasional cries for help. As she cleaned a new-caught salmon—and where had it come from?—she found herself automatically tensing, her eyes flickering from side to side, her ears stretched to their limits, her body ready at any moment to dodge a blow or rush to her mother's side. But none of that came. Instead Kalessa started talking about how the kitchen reminded her of her grandmother's kitchen fire, even though that place had been a pit outside a tent.

"It has the same feel," she explained, and picked up another knife from her seat behind the whirling whetstone. "Did you know your grandmothers, my sister?"

Aisa shook her head and carefully deboned the salmon. "My father's parents died before I was born, and I never even learned who my mother's parents were. She never spoke of them. I only knew that she came from somewhere far away from Irbsa."

The quiet, friendly talk continued while they worked and Old Aunt watched, and the scene filled Aisa as sweet liquor filled a jug. She'd had no idea how good simple talk could feel. A bit of the tension lifted from her shoulders. Even the hunger eased.

Supper was a fascinating and monumental event. How fine a thing it was to cook a rich meal and then sit down to eat it! As a slave, she had always eaten leftovers and crumbs at the smoke-filled hearth. The orcs and trolls, kind as they were, had given her strange food. This was food she could make as she liked and devour until she was full. Even washing up afterward was pleasant, with Kalessa to help and the soft scent of Old Aunt's pipe.

Afterward, Old Aunt pointed Aisa to a room with a strange bed in it—a shelf with a big bag of feathers for padding and a smaller bag of feathers for a pillow. Thick quilts were piled atop the entire affair for warmth. A lamp stood beside a pitcher of water and a bowl on a table in the corner for night and morning washing, and one of those incredible glass windows looked out over a moonlit beach, where soft waves lapped at brown sands. The luxury took Aisa's breath away. Her amazement grew when she discovered that she and Kalessa wouldn't be sharing the room or the bed— Kalessa had a room of her own.

"The door latches," Old Aunt said, "from the inside. Good night now."

After she left, it took Aisa a moment to understand what she meant. With trembling fingers, Aisa closed the latch with a solid *clunk*. Four thick walls stood guard around her, and the only way in was a door that she alone controlled. For the first time in years, Aisa felt completely, totally safe.

For a moment, she didn't move. Then she threw her hands wide and spun in a giddy circle. The relief was so powerful she didn't know what to do with herself. Suddenly her bindings felt too close, too confining. With a little cry of happiness, she unwound the rags from her hands, noticing for the first time that the blood from the elven boy's wounds had vanished, and flung them into the corner. Then she cast back her hood, tossed aside her dirty dress that smelled of sweat and wyrms, and unwound the scarves from her head and body. These she also cast into the corner, and she stood in the center of the room in her underthings with a feeling of lightness. Night black hair spilled down her back, and she ran her hands through it, feeling it rumple soft beneath her fingers and scratching her itchy scalp. It was a fine thing to wash from the basin and sponge away days of dust and travel, and never once did she have to hurry or worry that Farek with his hard hands or Hamzu with his piercing eye might barge in.

In a trunk at the foot of the bed, she found fresh new clothes, and a long, soft shift she assumed was for sleeping in. For all these things, Aisa decided she would work for Old Aunt as long as the woman—or whatever she was— would have her, and Hamzu could twist in the wind. As she slid between clean sheets on a delightfully comfortable bed, the butterfly sound of gentle singing wafted under the door. The tune had no words, just a melody soft as rising bread and soothing as a mother's touch. It sent Aisa into a deep, comfortable sleep.

In the morning, Aisa woke easily and dressed in the fresh white clothes she found, including a clean white scarf to wrap around her face and a hood to pull over her hair. There were, however, no rags to wrap her hands in. And her clothing from last night had disappeared. Aisa glanced uneasily at her bare hands and at the latched door. Well, it was only Kalessa and Old Aunt out there. No men to stare at her bare skin. Gingerly, feeling oddly naked, she left the sleeping room and found her way to the kitchen. Outside one of the windows, an orange sun was just creeping over the horizon. Old Aunt was just settling onto her stool by the fireplace, which had been banked for the night. Aisa hurried to stir it up and add wood as Kalessa wandered in wearing a new tunic—also white—and buckling on her sword in the absent way Aisa already recognized as automatic to her. Her golden eyes were still heavy with sleep, and her auburn braid was still down for the night. Kalessa was not a morning person.

"Just in time," Old Aunt observed as Aisa set the table with cheese, bread, and small beer for breakfast. Old Aunt poked at the fire with her stick. Aisa again thought of Bund and the shaman and even of Hunin's brother the priest. Did everyone with power brandish a stick to show it? She wondered what it would be like to wield one, be in such a position of power herself.

"Thank you, sister," Kalessa said with her mouth full. "You are so quick at setting a table. I'll fetch the water and more wood, since you have become our food maiden."

"I'm afraid not," Old Aunt said from her stool. Her plate was on the stone hearth. "You have other duties today. In fact . . ." She leaned back to glance out the window. ". . . you should finish that bread and draw your sword. Aisa will tend to the washing up."

Aisa tensed, and Kalessa was on her feet in a flash, her bronze sword out. "What are you talking about?"

The kitchen door smashed open. Sunlight slammed into Aisa's eyes. To Aisa's utter shock, Hamzu burst into the room. Foam and saliva flecked his lips. His left eye glowed like an angry sun, and its gaze penetrated Aisa's very soul until she stood naked before a jeering crowd. With a bull's roar, Hamzu rushed straight at Aisa. Cold terror washed over her and turned her ribs to ice. She couldn't move, couldn't think as he thundered toward her, overturning tables and benches along the way.

Kalessa was already moving. She interposed herself between Aisa and Hamzu, her sword up, and she roared a battle challenge of her own. He slashed at her with his claws—when had he gotten claws?—but she eeled aside. Her sword flicked out and scored his massive chest. Blood flowed. He bellowed thunder again and slashed. His claws raked Kalessa's off arm, leaving great furrows. Aisa cried out. Kalessa didn't seem to notice. She stabbed at Hamzu's heart, but he caught her wrist and twisted. Her sword clattered to the floor and slid away. Without hesitation, Kalessa kicked Hamzu in the groin. He grunted and let her go.

"She fights dirty," Old Aunt remarked from the heart. "What a delight."

Hamzu bent for a moment from the pain. Foam dripped from his mouth to the floor. Fear gripped Aisa in an iron vise. Her mind couldn't encompass what she was seeing. She wanted to run, but she was also terrified that Kalessa would be hurt. And Hamzu—what was wrong with Hamzu that he would come here and attack her this way? It made her sick.

Blood ran freely from Kalessa's wounds, and from the table she snatched the knife Aisa had used to cut meat. When Hamzu straightened, she leaped straight at him. The knife gleamed in the firelight. With a shout, she plunged it straight into his glowing red eye. Aisa flinched at the sound it made. Hamzu bellowed to shake the windows. He staggered back-

ward, his massive clawed hands over his face. Kalessa dove
for her sword, but Hamzu was already stumbling for the
door. He lurched into the sunlight beyond and his pain-filled
bellowing faded into nothing.

Aisa stared wildly about the room, her heart pounding
like a drum in her chest. Kalessa regained her feet and stood
with her sword at the ready until the last of Hamzu's yells
disappeared. Only then did she sheathe her weapon and
drop to one of the upright benches. Old Aunt poked calmly
at the fire with her stout stick, as if watching children at
play. Silence fell over the room. It lay thick and heavy. Outside, a bird called, and then another. At last, with a pang,
Aisa noticed the blood running down Kalessa's arm.

"You are hurt!" she said.

"Scratches," Kalessa said, but winced as Aisa gently
probed them. Aisa felt Kalessa's pain in her own arm, and
she got angry all over again at Hamzu, and then she felt confused. That couldn't possibly have been him, could it? He
would never do such a thing, and he certainly could not have
found this place.

"These must be cleaned and bandaged." Aisa leaped to
her feet, glad of something to take her mind off what she
had just seen. "I'll get my—"

"Everything you need is in the cupboard over there." Old
Aunt pointed with her stick. "And get me some more smoke-
leaf for my pipe, while you're at it. I'm nearly out."

Aisa opened the cupboard and found jars and boxes of
herbs and distillations, liquors and pastilles, all neatly labeled
in both pictures and words. Many she had only heard of but
never had the chance to use. A set of tiny knives and needles
hung on the door, and a large basket contained ample sup-
plies of thread, sinew, and bandages. She pulled down what
she needed and took it back to Kalessa, who bore Aisa's min-
istrations stoically, though the liquor she used to clean the

wounds must have hurt like fire. Aisa felt awful about causing her new sister more pain, but there was no way around it.

"I'll be quick," she promised, and set her jaw. "Old Aunt, who was that and how did he find this place?"

"You tell me, dear." Old Aunt drew idle designs on the hearthstones with her stick. "You brought him here."

"I did no such thing!"

"You are pressing that wound very hard, my sister," Kalessa said. Her white tunic was a wreck.

"Sorry." Aisa let up. "I did not bring Hamzu here. You know that."

Old Aunt blew out more pipe smoke. "Child, do you know why you're here?"

"No." Aisa continued to work. The wounds were clean. Kalessa was sitting in a puddle of blood and liquor, but at least the bleeding had slowed.

"You are here because if the Tree tips with you in your current condition, everything will go as wrong as a cat in a soap kettle. Hamzu there showed it."

"I do not understand." Aisa reached for bandages. "Why do people who have knowledge never speak plainly about it?"

"Hamzu did, and you found it unpleasant," Old Aunt shot back.

"That was unfair."

"Was it?" Old Aunt's voice was kind. "Tell me what happened, then."

Aisa started to refuse, but then her brown eyes met Kalessa's golden ones. Kalessa touched Aisa's hand in a quiet gesture she hadn't felt since her mother died. "I would like to hear, too, sister."

And so she talked while she wound bandages. Once she got started, it was easier to talk than she thought. She told the entire story, starting at Hamzu losing his splinters at the meeting with the Three, and ending with his betrayal. Kalessa and Old Aunt merely made encouraging noises and listened. When Aisa finished, she felt wrung out, and her eyes were wet.

"Hmm," said Old Aunt. "That was a difficult thing for you."

"To say the least," Aisa replied.

"Does he hate you that much, do you think?"

"Hate me?"

"Oh my, yes. To touch you with truth that way, he must despise you very much."

Aisa cast about, confused. "No . . . I don't think he despises me."

"Then why would he do such an awful thing?" Old Aunt said. "I'm not being sarcastic, child. That's an honest question. If he doesn't hate you, why would he hurt you so much?"

"I don't know," Aisa said shortly. Lying. Who did this old woman think she was?

"Kalessa is here for a reason, you know," Old Aunt said, abruptly changing the subject in the ruined kitchen.

"Am I?" Kalessa perked up a bit. Her bandage made a neat sleeve around her upper arm.

"You're Aisa's defender. I told you that in this place, illusions come to die. Aisa's half-troll love—"

"He's no such thing!" Aisa protested.

Old Aunt shrugged. "Half-human love, then. That image of him, the image that you hold, comes here to die, and it will keep coming here until it has no reason to return."

"I see. My sister is deceiving herself," Kalessa said.

"Indeed." Old Aunt sucked her pipe, and it made a dry sound. She set it aside. "You, my little orc, have an utter lack of self-deception. Refreshing, really. Since you have no illusions to fight, you can defend Aisa from hers. Until she stops calling them here."

"I have no illusions about Hamzu!" Aisa said. "None!"

Loud footsteps tromped outside. They grew louder.

"Really? Because it sounds like *none* is coming closer by the moment, and your champion is wounded."

Kalessa got to her feet and hid a wince. "I will defend you, sister. He will not hurt you."

Aisa saw the pain Kalessa was trying to hide, and she cursed the fact that she knew nothing of blades and armor. The coming footsteps grew louder, each one a doom.

"Why would he hurt you if he doesn't hate you?" Old Aunt repeated softly.

Aisa licked dry lips. "He wouldn't. Not on purpose."

Outside, the footsteps paused.

"Then why did he hurt you?"

"I don't know."

The footsteps started again, louder. The cottage floor shook, and dishes rattled in the cupboards. Aisa wanted to curl up into a ball on the floor. Kalessa moved stiffly toward the door.

"Speak, girl," Old Aunt said. "He's coming again."

The words spilled out of her. "He . . . maybe it was a mistake. He didn't mean to do it, but he still did it, and it hurt me."

The footsteps paused again, just outside the open door. A shadow fell across the threshold, big and black and heavy. Kalessa tensed, her sword ready. Sweat trickled around Aisa's hairline and ran down her cheek.

"It hurts most when someone you love betrays you, doesn't it?" Old Aunt said.

The shadow leaned forward.

"Yes," Aisa whispered in a tiny voice. That one word pulled the secret out of her like a baby bloody from the womb and laid it on the table for all to see. She squinched her eyes closed, waiting for the inevitable blow to come—either a physical blow or a blow of painful words. But none came. She opened her eyes and saw only Old Aunt nodding at the hearth and Kalessa reaching forward to embrace her, the sword in its sheath.

"I am glad my sister has a love," she said into Aisa's ear. "Everyone should be in love. Warriors fight better when they love together, and lovers love better when they war together. I hope you find Olar and Grick's own happiness with him."

The tension drained away, and Aisa felt strangely light. They hadn't judged her or said a single cruel word. She might float away, up the chimney and into the sky to Valorhame itself.

The shadow at the door paused, then slipped away without another sound. Kalessa let out a burst of breath.

"Well," Old Aunt said, drawing on the hearth again. "He betrayed you, no question, and it was cruel. But he didn't intend to do it, and you still love him. Can you forgive him?"

Aisa blew her nose on a spare bandage. "I hope so. I think so. Is this enough?"

"For today, yes. And now it is time for daily work. You haven't brought me any smoke-leaf, my kitchen must be put aright, and the feather beds haven't been touched. Work, girl! Work, work, work!"

Chapter Sixteen

Aisa spent days and days cleaning and cooking and sweeping and hauling. And when that daily work was done, she dragged each of a dozen heavy feather beds to the door and beat them until white feathers flew. Kalessa, meanwhile, rested her arm and sharpened metal and, once the bandages came off, helped lift what Aisa could not. Although the work was the same as the slave labor she had done for Frida and Farek, it was also nothing like it. Here, she woke up every morning in a room she could latch, she dressed in fresh clothes and scarves (though she still left her hands bare), she ate fine meals, and she enjoyed simple conversation with her sister and Old Aunt. Often, when she spoke, it was about Hamzu, of how they had met, and of his dreams, and how he had saved her life and of how she secretly hoped they could find a life together. It would be difficult—a human and a half-blood Stane, but when had life ever been easy for either of them?

One day, Aisa asked Old Aunt, "Isn't everyone at the tribe worried about us?" Strange that it had never occurred to her to think of this before. And she had forgotten all about the Iron Axe.

"Worried?" Old Aunt poked at the fire with her stick. When Aisa looked closely at it, she saw intricate carvings on the smoke-blackened surface, and the carvings seemed to writhe. The stick fascinated her, and she wondered where Old Aunt had gotten it.

"We've been here for days and days," Aisa reminded her. "They'll think we've disappeared."

"I wouldn't concern myself over it, dear. You have other problems to think about."

Aisa, who was scrubbing a tabletop, stopped. "Like what?"

The kitchen door slammed open. Farek stormed into the room. Aisa's blood chilled and her bowels ran with ice.

"I've found you, little slut!" He was taller than she remembered, and fatter. With every step, he grew bigger and fatter until the floor creaked beneath his bulk. Spittle drooled from his pudgy lips, and his sausage fingers reached forward, ready to press her under his body and suffocate her. Aisa's every muscle was paralyzed with fear. Suddenly she was back in the stable, with the smell of goat shit and the sound of cows lowing around her, and Farek was shoving her down and pushing aside her clothes and grunting in her ear and filling her with cold and ice. He was trapping her again, ready to take her to the floor.

And then Kalessa was there. She slammed into fat Farek from the side. He made an "oof" sound and went down. Kalessa went with him. They rolled across the floor, crashing into tables and overturning benches. Kalessa flailed at Farek with a fury, kicking and punching in a whirlwind fury, but Farek's impossible bulk seemed only to absorb the blows. He laughed and pawed at Kalessa as they fought. Somehow he managed to roll on top of her, and his heavy weight pressed her down. Kalessa gasped for air. Aisa's own breath strangled in her throat, and still she couldn't move.

"You're mine," Farek gasped into Kalessa's ear. "All mine."

The awful words spoken to Kalessa shattered Aisa's paralysis. Her fear evaporated, replaced with hot anger and desperation. She snatched a butcher knife off the table and slid it across the floor toward Kalessa. Her hand closed over the handle. Kalessa swung, and the knife connected with a meaty *thunk*. Farek howled in pain and outrage. Blood gushed down his side. He rolled off Kalessa and scrambled to his feet while Kalessa coughed and gasped. Farek tried to swing at her with his fist, but Kalessa ducked and sliced him with the knife instead. More blood flowed.

Clutching at his bleeding forearm, Farek snarled, "You'll pay for that later, little slut!" Then he lumbered out the door and disappeared.

Aisa ran over to help Kalessa to her feet. "You call up some terrible illusions, sister," she said. "Even for a human."

Guilt washed over Aisa. Twice Kalessa had taken pain meant for Aisa herself. Twice Aisa had come close to losing her entirely. Now that the fight was over, the realization that Farek—or this image of him—could have killed Kalessa made her shake with unrealized panic.

"I'm so sorry," Aisa whispered. "So sorry."

"No, no." Kalessa dismissed her apology. "It was foolish to let him close to me like that. My fault."

"You must not take such risks on my behalf." Aisa brought her to a bench while Old Aunt wordlessly relit her pipe at the hearth. "You must not—"

Kalessa flared. "What sister would deny me the honor of fighting for her?"

"I . . . I don't . . ."

"You, Aisa, must occasionally let people take care of you," Kalessa said, "instead of always taking care of others. Oh yes, I know. Your sharp tongue disguises your need to do this, but even the healer sometimes needs—ow!" She gasped, cursed, and gasped again.

"A pig fell on you and hurt your ribs," Aisa observed tartly. "You are to stay as still as possible while I make medicine." Then her voice softened. "And I will make no more remarks about your risks if you make no more remarks about my sharp tongue."

"Agreed. Sister."

"It's not over yet, dear," said Old Aunt as Aisa rummaged through the medicine cupboard. "Why did you bring Farek here?"

"I didn't bring—"

Heavy, fat footfalls fell outside the open cottage door. Aisa froze.

"Well?" Old Aunt asked. "You hated Hamzu, or you claimed to. Farek, another big man, is someone you fear. Why is that?"

Aisa stood paralyzed again in front of the cupboard. The words stuck in her throat. For some reason, the hunger for elves awoke and raged through her.

"He's an illusion," Old Aunt said. "He's only big and powerful because you remember him that way. How much power do you want to give him?"

"Farek has power," Aisa cried. "He hurt me."

"In what way did he hurt you?" Old Aunt asked in her relentlessly gentle voice.

The footsteps grew louder again.

"He *raped* me," Aisa shouted. "He took me into his stable two and three times a week and pushed me to the floor and he raped me."

The footsteps paused.

"The bastard," Kalessa spat. "I'll cut his balls off."

"I'm so sorry," Old Aunt said quietly. "That was a terrible thing he did to you. It was awful and unfair and horrible in the worst way. I can't think why anyone would do something so horrifying to someone so kind."

The acknowledgment of the pain ran through Aisa like hot water through ice. It was the first time anyone had recognized her ordeal for what it was, and she hadn't realized how powerful that simple act could be. Tears pricked at the back of her eyes and choked her throat. The hunger prowled through her like a ravenous tiger. Words spilled out of her.

"I'm not kind," she said. "I have a sharp tongue and Farek was punishing me for it. I deserved everything he did to me."

Farek's heavy shadow appeared in the doorway, and his harsh whisper wafted through. ". . . *you're mine* . . ."

"No," Old Aunt said. "No one deserves such things. Farek wasn't punishing you. He was a cruel man who only thought of his own pleasure."

"But—"

Old Aunt quietly got to her feet, leaning on her stick, and the presence of the goddess Grick filled the cottage. Walls groaned and shadows fled. "Remember who I am, girl, and remember the authority behind my words."

Aisa swallowed. It was true. Old Aunt was so down-to-earth and . . . grandmotherly, Aisa had forgotten who she really was. Resolve filled Aisa. Strength returned to her limbs, and she stormed over to the open door. Farek was just outside, leering and grasping with his sausage fingers. Blood ran down his face and side. The awful hunger raked at her, goaded her.

"You're *nothing* to me!" she spat. "You have no hold on me or mine. You are no man, and dog shit has more honor."

With every word, Farek shrank. His fat melted away and he grew smaller and smaller, until he was the size of a man, a child, a dog. He looked up at her in fear. The hunger abruptly let up.

"Go fuck a goat!" she snapped, and slammed the door.

"That's my sister!" Kalessa said from her bench.

Old Aunt sank back to her stool by the fire. "Very nice. Good delivery, fine timing, excellent grasp of the vernacular. But I wonder . . ."

Aisa, who was leaning with her back against the door and feeling amazing, proud, and powerful, gave a heavy sigh. "What now?"

"You once told Talfi that you never wanted a man to touch you again." Old Aunt blew out a cloud of aromatic smoke. "Is that really true?"

"I . . ." Aisa paused. She had been about to say it was indeed true, but suddenly she wasn't so sure. "I do not know."

"Well, then, how about we get this mess cleaned up?" Old Aunt said. "And by *we*, I mean *you*. I have a pipe to smoke."

Kalessa, it turned out, had a cracked rib. Aisa spent many more days—she lost count of the number—nursing her and keeping house for Old Aunt. Kalessa chafed at the time she had to spend immobile, but Aisa was firm with her.

"The more you move about, the longer it will take to heal," she said.

"Orcs heal faster than humans," she grumbled from the padded bench Aisa had set up for her in the kitchen opposite Old Aunt's spot at the hearth.

"Even so." Aisa handed her a mug of ale. "I still know so little of orcs. How do you choose your wyrm?"

Kalessa's eyes lit up. "Slynd. I miss him. I hope he is not worrying over me."

"Do wyrms worry?"

"They are very intelligent, much more so than simple serpents. You have to be strong to command one from the line of the Scarlet Wyrm." She drank from the mug. "When I was ten and a woman, our nest went to the hatching ground where the wyrms buried their eggs. It takes a week or more for them all to hatch, and we all wait for them to crawl out of the ground so we can claim them."

"Do you form a lifelong bond by looking into their eyes?" Aisa asked.

Kalessa laughed. "Nothing so simple. When Slynd came

out of the ground, I wrestled him. We rolled across the ground with the rest of the nest cheering for me and the other children who wrestled with the other wyrms. It was like fighting an iron band, and more than once I wanted to give up. Slynd tried to bite me several times, but his teeth hadn't come in completely, and he only scraped me. It still left scars." Kalessa held up her arms to show the marks. "But in the end, I wrestled him to submission. The contest made him hungry, so I fed him a baby sheep, and that made him mine."

"I fed a stray cat once," Aisa said wistfully. "He followed me home, and Mother let me keep him. I named him Sand because that was his color."

"But then something dreadful happened to him?" Kalessa said. "One of your brothers set him on fire, I suppose, or cut his tail off."

"No." Aisa shook her head with a smile. "He was my cat for years. He grew old and died, not long before my mother took sick. I still miss him sometimes." She paused a moment, and realized that her scarf had fallen away from the front of her face. She hadn't noticed. How long had it been like that? Kalessa and Old Aunt hadn't remarked on it. Nothing bad had happened, though the elven hunger still nagged at her. She offered a shy smile to Kalessa. For a moment, she felt completely naked, but Kalessa only smiled back with straight white teeth against faintly green lips, and Aisa relaxed.

"What happened with your wyrm?" she asked, pretending nothing momentous had happened.

Kalessa played along. "A few months later, he was big enough to ride, and I broke him to saddle with reins made from one of his own shed skins. My brother Hoxin helped me make them. That was a good day. My parents were proud of the status their only daughter brought the nest."

"That's an important thing, is it?" Old Aunt asked.

"It is the only thing," Kalessa said seriously. "When I die, my status will decide whether I go to Halza and Vik's realm or to Valorhame itself."

"Will it?" Old Aunt said mildly, poking at the fire with her stick.

Kalessa started. Like Aisa, she had forgotten whose house they were in. It was easy to do. Old Aunt didn't look like someone who was married to the King of Birds himself. Kalessa turned to her and winced as her ribs twinged.

"Is it not so, great lady?" she asked. "Your tone makes me doubt."

"She won't tell," Aisa said. "They never do."

Old Aunt puffed her pipe. "The Nine are more fair than you think. Status matters, little one, but only *your* status, not your family's or your ancestors'."

Kalessa looked shocked. "But . . . everything my parents and grandparents have worked for . . ."

"Means nothing for you," Old Aunt finished affably. "On the other hand, it also means that people who commit dreadful crimes do not also seal their children's fates. Every slave, every thrall, farmer, merchant, soldier, earl, and king has the same chance for Valorhame. And now I should like a nice horn of ale."

Aisa, feeling more than a little awed, set one on the hearthstones next to her like an acolyte leaving an offering on an altar. Old Aunt accepted it and drank deeply, then relit her pipe and fell into a heavy silence. Kalessa pressed her with more questions, but she gave as many answers as a stone.

While Kalessa's ribs healed, Aisa continued the work about the house. It was harder without Kalessa to help, but Aisa managed. At night, Old Aunt's haunting melody sent her to sleep, and in the morning, she woke sweet and refreshed. She stopped wearing a scarf over her face entirely, though she still covered her hair. And every evening after the work was finished and the supper dishes put away, Aisa talked while Old Aunt listened. She talked about whatever came to mind, though often the conversation came around to her mistreatment at the hands of Farek and her remaining anger at Hamzu. Despite the latter, she missed him with an intensity that surprised her. He had done something wrong, but so had she, and it was time they made good again, like grown people.

"So you love him," Old Aunt said one night after the feather beds were put away. Aisa had declared Kalessa's ribs healed, and the young woman had spent the day in a whirlwind of activity: hauling buckets, bringing wood, and toting feather beds. Even housework, she declared, was better than sitting still.

"Missing is not the same as loving," Aisa said tartly. "It's easy to miss someone. It happens all the time."

"Because people leave you all the time." Old Aunt lifted a coal to her pipe, lit it, and tossed the coal back into the fire, a trick that never ceased to amaze Aisa. "It's difficult to get past people who leave you—or who shove you out the door."

"Why?" Aisa asked. "You are not planning to—"

For a third time, the door smashed open. Aisa scrambled to her feet, heart in the back of her throat. How many times would Old Aunt put her and Kalessa through this?

Kalessa had learned from the previous visitor and always kept her sword close at hand. She leaped in front of Aisa, blade at the ready. "Come on!" she snarled. "I am for you!"

But the thing that muscled through the door made even Kalessa gasp and take a step back. It had eight legs sticking out from a single trunk of pink and brown flesh that looked melted together from too many other bodies. Eight arms stuck out in all directions, half of them holding swords or knives.

Atop this monstrosity perched four heads with dreadful, wild eyes and tangled dark hair. With a cold chill, Aisa recognized her family—her two brothers, Fayyad and Nasim, her father, Bahir, and her mother, Durrah. The monster that was her family rushed at Aisa, snapping and snarling.

"You failed in your duty as a sister!" Fayyad growled.

"You showed loose and wanton morals!" Nasim howled.

"You failed to stop me from gambling!" Father groaned. "It was your fault I had to sell you!"

"You let me die," Mother whispered, and that pierced Aisa's heart with an arrow of stone. She remembered desperately searching for herbs and rendering tinctures, listening to conflicting advice from male doctors who refused to enter a woman's sickroom, all while cooking and cleaning and sweeping for two brothers who wouldn't touch women's work and a father who gambled away so much money they couldn't afford to hire any help. And more than once, Mother begged for something that would end her pain, and Aisa wished she had the courage to give it to her. But in the end, Mother had slid slowly into death with Aisa helpless at her side. All the guilt she had been suppressing for the last eight years crushed her down, paralyzed her while the monster family stormed across the kitchen toward her.

For the third time, Kalessa leaped in front of her, sword out. She swiped at the monster, and even though Aisa knew this wasn't really her family, she wanted to shout at Kalessa to leave them alone, not to hurt them. But the words wouldn't come.

Kalessa slashed at the creature and opened a gash on its trunk. "Ha!" she shouted. "I have you—"

The creature flicked Kalessa aside with one arm. She flew across the room, crashed against one wall, and slid to the floor unconscious.

"You're a failure!" the creature roared in one voice. "A bad daughter! Bad sister!"

Kalessa, Aisa's defender, was gone. Old Aunt, meanwhile, sat on the stool, smoking her pipe and scratching at the hearth with that damn stick. Fear and loathing pulsing with her heart, Aisa spun and snatched the stick from her. She faced the monster that was her family, and the hatred grew. They had betrayed her, hurt her, and now they dared to call her names? She stood straight.

"Filth!" she shouted. "Stay back!"

But the monster lunged at her. The familiar but twisted features of her family leered down at her as they came. She raised Old Aunt's stout stick at them like a club. At Fayyad, who always lifted her so she could pick the juiciest pears from the tree behind the house. At Nasim, who conspired with her to stay up late and spy on the grown-ups during Rolk's feast. At Father, who took her on his shoulders to the market and let her listen to the men while they bargained. And at Mother, who made colored eggshell mosaics with her every spring until she became too weak to leave her bed.

Aisa faltered. Yes, they had betrayed her. They had also loved her. Her father couldn't stay away from the dice any more than her mother could force herself to stay healthy. Her brothers had been trapped by a culture that decided men didn't help in the house. The monster rushed toward her with its monstrous form and familiar eyes. Nothing excused what they had done. But none of it meant they hadn't loved her. And pain was not solved with more pain.

Aisa lowered the stick. In one smooth motion, she pulled her scarf off her hair and stood before them as she had before the slavers took her. "I love you."

The monster halted only half a step away, loomed over her. All four heads breathed warm, sour breath down on her face. Aisa's mouth was dry with near panic, but she forced herself to hold her ground. "Nasim, Fayyad, Mother, Father. You are my family, and I love you."

"You are a—" Fayyad began.

"Shh!" Aisa reached up and put a trembling hand over his mouth. His lips were rubbery. "You caused me pain. I hated you for it. Part of me still does. But you are my brothers and my parents, and I still remember the good things, too."

"You are—" Mother began.

"No," Aisa said gently. "I never was. No one is a saint, and no one is a monster. We are a mix of both."

"You—" Father began.

"I will no longer carry your pain," Aisa said with tears in her eyes. "I forgive you. All of you. Go now."

The monster stared at her. After a long moment, it turned and slunk toward the door. Aisa stood unflinching behind it, feeling tall and powerful with the stout stick at her side. Old Aunt puffed on her pipe at the fire. At the door, the monster turned.

"You were always a good sister," Fayyad said.

"We are proud of you always," Nasim said.

"I was wrong, and I am sorry you suffered for my weakness," Father said.

"No one else could take better care of me," Mother whispered. "You were the best daughter anyone could want."

Tears of relief and joy ran down Aisa's cheeks as the monster slipped out the door and disappeared. Aisa sank down on a bench, overwhelmed at the power of this day. A great weight lifted from her back. She felt strong and weak, powerful and meek, all at once. The stick lay across her knees.

"Yes," said Old Aunt from the fire. "Very good, my daughter."

A groan came from the corner. Aisa gasped. "Kalessa!"

Kalessa was already staggering to her feet by the time

Aisa got to her. She seemed unhurt except for a bump on her head. "I was of little help," she complained. "The monster still attacked."

"Your job as the defender," said Old Aunt, "was to do what needed doing. In this last case, you needed to stand aside. Now I'm sad."

"Sad?" Kalessa said, clearly not sure if she should be mollified or insulted.

"You have faced all the enemies you need to face," Old Aunt said. "It is time for you to leave, and I'm sad."

"Leave?" Aisa put a hand to her mouth. The entire idea seemed strange. She had been living here for so long, the rest of the world had all but faded away. Abrupt, new questions crowded her mind, questions she had been meaning to ask but hadn't done so because she'd been too tired or too busy or too occupied talking about herself.

And there was one enemy she hadn't faced yet. When she thought of it, the hunger, which rumbled quietly in the back of her head, came to greater life, and the desire for her former master's touch swept over her so hard she swayed.

"Old Aunt," she began, "what about—"

She touched Aisa's cheek and withdrew. "You have earned your face, child. You have the strength to face the world on your own."

"My . . . face?" Aisa put a hand to her bare cheek and thought of mermaids.

With a creaking of joints, Old Aunt stood up. "But first, you must have the reward I promised."

"Reward," Aisa repeated stupidly, trying to push the hunger aside. It was all the harder because she hadn't realized how much she had been hoping until now that Old Aunt would take the hunger away.

"Reward. When you arrived, you pointed out that you had met many powerful beings—three giants, Death, a trollwife,

and me—and that they were all women. You said that we
women are doing a terrible job of controlling everything if
we allow the men to kill and rape and steal and do anything
else they please. I also said that your question told me much
and that I would answer it for you."

"Oh." Aisa had all but forgotten. "I see. What's the answer, then?"

"I think you know already," Old Aunt said in that mad-
deningly affable tone. "Tell me."

Aisa forced herself to think through the hunger. She
thought about the three creatures who had come for her, all
of them pieces of her own thinking, all of them people who
had hurt her, all of them men—except for the piece that had
been Mother. Why was Mother there? She was a woman.
But Mother hadn't hurt her on purpose, like the others. The
others had chosen. It was about choice, wasn't it? And what
had Old Aunt said about those who got into Valorhame?

"The women I met don't run the world," Aisa said slowly.
"But the men don't, either. Everyone makes their own
choices. We get into Valorhame by our own choices. When
men do dreadful things, it is through choice, not because
fate forces them. We all are people, not monsters, and we tip
the Tree with our own choices."

"Very good." Old Aunt nodded. "Oh, the Nine and the
Fates and a few other entities may throw a few . . . sugges-
tions your way, but in the end you have to decide what to do.
You decided to help the elven child live, and you ended up
here as a result. You decided to forgive your family, and
we're having this discussion as a result. I truly had no idea
how this would come out when you walked through my
front door. By men's choices, you were hurt. By your own
choices, you became strong again."

And Aisa felt a small tremor beneath her shoes. Kalessa
glanced sharply about.

"The Tree tips," Old Aunt said. "We must move along. First to you, my dear little orc. You must choose."

"Choose what?" Kalessa asked.

In response, Old Aunt gestured with her pipe. On the walls blazed a dazzling treasure—swords of all sizes, shields of all shapes, suits of armor, ornate jewelry boxes, wands with runes of silver and gold etched into them.

"You may choose one object from my house," Old Aunt said. "Anything you like."

Aisa couldn't imagine how anyone could choose. Everywhere she looked, more and more sights awed her senses. She realized that each incredible, impossible object had been there from the beginning, but she had somehow failed to notice them. It was like looking at a picture of a tree and suddenly realizing it was a woman's face, and had been all along. Kalessa's mouth fell open in astonishment. She wandered among the treasures, reaching out to touch this sword or that lance, but not quite doing so.

"Come on, come on," Old Aunt said. "Before you're gray."

"Great lady!" Kalessa gasped. "I am not worthy of any of it."

"Don't insult me," Old Aunt said peevishly. "Choose."

Abashed, Kalessa looked at a long sword with a green emerald set in the hilt. Gold runes marched up the blade. She ran her hand along the iron, then set her mouth.

"I have done little here, and my honor will not allow me to take such a weapon." She strode to the kitchen table and snatched up a knife. It was the one she had stabbed Hamzu with. "This is more appropriate. I have used it, and it should be mine."

"Are you sure?" asked Old Aunt archly. "The choice, once made, cannot be unmade."

Kalessa slipped the knife into her belt. "I thank you."

"Very well. Now you, girl."

"Me?" Aisa clutched the stick to her chest, taken aback. "I have had my reward. You answered my question. That was our bargain."

"No. *You* answered your question, not I." Old Aunt gave her a small grin. "Therefore your reward is still forthcoming. Choose. Don't be shy."

Aisa glanced at the shining treasure. Any one object would make her a wealthy woman, or a woman of great power. But that was assuming she could even figure out how to sell a singular object, or wield its magic. And in any case, Old Aunt had already given her something even more powerful than treasure—her choices. Nothing that hung on the walls came close to being that important. Aisa turned her back on it all and looked at Old Aunt's lined face and her wild white hair. A rush of affection swept over her. This was a woman of true power and wisdom. Her eye went down to the old, stout stick, the one Old Aunt used to poke the fire with every day, the one Aisa now gripped in her own hands, the one Aisa had held to face her family. It was an ordinary chunk of wood, worn smooth with use, as thick as Aisa's wrist and as long as her arm. One end was black with ash.

Aisa said suddenly, "I want your stick."

Old Aunt pursed her lips with surprise. "My stick?"

"Yes. It will remind me of you and all that you gave me when I stir my own fire every day."

"But it's worth nothing, child."

"To me," Aisa said firmly, "it is worth everything."

Old Aunt shrugged with shoulders like stone. "You'll find your things by the door, then. Mind the Twist when you leave." And she stumped out of the kitchen. The treasure faded away and vanished, though it was also somehow still hanging on the walls.

"That is all?" Kalessa said.

"It would appear." Aisa looked about the kind kitchen one more time. "We should go. Everyone must be worried to death."

They opened the door, crossed the threshold, and felt the Twist take them.

Chapter Seventeen

Danr had prepared himself for a long, dull council meeting filled with speeches and arguments and discussions. It didn't quite go that way.

Kalessa's father, Hess, introduced Danr to the Council of Wyrms, eighteen lavishly dressed orcs who sat around the round stone table at the bottom of the crater. A fire burned in an open area in the table's center, giving both light and heat, and the shadows danced across Danr's face as he nervously rose to tell about the Stane coming from under the mountain. The fact that the trollwives were using *draugr* as power to open the doors and intended to use them came out fairly quickly, and Danr braced himself for shock and horror, but the orcs' reaction startled him.

"The dead live on to fight for the living!" roared one councilor.

"The more we kill in the battle, the stronger our armies will become," shouted another.

"Even our own dead will give us power!" declared a third.

"Uh . . . it will be so," Danr said, exchanging a quick look with Talfi, who was clutching Danr's old pouch at this throat. "And furthermore, the Queen Under the Mountain sends gifts as signs of her respect and admiration."

With that, he took out the stone box and from it produced treasure—coins and gems and gleaming swords and bejeweled daggers and more. He piled them on the table, and orcs pounded the stone in appreciation.

"Orcs of Xaron," boomed the councilor woman from the First Nest, "shall we go to war with the Stane against the Fae?"

The result was a resounding "yes." Talfi barely seemed to notice. He was holding Danr's pouch beneath his nose with one hand and fingering his silver medallion with the other. A strange expression slid across his face and he stared at Danr, then down at the table, then at Danr again. Danr wondered what on earth was going on now.

Almost as a side note, the Eighth Nest was promoted to Seventh Nest, which upset the former Seventh, as they were demoted to Eighth. And the meeting started to break up.

"One last thought, please," Danr spoke up, and everyone turned to look at him, including Talfi. Danr tensed. No matter how often he had spoken lately, he couldn't get used to all those eyes on him. "I'm seeking the Iron Axe. It's in three pieces—the head, the haft, and the power. A wise woman told me the Fae have the head, but I could find the haft among the orcs. Do any of you know where I might find it?"

The councilors murmured among themselves. Danr waited, trying to be patient, but gritting his teeth all the while. Without meaning to, he glanced at the sky. Night had fallen fully during the meeting, and the crescent moon, called Kalina's Chariot in this phase, rode high in the sky.

At last, the leader of the First Nest spoke. "We have never heard of the haft being hidden among the orcs," he said. "But, Prince Hamzu, we would be pleased to help you find it, if we can."

And the meeting ended. Danr trooped out of the crater with Talfi and the chattering councilors, trying to hold on to optimism and failing. The orcs had no idea where the haft was, and Danr had no idea where to look now, with only a few days left. What was he going to do?

At the top of the crater, the councilors scattered to their own nests to bring the news, and cheers erupted at campfires all over the great camp. Hess and Xanda declared a great celebration for the new Seventh Nest. Danr truthfully pleaded tiredness and withdrew. Talfi came with him.

"That was certainly easy," Talfi remarked. "I can see why we needed to get here ahead of Earl Hunin's envoy. I mean, Filo said Hunin sent all kinds of gifts to bring them to his side, but the orcs really just want to go to war."

"The orcs were waiting for an excuse," Danr agreed quietly, "and they'd ally themselves with whoever showed up first to— wait!" His mouth fell open and he stared at Talfi, who returned the look with guileless blue eyes. "Filo. That was before you were . . . before you lost your memory again."

"We killed a wyrm together," Talfi said. "I ran and ran, and you smashed it with a rock."

"You remember?"

Talfi grinned. "Later, we were in the stable and everyone came for you about those brothers who got killed, and then we met the *draugr* and you were put on trial."

"Rolk and Vik!" Danr wanted to dance with glee, but the orcs were still emerging from the crater behind them and he didn't want to create a spectacle. "You do remember! How?"

"Wonderful speaking, Prince Hamzu!" Hess appeared from the twilight and clapped Danr hard on the shoulder. "You acquitted yourself well!"

"Thank you, sir," Danr said, wishing the orcs weren't quite so exuberant.

"Have you seen Kalessa?" Hess twisted his head around as if she might appear from the shadows. "Usually she's in the middle of everything."

"I haven't. But I'll let her know you're looking."

Hess wandered away. Danr drew Talfi aside, nearer the grove of trees, so they could have some privacy among the spreading branches. "How?" he asked again.

"This." He extended the pouch on its thong. "And you."

"Me?" Danr blinked. "I don't understand."

"This pouch is a part of you, isn't it?" Talfi said. "I have strong memories associated with you. All that lifesaving and best friend being and . . . stuff. It all hovered at the edge of my mind, and it got stronger whenever I touched this pouch. Or smelled it. Like the way smelling certain foods makes you remember a holiday from when you were little."

"How do you know that if you don't remember anything from when you were little?" Danr asked.

Talfi thought about that. "I just do. Anyway, the memories just hovered there like hummingbirds, and at the meeting, I started really trying hard. The smell of the pouch and holding this medallion broke through, and I remembered. All at once." He leaned against the tree while insects chirped in the background. "It's a weird feeling, like I should have always remembered."

"Do you remember anything from before you came to Skyford?"

Talfi shook his head. "One thing I do remember—you and Aisa finding out from Bund that I'm *regi*."

"Oh." Danr's face flushed hot, and he automatically glanced around to see if anyone were within hearing. "Yeah. Uh . . ."

"You didn't say anything to me about it when we were talking about my past," Talfi accused. "No little thing for a truth-teller."

"Well . . . no . . . ," Danr stammered. "But . . . did you know?"

"Of course I knew!" Talfi crossed his arms. "That's not the kind of thing you forget, even with . . . whatever my problem is. But you didn't tell me the truth about what you knew, even though I asked. It's a slap, you know?"

"Sorry." Danr looked down. He had gotten into trouble by telling Aisa the truth, and now he was in trouble for not telling it to Talfi. He couldn't win. An uncomfortable silence fell. Danr felt he should say something, but he couldn't find good words.

"All right, look," Talfi said, "let's put this truth-telling stuff of yours to some actual good use."

Danr put up a hand. "Hey, I don't think—"

"How do you feel about me?" Talfi interrupted.

And Danr had to answer. "I like you. You're like a brother I never had. I'm nervous that you're mad at me."

"That's not what I meant," Talfi said. "How do you feel about me being *regi*?"

Oh no. The words piled up, pricking behind Danr's eyes. He tried to keep them back, but they wouldn't be kept in. His mouth moved. "It's strange and sometimes it makes me shudder, but other times I think, so what? You can like whomever you want, and why should I care?"

"All right," Talfi said, looking a little relieved. "That—"

But the words kept coming. "And I'm worried that you want me in your bed."

The words hung there in the dark, black and ugly. Danr turned his head, feeling heavy and more than a little nauseated. Why did the truth always come out so nasty? Why couldn't the truth ever bring beauty and light?

But to Danr's surprise, Talfi didn't turn away. "I figured it was something like that. You've been jumping around like an orc with a snake in his boots. It was the only thing I could think of that might be bothering you. Look, Prince Under the Mountain, that orc girl might think you're pretty hand-some, but to me, that nasty mask you wear is about as hand-some as a sheepdog with mange." He slugged Danr lightly on the arm. "You're not for me. Check me with your left eye, if you don't believe it."

"I can't," Danr said, and for the first time he was relieved to be called ugly. "You disappear in my left eye."

"I do? You never said."

Danr hurried to explain, and the awkwardness was smoothed over. "Why do I disappear?" Talfi said. "Does anyone else disappear?"

"I don't know," Danr said, forced to answer. "No one else does it that I've noticed."

"Huh." Talfi scratched his nose, his foxlike features showing simple consternation, as if he were being con-fronted by a child's riddle. "It probably has something to do with me coming back to life, right? We'll add it to the pile of mysteries we're carrying around. Maybe you can ask Death, if you see her again."

"That's a thought," Danr admitted, then yawned. "Huh. You once told me that you dream about someone who loved you. Was that a man? A *regi* man?"

Talfi flushed a little. "In the dream, yeah. He has red hair. I reach for him but can't touch him, and when I wake up, he's gone. I don't know what to do."

Danr tried to be sympathetic, but he yawned instead. "Sorry. I'm too tired."

"Me, too. You don't mind still sharing a tent with a *regi*, do you?"

"Long as you keep your hands under your own blanket," Danr said.

"Hey! Just what do you think I'm doing under there?"

They both laughed, and the last of their tension evaporated.

"Where's Aisa?" Talfi said as they approached their tent. Someone had built a small fire for them in front of it. "We should tell her what happened."

"You know she's been avoiding me," Danr replied, not sure whether he should be angry or sad. He settled unhappily on both. "I think she's made it clear she'll never talk to me again."

"Hamzu!"

Danr spun. A woman in white stood behind him. A loose hood covered her hair, though dark tendrils curled out from beneath, and she leaned on a stout walking stick. Her face was beautiful in a way that made Danr's heart jerk. It took him two breaths to recognize familiar brown eyes. Disbelief rocked him to his toes.

"Aisa?" he gasped.

"I have returned," she said, and smiled. Her smile reflected the moon itself, and all of Danr's anger evaporated. Joy overtook him. For another of those smiles, he would Twist across the continent nine, ten, a thousand times. "Did you miss me?"

He had to answer. "Every moment!" Danr rushed over to embrace her, then checked himself. "Why—? Your scarves— your clothes—what happened?"

Now he noticed Kalessa standing behind her, looking puzzled. "Were you not worried for us?" she asked.

"Worried?" Danr repeated. "I suppose. I was worried because Aisa was angry at me and I was angry at her, and I was sad at the same time." He paused for breath, cursing his truth-telling mouth, and rushed on. "But I wasn't worried about your safety. Should I have been? Aisa, what happened to your scarves? And your hand wrappings? You're beautiful! You're—"

He clamped his mouth shut, cursing again. He had answered the question, and could shut up. He *needed* to shut up.

"But we've been away for days and days," Aisa said. Then added, thoughtfully, "Haven't we?"

"I think," Talfi said, gesturing at the ground, "we should sit down so you can tell the entire story."

They did. And while Aisa spoke, Danr watched Aisa's face. It was like finding a flower in a snowdrift. He couldn't keep his eyes—both of them—off her. Her dusky skin looked soft and smooth, and her lips moved like petals in a quiet breeze. He hadn't realized how truly hungry he'd been to see her face until it actually lay bare before him, and now he was a guest at a feast that couldn't fill him.

When Aisa came to the part about a monstrous version of himself bursting into the house to attack, Danr's stomach turned to cold stone. That was how Aisa saw him? He wanted to flee, let safe, welcoming darkness swallow him up so he would never have to face her again. But even as he tensed to move, Aisa touched his huge hand with her small one, and he froze. That tiny gesture held him in place by the fire. Without further acknowledgment, she continued her story, and he stayed.

At last, when Aisa and Kalessa finished, the fire in front of the tent had burned to embers.

"That's . . . I don't know what," Danr said into the shocked silence that followed. "You were in the house of Grick? The queen of gods?"

"It didn't feel like it." Aisa took back her hand and poked at the fire with her walking stick, the one she'd taken from the old woman's house. "It was like visiting my grandmother, if I'd known her, and if my grandmother had been eight feet tall with big teeth."

"You could have had anything," Talfi said wistfully. "Any treasure, any magic."

Across the fire from him, Kalessa held up the knife from Old Aunt's table. "It did not feel right to take more."

"An ordinary stick and knife," Danr said, "but from the house of—"

A new voice said, "Lady Kalessa—"

Startled, Kalessa twisted in place and flipped the knife into a defensive posture. At the same moment, there was a soft, metallic sound. The orc, a servant who had stepped up behind her, blinked at the point of the long, sharp sword in Kalessa's hand.

"Apologies, my lady," the orc stammered. "I should not have—your father was wondering if you were going to attend the—"

Danr stared, astonished. So did Kalessa and the others. The simple knife had become a full-bladed sword. Kalessa recovered first. She lowered the blade and cleared her throat. "I am a bit on edge is all. Tell my father I will see him shortly."

The servant ducked his head and withdrew into the darkness. Kalessa, still seated, held up the sword again and turned it so the remaining firelight ran down the blade. The weapon was plain steel, unornamented but well made, with a wire-wrapped hilt and a heavy ball on the pommel.

"What did you do?" Aisa asked breathlessly.

"I do not know." Kalessa balanced the sword on the back of her hand. "One moment it was a knife. When I wanted a sword, it became one."

"Powerful magic," Talfi breathed. "I don't even see any runes."

"Can you change it back?" Danr asked.

"I do not know," Kalessa said again.

"Maybe we should look at it," Talfi said. "You know—*look*."

All eyes turned to Danr. He shifted uncomfortably. Things hadn't gone well last time he had done that. But Kalessa, who was sitting next to him, held up the sword on her palms. "Please," she said.

Danr glanced at Aisa's face, still a new experience. To his surprise, she only nodded encouragingly. He took a breath and closed his right eye.

The sword leaped into bright life. It seemed to twist in Kalessa's hands like a glowing, writhing vine. One moment it was a knife. Then it was a short sword. Then a longer one. Then it was a long, thin rapier. Then it was a curved cutlass. Then it was a thick, heavy sword longer than Kalessa was tall. Then it was a small knife again.

Danr let out a long breath and opened his eye. Kalessa was holding the sword. He explained what he had seen. Kalessa looked at the blade in wonder. "This is indeed a powerful gift. I should keep it a secret until—"

Even as she spoke, the sword flicked into knife size. Kalessa blinked, then grinned and sheathed it at her belt. "Wait until I face an enemy with *this* at my side! The great lady was generous indeed!"

"Aisa," Talfi said quietly, "she let you take that stick."

"It's only a stick," Aisa scoffed, still poking at the fire. "Nothing else. What she really gave me was—"

"Choices, I know," Talfi interrupted. "But we thought Kalessa had just a knife. Maybe we should look at that, too."

"Only if you want me to, Aisa," Danr said quickly. Embarrassed, he looked away. "Even though you saw a . . . a monster in that house, I would never want to hurt you. The real me wouldn't, I mean. I'm sorry."

He continued staring away into darkness, expecting a tart reply, or—worse—silence. Instead Aisa touched his hand again. "I know," she said. "We both did wrong things to each other by mistake. I was not truly angry at you—I was angry at Farek and my family and all the other people who had hurt me, and I pointed that anger in the wrong direction. Please accept my foolish apology."

Truly flustered now, Danr blurted out, "I won't look at you ever again!"

"Do not say that," Aisa laughed. "I did not throw these scarves away so you would not look on me ever. Do you like my face?"

And Danr had to answer. Suddenly he wished with every fiber of his being that Talfi and Kalessa were anywhere but at this dying fire. "I love your face," he said. "It's more beautiful than roses in moonlight. I knew it would be even before I saw it."

Now Aisa blushed and looked away. Kalessa coughed and drummed her fingers on her knees.

Talfi said, "Are you going to look at her stick now?"

"Oh." Danr cleared his throat. "Yes. Hold it up, Aisa."

Recovering herself, Aisa did as he said, balancing the stick on her palms the way Kalessa had balanced the sword. "I cannot think what you will—"

Danr closed his right eye.

The explosion blasted him backward. An invisible hand bowled him over, and he tumbled away from the fire. The wind burst from his chest. He fetched up gasping and flat on his back. Overhead the stars rocked sickeningly.

Three faces poked into view. "Are you injured?" Aisa demanded.

Still a little stunned, Danr checked. "No." He sat up with Kalessa and Talfi's help.

"What happened?" Aisa clutched the stick. "What did you see?"

"I'm not sure." Danr coughed, then told them what he'd seen. "It was . . . powerful. I didn't get a good look, though, and I don't understand what I saw."

"It's just a stick for poking at logs," Aisa maintained, but there was doubt in her voice.

"It definitely isn't," Danr said. A suspicion grew, bringing with it both dread and hope. "Let me brace myself and look again."

"If you are certain." Aisa sat in front of him and held up the stick again. This time Danr braced himself and closed both eyes, then slowly opened his left just a crack. Light spilled into his head, but it didn't hurt like sunlight. Cautiously he opened his eye wider and wider, trying to focus on the stick. The power of the object pushed at him, but this time he was able to keep more control. The stick was ancient, and it had been touched by ancient blood. It called to earth and water and blood, blood, blood.

"It's the haft," Danr whispered, and the words spun around him in a whirlwind. "The haft of the Iron Axe."

Talfi and Kalessa gave identical gasps. Aisa clutched the stick to her chest. "The haft?" she repeated. "But Old Aunt used it to poke the fire."

"That is why she brought us there," Kalessa breathed. "So you could prove yourself worthy of it."

"Bund said we should start looking for the haft in Xaron," Talfi said slowly. "She didn't say the orcs actually had it. Did she know?"

"Old Aunt said that she was all women of power," Aisa murmured.

"Does that mean Bund isn't dead?" Danr asked with hope.

"I do not think it means her body still lives. It is more like a . . . connection. They think and act alike. Rolk! I'm holding a piece of the object that sundered the continent a thousand years ago." She tapped it. "It feels like an ordinary piece of—oh!"

Her eyes glazed over and she wavered. If she weren't already sitting, she would have fallen over. Danr flung out a hand to steady her.

"What's wrong?" he demanded.

"I can feel it." Aisa's voice came from far away. "The head of the Axe. I can sense it. It lies in darkness in a case of glass surrounded by bronze. That way." She pointed to the northwest, then shook her head and came out of the trance. "I can still feel it."

"Does it hurt?" Danr asked.

"No. But I can feel it. It is nothing like my hunger for . . . them." Her face, her beautiful face, was pale. "Still, it is in Palana. With . . . *them*."

Danr gnawed his lower lip. Aisa had been through so much. "You don't have to go, Aisa," he said softly. "You're an exile anyway. They won't let you in."

"No." Aisa slowly shook her head. "To the elves, humans are like mayflies. They won't remember someone as unimportant as I. And I think I have to go." Her voice quieted. "Old Aunt all but said as much."

"You can't be serious," Talfi said. "They touch you and—"

"I am serious." Her tone was iron. "I will go."

"At least the haft calls to the head," Kalessa said. "This is helpful. Finding the power will be much more difficult, I should think."

"How do you find power?" Talfi mused. "I mean, an axe head and a handle, sure, but power? It's not something you can bury under a tree or stash beneath your bed. How will we find that?"

"One problem at a time," Aisa said.

"And how could you not notice what that thing was?" Talfi asked Danr.

"I didn't look with just my left eye," he said without taking his gaze off Aisa. "I see everything the usual way when both my eyes are open. People can lie to me and stuff can hide, unless I look."

"Maybe you should wear an eye patch," Talfi muttered. "You'd never be fooled."

Danr looked away and down. "No. Too painful in too many ways."

"Now we have to fetch it," Kalessa said.

"We?" Danr said.

"Of course." Kalessa drew her knife and flicked it. It became a long, heavy sword, and she gave a wide, orcish grin. "You cannot think I would let my sister continue this foolish quest without me."

"And finding the Iron Axe would bring a lot of status to your nest," Talfi said shrewdly.

"Enough to become Second at least," Kalessa agreed. "Perhaps even First. And I will step through the doors of Valorhame one day. You said the Fae hold the Axe's head in Palana, is that right?"

"Yes," Aisa said cautiously.

"Then I already have an idea. We must speak to my father."

Chapter Eighteen

The river barge slid from the Silver River onto Lake Ta, the middle of the Three Fate Lakes, which formed stepping stones from south to north. The city of Palana, the capital of Alfhame, lounged gracefully on the southern shore a few leagues east of the river's mouth. Aisa tried to keep her eyes on the deck of the barge, but it was difficult with the city coasting toward her at every thrust of the fairy boatman's pole. The city called to her. It was full of wine, and she was consumed with thirst. It was full of rich food, and she was starving. It was full of air, and she was drowning.

"Vik and Rolk," Hamzu breathed beside her. "What is going on here?"

Talfi's bronze chains clanked against the planking. "Fuck us all."

That brought Aisa's head up. Lake Ta straddled the boundary between Alfhame and Balsia, and it wasn't, in fact, all that far from the hills of Skyford, which was why Skyford was a favorite target for sprite tribute slavers and the humans they employed. The Balsian side, east of the Silver River, was flat plain. The Alfhame side, west of the river, was thick elven forest. What had caught Hamzu's eye was the human army.

A great encampment had set up army tents all along the lake—on both sides of the border. In fact, the encampment flowed along the shore all the way to Palana itself. Soldiers, some in careful uniforms and some in rough homespun, moved about the camps. Formations drilled among the trees. Soldiers washed in the lake or pulled fish from it in nets. Hundreds of horses snorted, grazed, and champed while countless banners floated on the breeze. Aisa was not conversant with different factions within Balsia, but she did recognize banners—hastily sewn—that sported a bejeweled skull. Fairies and sprites wandered about the camps, unnoted and unmolested. There were no signs of hostility, though the men did keep their distance from the Fae as best they could. No elves were in evidence, and the men displayed only weapons of bronze and wood.

Their journey had taken them ten days up the plains of Xaron, speeding north into humid summer weather on Slynd's back with the lush forests of the Fae a distant green haze on Aisa's right, well out of bow shot, though they'd been forced to leave the wyrm at the border, just as they had left Danr's sack and the Stane's magic box with Hess.

Aisa had been a bit startled to learn that, despite the constant skirmishes along the boundary between Alfhame and Xaron, a number of orcs sold slaves to the Fae.

"There are always those who are happy to trade their principles for money," Kalessa had observed. "On both sides of the border."

Massing the orcish armies would take less time than Aisa had expected, but more time than Hamzu wanted to wait to hunt for the next piece of the Axe, so the four of them ran ahead of the army, which needed to march—or slither— north to the plains between Lake Nu and the North Sea, which the Fae didn't claim. From there, they would move around south to Balsia and meet the Stane. Hamzu, Aisa knew, was hoping that Earl Hunin would finally see the wisdom of joining with a powerful force of orcs from Xaron and of Stane from under the mountain instead of fighting them.

Unfortunately the travel time had eaten up the remainder of their days. Overhead, the two stars of Urko had grown so bright that they were visible even during the day, and they were touching. Tonight they would merge. They had to find the head of the Axe, but they had no real idea where to look. Now this army was in the way. It looked as though Hamzu's hopes were smashing to pieces.

"Who are all these humans?" Kalessa demanded. "What are they doing in Palana?"

"The armies of men have arrived from Balsia," grunted the knobby-jointed fairy at the stern. "Summoned to be our allies in the eventual war. You're lucky you got here when you did. The borders will close soon, I'm sure. Great King Vamath has forged an alliance with the human who calls himself King Hunin." The fairy's saillike ears plastered themselves against his skull at the name of the human king. "We will purge Erda of the Stane and their allies"—he gave Kalessa a meaningful look—"for once and ever."

A sick dread stole over Aisa and ice water spilled through her bowels. She hadn't even considered this possibility. Humans would never ally themselves with elves! But here they were. Her fingers grew white around the haft she held. The orcish army would come around the lakes and discover an enemy twice as large as they had been expecting, and allies who were far weaker. Aisa shot Hamzu a glance. His face was absolutely stoic, but tension rode every muscle. They had to talk, and quickly, but there was no place to do it.

"You look pale, orc," said the fairy with a toothy grin. "Something wrong?"

Kalessa's hand had gone to her sword. "You are paid to steer a barge, fairy, not provide politics."

The barge passed the seemingly endless human army, row after row of men and tents and horses and equipment. The more she saw, the sicker Aisa became. The encampment ran right up to the edge of the city of Palana itself.

Their barge pulled up to a dock, and another fairy wearing a golden cap leaped onto the deck.

"Inspection," he said. "I assume these are slaves?" He reached toward Talfi, who flinched away.

Kalessa brought her blade around. "Keep your hands to yourself unless you want them cut off!"

The fairy pressed his ears flat against oak bark skin. "I inspect all of the wares before they enter the capital city."

Aisa kept her eyes firmly on the deck of the lake barge. The sounds and smells of Palana, the capital city of the Fae kingdom of Alfhame, washed over her in a steady rhythm. The hundreds of faint footsteps of fairies pattering about the pathways. The flutter of sprites in the trees. The soughing of the wind through the leaves. The lapping of water against wood. The call and conversation of fluting voices. And the smell of the Fae. How could she have forgotten it? Earth and peat and sweetness and cinnamon all mixed together in an intoxicating aroma that made her body cry out in need. Bronze shackles weighed her down at wrists and ankles, but she barely noticed those. The hunger drove nearly every other thought from her head, and every passing moment it seemed more and more foolish that she had insisted on coming along. Her fingers were white around the haft. Aisa tried instead to concentrate on Kalessa's voice. Listening to her harshly harangue the fairy inspector helped with the hunger.

"Look, yes, touch, no," she was saying. "Spoil my merchandise with your addiction, and I take the difference out in blood." Kalessa's new blade was in her hand. It was currently in the form of a large, sharp knife, and it made Aisa feel a little safer.

The fairy backed up a step. "Is that an iron blade?"

"I am aware of your cowardly aversion to iron," Kalessa sniffed. "But no, I did not break your precious laws. This is good bronze. Inspect now! You cost me money."

Small brown feet padded over to Hamzu, who stood on the deck next to Aisa, also in bronze shackles. Aisa wanted the fairy to touch her, run his knobby fingers over her skin so she could drink him in. It was worse being here than in Balsia or Xaron. There, she'd had no chance of touching the Fae. Here, it was like walking into a banquet hall filled with delicious food when she had not eaten for days, and forcing herself not to touch a single succulent crumb.

"This one has Stane blood," the fairy observed. "We haven't had any Stane in centuries. And won't ever again, if things go as His Royal Majesty plans."

"Which is why I insisted upon selling him here at the capital instead of at the border," Kalessa said, and only Aisa caught the agitation in her voice. "Do not bother to ask him questions. He cannot speak."

"He would be both strong, and a curiosity after his race becomes extinct," the fairy said, and Aisa felt Hamzu tense beside her. She prayed he would not become angry.

The fairy's feet moved over in front of Aisa. She kept her eyes down, though she automatically watched from the corners. Sickening how easily the slave's reflexes came back to her. The hunger raged. "And what is special about this one?" the fairy demanded.

"She is a healer," Kalessa said. "The best in the land. She can all but bring the dead back to life."

"And as Kin go, she's extremely attractive." A knobby brown hand extended into Aisa's vision, intent on lifting her chin. Even though he was only a fairy, her entire skin longed for that gentle exquisiteness as a parched farm yearned for rain. The flat end of the knife slapped the fairy's hand aside. Aisa risked a peek upward, both relieved and disappointed.

"Do not touch!" Kalessa barked. "You want to lower her price by addicting her to your kind and ruining her for sale anywhere outside Alfhame."

"It takes more than a touch, you know," said the fairy. "And only the elves can—"

"Do not touch."

The fairy sighed. Aisa glanced at the two stars merging in the sky overhead. This was taking up so much *time*, time they didn't have. But she was a slave again, and she couldn't speak.

"And what's special about this one?" the fairy asked with a gesture at Talfi.

"He comes with the Stane," Kalessa said. "Two for one. He keeps the big creature from exploding."

"How?" asked the fairy.

Kalessa leered in a way Aisa had never guessed an orc could leer. "Guess."

Talfi's sharp face had gone bright red. Hamzu's face remained stoic. Aisa prayed to Rolk they would stay calm. The fairy shrugged. "It will lower his price if he is attached to the Stane."

"My concern, not yours." Kalessa tossed a few coins to the fairy boatman.

The city of Palana arched and writhed through the great trees of the lush Fae forest, just as Aisa remembered it. A confusing network of bridges and boardwalks threaded through the branches, and bright, eye-twisting sprites flittered among the leaves, laughing as they went. Down below, the earthen, knobby-jointed fairies skittered about on errands of their own. And between them moved the elves, bright and beautiful with their luminous skin and silken hair and shining robes. They didn't seem to walk as much as glide. Every gesture was a dance, every word a symphony. Aisa wanted to rush up the gangplank and fling herself at the feet of the least of them to beg for a touch, but she stayed where she was. The shackles actually helped. Good, solid bronze weighed her down. The shackles were bronze instead of iron because the Fae couldn't bear the presence of iron, just as the Stane couldn't bear the presence of sunlight. Even a touch of iron caused pain to the Fae, and wounds from iron weapons festered into poisonous infections that killed the Fae within hours, or even minutes. Iron and steel were therefore banned within the borders of Alfhame.

The fairy said, "Once you pay the import tax . . ." Kalessa sighed heavily and dropped several more coins in the fairy's little palm. ". . . you are free to sell your wares."

Kalessa led Talfi, Hamzu, and Aisa onto the dock by their shackles, jerking them along as if they were dogs or cattle. Aisa knew she was only acting the part of a slave dealer with special merchandise so a group of Kin and a half Stane would have an excuse to enter Alfhame, but she still found herself resenting the way Kalessa treated her. Hamzu walked behind her, slouching a little as he did in the village back in Balsia. Hunger and need tore at her. She clutched at the haft in her hands and concentrated on his presence to ward it off. He was strong and he was always there for her. How could she have pushed him away for a stupid mistake? He was not perfect, but his imperfections were ones she could forgive, and she realized she wanted him to forgive her own imperfections. She wanted him . . . well, she wanted him.

It was a strange moment for her, shuffling along in shackles through an elven city, and avoiding their hunger by instead admitting to herself that she loved a man who was half Kin, half Stane. She felt the sun should shine on her, that her hunger should evaporate, and Hamzu should spin about and take her in his arms. None of those things happened.

But she was still afraid of him.

It was as hard to admit that as it had been to admit that she loved him, but it was so. He had never hurt her, not on purpose, but she had seen the sheer physical power of his body. If they became . . . became intimate, what would stop him from snapping her like the dry stick she now held in her hands? How much would it hurt to have him touch her? The thought made her shaky.

They shuffled through the city. Human slaves with silver collars around their necks pulled wagons loaded with stuffs and carried sedan chairs laden with elven lords or ladies. Bridges arched overhead; brightly colored birds with graceful tails and high topknots twittered in the branches. Nowhere was there any of the usual things Aisa associated with cities—mud or excrement or waste or clutter or poverty. Everything was grace and beauty and light, just as in her memory.

As if reading her mind, Hamzu muttered, "This place is horrible," in a voice that carried no farther than her ear.

Aisa cocked an ear, questioning without speaking to conserve and conceal communication.

"The trees and birds are twisted from their natural growth," he murmured. "They're unnatural, and in pain. Sewage runs so thick and heavy under the ground it curls my toes. So much here is wasted. The lake is ready to erupt with filth."

"It looks beautiful," Aisa said softly.

"Not to my eye. I can see it."

That was interesting. Aisa remembered emptying buckets of night waste into holes under the trees, and throwing away clothing that had a small tear, dishes that had a tiny crack. She hadn't given a thought to where everything went, or to how much the Fae wasted—or to how much waste they produced. When she did think about it, and how she was walking across elven filth, her hunger abated somewhat.

They passed a trio of *draugr*, two human and one fairy, standing huddled beneath a half-dead tree. A pair of living sprites, their chaotic forms flickering like fire, danced in the air above the ghosts as if conversing. The *draugr* stretched pale arms out to the group as they shuffled by.

"Release!" Their cold whisper made Aisa shudder.

Kalessa yanked the chains and hurried the group along. A number of Fae stared briefly, then went on their business. The elves took slaves in tribute from the Kin in Balsia and Irbsa, but since elven glamour stole away Kin fertility, and since the elves were hard on their slaves, slaves neither lasted long, nor reproduced. The elves always needed more slaves than the tribute agreements allowed, so they bought more. An orc slave trader in Palana was therefore an oddity, but not unheard of.

"This place is familiar," Talfi said softly. He looked about as if in a daze and inhaled hard. "The smells. It's like remembering a story from a long time ago. Around the corner there will be a small butcher's market beneath a beech tree."

There was. A cluster of booths run by fairies sold meat ready for the cook pot. Aisa licked her lips. "You've been here before, then. Before you died."

"I think so."

"The only humans in Alfhame are slaves. You must have been addicted like me." A bit of hope clutched her heart. "How—?"

"It's like Hamzu and I thought." Talfi shifted in his shackles, and they clanked. "When I die, I start over."

The hope extinguished, and Aisa dropped her head. "So if you form an attachment to your new master, we only need kill you," she couldn't help saying.

"I'd rather you didn't."

"You have no idea what you're saying," she whispered.

Hamzu stumbled and went to his knees with a low cry. Aisa went to him. Kalessa sighed heavily, as if annoyed that her prize slave had tripped.

"What is it?" she hissed in his ear.

"The drums." His voice was hoarse. "I can feel the Stane drums. Like I did in the caves. They're loud and powerful. I think the spells are ready, and they're going to open the doors. Tonight. We have to get the Axe!"

"We need not worry about the Stane," Aisa murmured, helping him up. "They're in Balsia, and all the armies are in Palana. It will take two weeks or more for the Stane to march here."

"But the stars are coming together tonight," Hamzu pointed out.

"Which way, which way?" Kalessa said as if to herself, and Aisa remembered with a start that *she* was supposed to point the way. The haft of the Iron Axe only responded to Aisa, so Kalessa couldn't use it to guide them to the head. Aisa slid her hands down the haft and let the pull come over her. The head was close; she could feel it. She let the haft draw her toward a trio of gigantic ash trees that supported an equally gigantic house of polished wood and glittering glass that, like all elven houses, looked as if it had grown out of the trees themselves. It was horrifyingly, hauntingly familiar.

"The palace," Aisa whispered. "The head is in the palace. Where I was once a slave."

"Will they recognize you?" Kalessa murmured.

Aisa's heart was pounding and fine sweat broke out along her hairline, but she shook her head. "It was years ago, and to elves, all humans look as alike as grasshoppers."

"Then why didn't you come back after you were exiled?" Talfi said. "You could have arranged to be sold to someone else and—"

Aisa rounded on him. "I would rather live all my days in hunger than feast upon filth!"

"Quiet, slaves," Kalessa said as a pair of fairies passed within hearing. Aisa hushed herself, and let Kalessa drag her toward the palace. Her back straight, Kalessa climbed a delicate-looking staircase into the branches to a side door and pounded on it. It opened by itself, revealing a luminescent sprite. It seemed to be a glowing ball of light hovering in the door, but when Aisa looked at it more closely, she could see the wavering form within. The sprite flickered and another Kalessa was standing in the doorway. Aisa remembered sprites changing shape during her previous time in Alfhame, but it was still unnerving to watch.

"Slaves from an orc," the sprite Kalessa said. "You sell cares with your wares."

"I sell the finest," Kalessa interrupted. "And only to your master."

"The king does not buy slaves himself, the elf," giggled the sprite. "My name is RigTag Who Sings Over the Stormy Sky, and you may sell to me, you see."

Kalessa folded her arms. "I do not sell high-class slaves to underlings."

Aisa's jaw tightened. Kalessa was pushing too hard, too far. The object was to get them into the palace, and quickly. Slaves went everywhere, and they could look for the Axe head in relative anonymity, since elven slaves never—almost never—disobeyed their masters and were trusted everywhere once they were addicted.

And that was the key. Aisa herself did not worry about becoming addicted to the Fae. She already was. The Stane did not become addicted, and Talfi, who had insisted on coming along, had his own way out, if he needed it. The basic plan was that once they used the haft to locate the head of the Iron Axe, they would figure out a way to steal it, hopefully within a day or two. They couldn't plan better than that, since they didn't know how well the head was guarded, but Aisa suspected it would not be. The Axe head was useless without the heft and the power, and after a thousand years of easy rule, it seemed likely to Aisa that the luxury-loving elves would treat the head more as a curiosity than an artifact of great power.

However, before all, they had to be sold into the palace, and Kalessa had fallen too deeply into her role of arrogant slave dealer. Aisa was trying to think of a way to signal Kalessa when an elven lord strode toward them. Aisa's breath caught, and beside her, Talfi drew in a sharp gasp. The lord was beautiful, even by elven standards. His hair was the color of maple leaves in autumn, and his wide eyes were the intense green of twining ivy. His face was chiseled from finest marble, and the intensity of his eyes contrasted sharply with his fair skin. Rather than the usual elaborate robes or heavy dresses favored by the other elves, he wore a tunic and half boots of heavy brown silk. Aisa wanted to beg him to touch her with one of his long, supple hands.

"What's this?" he asked in a light, boyish tenor. "All this shouting is—oh!" He caught sight of Kalessa and her charges. He blinked heavily, and his perfect face blanched a little.

The sprite popped back into its normal chaotic shape and bobbed uncertainly in the doorway. "My lord Ranadar, this orc—"

Kalessa jumped in. "I am selling exotics, great lord, and the sprite prevents me from presenting them to you. If Your Lordship would only—"

"I'll buy the lot," Ranadar said. His voice was shaking. "Give the orc what she wants and take the new slaves to the baths for cleansing."

"My lord!" said the sprite, shocked. "You are the son, the

one, who is done of the king, the thing. It is unseemly, meanly, that you buy—"

Ranadar punched the sprite hard. Its light dimmed sharply, and it dipped in midair, nearly falling to the ground. "Are you questioning me, creature?"

"C-certainly not. Rot!" the sprite whimpered.

"Good." Ranadar stalked away.

Aisa utterly failed to conceal her surprise and she exchanged glances with Hamzu and Talfi, who seemed as startled as she was. Only Kalessa appeared unfazed.

"Three thousand in silver," she said, a scandalous price, "and I'll need a room for myself in the palace for several days."

The sprite, its light still dim, paused a moment, then said, "It will b-be, you see, as His Highness Lord Ranadar wishes, like f-fishes and dishes."

A pouch of coins dropped into Kalessa's open palm, and the sprite, weaving dazedly, led them through the luxurious palace and past a number of other black-clad human slaves who barely noticed even Hamzu. They performed their tasks in a happy haze that Aisa recognized all too well. All of them had been taken from somewhere else, ripped away from family and friends and sold here, just as Aisa herself had been. A young man carried a chamber pot as if it were filled with gold. A little girl no more than seven scrubbed floors with a small smile on her face, not noticing the raw blisters on her hands. Aisa's outrage overwhelmed her hunger for a moment, and she gripped the haft even tighter. *This* was why she was here. *This* had to end.

The haft seemed to tug at her in response. The head was close by. Aisa could feel it.

The sprite took them to a bathing room and bobbled away. The room was sticky and humid, with several sets of small private bathing stalls—Aisa remembered stoking the great tubs of water on the roof that granted hot running water— where two smiling slaves helped them bathe and change into the loose black trousers and shirts that marked all slaves. A single small window, too small to climb through, overlooked empty air, and the blue lake beyond.

They bathed quickly. Aisa chewed her lip. How were they going to find the Axe with only a few hours to spare? When they finished dressing, Kalessa, without turning a hair, locked silver slave collars around their necks. Aisa caught no indication that she was anything but a slave trader who had struck a nice bargain. That hurt a little, necessary as it was. Then Kalessa ordered the bath slaves to leave, and they did.

"How are the drums, Hamzu?" Aisa asked.

"I'm all right." He passed a large hand over his face. "They just caught me by surprise. But I can still feel them. Sunset at the latest."

Another surprise came to them. Just as Talfi was pulling on his tunic, the door opened and Ranadar stormed into the room. Before anyone could react, he strode up to the startled Talfi and grabbed both his hands.

"How is it possible?" he demanded. *"How?"*

"My lord!" Kalessa barked. "You can't—"

But Ranadar kissed Talfi full on the lips. Talfi stiffened and his eyes slid shut. Aisa tightened her grip on the haft. She knew all too well what Talfi was feeling, and she both envied and pitied him. Kalessa's eyes met Aisa's. Her hand moved toward the shape-shifting sword at her belt, and Aisa's hands tightened on the heft. Maybe they should kill Ranadar now, hide the body, and move for the Axe head. Maybe they could—

Ranadar broke the kiss. Talfi staggered and opened his eyes. "Ran!" he gasped. "Vik and Halza, it's you! Ran!"

"How?" Ranadar repeated. His voice was hoarse, and it

sounded strange in an elf. "You died. Father cut your throat when he learned about us. He made me watch while Mother applauded."

"The dream man," Hamzu said in shock. "Red hair."

Talfi's face was ice pale. "How long ago was that?"

"One hundred forty-seven years. Not that I haven't counted every day."

"I should have charged more," muttered Kalessa.

"Is anyone watching us, my lord?" Aisa said quietly.

Ranadar's demeanor shifted. His face became more arrogant, his voice harder. "Of course not, girl. I should lash you for—"

Talfi put a hand over Ranadar's mouth. "Still the uppity elf."

"Rolk!" Ranadar crushed Talfi to him in a rush of emotion, not seeming to care that two other slaves and an orc were watching. "Only you would dare call me that. How, *Talashka*? I saw you die."

"I don't know," Talfi said. "I die and come back, but every time I do, my memory disappears—until you kissed me and brought some of it back, anyway."

"Wait!" Hamzu rumbled. "Do you remember all the last hundred-some years?"

"He speaks!" Ranadar said, taken aback.

"How about that!" Talfi said. "We found a way for you to lie. Sort of."

"I still think I charged too little," Kalessa grumbled.

"What is going on?" Ranadar shouted.

Aisa glided to the door and locked it. Ranadar clearly had no talent for subterfuge, and under other circumstances, she might have found his revelation about Talfi fascinating, but the Axe haft was tugging her toward the head, which was less than twenty or thirty paces away, and Ranadar was proving an obstacle. She shifted the haft, thick and heavy, in her hand.

Talfi caught what Aisa was up to. He stepped between her and Ranadar, who seemed unable to comprehend that he was in any kind of peril. "He wouldn't do anything to hurt us. We were planning to run away together when his father caught us."

"The worst day of my life, *Talashka*." Ranadar couldn't seem to stop touching Talfi, on his face, his arm, his shoulders. "And now you're here. It's real. Tell me everything."

Talfi started to speak, but Kalessa's sword was in her hand. With a quiet sound, it changed into a long, iron sword. Ranadar hissed through his teeth and groped for his own blade, but Kalessa's sword at his throat stopped him.

"He is Fae," Kalessa said. "He will betray us to his own people in a moment. We should kill him."

"I must agree," Aisa said grimly. It was growing more and more difficult to stand in the hot, steamy room with the elf and his damn beautiful hands. "Elves live for elves, no one else."

"You will pay for that insolence, human girl," Ranadar growled.

"That human girl is my sister," Kalessa retorted, "and for the rest of your short life, you will treat her with—"

"He won't hurt us!" Talfi interrupted. "I know he can be snotty, but—"

"What?" Ranadar said.

"—he *loves* me. It's a lot to take in, I know, but believe me. I remember now. I was captured by slavers and sold here a long time ago. Ranadar bought me. He looked a lot different then." He turned to Ranadar. "Your hair was longer, and you didn't dress like this."

"You are addicted to him now," Aisa pointed out. "You would believe anything he says."

Talfi thought a moment, then shook his head. "No. I want

him, but I don't need him. I mean, I do, but . . . not the way you do, Aisa."

Aisa didn't know whether to feel relief, envy, or anger, so she merely closed her mouth.

"After you . . . died, I went to the woods." Ranadar touched Talfi's face. "I barely come to the palace anymore. The army drove me back here."

"When you punched that sprite, I nearly swallowed my tonsils," Talfi laughed.

"Yes, well, I've been waiting to do that for a long time. RigTag Who Sings Over the Stormy Sky was always a bit of a—"

"You have a sword at your neck, elf," Kalessa reminded him.

"Uh . . . the short story is, we fell in love," Talfi said. "An elf for a human. Who thought?"

"Stranger things have happened." Hamzu looked at Aisa, who felt a little flush.

"Look at him with your eye," Talfi said. "You'll see!"

"Oh! I'm a fool." Hamzu closed his right eye. Kalessa's sword never wavered, but Aisa held her breath. Hamzu asked, "Would you give up your elven heritage for Talfi, elf?"

Ranadar hesitated for a tiny moment. "Yes."

"Would you betray your people? Turn traitor for them?"

Traitor, Aisa thought.

Again, Ranadar hesitated. Talfi took both his hands again. The young man's eyes were full of trust, and Aisa wondered what it would be like to trust someone so completely.

"Yes," Ranadar said. "There has been nothing for me here for more than a century."

Hamzu opened his right eye. "He's true. And I don't ever want to look at two people in love again. It's like drinking maple syrup."

Watch for the—

"Helpful traitor!" Aisa blurted out. "He's the helpful traitor! Death mentioned him."

"What?" Talfi and Ranadar said at the same time.

"Oh!" Danr clapped his hands hard. "I'd forgotten. Huh. If Death speaks for him, then, I can't say a word."

Ranadar was looking more confused by the moment. "Death?"

"Never mind," Aisa said. "Just know that we trust you, based on high authority."

The doorknob rattled, and someone pounded on the wood. "Open this door, slaves!" came a fairy voice from the other side. "What do you think you're doing in there?"

Everyone tensed. Ranadar, however, raised his voice. "I'm inspecting my merchandise, Joff. Leave me!"

"S-sorry, my lord." Feet padded hurriedly away.

Kalessa lowered her sword. "We should find the head. Now."

"What head?" Ranadar put a protective arm around Talfi, who looked ready to both melt and burst at the same time. "What are you talking about?"

Hamzu explained quickly. The more he talked, the paler Ranadar became, until he looked like one of the *draugr*.

"The Iron Axe," he breathed. "You want to piece it back together."

"What is happening outside?" Hamzu said. "Why is Hunin's army here?"

Ranadar sighed. "My parents and I don't speak much, not since Father killed my *Talashka*. I only know that this King Hunin has brought many human tribes together from all over Balsia. He waves a jeweled skull about and invokes a long-dead hero of some sort, and they fall all over themselves to follow him."

"Jeweled skull?" Talfi looked at Hamzu. "Didn't you give—?"

"I did," Hamzu said grimly. "What else?"

"We've heard rumors that the filthy Stane—"

"Watch it," Danr growled.

"Uh, yes. The . . . mighty Stane are coming out from under the mountain again, and when Mother saw Hunin was raising an army to defend himself, she offered Hunin an alliance, a new treaty. If the humans fight beside us, we will take no more slaves. For a hundred years." Ranadar cleared his throat. "Once the Stane are crushed—sorry—we'll have peace forever. And the *draugr* will be laid to rest. That's the hope, at any rate."

A short silence fell over the group as everyone digested this. Aisa fingered the haft. She had come to know every bump and every grain on its surface in the last several days.

"I do not like this," she said at last.

"No," Kalessa agreed. "We are missing something. Something powerful. The Fae would never ally with Kin. They see Kin as slaves or prey, not equals."

Ranadar shrugged. "When the Stane emerge, blinking and weak from their time underground, they will find two armies awaiting them. And we know the orcs are coming, but we outnumber both. You will have no hope."

"It won't be as easy as you think," said Hamzu with a sad pride. "Once the Stane have finished using the *draugr* to force the doors open, they'll keep using the *draugr* to fight the war."

"Mother is an excellent strategist, and Father is a powerful magician, so I can't imagine they haven't thought of this," Ranadar said. He was touching Talfi's hair, as if he still couldn't believe it was real. "But I also can't tell you what they might plan to do about it."

"We need to put the Axe together," Hamzu said. "Once we've done that, we'll know where the power is hidden, and it won't matter who can do what to whom."

"Will you help, Ran?" Talfi asked. "Can you help?"

"You ask a great deal, *Talashka*." The arrogant look left Ranadar's face and he gave a smile that was both frightened and hopeful at the same time. "When your blood spilled across the floor, I thought my life would end. All I could think was that I would never see you again, and how much I hated my parents. And when I saw you on the doorstep, I thought at first you were one of those terrible *draugr*, and then I simply could not believe it, and then I *had* to believe it. The Good Gardeners, the Fates, have handed me a second chance, and I will not throw it away."

"Even if it means trading away your entire country," Aisa couldn't help asking. "That seems terribly selfish, even for a prince."

"It's utterly selfish." Ranadar tightened his arm around Talfi's shoulder, and Aisa's hunger growled within her at the sight. "When have elves been anything but?"

"Hmm," said Aisa.

Hamzu was pressing an ear to the door. "We should move. Is the haft still pulling you toward the head, Aisa?"

She nodded. It still felt strange to show him her bare face.

"Then it seems a good chance that once the Axe is back together, it'll lead us to the power. And it won't matter whose army is biggest."

"What exactly do you intend to do with that Axe once you have it?" Ranadar asked.

Aisa saw Hamzu struggle for a moment, but the truth-teller in him was forced to answer. "I will free Death from her chains, and I will stand before all the armies and tell them that anyone who tries to make war will pay with their lives." He glanced at Aisa. "And I will tell the elves they can have no more slaves."

"Very nice," Ranadar said. "And then?"

"Then?"

"Yes. What will you do next, great one?" Ranadar's voice

was soft and steady, and Aisa could not tell if he was being serious or sarcastic. "What will you do when Death roams free, and the blood of those who disobey you stains the forest red, and my people have run home with their tails between their legs?"

"I . . . don't know," Hamzu said.

"Ran," Talfi said.

"You will own the most powerful weapon the world has ever known," Ranadar continued. "A weapon that can crack a continent. A weapon even the gods fear. What will you do with it?"

Hamzu took a step backward. "I don't have to *do* anything."

"A year from now, if the elves decide to invade Xaron," Ranadar said, "would you stop them?"

"Of course!"

"And if the orcs decided to invade Alfhame? Would you stop them?"

"I . . . suppose."

"And if the Third Nest tried to raid the poorer Seventh Nest for their ragged sheep and goats, would you stop them?"

Hamzu's voice was shaky. "Probably. If I knew about it."

"What gives you the right to do any of it?"

And Hamzu remained silent. The room filled with silence. It hung in the steamy air, heavier than the mist.

Aisa stared. Ranadar had asked Hamzu a direct question, and he had not answered. His compulsion to tell the full truth had not forced him to speak.

"There is no true way to answer your question," Hamzu said at last. He sounded sad and tired.

"No," Ranadar said. "You needed to be aware of that."

Hamzu slumped to a bench. Aisa quietly sat next to him but didn't speak.

"Speaking of truth," Kalessa said, "I would like to know how we will leave this place once we have the Axe. We have had no chance to plan an escape, and I have the feeling we will be heavily pursued the moment we find the head."

"We will Twist," Ranadar sniffed. "Honestly."

This brought Aisa's head around. "You can Twist?"

"All elves can Twist, at least a little. There is plenty of power in this tree. I will open a portal, and we can go."

"Why didn't you Twist away when you wanted to escape with Talfi the first time around?"

Here Ranadar actually dropped his eyes. "Because . . . I was a coward. I hesitated, and Father was able to seize control of the Twist. Then he killed my *Talashka*, and it didn't seem worth it to leave. Nothing was worth anything."

"But it's different now," Talfi said, taking his hand. "We're all different. Let's find the other half of the Axe."

Chapter Nineteen

The drums throbbed in Danr's head and heart, growing more and more powerful. They made him want to smash and rip and tear. His awful monster half demanded to come out, and he worked hard to keep it under control.

"Where is everyone?" Kalessa whispered. "We haven't even seen any slaves since the bath."

"Who cares?" Talfi said. "We have it easy for once. Let's go."

The hall ended in the throne room. They entered behind Aisa, who held the haft before her.

Like the rest of the palace, the throne room seemed to be deserted. The dark, burnished wood reflected high, arched windows that showed the bloody sun as it dipped down to touch Lake Nu. High above the sun, the stars that made up Urko were merging into a bright comet.

In the center of the room was a large round table of stone. Strange objects covered it. Curious and apprehensive, Danr crossed to it, his bare feet padding on the wood, and discovered a lifelike model of the city of Palana and its surroundings spread across the surface. Lake, trees, grassy plain—all there. There were even tiny tents and miniature men to show where the Kin were camped. The men moved, and Danr jumped back, startled.

"It's a projection," Ranadar said, joining him. "Father created it so he can see from up here everything that happens down there. Sometimes I think he imagines himself to be Rolk or Olar, watching the little people down below."

Aisa joined him at the table, standing between Danr and Ranadar. For a moment, Danr thought she might take his hand in that thrilling way of hers. Then he saw her eyes cut to Ranadar and his impossibly handsome face. Desire flickered across her features before she could suppress it, and he felt an unexpected heat of jealousy, accented by the drums. It wasn't fair. Only now was he able to see her face, and on it he saw desire for someone else. He knew her feelings were false, that none of this was Aisa's or Ranadar's fault, but right then he wanted to snap the elf's neck.

"Are you all right, Aisa?" he asked gruffly.

"I will be," she said, "once we piece the Axe together."

Kalessa glanced about nervously. "We are not safe here."

"We are perfectly safe." Ranadar sniffed. "I'm the prince. If anyone comes in, you are here at my bidding."

The people on the projection continued to move. The sun was setting at the edge of the table, pushing shadows across the lake and into the forest. Among the human army flitted a number of miniature glowing sprites. Dozens and dozens of them.

"Look at all the sprites," Talfi said. "Are they providing light for the camp?"

"Maybe they're lighting the way for that elf." Danr pointed to a spot near the lake. A tiny elven woman, resplendent in green and golden robes, strode down to the water with a scepter. More than a dozen tiny elves in bronze armor accompanied her. Other elves, hundreds of them, spread out in the forest behind. Fairies and human slaves stood with them.

"That's Mother," Ranadar said. "I don't understand."

"It explains why the palace is empty," Aisa said.

The drums throbbed harder in Danr's head. "Maybe it has something to do with the doors opening."

"How can it?" Aisa said. "They are many days' travel away."

"Your mother is the queen?" Danr said to Ranadar.

"You should refer to her as Her Majesty, Queen Gwylph."

"Who's that with her?" He pointed to a human standing beside Gwylph. His finger brushed the projection and he felt a quiet *wrench*, nowhere near as bad as a Twist, and abruptly he was standing on the shore of the lake. Trees reached across the slender beach to the water, and low waves lapped against pale sand. All the people Danr had seen, including Gwylph and the human figure, burst into full size. Danr felt hard boards beneath his feet instead of sand, however, and he realized he was experiencing the projection as a life-size image.

"—ready to begin any moment," the queen was saying. Up close, her perfect beauty was overwhelming. Her hair was spun from flax and gold; her eyes shone like jewels from the Stane treasury. Danr wanted to fall to his knees before her. "As soon as I receive the proper signal from my lord husband."

"Excellent," said Hunin. He was the human standing next to the resplendent queen, and he wore a king's violet cloak and gold crown instead of armor, no doubt because the elves wouldn't allow iron armor or weapons within their borders. The mourning ring, however, still made a black circle on his left hand. Behind him, on a litter chair carried by four soldiers, sat White Halli. His bruises had faded, of course, though he still had splints on his arm and leg. He was dressed in blue and gold, and even had a sword at his waist, but he'd been strapped to the chair to keep him upright, and his eyes remained vacant. A bit of drool oozed from the corner of his mouth. Guilt weighed black and heavy on Danr at the sight.

Hunin continued. "I—we—look forward to watching their blood flow, Majesty."

The sound of his voice jarred Danr from the half trance created by guilt and the queen's loveliness, and a pang jerked his heart. So it was true. Hunin had crowned himself king and brought great armies of humans here to Palana in Alfhame, all because he hated all Stane for what one of them had done to his son. He was obviously using Halli as a rallying point. For how many speeches had Hunin propped up his son in front of a crowd and shouted about the terrible Stane?

"Don't do this, my lord," Danr said hoarsely. "Please."

Both of them turned. Hunin clapped his hand to his bronze sword, and Queen Gwylph pointed her scepter. The other elves behind them came alert in a rattle of bronze. Only now that Danr had spoken did they seem to notice he was there. Hunin recovered himself first.

"What are you doing here?" he growled. "Did someone scrape you off a boot?"

The queen narrowed her perfect eyes. "He isn't truly here, Hunin. This is a projection. From my own throne room, if I'm not mistaken." With a fluid move, she swept her scepter through Danr's chest. It passed through him without a ripple. Danr felt nothing. "The time is very close now. Have you found your head, boy?"

Danr stared at her. He had to answer, but he didn't understand the question. "What are you talking about?"

"Poor child. Your head is made of clay and your brain is made of the cattle manure you shoveled up," she said with a tiny smile. "I mean the *Axe*, child. Did you find the Axe head yet?"

"No," he was forced to blurt. "How did you know we were looking for it?"

"The sprites are good at ferreting out secrets, and you travel so slow, slower than the rest of your kind." From anyone else, this would have sounded like a snarled curse, but from her, it sounded like silk gliding across marble. "Seek it all you like. You're short on time, and soon it won't matter what you find. When we're done down here, we'll find you up there."

"This isn't right," Danr said. "Lord Hunin, you've joined with the people who have taken thousands of slaves from the Kin and—"

"I miss Papa!" Rudin interrupted. He was standing between Hunin and White Halli's chair. "He's the monster who hurt Papa!"

Hunin's face was hard. "He did, and his kind will pay."

Something about the boy felt wrong. His words were too careful, too ready. And what was such a young child doing here, anyway? Hunin should have left him at home, or back in their tent. In a blink, Danr closed his right eye and looked at Rudin.

The boy's face and body twisted. He swirled into a formless blur of light and chaos. A shape-shifting sprite. Danr slumped his shoulder. He should have guessed. He should have checked. Rudin, whose badly timed words had stopped Danr from forging an alliance between the humans and the Stane in the first place. His words hadn't been so badly timed after all.

"When did Rudin die, Lord Hunin?" Danr asked quietly.

"I am king, you lying whelp," Hunin barked.

"That's right," the queen said smoothly. "He's nothing but the son of a troll's whore. He shouldn't even be speaking to someone with your greatness."

"I miss my papa," the false Rudin said, sniffling.

"You're not looking at the truth," Danr said through clenched teeth.

Hunin drew his sword and pointed it at Danr's throat. His black mourning ring weighed his finger down. The other elves watched intently but made no move to interfere. "You destroyed my son's life, Trollboy," he said. "Now you'll pay. You can't save your slave slut. You can't save your people. You can't save yourself. You were born worthless, you lived worthless, and when you die, you will slink into Halza's icy presence and beg to drink from her cesspool."

The words should have pierced Danr and slashed him to the bone. But even with both eyes open, he saw nothing but a small, frightened man driven by pain and desperation, a man who had missed true greatness by inches. Danr felt more pity for him than anything else. He felt the truth welling up inside him, and even though no one had asked a question, he spoke.

"You could have been a great king," he said quietly. "Instead you won't live to see the sun set."

"You make *threats*?" Hunin was almost howling.

"I'm leaving," Danr said. "But first, have you thought about who should give your grandson the warrior's blessing?"

"I—what?"

"He's a scary monster!" Rudin said. "He frightens me!"

"This is Rudin's first war, isn't it? He should have Fell's blessing from his father." Danr gave a hard grin. "But I nearly killed his father. And your grandson will go into battle without Fell's blessing on his head. Too bad. Human."

"Listen here." Gwylph raised her scepter, but Hunin was too fast for her. He raised his sword to Rudin and reached out with his left hand.

"Fell's blessing be upon you as you enter—" Hunin's left hand, and the iron ring on it, touched the top of Rudin's head before the boy could react. Rudin screamed. His face and body melted into liquid light. His scream melted into a liquid gurgle. Hunin snatched his hand back as the sprite slumped into a squirming mass on the ground.

"Rolk and Olar," the queen muttered.

Hunin's mouth fell open. Danr closed his right eye and saw the pieces falling into place for him, watched him realize how one of the slavers had killed Rudin during one of the many trips through Skyford, how one of the sprites who always accompanied the slavers had taken the boy's place, how the sprite had carefully goaded Hunin with both words and Fae glamours into refusing an alliance with the Stane, into assembling armies and marching them to Palana, all to benefit the Fae. But for what reason? Hunin didn't know, and Danr couldn't fathom it, either.

White Halli gasped from his chair. His eyes cleared and he blinked rapidly. "What's happened? Where—?"

Hunin spun, his sword still out. Shock whitened his face. The soldiers holding up the litter chair hastened to put it down. "Halli! How?"

"I didn't hurt him as much as everyone thought," Danr said, and the load of guilt he'd been carrying evaporated into air. "The sprite was keeping him under a glamour so you'd ally with the Fae and war against the Stane. You broke the spell when you touched the sprite with iron."

"Father?" Halli struggled against the bindings, and the soldiers worked to cut him free, though he couldn't stand with the splint on his leg. "What's happening? How did I get here? Where's Rudin?"

Hunin turned to the queen, his face filled with conflicting emotions—fury, pain, horror. "You! How dare you play with me this way!"

"It would have been easier to replace you yourself with a sprite, my king"—her curled lip let him know what she thought of the title—"but only a human with your charisma and speaking skills could have assembled such an army for us, and we thank you most kindly. Can you understand? You Kin always have a role to play in the wars of your betters. You just need to be persuaded to play it."

"Always tricking us, always preying upon us." Hunin was ignoring Danr now. "Our alliance is ended! I will take my army to the Stane, and—"

The queen touched him with her scepter. Hunin dropped to his knees, limp as a pile of rags. His eyes went shiny, and a line of drool slid from the corner of his mouth. He looked the way White Halli had a moment ago.

"Father!" Halli tried to stand but couldn't. The queen motioned at him. He and the soldiers went limp as well.

"You underestimate your importance, Hunin, now that your army has arrived." Gwylph touched the injured sprite with her scepter. It sprang into the air and swirled into a new shape—Hunin in his scarlet robe and gold crown. "Very good, RikiTak Who Glides Over Water. You'll do for the next few moments. As for you—" She turned to Danr. "You are—"

But Danr pulled his hand back from the projection. With another little *wrench*, he found himself back in the throne room. Everyone was gathered around him, and he became aware that Aisa and Kalessa were pulling on his arms, but they hadn't been able to budge him.

"I'm all right," he said. "You can stop."

They let go. Aisa demanded, "What happened?"

He told them, in terse sentences.

"Huh," said Talfi. "That's . . . I don't know what that is."

"The humans are here because the Fae want them here," Danr said, "but I don't know what they're planning. The queen has also figured out where we are."

"Then we must find the head quickly," Kalessa said. "Do you know where it is, elf?"

"I don't," Ranadar admitted. "Father always said it wasn't a toy for children."

Aisa held out the haft. It pulled at her, and she followed it toward the high, thin chair that made up the throne. Beside the throne on a small table was a box the size of a small treasure chest. It looked to be made of sheets of jade inlaid with gold leaves. The haft came around of its own accord, pointing at the box like a compass orienting on north. Danr came to stand beside her. Outside, the stars had come together into a single, bright point of light.

"There," she breathed. "In there."

Kalessa was standing at one of the doors with her sword out. "No one is coming. Be quick!"

Danr stood before the box, not quite believing it. After all this time, it didn't seem possible or real. The box didn't even have a lock. Aisa was standing beside him with the haft, her face looking tight with eagerness and apprehension. In the end, he had done all this for her.

And he couldn't imagine doing anything else. Because he loved her. Oh yes, he did, and he couldn't imagine living without her by his side.

But she had never once said how she felt about him. Suddenly he had to know. He had done all this—fought White Halli, become an exile, faced the Three, spoken to Death, Twisted to Xaron—because he loved her, couldn't imagine a world without her in it. None of it, not even the Axe itself, meant a thing if she didn't feel the same way. His hands trembled and his heart was heavy. He was tired of walling himself off. Tired of running away. Tired of being divided. The truth always hurt, but he had to know it, and he had to know it now. He pulled back from the box.

"What is it?" Aisa asked tightly.

"We should not wait," Kalessa said from the door. "The stars—"

Danr swallowed. It had to be fast, and it had to be now. "How do you feel about me, Aisa?"

"What?" She looked startled and puzzled both.

"How do you feel about me?" His heart was pounding and his breath came in short puffs. "I came all this way—we came all this way—together, and now I need to know. How do you feel about me?"

"I . . . this isn't the time, Hamzu."

She was avoiding his eyes. That meant only one thing. His heart became hollow clay in his chest. All right, then. When this was over, he would walk away. He could go under the mountains, or perhaps join the orcs. It didn't matter. Nothing did.

But how much of this was his fault? Had he told her how he felt? He searched his memory. He had not. But how could he, who was always forced to tell the painful truth, tell Aisa even a lovely truth without causing pain?

And then he knew.

"Danr," he said quietly.

"I'm sorry?" She looked up at him.

"My name." His voice was husky and thick with emotion. "It's Danr. The name my mother gave me. The name I've never said aloud to anyone. I can only say it to people I love."

She stood up on tiptoe. He leaned down, and their lips met. The drums swelled, and the entire world rushed through him, propelling him upward, higher and higher until his soul joined the stars. For the first time in his life, he felt complete, whole and undivided. He pressed himself to her and felt his strength merge with hers until they were the only ones, god and goddess, in the entire universe. Nothing finer could come after this. When they parted, there were tears in Aisa's eyes.

"Danr," she said, and the sound was music. "I love you. I always have."

"And I love you! By the Nine, I love you." Danr picked

her up and swung her around. She gave a breathless little laugh. Aisa loved him! And the world was a fine place, drums and axes and all.

"But—" Aisa added.

Danr set her down, wary and unhappy again. "But what?"

"But I'm not ready for you. Not yet." Her face softened. "I need more time to sort myself out. If that's all right with you."

Oh. That was all? Relief came back to him, and he felt as if he were floating. She still loved him. It was all that mattered. "I can wait forever," he said, "as long as I know you're coming. And that's the truth."

"We should move," Kalessa said.

"Yes!" With new energy, Danr opened the jade box. For a dreadful moment, he thought it might be empty, that this was a trick, but inside he found the head of a plain double-bladed battle-axe. He drew it out. Ranadar sucked in his breath and drew back. The head was battered and pockmarked, barely a foot across, with a cruel-looking spike set into the top. At first, Danr thought rust streaked its surface, but then he realized it was ancient blood.

What gives you the right?

"Give me the haft," Danr said shakily.

Aisa passed it over. Everyone, including Kalessa, gathered around to stare in awe. When the head came into his hand, Danr felt it pull toward the head like a lodestone toward iron. Outside the window, the two stars grew brighter in their merging.

"We are changing the course of the world," Kalessa breathed.

"The Nine and the Three move through us," Ranadar said.

Danr let out a breath and slid the wood into the socket at the bottom of the head.

Nothing happened. He looked at Aisa, who gave a small shake of her head by way of a shrug. Danr swung the Axe carefully once or twice. It seemed small in his hand, more like a hatchet, and not at all potent. It didn't seem like the weapon that had—

The Axe wrenched him around. New knowledge flooded Danr's mind. The power, the third piece, was nearby, so close the Axe could almost touch it. The Axe thirsted for it, wanted to drink it in and become whole so it could do what it was forged to do—destroy.

What gives you the right?

Sweat broke out across Danr's forehead. As the sun sank halfway beneath the horizon on the projection, the Axe's spike pulled Danr clockwise around the circle until it was pointing.

It pointed at Talfi's heart.

Aisa gave a small cry. Danr felt all the blood drain from his face in an icy wash, and his legs went weak beneath him. Talfi. The power was Talfi. Danr pulled back. It was too much, too big an idea, like trying to understand the sun itself. But it also made a terrible sense. Danr had just been avoiding the truth.

Talfi's blue eyes were wide. "It's me? How can it be—no, it has to be me, doesn't it?"

"It was right there in front of us this whole time," Danr said in a weak voice. On the projection table, the sprites were rushing about like shooting stars. "The Axe's power keeps you alive, but it takes your memory every time you die. That's why I couldn't see you with my eye—you aren't really there. You've been drawn to me as a friend from the beginning because the power somehow knew that I would find the Axe, even if you didn't understand that."

Ranadar looked at Talfi in awe. "You're the actual one. The squire they sacrificed a thousand years ago. It is *your* blood on that blade."

As if in response, the Axe swung itself at Talfi. Talfi

jumped back with a yelp. For a moment, Danr saw Talfi on
the floor, split in half, while the Axe drank his blood. Then
the vision was gone.

"The only way to fully remake the Axe," Danr said in
horror, "is to kill Talfi with it. How can we—"

A spear point emerged from Talfi's chest. Blood colored
his tunic. Talfi looked down at his chest with a surprised
look on his face. Then he crumpled to the floor.

"Talashka!" Ranadar flung himself to the floor beside Talfi.
Aisa stared down at them, not comprehending what she was
seeing. Talfi lay on the wooden floor, a floor she had once
spent hours polishing, his face already pale. A scarlet pool
spread beneath, and for a wild moment, Aisa thought she
would be required to clean it up.

Then Aisa heard a metallic sound. Vamath, the elven
king, was standing in the doorway. The spear had come
from his hand. Bronze links gleamed like gold in his armor,
and his sunshine hair flowed carelessly down his back. His
fine eyes and perfect face made her breath catch in her chest
and her skin ache with desire even as her stomach roiled
with nausea. After all these years, his smooth fingers, perfect in every way, would touch her face and make her shiver
with happiness again. Behind Vamath came a troop of six
elves in armor of their own.

Danr—not Hamzu—roared. He rushed at Vamath in an
avalanche of howling thunder, the Axe raised high. The
king stepped smoothly aside at the last moment, and Danr
slammed into the elves behind him. Three went down like
ninepins. The others raised their swords. Kalessa's sword
flicked into the shape of a steel great sword and she charged.
Ranadar stayed with Talfi's body.

Kalessa's blade stabbed—and went through Vamath like
empty air. His image vanished. Vamath, his true self, appeared

behind Kalessa, and he cracked the back of her head with his pommel. She sprawled across the floor, dazed. The six elven guards piled on top of Danr. He struggled, and flung two of them off. The Iron Axe flew through the air, flipped end over end, and bit into the floor at Aisa's feet with a *thunk*. Aisa held her breath in a panic. She wanted to fight, but she could no more have raised her hand against her former master than she could have slit her own wrists. Ranadar continued to weep over Talfi's body.

One of the guards hit Danr on the head again, and then again. The blows dazed him. King Vamath reached into the fight and stroked his face. The rage and fear left Danr, and he relaxed in the guards' grip. Aisa recognized the signs, and horror washed over her in a black wave.

"No," she whispered. "Not him, too. Please, no."

But when Vamath stepped back, Danr followed him with utter adulation in his eyes. They had been wrong—his Stane blood hadn't kept him immune after all.

"How do you feel toward me, boy?" Vamath asked him.

"You're beautiful," Danr said, his husky voice rising from a dream. "I adore you."

"Good," Vamath said. "What's happening to the Stane?"

Danr shuddered hard. "I feel the drums. The doors are opening now. Right now. I want to be with them. But I love you more, master."

The awful words slammed into Aisa like a hammer made of stone. But she wanted even more for Vamath to pay attention to *her*. And she hated herself for it. Most of the injured guards were trying to recover. Two of them bound Kalessa's hands. Vamath ignored Aisa and strode over to the projection table, which showed the last bit of sun vanishing from the horizon.

"What are you doing?" Aisa asked.

Vamath continued to ignore her. Instead he touched the

table and his eyes went blank. "My queen, we have the Axe
here and the Stane have opened the doors. Let it begin."

The tiny queen raised her scepter. A streak of light shot
from the top and burst in a scarlet flower over the lake. At this
signal, the bright sprites and bronze-armored elves and brown
fairies who had insinuated themselves among the humans
sprouted knives and axes and swords and fell on the surprised humans. As Aisa watched in horror, blood flowed in
miniature, and dozens, hundreds, of soldiers and officers and
camp followers—cooks, servants, grooms, porters, squires,
and more—died in fountains of blood. Many fought back, but
the elves, sprites, and fairies had caught them completely off
guard, and the resistance was short-lived. The flashing swords
hacked and sliced. Heads and arms dropped to the ground.
Aisa saw a boy, barely old enough to squire, flee in terror, only
to be cut down by an elven sword. A female cook with brown
braids flung a cauldron lid at an attacking sprite, but the fairy
behind her ripped open her back. A flock of thin screams filtered up through the high windows of the throne room.

"What are you doing?" Aisa cried. "Rolk, what is this?"

Then the *draugr* appeared. They rose from their bloodied
corpses by the hundreds. Ghostly hands reached up to the
darkened sky. *"Release!"* they howled. *"Release!"*

Gwylph, the elven queen, raised her scepter again. Countless firefly lights from the *draugr* flickered through the
forest and up the beach. For a moment, Aisa thought she had
it. The power and terror of it shook her through.

"You lured the humans here with trickery and false prom-
ises in order to slaughter them and harvest their *draugr*," she
gasped.

Vamath had released the table. "The trolls can do it in
their lands," he agreed absently, "and we Fae do it here.
Very nice of the Stane to give us the chance. With this kind
of power, we'll slaughter them with ease."

"But the Stane aren't here," Aisa said. "They'll find out in due—" But even as the words left her mouth, she realized she hadn't worked it all out. The fireflies that traveled up the beach weren't filling the queen or her scepter. The queen in the projection gestured gracefully with her scepter, and the lights gathered together into a river of silver light. The river flowed like mercury away from the beach and into the city of Palana. In seconds, it was rushing through the windows of the throne room with the sound of a billion whispering leaves. Vamath raised his hands and it flowed over—into—him. A bit of nausea crept through Aisa's stomach, just like the way she felt during a Twist.

"The doors are opening," Danr said in his dreamlike voice. "The Stane are climbing out."

"Father!" Ranadar said from Talfi's body, a corpse with no *draugr*. "Don't!"

"Go below," Vamath ordered his guards. "These whelps are no threat, and we will need every sword in the city."

The guards left, and Aisa had the last piece. Her knees went weak and she sagged to the floor next to the Axe. Vamath, a master of Twisting, was harnessing the power of the *draugr* to Twist the Stane to Palana as they emerged from under the mountain. The Twist and the long distance would separate them from the *draugr* in Balsia, and the Fae would slaughter the surprised, weakened Stane just as they had slaughtered the humans.

"You can't do this," she begged. "My lord, you must not."

But Vamath was glowing like a silver star. Light streamed from his eyes and mouth and fingertips. He was beauty and power and terror all at once, and Aisa felt as helpless as a baby in his presence. She knew it was nothing more than glamour, but that didn't change a thing. Vamath's hands swept in an arc, leaving a bright streak of pure light behind, and Aisa felt the sickening nausea of the Twist.

"You will not!" His eyes filled with rage over Talfi's death, Ranadar pulled the spear out of Talfi's body and threw it straight at Vamath's heart.

Vamath flicked a finger, and the spear vanished. It reappeared past him, Twisted there by Vamath's magic, and thudded into the back of the throne itself. Talfi's blood dripped down the shaft and stained the cushion.

"I have had enough of the traitor," Vamath boomed. A bolt of silver light flared from his hand and caught Ranadar in the chest. The elven prince flew backward and slammed into the wall. With a gasp, he slumped to the floor. Was he dead? Aisa couldn't tell. Then she realized he couldn't be; there was no *draugr*.

Vamath shouted, *"Now, my queen! Twist!"* The silver light exploded in all directions. Aisa shielded her eyes against the consuming brightness. Nausea roiled through her, and she felt the tears stream down her face. They had lost. After all the pain, all the death, all the fear and trials, they had lost.

The light went out. Tiny flares appeared all over the projection table, spouting like little geysers. In each one appeared a troll, dwarf, or giant—in the forest, on the beach, in the city, even in the lake. A giant with two heads rose out of the water with a startled look on her face. Hundreds of Stane stumbled and staggered about, looking drunk or confused. Several dropped to their knees and vomited. The queen, appearing cool and unruffled, raised her scepter again. Silver lights rushed toward her again. The other Fae readied their weapons, awaiting her signal.

"No," Danr whispered. "Leave them alone! They're my people."

Vamath's hands still glowed silver. He pointed to Danr. "You'll join them, Stane."

And at that, something inside Aisa broke. The elven lord could do as he liked to her, to Ranadar, even to Talfi, but not to Danr. Not to her Hamzu. She wrenched the Iron Axe out of the floor and rushed at him with the blade held high. A scream tore itself from her throat. Vamath was only a few steps away. The look of surprise on his face flickered into fear for just a moment. Aisa swung with all her might.

Vamath caught the Axe by the handle just above her hands. "You surprise me, little parrot."

"I won't let you hurt him," Aisa hissed, though being this close to him made her sweat with need.

"Join me, little parrot," Vamath said with a small smile. "I'll give you this."

He leaned forward and kissed her.

Vamath's touch swept over her. It was everything Aisa had dreamed—and dreaded—ever since her exile into the cold human lands. A light, delicious languor washed over her, and every inch of skin tingled. She was breathing honey and nectar, drinking light, bathing in music. She shuddered and relaxed. The Axe lowered. Vamath carefully stepped back from it. On the projection table, the elven queen was glowing silver now. Only a few seconds had passed, and the Stane remained unfocused and dazed from the unexpected Twist.

Talfi jerked upright with a deep gasp. He sat panting on the floor, looking just as dazed as the Stane. "What—?"

"Give me the Axe, child." Vamath held out his hand. "Once I split the vessel that holds the power in two with it, he'll die forever, and the weapon will be mine."

"Kill Talfi?" Danr said.

"Who's Talfi?" Talfi asked.

Aisa clutched the Axe, still in the clutch of Vamath's wondrous kiss. She would sell her soul for another one.

"Now, child." Vamath snapped his fingers.

It would be so easy, so sweet. Aisa's fingers slid over the wooden handle, and she thought of Old Aunt by her fire. *"You have earned your face, child. You have the strength to face the world on your own.*" It was as if Grandmother were standing behind her, and she let the strength fill her.

"I have my face," Aisa told the elven king. And she thrust the Axe at his chest.

The iron head pushed straight through Vamath's armor and hissed into his flesh. The smell of cooked meat tanged the air. Vamath screamed. He clutched at the Axe's handle, but it was already buried deep between his ribs. Aisa twisted the handle and pulled the Axe back out. Vamath staggered backward.

"You . . . you can't . . . ," he gasped.

Aisa raised the Axe. "I. Can."

Vamath dropped to the floor with a crash. His *draugr* drifted up from the body. *"Release!"*

The moment he died, the awful hunger drained away. It simply disappeared as if it had never existed. A burden heavy as stone lifted. Chains shattered and fell away, leaving Aisa feeling light and free. She could leap and jump and even fly. A laugh bubbled up and burst. She was giddy with delight. He was her master, her hunger, no more. Aisa dropped the Axe and skipped across the room to take Danr's hands in hers, drawing him into a little dance.

"I'm free!" she shouted. "The hunger is gone and I'm free!"

Danr seemed bemused. "What happened to us?"

"I . . . killed him. The elven king." A thought stole through her exhilaration. "That must be how it works. When an elf dies, all the slaves who hunger for him are released. They don't want anyone to know that." She was weeping now even as her heart soared with light. "It's just like the Three said—finding the Iron Axe would end my hunger! I'm free! By the Nine, I'm *free!*"

Talfi was getting uncertainly to his feet. "Who are you people?" he demanded. "Who am *I?*"

"The Axe!" Danr rushed over to pick it up. "The Stane! What's happening to the Stane?"

Chapter Twenty

D anr rushed to the table with the Axe in his hand. So much was happening he could hardly keep track. The overwhelming need he had felt for Vamath had vanished the moment Aisa killed the elf, and what a moment that had been! But now—

On the table, the tiny projection of the queen seemed to have gotten tired of waiting. Filled with silver power, she let a burst of it pop from her scepter. The elves, fairies, and sprites fell on the Stane just as they had done on the humans. The Stane were a little more able to defend themselves, however. They were carrying iron weapons and wearing iron armor, which slowed the Fae attacks, but they were still dazed and surprised from the unexpected Twist, which gave the Fae an advantage. The giants—and there were more than three dozen of them tall as trees—stomped through the woods, swinging clubs and smashing with their fists, but the agile, chaotic sprites darted at their eyes and blinded them with popping lights, confused them with fireworks. Elves and trolls squared off, trading quick feints and powerful blows. Fairies and dwarves rolled across the ground in a tangle of arms and legs. But it was clear the Fae had more power.

Through it all, the human *draugr* shouted, *"Release!"* and Gwylph fed her subjects a steady stream of silver light from her scepter. It healed their wounds, boosted their strength, raised their morale. The confused, scattered Stane couldn't rally. Their commanders gave no orders. Their regiments fell apart. Stane fell, and their *draugr* appeared, giving more power to the queen. It wasn't a war; it was a slaughter.

The two stars that were Urko gave off a great burst of silver light. It overpowered the dying sun and shone straight through the window. The glass created a slanted silver column, and Talfi sat in its center.

Ranadar, consciousness newly regained, got to his feet. He seemed torn between his father's *draugr* and Talfi, who looked confused. The sounds of battle filtered up through the windows—screams and shouts and clashing of metal on metal. The earth trembled beneath giant feet. Danr looked at the Axe in his hand.

"Talfi!" Ranadar had made his choice. He ran to his lover and gathered him close, ignoring the blood on Talfi's tunic and the slanted column of light he lay in. More of Talfi's blood still spattered the far wall beneath the spear that had killed him.

"Who are you?" Talfi asked.

Danr and Aisa hurried over, though a cold dread was gathering in the pit of Danr's stomach. He knew what was going to happen, could see it coming, but he couldn't bear to think of it. Not Talfi. Not his friend.

"Why doesn't he remember me?" Ranadar demanded. "He did before."

"Talfi," Danr said, his voice growing thick. "We're your friends. Touch the amulets at your throat. The pouch and the medallion."

With a puzzled look, Talfi fished around in his tunic and came up with both objects. He clutched them in his palms.

"Ranadar, Aisa." Danr set down the Axe. "Hold him."

"Hey!" Talfi protested. "What are—"

They all three embraced him in the cold light of the two stars. Danr felt Aisa beside him and met her eyes over Talfi's head. She nodded, and he knew she was thinking the same thing he was: only the Axe could stop the one-sided battle raging outside. Sorrow broke through Danr, and anger, too. Her hand tightened around his arm. She was with him, and that meant everything, but the thing that was coming . . . he didn't know if he could bear it.

In the center of their circle, Talfi inhaled sharply. "I remember! Rolk and Vik! I remember!"

They stepped back, except for Ranadar, who kept a protective arm around Talfi. Danr couldn't meet his eyes, but he picked up the Axe. Talfi looked at it. "Oh."

"What?" Ranadar said. "What is—?"

"Talfi is the vessel of the power," Danr said, still looking at the floor. "He was the squire who was split in half a thousand years ago to create the Axe in blood and iron. When the Axe was sundered, the power went into Talfi. It won't let him die, but it erases his memory every time he comes back to life. You might say there is no Talfi anymore. It's why I can't see him through my true eye."

"So?" Ranadar said, but the truth was written across his face.

"Ran." Talfi's voice was quiet. "The only way to stop your kinsmen from destroying the Stane is to reunite the Axe. To do that, Danr has to take the power back. He has to kill me with it. And this time I won't come back."

The awful truth wrote pain across Ranadar's face. "No!" he cried. "Never again!"

"I've lived a thousand years, Ran," Talfi said. "It's my time. I'm sorry."

"I just found you again." Ranadar buried his face in Talfi's shoulder. "I can't lose you now."

Talfi touched his sunset hair for a moment, then gently pushed him aside and stood before Danr. "Do it. The stars are coming apart!"

They were. The silver light was already beginning to fade.

Danr looked down at Talfi, the friend he had faced a wyrm with, shared bread and salmon in a stable with, laughed and shared dreams with. "How can I kill my best friend?" he said thickly. "Not even Death and the Nine can ask this!"

"Danr," Talfi said in a quiet voice, "I died a long time ago, before the Sundering. It's all right. You need to do this. Everyone else will die if you don't."

Ranadar put his own hands over his eyes and moaned. The sound was a thousand years of pain, but he made no move to get in the way. Danr's heart wrenched for him.

"I've learned so much from you, Talfi," Danr choked. "I—"

"Just do it, you big oaf!" Talfi shouted. "They're dying!"

The light continued to dim. With trembling hands, Danr raised the Axe high. He felt the blade's thirst, and tears gathered in his eyes. Talfi looked up at him with expectant, sky blue eyes. Danr's muscles tensed to swing. But he lowered the Axe instead.

"I can't," he whispered. "I can't kill my friend."

And then Aisa was beside him. Wordlessly, she put both her small hands on his arm, and through those small hands came great strength, a strength greater than anything he had ever felt. It was the same strength he had felt when they kissed for the first time.

"You don't have to do it alone," she said. "I'm here. Before, and during, and after, my Hamzu. My Danr."

The silver light was nearly gone. Talfi spread his arms wide, raised his chin, and closed his eyes. "Please," he said.

Danr looked at Aisa, her eyes filled with compassion and love. Yes. She was there for him. Had always been there for him, and would always be. With her help, he raised the Axe high and swung it through the air toward Talfi's head just as the last of light faded away.

The blade cleaved Talfi neatly in two. To Danr, it felt like a hair slicing through glass. Without a sound, the two halves of Talfi's body fell to the floor. There was no blood this time, only the soft chime of a bell. Red and golden light flowed from the two sides of Talfi's body and rushed into the Axe. Talfi's split body crumbled into dust.

The Axe crackled and snapped. Power coursed through Danr. He felt the underpinnings of the world, the great continent moving slowly beneath his feet like a great raft on an ocean, and he felt the air moving above him like a silken river. He felt the water in the oceans and the lakes, heavy and swirling, and he felt the heat of every bit of fire and light in the world. He felt nine forms of light—Olar and Grick, the twins Belinna and Fell, who fought as one, Urko and Rolk, Kalina and Bosha, Vik and Halza, and even trickster Tikk, who was only pretending to be light—and he felt three forms of shadow—Nu, Ta, and Pendra. And behind them, Death in her chair.

His attention snapped back to the throne room. The dust that had been Talfi drifted at his feet. The elves had done this, forced him to kill his friend. The monster half raged within him, and this time he gladly let it out. The creature took over. A roar burst from his chest, and he leaped at the high window with the Axe high over his head.

The windows disintegrated. The leap, powered by the Axe, carried Danr all the way down to the shore. He slammed into the beach a dozen paces away from Queen Gwylph and her scepter in an explosion of sand that splashed up and froze in a wave of glass from the Axe's heat. The Axe snarled and glowed an angry red. All around was the Fae army, butchering the desperate Stane.

Danr the monster threw the spitting, glowing Axe, and it spun through the air. It sliced through twenty elves and fairies, spraying elvish blood in all directions, then turned and flew back toward Danr's hand. On the way, it slashed through ten sprites and a dozen more elven warriors. Their screams mingled with the cries of dying Stane. Danr put out his hand, and the Axe slammed into his palm, solid and powerful. He stood tall and terrible while power coruscated over and through him.

"Who are you?" demanded Queen Gwylph. "What are—?"

Danr slammed the Axe into the ground. The very earth shook all around Palana. The stones groaned, and the lake churned. Trees cracked. The tallest one leaned precariously, then fell with a great and terrible crash. All fighting ceased as everyone, Fae and Stane, lost their balance. Giants thudded to the ground, crushing the sprites they were fighting. Even the queen staggered.

"I am power!" Danr roared. "I am fate! I am death!"

He raised the Axe, and a dozen balls of fire rained down from the sky. They slammed into the elven city, setting trees ablaze and sending Fae and Stane alike running for the lake. Danr reveled in the destruction like the monster he was.

"What gives you the right?" shouted Gwylph.

"The same thing that gave you the right to kill both my people!" Danr roared. "You took the power and used it! Now I will use mine!"

Fire raged all around them as more and more people raced for the lake like animals fleeing a forest fire, friend and foe side by side. Danr leaped at the elven queen. She fired a bright silver light from her scepter, but the blazing Axe sucked it in, a volcano devouring a candle. Desperately she backed up a step and wove a shield of silver energy. Danr split it like kindling. He was close enough now to smell her, but now he saw the truth of everything. Her glamour was gone, and she was no longer beautiful. Her skin was rough as oak bark. Her scent was of dead leaves. Her sticklike skeleton propped her up from inside. The rage consumed him. He swung at her neck—

—and she vanished. Twisted away.

Outrage boiled over, and the Axe's power thundered through Danr. He'd had enough! The Fae had called him filth, but they were the ones who took slaves, dealt death, tricked and lied and deceived. The Axe's easy power called to him. All his life he had been forced to keep the monster in check, never show what he could do. Now, at long last, he could do *anything*, and he would. He would carve the entire elven country from the continent, flood it with ocean water, and let the merfolk swim through its ruins. He was a monster, and monsters destroyed.

Aisa and Ranadar stepped out of thin air. Ash smudged their faces, and their clothes were torn. Kalessa was with them, too.

"There he is," Ranadar gasped.

Kalessa groaned and clasped her shape-shifting sword. "I did not enjoy that at all."

"Danr!" Aisa ran to him. "You have to stop!"

"Don't give them the satisfaction. Don't give them a reason to hate you."

Danr raised the Axe, and another fireball slammed down from the sky, engulfing half a dozen trees and the homes within them. "It's too late. They hate the monster anyway. Why not stop them in the bargain?"

"Keep the monster inside."

She grabbed his arm. "You're not a monster!"

"You're not my mother!" the monster snarled, and she stepped back, aghast. "You have no right to tell me what I am!"

"Your mother thought there was a monster inside you!"

Aisa said as the flames continued to burn. Heat washed over them in waves. "She was wrong!"

"She was right!" He raised the Axe again. "Watch the monster work!"

"Don't you see?" She took his arm again, and he saw she was crying. "You want to blame your monster half, but he doesn't exist. It's only you. You're a person, a good and fine person. Look at yourself with that true-seeing eye, and you'll know. Look at yourself—for me."

He halted and looked down at her face, still naked and filled with raw emotion. For him. And so he did as she asked. For the first time since the Three knocked the splinters out of his eye, Danr looked down at himself and closed his right eye.

He was expecting a monster, the creature that had lived inside him ever since he was born. But he only saw . . . himself. A person in a plain tunic and dark trousers. Not a prince, not a truth-teller, not Hamzu, not Trollboy, not Danr. A *person*. His true self.

"It doesn't matter if the world doesn't accept you," Aisa said. "*You* have to accept yourself."

The truth came over him. There was no monster. There never had been. The monster was nothing but his own anger, his own rage, his own self. There was no separate Stane half and Kin half, no monster half and normal half. No one to blame but himself. He'd been avoiding the truth.

This new truth lay before him, naked and harsh as a tree stripped of bark. But why did it have to be harsh? This truth gave him new knowledge. If the monster didn't exist, it meant he was in control. He made all the decisions; the monster made none.

Once he accepted this, the desire to destroy left him. The monster disappeared—it had never existed anyway—and

Danr let the Axe fall to the sand. His arms went around Aisa. New emotion swept over him.

"I'm sorry," he cried into her shoulder. "I'm so sorry."

"You need never be sorry with me," she said. "Never, ever. My Danr, my Hamzu, my friend, my love."

They stayed like that for a long time, with Ranadar and Kalessa standing guard, while the fires died down all around the forest, and warriors and citizens alike from both sides found refuge in the lake.

At last, Danr and Aisa parted. The Axe lay on the beach, still glowing like a demon. Kalessa eyed it speculatively.

"Don't," Aisa said.

"What do we do now?" Ranadar said. His voice was flat. "Everything's destroyed. My *Talashka* is dead."

New sorrow speared Danr's heart. Gingerly he picked up the Axe. The power rushed through him, but this time he was ready for it, and he was able to hold it in, though it was like checking a team of unhappy stallions. The Axe demanded to be used.

"Twist us, Ranadar," he said through clenched teeth.

"Where?" the elf asked. "There's so much energy about, I could probably send us halfway across the world."

"Anywhere you want. Just go."

Shrugging as if nothing mattered to him anymore, Ranadar drew patterns in the air with his fingers, the way Bund had drawn them with her stick. He clearly wasn't as skilled as his parents, for it took him longer. The fires were dying down now, but a small aftershock rumbled through the ground as a reminder of the previous earthquake, and the Fae and Stane in the lake looked at one another in fear.

"Ready," Ranadar said, and nausea overtook Danr. There was the usual *wrench*, and the four of them were standing in the low, sandy cave with the tree root ceiling. No, not the four of them. Five. Queen Vesha of the Stane was there as well, looking entirely confused. Water streamed from her mail shirt, and she gripped a long sword with runes etched on it. Her head touched the ceiling.

Death sat in her rocking chair, knitting needles clicking in her lap. The candles still burned on the table next to her, the heavy door in the cave wall remained firmly shut, and the thin thread still made a chain around her neck.

Ranadar looked about in bewilderment. "This isn't where—"

"I pulled you here, dear," Death said. "You know who I am."

The elven prince noticed her for the first time and paled. So did Kalessa, who knelt. Vesha's face also went white, and she dropped her sword. Aisa moved over to them to make hurried explanations while Danr approached Death's chair. His mouth was dry.

"I have it," he said simply.

"So I see." Death rocked faster and her fingers were tense around the needles. Her lips were tight. "What do you intend to do with it?"

For once, Danr felt no compulsion to answer. It was probably because his actions spoke for him. Danr raised the Axe. Death stopped her breath.

"Wait!" Vesha flung herself in front of him. Her eyes were wild. "You can't! You have no idea what we sacrificed for this."

Danr looked at her. "I know exactly what you sacrificed. What *everyone* sacrificed. This is a wrong."

"The death of our people is a wrong." Vesha was trying to draw herself up in the cavern, but the ceiling was too low. "The Fae—"

"Paid a heavy price for what they did," Danr finished for her. "The Stane paid, too. You're only afraid of what she'll do."

"Yes," Death whispered.

"Aren't we all?" Vesha's low voice had a quaver in it. "You don't know what'll happen if you free her."

"Yes," Death whispered again.

Danr hesitated, but only for a moment. "But we *do* know what'll happen if I leave her. And that's worse."

The Axe left a glowing trail as he swung it through the air, and the blade met the thin thread with an earsplitting screech. A cold shock bolted up his arms and shoulder. Darkness and light exploded in all directions. The earth rocked. Dust and small rocks filtered down from the ceiling.

"Yesssss." Death rose from her chair, leaving her knitting behind. She stretched, and the sound of her joints popping was the sound of suns exploding before they went out. Her presence filled the chamber, pressing everyone back with a force Danr couldn't name, and her voice became rich and deep, like stones rubbing together. "Step aside, little ones. I want a parade."

Danr and everyone else stepped hurriedly back. Vesha pressed herself against the back wall, clearly wishing she were somewhere, anywhere, else, but where, Danr wondered, could she hide from Death?

From nowhere appeared a stream of *draugr*, thousands of them: elves, sprites, fairies, trolls, giants, dwarves, humans, orcs, and even merfolk. They paraded past Danr and Death, leaping, hopping, storming for the door, and somehow the cavern was large enough to fit them all, even the giants. Joy lit every face. *"Released! Released!"* they cried in a thousand gleeful voices, and their happiness leaked into Danr's eyes and brought little tears. *"Released!"*

With a deep clatter and an absolutely appropriate groan of hinges, Death dragged the wooden door open, and the *draugr* flowed through it, neither hesitating nor pausing before they crossed the threshold into the darkness beyond.

A familiar figure separated from the stream. Grandmother Bund paused at the door. Danr's heart lightened, and he couldn't help smiling. The pain was gone from her face, and her body was straight. She waved her stick at them. A simple joy filled Danr, and he ducked his head.

Good for you, she mouthed. Then she turned and strode through the door with the other spirits.

Danr caught sight of White Halli in the crowd and his breath caught. The Fae must have killed him during the battle at the lake. Halli paused. The other *draugr* rushed around him. Halli's eyes met Danr's for just a moment. Danr held a cold breath heavy with guilt. Then Halli saluted Danr with a wry grin.

"Released," he said, and the word carried more meaning than ever before. Danr let the breath out, long and shuddering. The guilt, every last particle, went with it, and he felt weak and shaky inside.

Halli turned and stepped through the door. For a moment, Danr thought he caught a glimpse of a little boy on the other side, reaching out his arms for his papa. Danr wiped at his eyes for what must have been the fortieth time that week. Aisa squeezed his hand.

The last *draugr* slid through the doorway, though the door itself remained open. Nothing was visible beyond the lintel. Danr was enormously curious about what might lie beyond it, but not curious enough to actually ask for a look. Death gave a world of a sigh, picked up her knitting, and took up her chair again.

"Thank you," she said in her new rich voice. "You have restored balance."

Danr didn't know what to say to that, so he simply nodded.

"But," Death continued, her needles moving and clicking

without fail, "your actions have, in their turn, created imbalance."

Danr tensed, and his hands tightened around the Axe. "What do you mean, lady?"

"I mean, child, that no one in history has ever performed such a service for the Nine or the Three or me. You created a debt, and it must be repaid."

"Oh." None of this seemed quite real to Danr, and he felt completely at sea about it. Only Aisa beside him kept him from floundering completely. "There isn't any need for—"

"Shush. I'll decide that. Aisa, come forth."

Aisa shot Danr a look and came forward. Danr started to come with her, but she waved him back with a small gesture. She was literally facing Death, and without flinching. After all the events of the day so far, Danr hadn't thought he could be impressed again, but he was wrong.

"You've vanquished your elven hunger, I see," said Death.

"Yes, lady," Aisa said, her head held high, and Danr felt a flash of pride for her.

"Still, the elves stole something else from you, something no agency on Erda can restore. Fortunately I am not of Erda."

Aisa said, "I don't understand, lady."

"They took your fertility, dear." Death tapped her chest, and Aisa staggered. "From death comes life. Be restored!"

A tiny moment arrived. It hung in the air like summer mist, then finally passed. Aisa regained her balance. "Thank you," she whispered.

"Kalessa, come forward."

Looking a little startled, Kalessa obeyed. "Lady, I didn't—"

"Do much here, I know. Your contributions have been rewarded with that sword you carry. But know this, girl: your deeds will not die with you. The bards will tell your stories long after you have passed through my door. Be renowned!"

Kalessa flushed. "I . . . thank you, lady."

"Hamzu, Truth-Teller, Trollboy, Danr, come forward."

"Lady," Danr began, "I can't think what you might give—"

"My son?"

Danr turned, and he was no longer in a cave, but on a hillside just above Alfgeir's farm, the place where he and his mother came to escape the daily drudgery of the farm. The day was cloudy, so he felt no headache, the leaves were green, and the grass was soft beneath his feet.

Halldora, his mother, stood next to him on the hill. She was young and vital, her long black hair sleek and glossy, her face unlined by fear or worry or sickness, though he topped her by more than a head. She wore a simple blue dress he remembered as one of her favorites, and she smelled of flour and wood smoke.

"Mother?" His throat thickened and his entire body shook. "Mother!"

"Danr!" She threw her arms around him, and he realized he was no longer holding the Axe, but he didn't care.

"What are you doing here?" he asked. "Where are we?"

She pulled him down to sit beside her on the hill with the callused hands he remembered, the hands that had soothed him when he was afraid or hurt, the hands that had long ago fallen still and cold. "We have only a moment, my Danr. We mustn't waste it."

"I've missed you so much." He was trying not to cry, and feeling stupid about it. "Every day, I miss you."

"I miss you, too." She put an arm around him, barely able to reach, and her touch returned him to childhood and happier days. "But we'll see each other again, and I have things to say."

He knuckled his eyes. "Then tell me."

"I'm sorry, my Danr. So very sorry."

That took him by surprise. "Sorry? For what?"

"For all the mistakes I made. For leaving you the way I did. For not telling you about your father. And for making you think you were a monster."

"You didn't make me think I was a monster, Mother." He turned to face her so he could study her face, etch it into his memory before it was taken away again. "Never that."

"I did. Because of me, you thought there was an evil creature inside you, one you needed to deny. But it was the world that needed to change, not you. I'm so sorry. Always know, my darling boy, that I'm proud of you and everything you've ever done."

He touched her face, feeling adult now. "You don't need to be sorry, Mother. I'm not."

"I will try," she said with the little laugh he knew so well.

"How did you become a truth-teller?" he asked suddenly.

"Kech was stuck in a loveless arranged marriage because he was prince," she said quietly. "We met on the mountain and fell in love. When I became pregnant with you, we journeyed to see the Three, in order to ask if the world would ever accept a troll who loved a human. The answer was a harsh one—it would happen, but not while either of us lived. And they knocked out my splinters. Your father was appalled and terrified, and he went back to his wife. I was left with you and the truth." She rose to her knees and kissed his cheek. "But I wouldn't change a thing. You were the best thing that ever happened to me. Never forget that, my son. Never."

"I won't," he said, "I—"

And then Danr was back in the cave, clutching the Iron Axe to his chest. The hillside and his mother were both gone.

"I trust that is reward enough?" Death said from her chair.

"What happened?" Aisa asked. "You're pale."

"Thank you, lady," Danr whispered. "Just . . . thank you."

Death nodded. "Be well."

"You should have this," he added quickly, and held out the Axe to her. "We can't keep it."

Vesha made a small sound but didn't move from her spot at the back of the cavern.

Death took it from him. "Are you sure? You put it together, you sacrificed your friend for it, and you have to live with the deaths it caused. You earned the right to wield it."

"No," Danr said firmly. "It must never appear in the world again."

"As you wish." She set the Axe on the table beside the candles. It vanished, but also didn't vanish. Somehow it was there and not there at once, untouchable until the end of time. "And now, Ranadar, step forward."

"Me?" Ranadar came hesitantly toward her. "But I didn't do anything."

"Without your willingness to turn traitor, Danr and his friends would never have freed me," Death replied amiably. "This must be rewarded. And there's another one I owe."

"I don't understand," Ranadar said.

Death set her knitting aside, picked up one of the candles, and waved it at a shadow near the door. The shadow faded, revealing Talfi.

Danr's heart jerked, and he grabbed Aisa's hand. It was cold.

"*Talashka!*" Ranadar ran toward him, but when he tried to touch Talfi, his hands went through him.

"*Release!*" said Talfi.

"He's not alive, dear," Death said.

"Then you know what I want," Ranadar said. "What *he* would want."

"The dead can't return to life. It's just not possible."

"Except Talfi—" Aisa began.

"Talfi died long ago. The power of the Axe only kept his body going. Even I can't bring him back. Unless . . ."

Hope flickered in Danr's chest, and he kept his breath close. A similar hope blossomed in Ranadar's eyes. "Unless what?"

"Life must balance out. Talfi could come back, but for every day he lives past his allotted time, someone else must lose a day."

"Take my remaining days," Ranadar said instantly. "Give them to him."

"How about half?" Death snapped her fingers. "Be alive!"

Talfi flickered. A swirl of stars surrounded him, trailing bits of light. His feet lifted off the floor and an unseen breeze tousled his hair. He gasped sharply once, twice, and a third time. Then he came to rest on the floor. Ranadar caught him, and this time he was solid. Danr, Aisa, and Kalessa ran forward and caught him up as well. Danr's heart swelled until he thought it might burst.

"Hey!" Talfi protested. "Not so hard!"

They separated, and Aisa wiped her eyes with the back of her hand. Tears streamed down Ranadar's cheeks, and he seemed not at all ashamed. "What do you remember, *Talashka*?"

Talfi thought. "Everything. Well, everything from the time I came to Skyford. And my time with you in Palana, Ran. The other stuff is . . . blurry."

"Queen Vesha, come forth," said Death.

Vesha flinched, then visibly steeled herself and stepped forward under the low ceiling. Danr watched her come with mixed emotions. She had caused all this, but she had also *needed* to cause all this. He could see her now, the queen, representing her people.

"I accept your consequences, lady," Vesha said in a rock-level voice. "I only beg that you lay them on me and not my people. They only did as I ordered them."

"Your people have reaped many rewards and paid many consequences," Death said. "Restoring your balance was difficult. They and the humans have been Twisted back to their homelands where they belong, while the Fae slink through their ruined city. The doors under the mountain remain open, yet no one will make war for quite some time."

"Yes, lady," said Vesha. From her voice, she might have been discussing a harvest of mushrooms, though a tremor crossed her hands.

"But you may not escape what you have done." Death's own voice deepened. Ice curled through it, and a palpable cold pushed against Danr's bones. His teeth chattered in his head and his insides shriveled. Death hadn't moved from her chair, but her presence thundered through the room. Danr's knees weakened, and he felt like a gnat that didn't see the boot about to tread on it. "Know, then, little queen, that I will not come for you out of old age or disease or injury. I will not come today, or tomorrow, or in a hundred years. Instead I will come for you at the very moment you set foot above the mountain. Be *cursed*."

The last word thudded through the cavern like a bolder. In the silence that followed, the cold retreated. Danr swallowed, and the color left Vesha's face. She had spent her entire life wishing to leave the warrens under the mountain. Now her life would end the moment she did so. Vesha sank to the floor with her hands over her face. Suddenly Death didn't seem so kindly anymore.

"So, then," Death said as if she had just realized someone might want a berry tart, "it seems to me that I may need someone to act on my behalf in the mortal world now and then. The risks would be enormous, but the rewards would be powerful."

"I do not understand," Aisa said.

"The Tree," Death replied. "It's tipping. Did you think we were finished? That the Iron Axe was the end of it all?"

"I hadn't thought about it," Danr said.

"We're just getting started, sweetie." Death smiled. "If you're interested, dears, I'll call on you again."

Oh," said Danr, still a little stunned from watching the curse, "uh . . . I don't—"

But the *wrench* of a Twist took them, and moments later, Danr and the others were standing in the street outside the house of Orvandel the fletcher. Vesha was nowhere to be seen.

"Uncle Orvandel!" Talfi said. "Have we got a story for him!"

The last of the roast salmon and stewed chicken had been cleared away. Orvandel reached for his ale horn, but Ruta slapped his hand away. "You've had quite enough, oh mighty lord."

"Hmf," grumped Orvandel, but he didn't take more ale. Karsten and Almer, his sons, had remained quiet throughout the meal, clearly in awe of Danr and Ranadar. Almer had shaken hands with both Talfi and Ranadar, and neither of them mentioned their previous awkwardness. Orvandel had remarked that it was a historic day, setting a table with Fae and Kin and Stane, and a pity no one was here to record it.

"So, what's going to happen now?" Kalessa said.

"Everyone's in a weakened state," Ranadar said. "Palana was nearly destroyed, and we—they—have to deal with the fact that the secret of how to cure a human's addiction is public knowledge. Slavery will soon end."

"The Stane can come out when they need to," Danr added, drinking some ale of his own. It was sweet and light. "And they don't need to worry about getting attacked, now that Hunin's army has been destroyed."

"You know," said Talfi slyly, "with Halli and Hunin and

Rudin all dead, we'll need an earl. It wouldn't be difficult for a great hero such as yourself to take such a position."

"Oh no." Danr held up his hands. "I don't want it. Besides, I'm too truthful. Let Hunin's brother the priest take it."

Kalessa stretched. "What are you going to do, then? What are *we* going to do?"

And Danr had to answer. "Well, the Noss Farm is vacant, and it butts right up against Stane land. Perfect place for a half-blood. But . . ." He took Aisa's hand under the table, and she gave him a questioning look. "There's no hurry."

"I," Aisa said firmly, "want to find mermaids."

"Then that's what we'll do next," Danr replied, just as firm. And the smile that spread across Aisa's face sent a river of joy through his heart.

Together they turned back to the table.

ABOUT THE AUTHOR

Steven Harper Piziks was born with a name no one can reliably pronounce, so he usually writes under the pen name Steven Harper. He sold a short story on his first try way back in 1990. Since then, he's written twenty-odd novels, including the Clockwork Empire steampunk series.

When not writing, Steven teaches English in southeast Michigan. He also plays the folk harp, wrestles with his kids, and embarrasses his youngest son in public. Visit his Web page at http://www.stevenpiziks.com.

CONNECT ONLINE
stevenpiziks.com
twitter.com/stevenpiziks